LAST
OF THE
OLD SCHOOL

RICHARD JOHN THORNTON

LAST
OF THE
OLD SCHOOL

To Debbie,

Thank you so much for your amazing support. Hope the book delivers

3/11/23

DEDICATED TO TEACHERS EVERYWHERE.

PAST, PRESENT AND FUTURE.

Dear reader,

The following story is a work of fiction. All characters and situations are inventions of imagination.

But if you should find your memory being jogged to any slight degree regarding your own personal experiences as a former secondary school pupil, then I would be inclined to say I have succeeded in my aims.

In advance, I thank you for reminiscing with me.

RJT

PROLOGUE

Littleholt Secondary School
1988 Leavers' Journal (excerpt)
Entry no. 74

We'd all heard the rumours about Mister Reynolds whilst still at junior school. I can still remember our first encounter as though it was yesterday, although it would be about five years ago now.

He certainly lived up to our expectations. Just the sight of him sometimes made the hairs on the back of my neck stand on end. When he glanced in my direction, I'd just look at my feet if I was standing, or the top of the desk if I was sitting, hoping that he wouldn't notice me.

But I could still feel the cold stare through those mysterious dark spectacles of his.

Yet I soon discovered that he wasn't the ogre that most people thought he was. He was a very kind, genuinely caring man.

He was most generous to me and remains a great inspiration.

Though of course, there was the side of him that scared the life out of many kids in the school.

But you know what? Deep down, I reckon he loved the notoriety and the image that went with it.

One thing was certain.

He wasn't a teacher that you could afford to make an enemy of.

He was Kingpin in our school.

The kids knew it.

The other teachers knew it.

He absolutely ruled the place.

He was a hard man; and perhaps not always fair.

And of course, like me, his ex-pupils would always remember him.

It's a safe bet that not many shed a tear on the day he retired.

But I did.

Jennifer Douglas

AUTUMN TERM 1983

1

The seventh. The first Wednesday of September.

Traditionally a day to induce a combination of dread and anticipation for most schoolteachers.

But for one teacher in particular, the new dawn not only brought with it the beginning of a new academic year, but also the enthralling premise of unforeseen challenges.

He would actively relish the annual opportunity to introduce himself to the influx of new arrivals.

Fresh young minds which would undoubtedly be keen to make his acquaintance.

Most of them would have heard the myth about him being a teacher to be feared, but that same myth was a long-standing and occasionally pleasurable shroud under which the man resided.

And indeed flourished.

And if the children thought such fiendish stories about him to be gospel, then who was he to dispel their delusion?

Let them feast on the false legend.

For him, today was not a day for trepidation.

It was an event which enabled him to embrace the prolonged warmth of the late summer sun and venture beyond the walls of comparative captivity that had housed him for six long weeks.

It was time for some real action once again.

He could vaguely hear the distant cries of battle calling him to arms as he spied from the kitchen window, preparing to confront his first opponent of the hour.

'Oy! Go and shit on your *own* bloody lawn! Go on, you dirty little animal! Get out of it!'

Ivan Reynolds' appearance at the back door startled the tortoiseshell kitten into an immediate and frantic withdrawal across the vegetable patch.

Yet this did not prevent the angered observer from continuing the pursuit.

Bounding onto the concrete patio still dressed in tartan bath robe, striped pyjamas, and leather slippers, he stumbled down the garden path waving a tea towel aloft, as though warning a pirate ship to retreat from his own private stretch of coastline.

The young cat leapt into the comparative concealment of the conifer row. However, the apparent truce between man and beast was to be short-lived.

The feline antagonist knew it wouldn't have to wait long to recommence the mission to deposit its morning refuse on that pristine, manicured plot of primed earth.

Ivan Reynolds was now the subject of intensive scrutiny through the base of the hedgerow.

The furry trespasser had learned of his neighbour's rigid routine which had been studied carefully over the past few weeks. Yet during the previous couple of days, that routine had altered noticeably.

The man in the striped pyjamas was suddenly absent during the day.

And each of the past two days had heralded the same departure time.

The kitten sensed that the man would be gone again within the hour, and that his garden would be rendered vulnerable for the taking.

Squinting furiously without the aid of his spectacles, though eventually satisfied that he had seen off the offending creature, Ivan checked the borders of his prized vegetable plots and flower beds. There was no obvious sign of defecation, but keeping the soil clear of the stuff was now a daily chore.

Still, it thrilled him to see the tiny combatant run for cover as he wielded the nearest weapon to hand such as a sweeping brush or watering can.

The game of life, no less.

Ivan Reynolds thrived on showing his feline foe who was boss.

Authority was a way of life to him and every victory, however small or insignificant to the casual observer, was savoured with personal relish.

'You need to calm down a bit, Ivan! You'll have a bloody fit with yourself one of these days! It's only a cat, for Christ's sake!'

Ivan's retired neighbour George Breeden peered over the low wooden fence that separated their properties.

Still weaving around the lawn, Ivan looked up and smirked wryly at the rose-cheeked expression of his friend, not remotely ashamed by his futile act of territorial defence.

'Bloody dirty things! It might only be a cat, but it's not *my* bloody cat and I don't want its crap on *my* cabbages and carrots!'

George chuckled again as Ivan stood gesturing with a fist towards his beloved crops.

'I thought animal muck was good for plants?' offered George.

Ivan spat his reply with venom.

'Manure, yes! Fertilizer, yes! Cat shit - *NO!*'

George chuckled at the farcical exhibition.

'I don't know, Ivan. What are you like? You should be in a good mood today, shouldn't you? First day of your retirement year, isn't it?'

Ivan nodded and rolled his eyes with barely concealed excitement.

'Yes, indeed! The triumphant last hurrah! Two more terms of stalking the corridors and scaring the younglings! I did hear a rumour they've even started calling me the Dark Lord. You know, from those popular kids' movies.'

George was now creased at the midriff in full guffaw.

'Yes, I think I know who they mean. I'll bet the kids call you far worse than that, too!'

Ivan stood straight and pushed his not inconsiderable shoulders back. The smirk had vanished, to be replaced by a stern expression of foreboding that even unnerved his neighbour for a second or two.

'I'm sure that they do, George...I'm sure that they do. But I've never once heard them yet! Not once in over thirty years! There's a hell of a lot to be said for a man's reputation, you know.'

George nodded, aware of his friend's infamous persona.

'Well, you've certainly got that! I'd better let you get ready. You can give me a report on the little horrors tonight.'

Ivan began to make for the back door, then stopped himself mid-stride.

'By the way, George…how are Jillian's feet? Did she have the op yesterday as planned?'

'She did, Ivan yes, thanks. She'll be up and about by the weekend. Bloody bunions! Still, at least it'll give her chance to be quiet and relax for a few days.'

Ivan's lips creased with mirth as he swept his lengthening grey-brown hair back across his forehead.

'Yes. It's a shame for you that the recovery is so swift these days! Give her my blessing.'

George put his hand over his mouth in mock horror.

'If she could hear you now! She'd clip you round the ear!'

'Have a good day on the allotment, George!' Ivan grinned.

The men waved to one another and re-entered their respective kitchens.

Ivan gave a cautious glance through the window just to check that the seemingly fearless feline had not ventured back into forbidden land.

It was a bright and alluring day for the start of a new term. The seasonal sunshine was still strong, but the onset of Autumn was indicated by the faintest layer of dew on the grass.

Many times had Ivan Reynolds been in this position.

The new First Year admittance at Littleholt Secondary School would now be trying on their new uniforms, packing their new pencil cases into their new bags, and putting on their new shoes.

He couldn't wait for them to meet him.

Every new year brought with it a new surprise.

Every new year an untried adversary would chance their luck.

The expectation was almost too much for him to bear.

Finishing off the breakfast pots, Ivan hung the tea towel over the cooker rail and flicked off the radio, murmuring with frustration as he stomped upstairs.

'Scargill and the bloody miners. Thatcher and the bloody Falklands. Any *positive* news? Or don't we get to hear about the good stuff anymore?'

Ivan had become slowly disillusioned with the greater scheme of things in recent times. Even the teacher's union was deliberating on industrial action. He would often ring the ear drums in the staff room about his satirical theory that politicians were beginning to take over the country as opposed to running it.

So far as he was concerned, the forecast on all fronts was bleak for Britain and he would never tire of telling people so.

It almost made him glad to be retiring at times.

Studying his reflection into the bathroom mirror, he washed and shaved, inspecting his even, tanned skin for signs of ever older age.

He clipped the hairs in his nostrils and ears before brushing his teeth and finally affirming the image with a final inspection.

In truth he thought he looked pretty good for fifty-nine.

By next Easter he would be sixty.

Six complete decades on the mortal coil. Three and a half of which he had spent cultivating an image of dictatorial proportions around several district schools.

It was somehow suitable that Littleholt was to be the theatre for his final curtain. Comfortably close to home, the school had accommodated his good-natured wrath for the bulk of his career.

Not long to go now.

He resumed the physical analysis. Some streaks of dark brown still accompanied the shoots of grey and white in his scalp. No signs of baldness though.

A reliable fitness regime and plenty of time in the garden had awarded his features with a natural healthy glow. The flesh around his eyes and cheeks was taut and smooth.

It was an impressive visage for this most hardened of warriors.

A dab of aftershave completed the masculine façade. Not that Ivan Reynolds was in any way persuaded by the need to act masculine.

His aura of strength was inherent and needed no artificial supplement.

His wife had always complemented him of being the manliest of men. A description he still recalled and fully appreciated.

Across the landing into the bedroom, he opened the wardrobe doors to reveal the choices of regalia. Dropping his pyjamas onto the bed, Ivan put on a crisp, white cotton shirt and linked the cuffs with gold studs. A navy-blue silk tie was knotted perfectly around his neck before taupe-coloured trousers were added.

A matching waist coat was then donned, the left pocket of which contained his father's silver watch on a chain. It had never missed a beat or slipped a minute for nearly ninety years and was a much-preferred keeper of time that the droning school bell that invaded his concentration every hour of the school day.

Highly polished leather shoes matched the trousers. The toes were avidly shined to a mirror finish, so that pupils performing penal press-ups could clearly view the sufferance etched on their own faces as they strived to bob up and down at his command.

He decided that the suit jacket would be carried into school over one arm due to the pleasant temperature outside. Inside the jacket were inserted three fountain pens that had never dared to leak so much as a smidgeon of ink since he first purchased them for his posting at Littleholt some three decades earlier.

Two pairs of gold-rimmed spectacles were always on his person. They were distinctive in design, fitted with new-fangled lenses that reacted to bright daylight by tinting themselves to a darker shade. One of the pairs he removed from its case and placed on the bridge of his nose. The other pair he secured in the inside pocket of his jacket with the pens.

Having made the bed, Ivan then folded his pyjamas and placed them neatly into the top drawer of his dresser. Then came the time to bid farewell to his wife, Meg, and his only son, Nicholas, by placing a gentle kiss on each of their right cheeks and then kissing the thick gold wedding band that adorned his ring finger.

Their radiant smiles never seemed to alter.

The lights in their eyes never seemed to dim.

'See you both tonight, darlings! Wish me luck on my first day!'

He hummed to himself as he descended the stairway and eyed the dark brown leather briefcase that lay below the mirror in the hallway.

It had been completely empty until the beginning of the week, but Monday and Tuesday had been designated as inaugural teacher induction days, during which Ivan and his colleagues could reconvene after their long, lazy holiday and talk about their long, lazy holidays.

Such days were not to the personal preference of Ivan Reynolds, but he played along with the charade. The modern teaching curriculum obliged teachers to walk around carrying reams of legislative paperwork which would never be read in earnest and must have required entire forests to be felled to produce such waste.

An argument he had professed many a time to an arena of deaf ears in the staff room.

It was officially purported that induction days were a useful way of preparing the school staff for this moment - the day of reckoning.

Most teachers agreed that school was a much more abiding place without the children. For the staff, a couple of days alone in school acted as a valuable calm before the inevitable storm.

But for Ivan Reynolds, the opposite was applicable.

The thrill of locking horns with pupils new and old could not come soon enough.

Securing the back door, he picked the morning paper from the worktop and then retrieved the briefcase from the hallway floor. He didn't need to check its contents.

Everything was in place for this much heralded occasion.

The one day he needed to look his pristine best.

Ivan checked his appearance in the hall mirror one last time.

Every aspect of the ensemble seemed to be in place.

The tinted shades of his spectacles were a useful tool in playing mind games with pupils. The theory of hiding the whites of the eyes derived from the outlaws of the Wild West; hence their wide brimmed hats that cast shadow across their wary features.

The children could not see the emotion in the eye of their master, so it stood to reason that they had little idea of where or at whom Ivan was looking.

Particularly when he was on playground duty.

When the true daylight turned the glass to an even blacker, more menacing shade.

The image in the mirror gratified him.

The neatness of the hair.

The glimmer of the gold ring against his tanned fingers.

The symmetry and cut of the suit.

Yes, He was ready.

Turning the front door key in the latch, Ivan took a deep breath.

He stepped outside, locked the door behind him and squinted up into the morning sunshine. An inner smile encroached as the prospect of the next few hours fuelled his veins with enthusiasm.

Moving toward the car along the front lawn he stopped and admired the motor's streamlined gleam.

The Austin Princess in metallic copper was his pride and joy.

On his first test drive, he recalled describing it to the salesman as motoring *'like shit flying off a hot shovel'*. An automatic gearbox added to the sense of effortless acceleration and power.

Successfully engaging the ignition at the second attempt, he welcomed the eventual hum of the engine, although the choke knob was a still a little uncooperative - a reliable source of frustration during the cold winter months.

At last, the familiar route to school beckoned again.

One last touch - music.

His favourite *Sounds of the Sixties* cassette resonated through the speakers.

Reversing off the drive and pulling away from home, Ivan Reynolds felt positively inflated with anticipation.

As did another local resident.

Just two minutes after Ivan's eventual departure, the tortoiseshell kitten emerged from the undergrowth next door.

It gave a final cautious check of the surroundings and gleefully laid its unwelcome deposits near to the cabbage rows in the soft, clean soil.

Burying the evidence without raising further suspicion, the young cat disappeared back through the hedge bottom leaving no trace of its visit whatsoever.

2

From a distance, uninitiated observers may well have mistaken the Austin Princess of Ivan Reynolds for a travelling roadshow.

Audibly singing along to the sound of Roy Orbison with the front windows wound fully down, the buoyant image and capable voice belied the usually affronting persona of the man behind the wheel.

The journey came to a temporary halt at the main town centre traffic lights, whereby the car signalled left and duly glided onward along the route to school.

Slowly passing the allotments where he had spent much of his summer holiday digging, turning over, and growing, Ivan glanced across the carriageway and through the green metal-mesh gates.

George Breeden was his regular gardening companion and would be along to open them up any minute now. Such a duty was considered something of a privilege. Only certain appointed members of the village growers' association possessed a key to that large silver padlock.

As yet, Ivan was not one of those privileged few, despite George having promoted his friend's worthy claim for the better part of a year.

Yet the allotment committee was undecided as to his friend's credentials.

Indeed, the jury was still out on Ivan Reynolds.

It was a bemusing process, and the man in question had little time for such tardy decision-making.

However, being the supremely confident individual that he was, Ivan had already affirmed in his own mind that he would one day have a key to those hallowed gates.

One day.

Considering the pending events at school as he left the allotment grounds behind, Ivan suddenly wished he was entering those gates and preparing for another blissful day in the sunshine.

Sitting outside his ramshackle shed with the radio on listening to the cricket; sipping his favourite tomato soup from a flask; observing the ineptitude of other gardeners and telling them where they were going wrong with their plots.

Plus, George was good company and had been a reliable friend and neighbour for years. It was rare for Ivan to tolerate anybody for longer than necessary, but George was of a similar age, thought along similar lines and had a sense of humour that complimented his own.

George also rented a grocery pitch on the thrice-weekly local market and a good proportion of what he sold was home produced on the ground he tended every day of the year.

Indeed, much of Ivan's personal annual - if somewhat less impressive harvest - also ended up on his friend's stall as Ivan always grew more than he could ever possibly eat.

Yet making money was never Ivan's motivation for rural creativity, anyway.

It was the therapy of the process that sated him most.

Preparing the soil and setting the seed. Nurturing, observing, encouraging, and taking pride in the finished products that had evolved through nature's wondrous magic. A studious daily attention to detail was vital, just to make sure things were progressing as they should be.

He supposed gardening to be comparative to his approach to teaching.

But not nearly as much fun.

Carefully navigating a roundabout, the thought entered Ivan's head that he hadn't been to the allotments since Sunday. Tonight, he should maybe afford himself just an hour of peace in that halcyon place on the way home from school.

Tonight, he would surely be ready for some solitude after eight hours in the gladiator ring.

The landscape became evermore familiar and enticing as the journey toward Littleholt Secondary neared its end.

The smatterings of pupils meandering along the local streets gradually drew together in the direction of the school premises and were slowly amassing into larger gatherings as the destination loomed.

In turn, the casual pairs and trios of amblers soon developed into tightly knit uniformed groups, trooping solemnly along to their united fate.

Ivan readily recognised many of the juvenile faces on route.

Either they were pupils he had taught in previous years or unscrupulous scrappers he had intervened among during many a testing break time.

It was a tried and approved dictum for the experienced hand.

Some students stood out because of what they had done. Some because of what they said. Others because of who they were.

And then there were those children who were too scared to come out of the shadows at all. Those with whom Ivan Reynolds had never had chance to properly acquaint himself.

The September newcomers were always easy to identify - even from afar in a moving vehicle.

For a start, they were always the smallest in physical stature. Invariably, particularly the boys, their uniforms did not fit properly, usually being slightly oversized for the purpose of accommodating growing bones.

They did not find reason to smile and invariably walked with a wary hesitancy as the dominant form of the school building beckons them ever closer.

Inaugural First Year pupils were also easy to identify for one other telling factor. The new influx did not recognise Ivan's car as he drove slowly past, sounding his horn at them to encourage use of the newly installed pedestrian crossing, instead of randomly jumping out into the road in front of his Princess.

When halted in their innocently misguided tracks, they would of course stop and dare to glimpse at the driver of the sizable metallic-brown motor vehicle that had unceremoniously made them jump out of their tiny skins.

But even then, they showed no curiosity or even the slightest trace of alarm as to who the mysterious man behind the wheel might be, as he stares back at them through those impenetrable lenses.

Holding the wheel; peering at the pristinely uniformed young ones; without the slightest sign of emotion or the merest expression.

Of course, the new children are not afraid of him, because they do not yet know of him.

But such understandable ignorance would indeed soon become enlightenment.

By this time tomorrow, by their second day, every single newcomer would come to know of him.

By *tomorrow* morning, every First Year pupil will be using the designated and newly installed pedestrian crossing.

By *tomorrow* morning, indeterminate caution should be the single ally of every First Year pupil if they wanted to avoid crossing paths with Ivan Reynolds.

Or indeed, crossing *swords*.

Hovering outside the school gates with his foot on the brake pedal, he allowed a small cluster of Third Year girls the right of way before pointing the car along the driveway, across the tarmac and into his assigned parking space.

Disengaging the engine and selecting park, he sat and studied the scene in his rear-view mirror for a few contemplative moments. He watched as children dashed back and forth or simply stood talking in small groups at varying locations on the playground and sports field.

Then he gazed forlornly at the school building. How he hated the architecture of the place. Prefabricated sheets of coloured plywood, interwoven with large, featureless windows.

Built in the late nineteen-fifties, this cheap post-war alternative to the original schoolhouse at Littleholt was a crass insult to exterior design.

It beheld no character; held no visual appeal. And it offered budding graffiti artists plenty of bare canvas both inside and out.

How Ivan wished for the solid, curved sandstone brickwork of yesteryear.

Huge, thick wooden doors with their ornate panelling and weighted cast iron features.

He supposed, like everything else that was being altered in the dubious name of progress, the proud history of Littleholt Secondary School was now relegated firmly to the past.

Forgotten forever by its previous generations of attendees.

But one thing remained certain.

Ivan's tried and tested methods of teaching were not quite past their sell-by date just yet.

The majority of pupils on the premises watched intrigued as the driver remained unmoving behind the wheel during his moment of reflection.

And they might have held their breath just for a moment or two as he finally, slowly emerged from the driver's seat.

Ivan noticed the muscular adolescent appearance of the Fourth- and Fifth Year boys and it struck him how some youngsters changed so quickly over the summer months. It was as though the long days in the sun actively encouraged sudden spurts of physical development.

Boys who were barely showing signs of a whisker back in May now appeared to exhibit stubble.

But Ivan hated whiskers - especially on youths.

It looked lazy.

Unkempt, and undisciplined.

His attention transferred to fifteen-year-old Shaun Peterson - the alleged finest athlete of the Fourth Year.

Of *any* year, come to that.

The cricket, football *and* rugby captain, no less.

Also, the biggest head in the school, by far.

Ivan actively encouraged exercise for all children.

He also advocated a sense of humility and modesty in his pupils.

Any strain of arrogance or bullishness immediately repulsed him.

And Shaun Peterson was certainly no wall flower when it came to the art of self-promotion.

Having been told since infancy that he would one day become an achiever in any sport he wished, Peterson quickly began to believe the hype surrounding his potential future status.

Ivan secretly despised the boy's pubescent swagger and would one day hope to hold him up as an example *not* to follow.

The boy had needed cutting down to size for a long time, now.

To his credit, Peterson was talented - and he knew it.

This wasn't the problem.

The thing that frustrated Ivan so was the fact that the teenager would insist on *boasting* to everyone that he was talented and that he knew it.

'One day, Peterson. One day.' Ivan mumbled to himself.

Cranking open the passenger door handle, he reached in for his briefcase and jacket.

As he did so, Ivan was suddenly surprised to see a face at his window as he began to wind it up.

The pale features of Kerry Meadows paraded themselves before him, temporarily blocking his exit from the car. She was an intelligent girl - unusually confident and outgoing for her age.

In truth, she was advanced far beyond her now Second Year peers in many ways. Sadly, this was considered an affliction by most of her classmates, who treated the girl with distrust and shunned her natural sociable disposition as being something rather odd.

Which indeed, it probably was.

'Good morning, sir. Lovely day for the start of the term, isn't it! Did you have a good summer, sir?'

Managing to manoeuvre Kerry away from the car door so he could close it, Ivan finally responded with feigned enthusiasm to her evidently genuine interest.

'Ahh…Miss Meadows! A friendly face to greet me! Yes! Thank you for asking. I had a blissful summer holiday. Did you?'

Jumping up and down on the spot as Ivan rose to his full height of just over six feet, the girl smirked up at him and narrowed her eyes against the sunshine.

'My sister had a baby! I'm an Auntie, now!'

Considering her perturbing revelation for a moment, Ivan ultimately opted to deliver the only plausible reply to her claim.

'That's absolutely *splendid*, Miss Meadows! Splendid! But if you don't mind…I'm running a little late…'

Now fronting an inane grin, Kerry watched as Ivan locked the car.

'See you around then, sir!'

Ivan forced a weak smile before turning toward the playground once again.

Kerry Meadows disappeared joyfully into the crowd, leaving Ivan to stand motionless among his reluctant disciples. The children tittered and whispered as he slowly began to walk among them.

His steady stride and still head concealed an ever-eager eye for potential perpetrators of any unlawful activity that might be occurring at that moment.

Ivan loved to catch criminals red-handed.

He could rarely muster the stamina for a protracted hunt.

The opportunist strike was much more invigorating.

He floated ghoulishly between the groups of pupils, saying nothing, and offering no clue to his intention.

The deeply tinted mask of the Dark Lord was now fully blackened in readiness to detect trouble.

He weaved around the children in silence. Those falling nearest to him felt compelled to second guess the purpose of his covert mission.

An imminent culprit was never far from his grasp.

The element of surprise was an addictive tool in the approach.

Ivan Reynolds had developed the keen eye and the sensitive nose for the sight and scent of dissent.

In fact, he had nurtured a sixth sense over time.

A built-in radar: that rarely failed.

And it continued to serve him well.

The uncertain murmurs of the playground were suddenly eclipsed by an explosive roar of fire and fury that shook all around to attention.

'MISTER HARPER! HERE! TO ME, BOY! NOW!'

The occupants of the vicinity braced themselves and turned into uniformed statues as all attention focused on the subject at hand.

Mark Harper was deemed by most to be a Third Year waste of time and space.

Ivan didn't particularly hold this against him.

But for all pupils, smoking within the school boundary was banned - even for the hopeless and the disinterested.

The alerting bark from the teacher was obeyed without question, although the scowl on young Harper's face suggested more than a streak of rebellion in his soul.

The young man dropped the barely concealed cigarette butt and emerged from his attentive throng of cohorts.

He casually approached the dominant figure in dark spectacles.

The treatment for such lawbreakers was short, sharp, and shocking for observers and criminals alike.

Grasping him by the back of his blazer, Ivan drew the schoolboy onto the tips of his toes to pull him closer and display him to the audience as some exemplary captive.

Mark Harper felt the shirt stitches under his arms begin to fray as his sense of defiance quickly evaporated in the heat of confrontation.

'Hand me those cigarettes please, Mister Harper. Before I tip you upside down and shake them from your pockets. I don't wish to lose my temper so early in the term. So, I suggest you play along, boy!'

There was no verbal reply from the pupil.

Only a trembling gesture of angered compliance as he surrendered the cigarettes.

Releasing his shamed quarry, Ivan took the packet of smokes and placed them in his suit jacket pocket.

'Ah! Embassy filters! My neighbour likes these! I'll be sure to pass them on to him. That is all, Mister Harper, thank you so much.'

Even with the dubious entertainment over, the transfixed audience stood with bated breath just in case Ivan Reynolds should identify another pupil suitable for public reprimand.

They watched and waited as their superior resumed his inspective stride.

Slowly he manoeuvred, in and around the various gangs and gaggles, which gradually emitted an atmospheric sigh of relief to watch him finally enter the main school building.

Via the large glass double doors and then taking a sharp left turn, he seemed to float along the corridor towards the staff room and reception area.

Scores of boys and girls observed his silhouette glide past the row of windows before finally disappearing from view.

Contented that he had satisfied his whim for administering the immediate upper hand, the playground banter quickly resumed its customary volume.

But each and every pupil in that playground now knew, that they should maintain at least one eye firmly focused on those main glass double doors.

Just in case.

3

Pushing open the staff room door, Ivan was greeted by the customary curtain of cigarette smoke which partially obscured the activity within.

By no means an advocate of the habit, he took one step inside and waved his free hand to mimic carving a path through the wall of nicotine. It may have appeared to the observer as an exaggerated gesture of disapproval, but Ivan never tired of performing it.

'What's the damned point in me keeping fit at my age if you lot are trying to poison my lungs on a daily basis? I know I'm getting on but I'm not ready for the box just yet!'

Colleague Matt Jenkins smiled as he stubbed out the remains of his filter tip onto a saucer.

'It's alright for you having nerves of steel, Ivan. We weaker-willed mortals need something to calm ourselves before facing the onslaught!'

Barely amused by the complimentary retort, Ivan shook his head and covered his mouth, muffling a final declaration.

'Well, if I were headmaster, I'd send the bloody lot of you *outside* to chuff to save you all polluting my breathing space!'

Again, Matt accepted the invitation for a verbal joust.

'If you were headmaster, you'd stop people having kids as *well*!'

Now Ivan was inwardly smiling, although his stern expression belied the fact. Placing his briefcase by his favourite armchair and draping his suit jacket over the back, he offered Matt the cigarettes that had been confiscated only moments earlier.

'There you are. Your brand, aren't they? Young Harper won't be needing them anymore.'

Matt Jenkins shook his head whilst avidly lighting up one of the unexpected gifts.

'Been on community patrol already, have we, Ivan?'

The knowing glance between trusting counterparts needed no further expansion.

Matt Jenkins was the unofficial yet accepted understudy to Ivan Reynolds.

At the age of forty-one, he was a few years the junior, but had aspired with learned enthusiasm to wear the mantle of respect that his mentor adorned so graciously.

Both men were tall and slender and regularly adorned their facial expressions with indeterminable grimaces. Both wore metal rimmed spectacles, and both had a penchant for terrifying pupils from a fair old distance with their emphatic vocal ability.

However, where Matt Jenkins was prone to become mildly affectionate toward those in his care over time, Ivan maintained little faith in attaching himself to those under his supervision. To the casual onlooker, this was the only apparent difference in mentality between the pair.

The understudy watched as his master shuffled his way through the myriad of outstretched legs towards the urn in the corner.

'I've already made your drink, Ivan. Five minutes ago, when I saw your car pull in. It's on the table. Sit down and relax for before the big push is called.'

Ivan puckered his lips and nodded in earnest gratitude.

'Thank you, Matthew. Black and no sugar, I take it?'

The apprentice replied behind a garland of grey smoke.

'Of course…and in your favourite Royal wedding mug.'

'That's a relief. So long as you don't think I need sweetening up. I'd hate to feel the need for such artifice. Much obliged to you.'

In truth, Ivan secretly appreciated Matt's unspoken admiration. It offered the possibility that even when he eventually did depart Littleholt's hallowed arches in a few months' time, his legacy of law and discipline would continue to thrive.

'And how's my little pot doll, this morning?'

As he reclined and unfolded the newspaper, Ivan's attention focused on Sarah Green. Like Messrs Jenkins and Reynolds, she was a fellow teacher of mathematics.

A very capable and accomplished tutor, Sarah had only started her career at Littleholt a couple of years ago but had soon become familiarised with the regimental attitudes of her elder, more experienced departmental associates.

Although, she did not always agree with the hard-line dictums that they frequently preferred to employ.

Ivan referred to her as such because of her preference for calf-length dresses, shoes with buckles and a shoulder-length arrangement of blonde curls.

Her blush-red cheeks usually made an appearance when angered or embarrassed. Either of which would invariably occur in Ivan's company given the scenario.

However, despite her somewhat dainty appearance, Sarah was never intimidated by her more aged contemporaries, and they rarely breached the accepted boundaries of gentle mockery.

Her mood this morning was certainly not one to encourage such exchanges.

'Well...I'm not very happy with the workload, Ivan! I'm still concerned about this syllabus we've planned. Matt and I agree it's too much to cover in three terms. Especially for the new First Year pupils.'

Ivan did not look at her as he lowered himself further into his chair and sampled the coffee as well as his newspaper.

'Perfect caffeine, Matthew! Perfect!'

Sarah was not accustomed to being ignored by her colleagues *or* her pupils and was certainly not about to accept being blanked by the head of the department.

'Ivan...did you hear me? All *this*...in *three terms*? Tall order, don't you think?'

Matt smirked and ventured for a seat close by to gain a better view of the ensuing debate.

He might have been a crusty old traditionalist, but Ivan Reynolds was also wonderful entertainment first thing in the morning.

His effortless ability to frustrate the younger members of staff through sheer desire to do so was unsurpassed and regularly successful.

'Sorry...Sarah, darling? Were you addressing *me*?'

She began to fume inwardly at Ivan's supposedly minimal interest in her opinions whilst also striving to ignore the mildly offensive term of endearment.

'I think this year's First Year schedule is too heavy! Way too much material to cover! Never mind the kids struggling! It needs reducing for *our* sakes!'

With one eye on the sports' pages and one ear on his despairing young colleague, Ivan cast a quick glance across the room to ascertain who else might be present.

Still Sarah persevered with her point as she ascertained a glint of responsiveness from behind the darkened shades.

'Ivan! It's now the first day of term! I told you back in June that it needs trimming! Though I think we've left it a little near the knuckle to start pruning at timetables now! We're up the creek without a paddle, rather!'

Finally, Ivan laid his paper on his lap, sampled his drink again and looked up to his fretting female teammate whose cheeks had now adopted the familiar crimson hue.

'My dear Sarah…if you feel that there is a problem with the topic syllabus for this coming academic year, then I shall be glad to discuss it with you in the first departmental meeting of the term. Okay? Is that fair? Am I being reasonable?'

Sarah clenched her teeth, knowing full well that she had little other alternative but to comply. Ivan requested some reassurance that she understood his stance on the issue and in turn continued his attempts to gently shut her up.

'But today, I have other matters of prior importance. In approximately thirty minutes, I shall be escorting my new First Year form group to their new form room whereby I will undertake various menial tasks with them for the duration of the day. This plan I would like to commence…*without* a headache…if possible. Because I bet you a penny to pinch of shit, that I will be *concluding* the day with one! Am I clear enough for you *now*?'

Matt Jenkins could barely conceal his mirth and offered another option as Sarah dithered, hovered, and silently contained her frustration.

'Sit down with us and have a drink. The first department meeting is tomorrow night. Calm yourself, Sarah! God knows you'll have enough reason to get aggravated over the next few weeks as it is.'

Resuming his read, Ivan indulged in the latest predictions of the England cricket captain and cast an eye over the recent football news. Intermittent slurps of coffee allowed him to mull over a suitably flippant solution to any departmental concerns.

Always one for the last word was Ivan Reynolds.

Eventually, the phrase was mentally assembled and duly emitted.

'Sarah, my dear, I've just realised! I'm glad you brought the subject up, actually! It's just occurred to me! It doesn't really matter if the schedule is rather overweight…'

She smiled with caution, knowing that sarcasm was probably imminent. Rolling her eyes with expectancy, she tilted her head toward the older teacher.

'Oh? Why? Enlighten me, Ivan, please do.'

His face creased with a pleasured grimace, giving an even more intimidating gleam to his shaded mask.

'…well, it doesn't matter to *me*, anyway, because I'm only here for the next *two* terms! Then I'm finished with the lot of it!'

Bob Davidson watched appreciatively from the drinks table in the corner. He had been on the staff at Littleholt Secondary School for as long as Ivan, and over the years had mastered the art of capably digesting everybody's conversations and offering very little by way of response.

Some - including it should be said, the great Ivan Reynolds - considered him to be the unofficial yet fully accepted voice of wisdom within the staff room. Hence, on the infrequent occasions that Bob was invited to venture an opinion, those in earshot tended to pay very close attention.

'Ivan…I'm rather puzzled…' he declared, with a slight hint of drama in his tone.

Ivan sighed and looked up from his newspaper once again to raise his brow and cock a ready quip in the barrel.

'My dear man…I'm not surprised you're confused…teaching bloody French *and* German at the same time! I couldn't get the hang of *either* of them!'

Bob remained undeterred in his aim of conveying some common sense to the eager throng.

Despite being distracted by Matt, who continued to giggle quietly behind his swirling cigarette fumes.

'What I mean is I'm a little puzzled…as to why the Head gave you a First Year form when you're not going to see out your full tour of duty with them?'

Ivan laid down the newspaper across his lap once more and drained his coffee mug. Sensing the growing audience waiting for his reply, he obliged with a typical combination of logic and humour.

'Bob. Great question as always. The Headmaster gave me First Year pupils…because I *asked* for First Year pupils. Thus, I hope to have dispelled your confusion in the matter.'

Now fully intrigued, Matt joined the debate.

'You…*asked*…for a First Year form group? In your hour of retirement? Have you gone barking mad?'

Placing the empty coffee mug beside him and sinking even lower into his favourite chair, Ivan rebuked his colleague's apparent astonishment.

'Mad? *Me*? Of course, I am, Matthew! I'm mad as the bloody hatter! But I'm also very considerate when it comes to my fellow members of staff…'

Bob, Matt and Sarah gazed at one another, knowing that some form of ironic justification was due to follow.

'…well, my friends…I couldn't leave the young ones to suffer some poor student teacher now, could I? First Year pupils need breaking in rapidly. And I'm by far the most diligent at showing our freshers how the land lies around here. I simply couldn't bear to think of the hurdles facing a lesser mortal than myself.'

The laughter soon echoed around the staff room and was duly interrupted by Sarah who moved quickly and appropriately to introduce a new colleague to the teaching fraternity who had just entered the fray.

'Listen up please, gentlemen. This is Phil Holmes. He supplied here most of last term. Do you remember?'

Matt stood to his feet and shook the newcomer by the hand whilst Ivan observed the pasty complexion, innocent eyes and unkempt hair of the stranger. In truth, he did not recognise the man standing uncomfortably before him.

Sitting cross-legged with newspaper still on his lap, Ivan took little deliberation in mounting a typically critical if completely fabricated appraisal of the figure standing next to Sarah.

'Oh yes! I recall that tatty suit and wonky tie! Of course…Philip! So, they snaffled you with a contract, hey? Poor soul! You have my deepest sympathies.'

Sarah handed Phil a mug of tea as he stooped to sit into the one vacant armchair in the circle. Again, Ivan took the opportunity to anoint him with an extended forefinger.

'Don't sit there. Philip! Carol sits there! We are very strict about parking arrangements in here, you know!'

Unwisely and in all naivety, the newcomer chose to strike back at Ivan with a few responsive doses of his own sense of sarcasm.

'Well, I don't see her name on it, anywhere. By the way…its Phil…not *Philip*! Not even my mother calls me Philip, anymore.'

Ivan was un-swayed by the young man's witless repost and continued with his own carefully honed script.

'And I do believe that you're holding Carol's tea mug in your hand as well! This is *intolerable*! *Two* sins for the price of *one*! Dear me, Philip! I do hope she comes in and catches you red-handed! It'll be confessional for you come Sunday, my boy!'

Phil Holmes looked at the half-smiles on the faces of those nearby and opted to return serve with a verbal volley once again.

'I'd heard about you before I came to this school. The great Mister Reynolds! Only two more terms left, haven't you?'

The audience gasped as Ivan leaned forward in his chair and presented his widest, zaniest grin which suitably underscored the foreboding black lenses of his spectacles.

'Unfortunately for you…and the children…yes. You're stuck with me for quite a while yet. By the way…what subject do you teach, Philip?'

Phil Holmes was becoming quietly incensed.

But he had been warned by several of the staff not to rise to the bait that Ivan Reynolds was so adept at dangling. Calming himself by mentally counting to ten, he adopted a renewed air of civility and spoke with undue courtesy.

'General science, though physics, specifically.'

Now pressing his back firmly into his chair, the elder opponent clasped both hands on top of his head before firing his next shot.

'Physics, eh? What a frightful bore! Hope you give out pillows to the pupils. I'd hate them to nod off and crack their little heads on the desks…'

Carol Shaw entered the room just as Ivan's performance against the younger protagonist was beginning to simmer.

She carried a stern demeanour.

Short, stout, and bespectacled, Carol sported a thick mop of white hair and a thin line of a mouth.

Being a very vocal geography teacher by trade, Littleholt pupils had traditionally deemed her to be Ivan's female equivalent.

Possessing a very similar temperament and principles to Ivan, she had become secretly enamoured by him over the fifteen years they had worked alongside one another.

It wasn't a romantic attraction, however; more a strictly respectful, professional one.

She too viewed schoolchildren as needing commandment as a forerunner to commendation. The former being preferable to the latter even if both treatments were deemed applicable.

And her occasionally explosive temper had been audibly indicated across the playing fields many a time during her auspicious secondary school teaching career.

Now undertaking the pertinent role of Head of First Year, she was eager to see that the morning of introductions and roll-calling went as smoothly as possible. With an unconvincing expression of pleasure, she bid good morning to her fellow staff mates.

After the courteous responses, Ivan ventured forth with a well-received line.

'Carol! How I've so missed your scornful smirk these past few weeks. And another thing…how come you managed to excuse yourself from the past two days' induction training?'

Adopting the toothy glare reminiscent of a crocodile at feeding time, Carol addressed the enquiry with equal proficiency.

'Because I heard *you* were here, Ivan! And I don't want to endure you for any longer than is absolutely necessary!'

Feigning a sense of deep emotional hurt, Ivan quickly rose to his feet and shook a large fist gamely in her direction.

'I may look hard and nasty, Carol! But I am still only a mere man. If you cut me…I do so bleed!'

She chuckled unreservedly before offering a genuine reason for her recent absence.

'Monday I was still on holiday in Portugal…and Tuesday I was still knackered from my holiday in Portugal. Is that okay with everyone?'

Matt Jenkins moved forward to stub out his umpteenth cigarette of the morning.

'Portugal, eh? Someone's being paid far too much money by the sound of it! We only made it to Salcombe, this year!'

'Lucky Salcombe! Did you bring me any rock back, Matthew?' Ivan chipped in, just as the signature bell for registration resonated throughout the building beyond.

'Not with your dodgy teeth, Ivan! Too much of a risk at your age!'

More laughter ensued among the throng as the door swung open yet again to reveal the slightly troubled features of headmaster Geoff Taylor. He appeared a trifle hassled as his immaculately dressed form hung from the frame half-way into the room.

Without pausing to pass even so much as a good morning greeting, he silenced the idle chatter with an important announcement.

'Okay, guys and gals! When you're ready! Matt and Sarah could you do the honours in filing the First Years from the playground and into the dining hall, please? Anyone here with a First Year form group needs to make their way in there also. Come along. No time to dilly-dally.'

And with that, the Headmaster was gone from the room as the first siren signified the commencement of the new term. Ivan juggled the newspaper on his lap and attempted to resume with the cricket story he had diverted from few minutes earlier.

As the rest of the teachers hurriedly finished their drinks and extinguished their smokes, he sighed with practised resignation and imparted a few words of inevitability to the oblivious departing group.

'So, my friends…this is how liberty ends…to the sound of an endless, droning bell…'

4

He watched as the remainder of his colleagues steadily trickled from the staff room. Eventually completely alone, Ivan sat among the silence and observed the scene of destruction that had been left behind.

Open and empty cigarette packets lay on every surface. The aroma of weak coffee played under his nose and dissipating smoke rings hung like small wreaths around the ceiling fixtures.

He pulled his father's silver watch from its home in his waistcoat pocket and flicked open the face cover.

Ten minutes to nine.

As he contemplated the unavoidable annual introduction that awaited his presence in the main hall, it really did seem like too much effort to move a single muscle at that moment.

Those pure undisturbed seconds of solitude each morning before registration were now so precious to him.

It never troubled his senses before, but so much of the modern school day had become a relentless assault on the ear drums.

A persistent crescendo of scraping footsteps and screaming playgrounds; the scraping furniture and the screaming dining hall; scraping for exam results and screaming of teachers.

Crossing his legs once more and arranging the pages of the newspaper back into some semblance of order, he dropped it on the coffee table and glanced beyond the window through partially closed horizontal blinds.

The window that coincidentally offered him a prime view of the playground.

He watched as the older pupils made their way to pre-designated form rooms. They were in the fortunate majority that were undoubtedly content in the knowledge that they had already trodden the uncertain and wary path that today's new arrivals were about to endure.

But nothing was a steadfast guarantee for any schoolboy or schoolgirl whilst Ivan Reynolds still trod such upon such holy ground.

The phantom was never far away from their thoughts.

The labyrinth of shadowy corridors concealed many hidden surprises; but none so surprising as he was to those little ones.

The minutes lingered peacefully on as the long line of innocent new faces were organised and subsequently paraded by Matt and Sarah, from the relative haven of the car park and into the maw of unchartered territory.

He casually listened as two hundred pairs of impish footsteps in two hundred pairs of brand-new shoes shuffled tentatively beyond the closed staff room door along the brightly lit passageway.

He visualised the scores of eleven-year-old boys and girls in their spotless new uniforms that would now be hesitantly amassed in the school's main assembly hall. With its recently polished wooden tile flooring that caused rubber soles to instantly squeak on contact, that would then reverberate for a second or two around the high corners of the chamber.

Soon the new innocents would be seated and cross-legged.

Seated and cross-legged and waiting.

Waiting for their calling.

Soon it would be time for his grand entrance into the arena.

He checked the hands of his pocket-watch once more.

Five minutes before nine o'clock.

Carol had specifically requested a prompt nine am start.

Ivan imagined her standing before the expectant and unnerved throng with clipboard in hand, ready to announce the names and despatch the children to their differing destinies.

He continued to scrutinise the now deserted playground through the blinds. All children looked to have been dispersed within the building.

Not a soul was to be seen in the warm morning light of that late summer day, but any remnants of the long holiday would soon become overcast for those blissfully unaware newcomers.

Still Ivan remained, embracing the tranquillity, and checking the silver pocket-watch again.

One minute to nine o'clock.

It was now time to move, he supposed.

Ivan would readily push any schedule to its absolute limit, but not in a purposed attempt to show any discourtesy to Carol as the mistress of ceremony.

It was more by way of lulling the new influx into a false sense of security. In the recent few minutes since being called into the main hall, the intake of First Year pupils would have observed every single teacher that sat around the edges of that echoing auditorium.

They knew not who their designated form tutors would be until the entire list of names had been exhausted. Only then would the respective leaders be fully assigned to their groups.

But of course, it went without saying that nobody wanted to be in 1RY.

Nobody in their eleven-year-old right mind wanted Ivan Reynolds as their form tutor.

Seeing him; watching them.

Every single morning; every single afternoon.

Listening to his gravelled, rasping voice as it verified the twice-daily attendance register.

The little ones having to explain any excusing adversity that may have fallen in their path should they ever dare to be late to his registration calling.

To the younglings who had listened to the myth, he was a symbol of immense power and authority.

Across the local district, junior schools had been rife with unsettling rumours during June. And then July. It was an unwritten wish of every new child attending Littleholt Secondary School for the first time.

The last teacher of choice was Mister Reynolds.

Nobody wanted to be in 1RY.

And so, Ivan let the little ones breathe their sighs of faint, futile, hopeful anticipation as they inwardly yet slowly began to rejoice at the realisation of his possible and apparent absence.

Absence that was, in fact, a deliberately delayed arrival to the scene.

As if by some incredulous, miraculous twist of fate, the eleven-year-old boys and girls might just convince themselves in those precious few minutes of false prayer that Mister Reynolds was perhaps no longer even residing at the school.

That he had perhaps gone forever and was never to return to haunt the dreams and occasionally validate the nightmares of those local little ones.

Together, those boys and those girls sat with the united and gradual belief that the ghost they feared had duly been exorcised once and for all.

But alas, no such chance would they be allowed to embrace.

Not on this day.

This most anticipated of all days.

Ivan finally resigned himself to duty. He checked his appearance in the staff room's cracked mirror and slipped on his suit jacket.

Brushing imaginary dust from his lapels and coaxing his cuffs through the jacket sleeves, he silently pulled open the staff room door, stepped out into the reception area and quietly closed the door behind him.

Then he commenced the walk along the main corridor toward the assembly hall.

A measured and soundless approach that could never be detected by mischief-makers until way too late in the game.

Stealth was a major attribute for any teacher.

Smiling and nodding at the receptionist as he passed the glass portal of the visitors' hatch, at that moment he felt every inch the demon that those innocent little children dreaded so.

'Morning, Mary.'

'Good morning, Ivan. Glad to be back?'

'Elated, Mary. Elated.'

Leaving the receptionist in his wake, she chuckled at his mild yet always effective sarcasm.

Along the corridor ever further, towards the double glass doors of the hall, where he could already sense the gradually dissipating trepidation among its juvenile inhabitants.

Yet the crucifying woe was almost upon those many young heads that faced the stage. Their subsiding worry would return imminently and swiftly.

On reaching the entrance, he looped his right forefinger around the right door handle and gingerly pulled it toward him, allowing a sufficient gap to form that would enable his subversive entrance.

Slowly, silently, studiously he entered the assembly hall.

And gradually, mournfully, one by one, those young heads of those First Year boys and those First Year girls began to turn in acknowledgement of the dreaded black cloud looming over their blue-sky land of hope.

Hope which had been nurtured over previous weeks and days.

Hope that was now ground to dust in one, single second of realisation.

First, two pairs of eyes. Then ten. Then two hundred, warily observed the figure in the darkened spectacles move beyond the door in the corner.

They studied him, numb and transfixed, as he selected a convenient position to stand, before leaning back against the wall and casually folding his arms.

Aware of the scrutiny he was under, his mouth formed into an indeterminable line.

He looked back at their cherubic faces from the dark seclusion of his mask.

Their crossed legs; their sharp haircuts; their new clean shoes.

This was Ivan Reynolds' territory.

Their growing despair was tangible as they soaked up his belated appearance in all its awesome, intimidating glory.

He readily sampled their dread whilst offering a tilt of the head to Carol who tried and failed miserably in her attempt to refrain from smirking.

In practised desperation, she hid her evolving mirth behind the clipboard held firmly in her grasp.

And even as she began the introductions and commenced the announcement to the fortunate majority, most of the little angels sitting on that shiny wooden floor had no true idea who was destined to meet with the ultimate force in the school.

Nobody wanted to be in 1RY.

Yet nobody knew who would be called to comply with that terrifying ordainment.

Still the young eyes turned to bore into him at random intervals. Their fingers crossed and their hearts twitching with wishful ambition that they might be saved from entering his frightful lair.

And still Ivan stood with arms folded.

Expressionless and staring straight ahead.

He remained motionless as the names were read out by Carol.

Child by child and class by class, was slowly extricated from the doom-laden few that could be and would be eventually designated to his form group.

Having imposed such a searing presence on many similar occasions over many years, Ivan simply stood by as each of his colleagues in turn gradually escorted their newly recruited infantry of soldiers from the main hall.

He sensed their almost tangible relief as they passed him by, never daring to look up at the tall giant with the blackest of eyes.

Indeed, they now strived to avoid his glare, just in case a mistake had been made and they had been placed in the wrong tutor group.

Matt Jenkins led his joyless throng of youngsters from the hall and out through the glass double doors, but not before offering a sympathetic wink to Ivan.

Yet the elder teacher did not emit a flicker of response.

Instead, his attention craned to hear the closing words from Carol, whose initial duty as Head of First Year had been carried out to regimental perfection.

And then it finally hit them.

The last remaining pupils scattered across the floor.

Sitting cross-legged in their brand-new shoes.

Newly uniformed boys and newly uniformed girls with their sharply cut hair and their tightly bound pigtails.

Now oh so anxious and facing their vulnerability.

Thirty-one pupils in all - fifteen boys and sixteen girls - remained to be confronted with the unavoidable, inevitable revelation.

The Head of First Year spoke softly as she introduced them to their new form tutor. Just as Ivan had requested, Carol had left the announcement of those to be seconded to him until very last of all.

The names in the final group needed no further confirmation. Those left stranded to meet with such a perilous fate were eagerly ordered by Carol to centre their full attention to the rear wall of the main hall.

To cast their frigid gazes unto the imposing, unsmiling figure in the three-piece taupe suit.

To the rear of that echoing, ghost-riddled chasm; where their new form tutor duly stood; with arms still folded and dark lenses now conveying more uncertainty than those children could ever have imagined them to.

The incoming, newly pronounced members of 1RY watched with racing pulses and worried brows as he eventually moved from his post and floated purposely and silently toward them and among them.

His pupils.

His form group.

His for the next two terms.

And then, as the children vainly grappled for a last possible chance of respite, their imminent damnation was confirmed as the Head of First Year handed over the ceremonial reins.

'*Yours*…I believe, Mister Reynolds?'

Ivan smiled at her invitation.

'Thank you so much…Miss Shaw.'

1RY shuddered in trepidation as the acidic yet strangely soft tone of their newly appointed leader cut the atmosphere with his opening statement to them.

'Good morning…you…lucky…lucky…people.' Ivan exclaimed, as he cast his imposing glare over the transfixed gathering.

Watching their features frozen with fearful resignation, he wallowed in the sense of respect they unwittingly yet automatically conveyed.

No one dare speak; no one dare swallow.

Fifteen boys and sixteen girls - the butterflies that inhabited their stomachs earlier now swooped in and around the depths of their guts like giant bats.

And then, the teacher spoke again.

'My name…is Mister Reynolds. I am your form leader for this year. You are collectively to be known as…1RY…'

Thirty-one children mentally cried out for their parents to rescue them as a crooked forefinger beckoned them upwards and onwards.

'Ladies and gentlemen…to your feet if you please. I will escort you to room ten. I shall expect everyone to memorise the route as I shall not be on hand to chaperone you *every* morning. Follow me.'

Thirty-one schoolchildren congregated.

Thirty-one brand new school bags were retrieved from the newly polished, shiny wooden floor.

Following their new master from the hall, one or two echoed murmurs were heard to ascend to the ceiling rafters.

Those occasional remarks from among thirty-one concerned children were soon thwarted by a shrill command from the front of the line.

'QUIET PLEASE, 1RY! Thank you, so much.'

Carol Shaw watched with concealed admiration and only a mild pang of sympathy for the young chosen ones, as the final group reservedly followed along the main corridor.

Past the staff room and reception area, and towards the bottom of the distant stairwells.

Ivan Reynolds did not need to glance over his shoulder at the flinching flock, as he calmly escorted them along the murky spinal pathway to the furthest of the two flights of stairs.

Then the ascent to room ten would commence.
Ivan Reynolds leading his disciples from the front.
Never looking back.
Now only looking forward.
Really looking forward.

5

Listening to the soles of their shoes scuffing the recently scrubbed faux-stone staircase, the pupils of 1RY tentatively kept pace with the ominous silhouette of their form tutor up ahead, who led the throng without any further vocal instruction.

Any willingness in the group to emit the lowest of low whispers had been quashed by the prior diktat of their leader.

Eyeing one another to ascertain faces both familiar and strange, the children gradually assembled themselves in a trembling formation on the third level landing outside room ten.

Ivan positioned himself at the door and removed the keys from his pocket before dangling the fob from his right forefinger.

The left hand then reached into his waistcoat for the silver pocket-watch. He flipped open the cover. After studying the face of the timepiece for a moment or two, he then returned it to the pocket and scrutinised the thirty-one sets of angelic features through his mysterious visor.

Then the voice of authority was heard once more, accompanied by a gesture to the rear of the landing.

'Coats on the hooks behind you, please. Gentlemen…I would like you to form a line in any order of your choice. Ladies, when this is achieved, I would like you to form a line parallel to them. Double file…as opposed to single file. Do we all understand?'

The newly elected members of 1RY gazed at one another dumbfounded as if their teacher's request had just been issued in a foreign language.

Ivan scanned their youthful uncertainty and tried not to display any sign of frustration as he began to spin the room keys around on the end of his finger. Evidently causing some confusion, the repeated version of the instruction was laced with sarcasm and slightly higher in volume.

'Two lines! Boys…and girls! Not at all difficult! Previous generations have managed to solve this initial puzzle without a single hitch.'

The group hastily began to rearrange itself according to Ivan's design.

Eventually, two straight rows of pupils evolved from the huddle. They each returned the discerning stare of their new master as a litter of puppies would wait for a loyalty reward.

Ivan begrudgingly accepted the final arrangement that stood quivering before him and sighed with feigned annoyance.

'Ten minutes! That's how long has transpired since I first introduced myself to you all in the dining hall. In precisely ten full minutes, we have managed to walk upstairs and stand outside the door. I can see its going to be a very long day.'

One or two amused if confused responses emerged among the apprehensive group, prompting Ivan to explain the logic behind the baffling design.

'In my form room…nobody sits next to their friends. Everybody is invited to make a *new* friend, today. So, each of you now will turn to face the boy or girl standing adjacent to you.'

The class complied with a natural sense of coy hesitancy as one or two exasperated groans of embarrassment slowly arose from the rear of the pack.

'I shall now unlock the door. I wish for you all to enter in your pairs as you are and take a seat next to one another. Starting at the farthest table nearest my desk and snaking your way to the back and then to the front once again and so on. Is this clear to all?'

The gentle rumble of disgruntlement was quickly confirmed with a resounding voice of disparity from the end of the boys' line.

'I'm not sitting next to *her*! No way!'

Ivan's ears instantly twitched as he withdrew the key from the lock, his attention becoming drawn toward the source of discontentment.

He began to move along the giggling ranks to decipher the cause of the unwarranted outburst.

'So…as expected…somebody wishes to lodge an early complaint, do they? Do we have a mutineer on board? Well! Hands up the one issuing the cry of objection!'

A rough-looking urchin of a boy with a very short haircut and a single stud in his left ear spoke out to repeat his disapproval.

'It's *her*! I'm not sitting next to *her*! She *stinks*!'

More laughter bounced among the group as Ivan stood over the overly vocal youngster before stooping down to his eye level.

Simultaneously and without warning, he placed a hand on the back of the boy's shoulder and ushered his subject even closer to afford the conversation to continue in a lowered tone.

'What is your name, son?'

His features still sporting a frown of distaste, the lone rebel stared vainly into the murky lenses of his form teacher.

'Trevor Sims.'

'Trevor Sims...*sir*. In future, you address me as *sir*. Now...let's try again shall we, Mister Sims?'

Evidently one with a nose for trouble, young Trevor reluctantly opted to play the game by the rules.

'Yes...sir...'

'We do not allow children to shout out in this form group. Nor do we allow boys to wear jewellery. Nor...are boys allowed to wear...white... socks...'

The churlish youth continued to stare blankly into the intimidating facade of his school master.

'Not a positive introduction to your tenure here at Littleholt...is it...Mister Sims? But...it's your first day and everyone deserves a second chance. Please remove the ear stud now this moment. I don't want to see it again. Your socks will be either black, grey, blue, or brown come tomorrow.'

Ivan quickly discharged the grimacing youngster and re-positioned himself at the classroom door. Again, he scrutinised the now ashen faces for any further sign of resistance.

'I do not bow down to anybody's personal preference. If anything, *you* are all here to satisfy *mine*. Now...in we go...before I become ever more agitated at this tragic waste of time and oxygen. Stand behind your chairs until I give the word to be seated.'

Hovering around the landing, Ivan discreetly peered through the glass portholes in the adjacent classroom doors.

Matt Jenkins had seemingly made a more successful start to inducting his new arrivals.

Sarah Green; likewise.

But Ivan had always felt his younger colleagues tended to rush into the menial details of school duty and forego the more important aspects of familiarising the new influx to the school codes of conduct.

Such as establishing, without leaving any strain of doubt in the minds of the pupils, who was in charge.

Modern teachers were increasingly too casual and indeed far too sociable for his liking.

And consequently, many modern pupils were becoming increasingly informal and belligerent.

Despite his unspoken acknowledgement of Matt's respectful admiration, Ivan was aware that those true to his own ilk were a dying breed. But his methods would never be compromised.

Even in this closing chapter. His last stand.

Turning away from his colleagues' classrooms, he re-engaged with the task of organising his own form group.

With the two rows of boys and girls now ensnared into the grey-walled cell that was room ten, Ivan followed them in and quietly pressed the door into the frame.

Once standing behind his desk, he observed the random pairings from behind the veil of his shaded spectacles.

A class of thirty-one, indeed.

Fifteen pairs of boys and girls.

And one girl left over.

Ivan studied the lonesome figure hunched disconsolately over the last table in the end row.

He was very adept at analysing pupils and their personalities simply by studying their appearance and body language.

The plump, uncomfortable looking girl stood alone staring down at the desktop. Her comparatively large adolescent build was accentuated by two thick pig tails tied in emerald ribbon which matched the bottle green cardigan, skirt, and tie.

He noticed she had greasy hair, sensing this was probably due to an unhealthy diet and evident lack of exercise.

Undoubtedly being fully aware of her own sizable proportions she was also evidently conscious of her subsequent lesser standing among the rest of her peers.

With hands linked across her stomach, she looked every inch the dejected First Year pupil.

Ivan pondered her supposed personal predicament for a second or two before letting his attention fall to the table at the front of the same row.

The table that Trevor Sims was standing behind.

The youngster's smirking face mirrored that of his teacher.

It appeared that this seemingly willing opponent wished to nail his individual colours to the mast with some immediacy.

Although Ivan noticed to his pleasant surprise that the offending ear stud had indeed been removed.

'I have examined everybody's uniforms…and you will be relieved to learn that everybody has passed the test. Everybody that is, aside the aforementioned Mister Sims, who has assured me that he will endeavour to rectify his appearance in time for tomorrow morning's registration.'

Ivan smiled at the young pretender, who's silent yet telling sneer conveyed a thousand unspoken insults.

Young Sims was evidently a cheeky rogue.

And Ivan Reynolds adored cheeky rogues.

When opposed by such he found himself in his element.

Assuming the upper hand was his forte, with pupils and adults alike. He believed this moment was the ultimate position of strength for any teacher in any school.

The first exchanges with the new First Year incumbents were crucial in determining the balance of power from the outset.

Should any sign of weakness be displayed by the tutor, the pupils would harvest, expose, and promote that frailty.

Yet unbeknown to them at that moment, 1RY would not uncover any chinks in this particular teacher's armoury.

As all children in his classes had discovered over time, Ivan Reynolds possessed no deficiency.

He was infallible; to the last.

The seating exercise was a simple, yet tried and tested charade designed to implement a realm of order. It didn't really achieve very much aside placing the pupils on their backsides - but also very much on their guard.

Once immersed in unfamiliar territory with unfamiliar faces, all children were quickly rendered compliant.

It was an efficient way to garner the room's full attention.

An effortless method of exerting tutorial authority.

And the tranquil sense of anticipation now ensuing among the group was music to Ivan's ears.

'1RY…you may now…be seated.'

His almost whispered request encouraged the momentary scraping of chairs and positioning of school bags.

With his back to the group, Ivan wiped the blackboard clean and scrawled a single word across it in high, chalky, bold capital letters.

RULES.

Rubbing his hands to clear them of chalk-dust, he then clasped them behind his back and began to walk slowly in and around the attentive congregation as he conveyed the first sermon of the day in controlled, velvet tones.

'There is no need to delve for paper and pencils just yet. The only tools you require are a capable set of ears and an absorbent brain. Firstly, let me welcome one and all to Littleholt Secondary. Putting things literally and concisely, it is now time for all of you to grow up.'

His indeterminable smile returned as he bathed in the united attention and cleared his throat.

'This is not a junior school environment, and as such you are no longer to be classed as junior school pupils. Your future from here onward is a two-way street.'

He had their full attention as he moved up and down the aisles.

'You are going to be treated as *adults* from this point on…if, of course, you show sufficient capability of *acting* like adults.'

Ivan stopped speaking once again and let his eyes focus on the captive audience for a few seconds before continuing his stroll.

'If such a premise appears too challenging, then I can assure you that your life here will be difficult. In short…if you play fair with me, I shall consider playing fair with you. Those that aren't willing to behave and toe the line…are…PLAYING…WITH…FIRE!'

Ivan stopped in his stride and quickly turned his head as if to specifically jolt those nearby that might just be daydreaming.

To his surprise, all still seemed focused to his each and every word.

He smiled once again and continued to float around the room between the desks.

'It goes without stating that, at this moment, this is a foreign environment to you all. A new lay out. New corridors. New hiding places. There are also lots of new toys that you might be tempted to play with. These toys are strictly forbidden territory! For instance, this school has its own science laboratories. Anybody found to be misusing the equipment - such as igniting gas taps with cigarette lighters or pouring acid into sandwich boxes - will be set alight themselves and…LEFT…TO…BURN!'

Warmth began to spread among the group as the tutor's speech adopted a distinctively entertaining slant.

'Anybody found swimming or fighting in the biology ponds will be tied to the bottom and permanently left alone to study the contents therein whilst fully immersed!'

Now those once wary children began to giggle in ready response.

'There is also a fully equipped gymnasium. Any playful monkeys among you who so much as hang onto a rope without asking permission…or having supervision…will be hung from a rope…without having to ask permission or having supervision.'

1RY was now engulfed by laughter as the very adept ringmaster continued to impress the gathering.

'This school also boasts a working kitchen for those of you undertaking your cookery syllabus. Anybody tampering with the ovens…will be duly roasted alive and basted every hour until VERY…WELL…DONE!'

Ivan continued to encircle his classroom, covertly watching the group of gigglers from behind the semi-darkness of his mask.

They carefully listened to the good-natured warnings. And yet he could see that Trevor Sims was still scowling. But he also sensed that the plump girl with the pig tails sitting alone, was now looking directly at Ivan and was obviously very amused by her teacher's light-hearted approach.

This was the sight that offered Ivan Reynolds his first pang of joy that day.

That a young lady's sorrowful frown had rapidly evolved into a beautiful smile.

'Those…basically…are the RULES! There are many other minor regulations that will become apparent as time goes on, but I won't bore you with them all now. We have one or two other supposedly more important tasks to perform together.'

As Ivan continued to address the group, he detected whispers emanating from the back of the room.

This was a habit he despised.

A pet hate that instantly fuelled him with vexation.

Any sign of wilful ignorance in the domain of 1RY was strictly forbidden. As the culprits would soon discover.

He coyly advanced toward the ongoing and oblivious distraction, whilst casting implicit warning of his approach for the benefit of all present.

'You will strive to annoy me, ladies. Yet I am a very patient teacher. But one of the things that I cannot tolerate is blatant bad manners.'

Ivan homed in on the preoccupied targets, stretching the fingers and thumb of his right hand before making a large fist and continuing to engage the full attention of the rest of the group.

'When I am talking, no one else is permitted to speak unless I *grant* them permission. If you wish to interrupt me, please raise your hand and I will duly invite your contribution.'

With his back to the chattering offenders, Ivan suddenly turned on his heels to face them.

'IS...THAT...CLEAR?'

With each word, the base of his fist came crashing down onto the tabletop, giving cause for the entire room to shake violently.

The shattering din engaged everybody in the vicinity, including Matt Jenkins in the adjacent classroom, who quickly assured his new form group against the theory that the noise may have been a bomb or distant gunfire. Or an earthquake.

With his hand still placed firmly atop the desk, Ivan closed in on the faces of the two girls, who instantly drew their attention back to his imposing presence, whilst cowering in the glare of the spotlight.

He continued to stare at the offenders for a full half minute, until satisfied that they had understood the short, sharp lesson in classroom etiquette.

Rising again to his full height, a faint grin re-emerged as he headed back to the blackboard.

'And that...is how...ladies and gentlemen...I acquired the nickname with which I am sure you are already familiar. Rest assured...*Ironfist* is not a term of endearment. It is a reputation that I uphold to the letter. It is also a warning.'

Taking certain pleasure in the stunted responses of his form group, he gestured once more with his tightly clenched fingers and thumb, so as the knuckles pierced white against the tanned skin.

'So...1RY...consider yourselves *warned*...'

6

'I abhor this period of clerical necessity but alas it is unavoidable.'

Under the scrutiny of thirty-one bemused schoolchildren, Ivan was now perched in his chair with both feet crossed firmly atop his desk. With hands clasped on his lap, he looked anything but the ominous character of Littleholt folklore.

For a brief sun-kissed moment he mentally removed himself from the classroom and was transported across town to the allotment, admiring his plot whilst browsing the newspaper and listening to the cricket commentary on the radio.

But only for a brief, sun-kissed moment.

It was time for the new regiment to perform their kit check as Ivan rasped idly from the front of the room, staring beyond the large windows into the wide blue yonder as he delivered the well-trodden procedure.

'Am I correct to hold the presumption that your parents have done you all proud in obtaining the recommended supplies?'

The class simply stared back toward their teacher without reply, causing him to centre his gaze to the rear wall of the room.

'Do I take the collective confused silence as a *yes*? Can I truly sleep soundly in the knowledge that everybody has pencil cases, calculators, P.E. wear, and the like? Is everybody equipped to this effect? Fine! There's no need to begin rummaging through your bags. I shall not be inspecting today. I believe you. Well, maybe not Mister Sims, but most of you…'

The young imp was again alerted to the mention of his name and glared towards his form tutor, who in return remained utterly expressionless as he covertly returned the young man's stare over the shining leather toes of his shoes.

Reluctantly lowering his feet, Ivan then reached for a white cardboard box positioned underneath his desk. With the box placed securely under his right arm, he then embarked on another slow-motion ramble around the classroom, in turn dropping a pink-covered booklet in front of each pupil.

'As you will have hopefully gleaned from the wording on the front, these are your school diaries. They are to be utilised specifically for the subjects you will be studying in school. They are *not* for doodling poems about boyfriends or scrawling rude words about form teachers. They should be signed each week by your parents, who can also add their own comments should they wish to do so. You may *not* add any commentary of your own. By such commentary, I offer as example "UNITED RULE OK" and similar futile references.'

Again, the members of the class responded in amusement as Ivan continued with his well-rehearsed monologue.

'During our first official form period, which will take place one week from today, I will need to sign them as well. You must record all homework duties when issued, so as not to conveniently forget to do the homework once beyond school premises and in front of your televisions. Your subject teachers will also ensure that the diaries are being used correctly. One thing you will *all* do before next Wednesday's form period is to cover your school diaries with brown paper. *Not* newspaper. *Not* wallpaper. *Not* fish and chip paper. *Not* toilet paper…but *BROWN*…paper. Consider this task to be your first homework assignment of the term.'

Ivan turned his head sharply at ninety degrees and hissed.

'Especially…you…Mister…Sims.'

A begrudging display of acknowledgement emerged across the face of the grubby looking boy.

Ivan continued his tour of the room with the now empty box, which was dropped conveniently next to the dustbin.

With hands inserted into trouser pockets, Ivan then spoke with his back to class and facing directly at the blackboard.

'This form group will stay together for all lessons for at least the entirety of this first year…possibly the second year also depending of course…on any expulsions…Mister Sims. You will have your registration taken here twice a day in this room every morning at eight-fifty and every afternoon at one-twenty-five. Your form periods will also take place in this room…with me...every…week…'

As his wandering gaze travelled back through the windowpane and down onto the manicured green swathes of the sports field, Ivan felt sure he heard a whine of discontentment emit from someone in the vicinity but could not decipher the source.

He opted to ignore it.

The late summer sun continued to illuminate the arena of room ten as he turned once more to face the attentive faces of 1RY.

'Who knows, ladies and gentlemen? Fortune may well smile upon you. I might just bump into you for the odd maths lesson should Mrs. Green be inconvenienced. Or maybe even a P.E. lesson if Mister Rogers is unavailable. I am very adaptable you know! I can be anywhere and anything...at any one time!'

More winsome sighs hung in the air, causing Ivan to nod his head in appreciation of the perpetrator's honesty of opinion, although their identity remained undisclosed.

Trevor Sims suddenly put up his hand to speak which was duly referenced by his superior.

'Do you not usually teach First Years then, sir?'

Ivan could detect the anxious expectancy in the boy's tone as he ventured a reply to the perfectly justified curiosity.

'Only...and I mean *only*...if I've been desperately unlucky in the draw, Mister Sims. But yours was a fair question, nevertheless.'

Trevor grinned with short-lived satisfaction as Ivan hooked his thumbs into his waistcoat pockets and began to float among the tables yet again.

He was not quite prepared to let the youngster feel so pleased with himself just yet.

'However, Mister Sims...I'm pretty certain that our paths will cross regarding other matters during the course of the next few months...you won't shake me off that easily...I can assure you.'

Trevor mockingly wiped his brow and emitted an exaggerated expression of relief that caused a girl sitting across the aisle to burst into laughter.

'Was there something humorous you'd like to share with us, Miss...?'

The scrawny, fair-haired girl immediately ceased her giggling whilst placing a hand to her mouth.

Through her fingers, she issued her name.

'Johnson...sir. Hilary Johnson. No, sir. Nothing's funny, sir.'

Ivan eyed the girl with guarded suspicion until she gathered some composure after her mirthful outburst.

For now, he let the moment pass.

But only for now.

'Next for despatch are your timetables, canteen menus and plans of the school layout. When combined, these resources should ensure that nobody has any excuses for *not* being *WHERE* they should be...*WHEN* they should be there. Please feel free to memorise these documents *before* you mislay them. Absent-minded schoolchildren are the bane of my life. Lost schoolchildren drive me to utter madness. And we don't want that, do we? Suffice to say, I expect you to be punctual at all times. Delay me during *my* day...and I shall feel free to delay *you* at the end of *your* day. Is this clear to one and all?'

The class mumbled in reserved agreement as Ivan distributed the relevant paperwork.

And unbeknown to the thirty-one pupils in the room, he found himself already developing certain affinity for his new form group.

But of course, it was very, very early days.

*****

The next two hours were spent complying with the school records requirements, clarifying anomalies regarding timetable arrangements and generally light-hearted - and mostly one-way - conversation about the high expectations of the Littleholt teaching staff concerning conduct and behaviour.

Far from stimulated by the annual rigmarole, Ivan sensed the urgent need for a rather more informal approach to class discussion which would enable individuals within 1RY to interact with a little more confidence.

The hands on the silver pocket watch designated that there were exactly ten minutes to the dinner bell.

'Well, you will all be overjoyed to learn that my voice is now quite hoarse and needs a rest. After lunch and for the remainder of the afternoon I wish for everybody in the form to have the opportunity to speak about themselves, to attain some degree of familiarity with one another. No doubt you are all experienced in the art of vocal competition, but this exercise will act as a mutual form of introduction. I shall exemplify my instructions by speaking about myself and we shall then break for lunch.'

Ivan cleared his throat whilst briefly deliberating on the content of his personal presentation.

'Whilst you devour your fish fingers, chips and baked beans during the next hour, I want you to think seriously about what you wish to reveal to your new school friends...and also consider that which you do *not* deem suitable for public announcement.'

Trevor Sims was the lone voice of inquisition once again and attempted to decipher his form tutor's convoluted vocabulary.

'So, you basically want us to give a speech about our lives, then, sir?'

Ivan gleefully pointed at the enthusiastic youngster and nodded in affirmation.

'In short, Mister Sims...yes, please. Got it in one, son!'

The boy's response was rapid and energetic - though possibly unpredicted.

'Go on then, sir. You go first!'

Ivan folded his arms and began to glide amid the attentive throng once more as he commenced his brief presentation.

'Thank you for your permission, Mister Sims. My name is Ivan Reynolds.'

He fully anticipated the titters of mild amusement that arose as his Christian name was revealed for the first time. Such immaturity was in accordance with time-honoured tradition for all teachers when their first names became public knowledge and it served neither to offend nor deter him.

'I am fifty-nine years of age, and my country of birth is Scotland.'

Trevor Sims did not falter with his curious interlude.

'Do you wear a kilt, sir?'

Ivan ignored the fact that he had been interrupted and opted instead to politely address the point of interest.

'Yes, Mister Sims. I own a kilt. Three…in fact.'

'Will you wear it for us, sir?' quipped young Trevor.

Ivan paused, momentarily fazed by the boy's earnest nature.

He also noticed the smirk adorning the features of Hilary Johnson.

'Perhaps…I'll wear it for you…perhaps, one day…Mister Sims.'

Waiting for any further questions which did not emerge, Ivan continued.

'I teach mainly mathematics. I have taught at this school for over twenty-five years. As a younger man I undertook national service in the Royal Air Force before going on to teacher training school.'

Trevor Sims raised his hand once again and was granted another opportunity to reveal his thoughts.

'Did you kill anyone when you were in the Army, sir?'

More laughter abounded as a knowing grin underscored the provocative mystique of Ivan's tinted shades.

Not the *Army*, Mister Sims. The *Air Force*. And I'm so sorry to disappoint you. I have never actually endured the dubious privilege of partaking in military conflict and therefore didn't have opportunity to take any casualties. But there is time…*yet*…'

Again, young Sims pressed keenly for answers.

He was a spritely boy with an engaging manner.

Ivan Reynolds was already becoming very fond of him.

'But…you must have had a gun, sir…or a rifle?'

Ivan could not help but pander to the cheeky rascal's innocent flashes of whimsy.

'Yes…of course. Now, if you don't mind…can I continue?'

Trevor nodded avidly and rested his chin on folded arms.

'I have a wife, Meg, and a son, Nicholas. I like cricket, Roy Orbison and growing vegetables. I abide dogs but hate cats…and, as I have already stated, I thoroughly detest…*schoolchildren*!'

The strand of persistent wariness that pierced through the amusement descending upon the room was tangible.

'Who is Roy Orbison, sir?' uttered the voice of eternal wonderment.

Ivan briefly explained the origins of his singing hero. The smiles on the pupils' faces were now emerging with some regularity. There was a relaxed atmosphere enveloping room ten. To his own surprise, Ivan felt gratified by the gradual thawing of ice and sensed the morning's schedule had been accomplished with unprecedented success.

He could also detect that the members of the class were possibly beginning to take to him, despite his unwitting predilection for scaring new pupils witless.

Yet his approach to the First Years was uncannily different this time around.

Ivan Reynolds, giant of fable, had seemingly endeared himself to 1RY at an untypically early juncture.

The once daunted group were now obliging and attentive.

He had seemingly lured their genuine interest with apparent ease.

In turn, the children now felt strangely secure in his company.

Yet in previous years, it would have taken weeks for such a relationship to even begin to blossom.

And most puzzled of all by the outcome of the morning's events, was the man at the centre of their attentions.

Checking the face of his pocket-watch, Ivan confirmed that lunch was imminent.

'And that…1RY…for now…is all that I have to say.'

His concluding words were interrupted by the timely drone of the midday bell. The class were given permission to rise to their feet and slowly file from the room. The soft resonance of the tutor's voice battled against the increasing volume of babbling discussion.

'After lunch, we shall reconvene, and I shall listen intently to all of you relating your own life stories. Be back outside the door in double file for one-twenty-five sharp.'

*****

Trevor Sims was late.

The last pupil back to class after the dinner break would always be made to suffer for the sin.

Temporarily forgetting where room ten was located, he eventually scurried up to the third level landing to find his form tutor standing at the open door with silver pocket-watch in hand.

The boy quivered and swallowed a large gulp of trepidation as he approached.

'Sorry, sir. I got mixed up, sir. I went up the wrong staircase, sir.'

Replacing watch into waistcoat, Ivan issued his response in time-honoured military fashion.

'Don't overly concern yourself, Mister Sims. Excuses for crime cannot evade the penalty. Hit the deck if you will, please. Twenty press-ups. I'll supervise the counting.'

Penance was duly served by the youngster.

Red-faced through a combination of nervous exertion and embarrassment, the mischievous boy was finally allowed to claim his seat among his classmates as Ivan followed him into the room and closed the door.

'I trust everyone is happily fed and watered and ready with their verbal resumes?'

1RY offered no reply aside a stony, awkward silence.

'I'll take that as a positive reply and that you are all raring to go.'

Ivan perched into his chair and performed the leisurely reclining position of earlier. The pupils observed dubiously with some faces quickly becoming etched with unbridled amusement at their tutor's irregular physical display.

'By the way…the placing of feet onto tables is a luxury preserved only for weary teachers in their late fifties. Any pupil found guilty of imitation will be handed a toothbrush and ordered to scrub every tabletop in the room until they shine like mirrors.'

The thirty-one schoolchildren studied their mentor as he interlinked his fingers behind his head and looked up to the ceiling as he spoke.

'Starting with the table nearest to my own and working backwards, I wish for every pupil to stand. I then wish to hear them loudly and clearly introduce themselves to the rest of the form. It can be as in-depth or brief as you wish, but I do hope to hear more than a simple confirmation of your names.'

Ivan peered at the first victim through the tinted facade of his lenses and opened his palm to her in a gestured plea of commencement.

'Well? Off you go, Miss…'

The pale-faced girl quickly blushed purest crimson and glared helplessly into her sweating palms.

'Andrews, sir. Louise…Andrews.'

'Listen carefully, 1RY. Miss Andrews is about to get our afternoon ball well and truly rolling…'

Ivan focused intently as one by one, the sound of quaking male and female voices stammered tentatively in attempting to address the form room. As they spoke by turn, he covertly wrote their names into a pre-drawn seating plan which would prove invaluable in the coming days.

The pupils soon took to the task of promoting themselves to their peers. Such an exercise in building confidence had proved very useful over previous years.

Ivan believed that it quickly eroded any inhibitions and gave individuals a sense of standing among their new classmates.

Ivan smiled inwardly as the young pupils offered details of their varying domestic arrangements, ranging from tales about their father's leaking motor car, rabbits with toothache and favourite aunties.

The subject matter intertwined with football, moulting dogs, and ballet lessons.

The group seemed to embrace the idea with enthusiasm once the first dozen or so participants had relayed their unique tales of home life. Indeed, the session became a surprising source of enjoyment for one and all, with Ivan even allowing his admiration to become apparent through what would just about pass as a genuine chuckle.

Then it was Hilary Johnson's turn.

For some unknown reason, Ivan's personal radar was alerted to the possibility of dissension.

It was as if he expected her to bring more than a little disruption to the affable proceedings.

His instinct would be proved correct in its predictions.

The mean-featured girl stood up and stared at Ivan, boring straight through his darkened visor before announcing her feelings of the moment.

'My name's Hilary. I hate my mum and dad cos they're always shouting at me. I hate my elder sister cos she's got the bigger bedroom. I hate school and hope it burns down. I hated my school dinner cos it made me feel sick. I hate my classmates, cos they think they're better than me. And I hate my form tutor cos he's just an old man who thinks he's a hard case...'

All present in room ten were suddenly shocked back into their shells on receipt of the unwarranted outburst.

Ivan calmly removed his feet from the desktop and sat up to engage with her youthful yet determined expression of distaste.

The indeterminable signal conveyed by his own visage remained in place, although it was now in danger of becoming slightly contorted by a swelling inner anger.

The opponents wordlessly encouraged each other in a mutual battle of wits as the surrounding throng anticipated an eruption of volcanic proportions.

Ivan observed the slyness that daubed itself across the girl's face.

This one certainly looked to have quickly promoted herself as the chief adversary to his position of authority.

But he would not be lulled to enter such a contest.

At least, not today.

The upbeat mood already established by the other children called for a rather more subtle reproach to her audacity.

'So...Miss Johnson...apart from those items that you opted to mention...would you say you're generally quite a contented soul?'

The rest of the class burst into unforced laughter as Hilary suddenly realised she had inadvertently made a target of herself.

Mission accomplished.

She rapidly glanced around at her giggling counterparts and became increasingly frustrated by her abject failure to intimidate the teacher.

Ivan had effectively said very little, but the words he had chosen had made her look foolish, just she had begun to nurture aspirations to establish herself as the smarter of the two.

Again, they engaged with one another's stare, before Ivan called an end to imminent conflict.

'Thank you, Miss Johnson. A most...constructive contribution. You may now be seated.'

1RY correctly sensed that Ivan Reynolds was not quite finished with his summing up of Hilary's first foray into competition.

His voice carried a definitive message to all in the room.

'I do so appreciate it when the loud mouthed and potentially troublesome pupils willingly show themselves to me so early in the game. It saves me so much time and energy trying to discover them for myself.'

Now inwardly fuming, Hilary parked herself heavily on the chair; her disquiet fuelled by the mocking conclusion of her more than worthy antagonist.

Ivan, meanwhile, casually resumed his horizontal position, replaced the heels of his shoes on the desktop and called the next act from the wings.

'Mister Sims. You have been itching to be ceremonial master all day. Time to entertain us with your personal autobiographical appraisal. And tuck your shirt in before you commence, please...'

Complying with the order to quickly rearrange his attire, Trevor Sims' eyes widened as he embarked on his intriguing story.

In turn, the youngster glanced around at the open-mouthed individuals around the room as he spoke.

'My name's Trevor. I live with me mam. Just the two of us. My dad left us when I was little. I don't know why he left, and I don't know what he looks like. I've got no brothers or sisters. Me mam works at the supermarket in town.'

Ivan's focus immediately became drawn to the boy's disclosures.

'I've got a grandma who lives in the next street, and I sleep there on Saturday nights when me mam goes to the pub with her mates. I've never been on holiday or even seen the sea, but me mam says she'll take me one day when she's got enough money. Me favourite food is sausages and me favourite film is Star Wars. But I've only seen it on telly cos me mam can't afford to take me to the pictures. She promised we will go one day.'

Ivan was compelled once again to abandon his supine posture as he sat up and listened with heartfelt enthusiasm, as the youngster relayed the key elements of his short life history.

Quietly enamoured and slightly saddened by the hard-hitting honesty of the declarations, Ivan mentally encouraged the end of a hiatus in Trevor's momentum by giving a nod of the head.

'Please continue, Mister Sims.'

'Erm…what else can I say, sir?'

'Anything you wish, Mister Sims. But no swear words, please!'

The boy's chuckling attentions wandered around the class again, before his eyes lit up with renewed inspiration.

'I could talk about the day I broke my neighbour's greenhouse window with me football, if you want?'

Genuinely touched by the earnest manner in which Trevor Sims had laid bare his own circumstances, Ivan swallowed a betraying lump of sympathy as he observed the forlorn-looking specimen before him.

Indeed, most of the class were also taken aback by the humility of the boy.

Finally, Ivan summoned a response as Trevor's eyes bored into him for the merest hint of approval.

'No…that…is…quite ample…Mister Sims…thank you. Thank you very much. You may sit.'

The teacher stood up and delved into his waistcoat pocket to assess the time.

With a check through the window to scan the playing fields below, he invited the final pupil in the form to contribute.

'And finally…can the young lady at the back of the room on the final table bring closure to the afternoon? Your name is?'

Slumped at her desk, the shy girl flushed with embarrassment as all eyes rested in her direction.

She evidently did not wish to speak whilst under such unwelcome scrutiny.

Ivan could sense the immense discomfort in her demeanour.

'Come along, now. We have two minutes until the last bell of the day. There's no need to be shy, my dear. Stand up. What is your name?'

Finally rising to her full height, she noticed Trevor Sims out of the corner of her eye, grinning and making faces to distract her.

Unfortunately for him, the teacher noticed also.

'Mister Sims! Face front - or you will be doing forty press-ups on my next count!'

Ivan nodded back to the girl as a measure of encouragement.

'Jenny Douglas, sir.'

'Miss Douglas…would you please continue…'

Having finally decided on something potent to say, Jenny plucked up the courage to vocalise it.

Then, on opening her mouth, the home-time siren whined into life on the outside landing, immediately inciting 1RY to pack their bags and create a crescendo of chatter.

Ivan halted the ensuing noise and bustle with a heavy slam of his fist on the desktop.

The technique worked as potently as always.

Silence quickly descended on the room again as all eyes focused on the irate-looking teacher.

His previous good humour had rapidly switched, and a voice of distinct discontentment reigned over all under his supervision.

'NEVER…EVER…STOP WORK…UNLESS GIVEN THE WORD TO DO SO. THAT BELL IS A SIGNAL FOR *ME*! *NOT* FOR *YOU*!'

Thirty-one pupils held their breath as the form tutor's tone suddenly lowered back to its previously sociable volume.

'Yes. It is the end of the day. Subsequently, we shall hear Miss Douglas' story at a later date. Now…please stand quietly behind your chairs and push them under the desks.'

Obviously excited at the realisation that their inaugural day at Littleholt was now at a conclusion, the pupils of 1RY began to fidget wildly as they watched the teacher move to the door.

'Do not forget…there is no registration period tomorrow morning. When the first bell sounds make your way from the playground to the main hall for First Year assembly.'

He scanned the room, confirming all were in order and ready for the off. Eventually, the class was granted permission to depart the room row by row. Having despatched his pupils, Ivan plucked his briefcase from below his chair.

He then checked the surroundings to verify that room ten had been abandoned in a reasonably tidy state.

He was secretly relieved to have completed the first day back of the new term, yet a customary sensation was seemingly amiss.

His typically abrasive personal approach was of a decidedly lower key. He could not summon the inner will to exert the looming presence that his formative classes had been privileged to endure in previous years.

The time-hardened edge to Ivan Reynolds had suddenly been blunted for some bizarre reason. He found himself genuinely becoming attached to his new form group.

And he found himself slightly bewildered by the fact.

Pondering the quandary, he closed the door and locked it behind him as Matt Jenkins emerged across the landing and strived to make the first obvious enquiry of his colleague.

'Well? Enjoy yourself, Ivan?'

The elder man pretended to be amused.

'Oh yes, of course, Matthew! Nearly as much as the time I visited the allotment only to find it completely flooded by sewage!'

Matt laughed heartily before pressing with another query.

He could see that Ivan had actually ended the day positively.

'So…how were the little darlings? We didn't hear you shouting very much, today. Have you got a sore throat or something?'

Ivan dropped the keys to room ten into his jacket pocket and presented a somewhat reflective figure as they began to descend the stairway.

'Do you know something, Matthew? Believe it…or believe it not, I honestly felt they didn't really *deserve* being shouted at!'

Matt chuckled again at the elder teacher's incredulous revelation.

'Don't tell me you're going all mushy in your final year, Ivan! Not *you*! Please! Tell me I'm wrong!'

Ivan stared through his shaded spectacles with a stern look of sincerity and a parting comment that left his younger colleague in hysterics.

'Well, it is a bit of a concern, isn't it, Matthew! I must try harder tomorrow, I suppose! Anyway…I bid you a good evening.'

Declining the offer of a sociable coffee in the staff room, Ivan made directly for the car park. With the sun still relatively high and warm he fully intended to visit the allotment and spend a couple of hours inspecting his season-end crops, yet his intentions were literally diverted by an uneven flow of traffic due to roadworks.

And then before he even realised, the metallic copper Princess had glided straight past the open green mesh gates that led to his little slice of horticultural heaven.

With diminished inclination to turn the car around at the next available junction, Ivan resigned himself to a quiet night on the back patio with the cryptic crossword and bottle of beer.

*****

As Ivan sat and watched the late summer sun setting behind the distant rooftops, George Breedon leaned over the fence and the pair duly enquired about one another's day.

The conversation was typically brief yet always welcome.

He enjoyed chewing the cud in the company of his friend and neighbour.

It was pleasing to recount that one or two personalities in the new class had been uncovered, which certainly looked to be likely candidates in stimulating his interest over the coming months.

With the air turning notably chillier as daylight was gradually replaced by shadow, Ivan drained the beer bottle and continued reading his newspaper indoors.

The evening passed quietly. After watching the ten-p.m. news he downed a double malt whiskey as a nightcap before embarking upstairs.

Retiring to the bedroom, he set the alarm clock, changed into his striped pyjamas, and made sure to kiss Meg and Nicholas goodnight as he had done every evening for many years.

Their comforting presence and loving smiles were enough reason for him to sleep soundly before a new dawn brought its next instalment of untold surprises.

Beyond the staff room door, the main corridor housed its customary morning crescendo of chatter and clatter. Ivan casually checked the pocket watch as he rankled with ideas for a possible solution to three across.

Unfortunately, the first bell of the day had long since sounded and the hands of time declared that the First Year assembly was about to commence in the main hall.

As usual, Ivan was particularly comfortable in the staff room's smoke-riddled yet somewhat homely atmosphere. He glanced up to assess the dissipating population of the playground beyond the window. The sun glared back at him through the ill-washed pane causing his spectacles to evolve a shade darker.

How he wished at that moment to be among his allotment plot with the radio humming from the shed table. It was a source of increasing frustration to him these days that he was only truly at peace with sweat on brow and spade in hand. Retirement would bring such reward in good time.

The possibility that his fanaticism for the regimental disciplines of school life had waned in the past twelve months was an issue that bothered him.

Whilst still upholding the performance of duty on a daily basis, no longer did the environment of Littleholt serve to fully sate his inherent inclinations.

Carol Shaw stood at the coffee table idly swishing a spoon in her mug as she observed Ivan's relaxed pose, whilst his features contorted with concentration in attempting to complete the crossword.

'Ivan, I'm giving my first speech to the younglings in about five minutes. I'd like you to hear it if you can be bothered to shift yourself from that chair.'

Always amused by her blunt mode of banter, he forcibly raised the corners of his mouth and issued an automatic repost.

'My dearest, Carol…I truly fear that I cannot in fact be bothered to move. However, if you shout loudly enough, and I know you are fully capable, your voice may just carry through the doors of the main hall, and I may just be able to hear you from the comfort of said chair.'

Carol drained her mug and retrieved a clipboard from her large holdall before setting herself down next to him. She was evidently in an affectionately sarcastic mood.

'Just thought you might like to display some solidarity among your colleagues for once…that's all.'

Pretending to ignore her, Ivan scribbled one or two solution possibilities onto the corner of the page. His carefully honed act of feigned ignorance did little to impress another occupant of the room who felt obliged to correct the elder statesman of the staff with regard to his seemingly cavalier attitude.

Phil Holmes had never been unduly overawed by Ivan's disposition on most traditional schooling issues and suddenly felt compelled to elaborate on the fact.

'You should really have more respect for your fellow teachers, Ivan. It wouldn't do you any harm to offer a little more concern for the social aspects of education as opposed to pushing all your energies into playing the disciplinarian.'

Matt Jenkins' nose suddenly lifted from the magazine he was submerged in as his senses twitched to the prospect of another public joust between Messrs. Holmes and Reynolds. Closing the glossy read, he shuffled closer to the action to gain a better vantage point.

Although fully aware of the irritating younger pretender in his midst, Ivan prolonged the performance of crusty indifference and offered no immediate reply to the challenge.

A tactic which only served to add fuel to Phil Holmes' steadily lapping fire.

'What's up, Ivan? Cat got your tongue this morning? Assemblies are a vital part of the school week. You should be in there to greet the children as they arrive. Not sneak in and spy on them. A positive method of interaction between teachers and pupils is what's required. A clear channel of communication is paramount if the school is going to achieve its future targets.'

Ivan began to ruffle the edges of his newspaper in a gesture of mild annoyance.

Phil Holmes took such body language as a sure sign that the elder man's feathers were becoming ruffled. Matt and Carol exchanged a wary glance as Ivan emitted a deafening, wholly exaggerated yawn.

Yet again, the younger teacher chose to aggravate the situation as he played to the supposedly attentive audience.

'Say no more, ladies and gentlemen. I mention something contemporary and proactive, and he pretends to be bored. Typical! You're a bloody dinosaur, Reynolds! You're finished! And you know it! Your retirement is just what we *all* need!'

Ivan scratched his forehead and swallowed the dregs from his coffee mug as the dwindling throng sat in eager silence.

Now at last he was ready to embrace the invitation of a duel with Littleholt's newest recruit.

'My dearest, Philip. I have been bored rigid by assemblies for many, many years. Probably from the time you were sitting in them yourself and pretending to be interested. I do not purport to enjoy them. I attend them under extreme duress as an act of civility and compliance with the school regime. Please do not argue to me or anyone else that such events serve any true purpose other than to encourage sheer tedium and waste twenty minutes that could be better spent doing crosswords.'

Mister Holmes was not impressed by the insincere logic of the veteran.

Yet the lure of extending the argument was too tempting to resist.

'It's *Phil*. Not *Philip*…okay? I'm just saying that a little more enthusiasm from you might just rub off on the pupils…that's all. So, sue me for being forward thinking.'

The young science teacher pursed smugly as though having established some moral victory.

But the chosen foe was never one to be defeated so easily.

'Believe me, Philip…there is only one thing in the world more tedious than assembly.'

'Really? Such as?'

Ivan looked across to Carol as he spoke.

Her responsive smile indicated she had already anticipated his next words.

'A physics lesson.'

Unimpressed by the jibe, Phil Holmes moved to the door and pulled it open.

'Cheap, Ivan. Humourless…and cheap.'

Carol and Matt made no attempt to disguise their appreciation of the entertainment.

Ivan folded up his newspaper and let it fall onto the floor by his briefcase. Clasping his hands over his left knee he addressed the now flustered scientist who hovered in the doorway.

'Philip…thirty-five years I have taught and lectured. I am not about to be brow-beaten by someone who has supervised a class for barely thirty-five days! Now, be a good little boy and go and mark some books or something. If you don't mind, you're delaying me for this very important assembly…'

Ivan stood to his feet, brushed himself clean of imaginary dust and then brushed past Phil Holmes, to be quickly followed by Carol and Matt.

*****

The main hall was now fully occupied by the First Years.

The resonance of their vibrant conversations quickly dissolved into silence as the masters of ceremony entered the arena.

They listened intently as the Head of Year spoke for a few minutes in front of the stage to relay her thoughts and hopes for the coming term.

Standing customarily at the rear of the hall with arms folded, Ivan began to scan the congregation for the now partially familiar identities of his form group.

He was adept at matching faces and names and played a mental game with himself as the assembly crawled pointlessly onward.

He readily identified Jenny Douglas because of her pig tails.

She sat on the end of a row next to fire doors that led onto the playing fields. Hilary Johnson was perched amid a collection of similar looking girls that all carried a united expression of anger and distaste.

And of course, there was Trevor Sims.

Ivan spotted him picking his nose as Carol offered some sound advice on school uniform and the importance of presentation and image.

'Trevor bloody Sims…' muttered Ivan under his breath. '…with bloody white socks on yet again.'

With assembly enduring for only fifteen minutes, Ivan was keen to make his exit quickly before the inevitable crush. He waited patiently beyond the glass double doors in the main corridor opposite reception.

Avidly scrutinising every pupil as they passed him barely daring to breathe, he nearly surrendered the hunt before finally locating the chattering target of choice.

'MISTER SIMS! COME HERE TO ME! NOW!' echoed the familiarly authoritarian tone around the brightly lit walls of the corridor.

The unkempt boy shuffled between the moving lines of children before finally positioning his nose only inches from the crooked forefinger of his form tutor.

As was his habitual preference, Ivan then lowered his face to the pupil's own to encourage a clear dialogue.

'What did I tell you yesterday, Mister Sims?'

The youngster was evidently confused as to the nature of the random encounter.

'What, sir? What did you tell me? I forgot.'

Trevor felt a large hand fall onto his shoulder as Ivan pointed to the floor with the thumb of his other hand.

'What did I say…about those socks of yours?'

Trevor glanced down at his feet before once again engaging with Ivan's dark gaze.

'Oh yes. Sorry, sir. I forgot, sir.'

Ivan now placed both hands on Trevor's shoulders and moved his mouth even nearer to the young man's ear as other pupils weaved past and warily observed the pair.

The boy stiffened as he briefly glanced at the concerned faces of his passing peers.

The teacher stood behind him and hissed.

'How can you possibly forget when you only put them on your feet less than an hour ago?'

With all the untouched innocence of a new-born, Trevor twisted his neck and looked vainly into Ivan's tinted glare.

'Oh…no, sir. I never took them off at all last night cos me mam hadn't done a wash. So, I went to bed in them. That's why…when I got up today…I forgot I had them on in the first place…sir.'

Ivan let the unblemished words of the likeable urchin register slowly in his brain. He then tried desperately not to smile at what was potentially a most plausible story.

Looking up and down the corridor, Ivan chose to word his conclusion on the matter carefully before again whispering into the boy's ear and releasing his grip on the youngster's blazer.

'On your way, Mister Sims. But tomorrow! No…white…socks! Is that clear?'

Now liberated, Trevor walked quickly away from his detainer, but not before pledging his compliance with the order.

'I think its wash night tonight, sir. So, I should have a different colour on tomorrow.'

Ivan shook his head in mild disapproval before venturing into the staff room for his briefcase.

*****

The Fourth-Year maths group always provided an examination of Ivan's mettle.

The pupils in the class were now fully accustomed to the regimental inclinations of their teacher. It was only natural. Ivan had nurtured them from Second Years.

Their resolve and resistance had grown over time, yet still they were still careful not to overly test his patience.

Standing at the top of the stairway, Ivan dangled the keys to room ten around his little finger.

A hush descended on the two lines of fifteen-year-olds as he unlocked the door and gave permission for them to enter class. After observing their individual appearance with an eagle eye, he followed them in and positioned the door gingerly into the frame.

Placing his briefcase on the floor next to the chair, Ivan stood with hands in trouser pockets to assess the collection of young adults.

So many former opponents; so many previous conflicts over the years.

Ah yes.

There he was.

Shaun Peterson sat at the back of the room with the usual suspects on either flank.

The policy on seating arrangements in Ivan's subject classes was rather more casual with the teenagers. No longer did he deem it necessary for the pupils to be forcibly separated from favoured friends.

After all, he figured they were supposedly maturing and would presumably find less distraction in one another. Plus, after three full years together, the issue of individual confidence had long since evaporated.

However, certain young men found maturity to be a useful baton to pass around the room in their predictable attempt to disrupt proceedings.

With physical stature also relatively imposing compared with many of their peers, certain young men were no longer averse to contesting the stringent personality of the experienced maths teacher.

'You're not going to go on about Scotland again are you, sir? We heard enough about it last year!'

A substantial proportion of the pupils laughed in response to Peterson's opening foray into combat.

A little harmless warm-up was probably just what Ivan Reynolds needed after the uninspiring rigmarole of assembly.

Yes, Ivan needed the early challenge that had been provided.

'My dear, Mister Peterson. Being as you raise the issue of my native country to the fore, it only seems appropriate to oblige with one or two snippets of interest to lovers of all things Scottish, such as my good self.'

The dark lenses hooded a pleasured expression that even perplexed the Fourth Years into guessing the nature of their teacher's mood and tolerance threshold at that moment.

It was all an easy game to play for Ivan.

A game he had yet to lose.

Shaun Peterson indulged in exaggerated groans and winces, much to the amusement of his collection of accomplices. As Littleholt's self-appointed sporting superstar of the past couple of years, hero-worship was a process that only a handful of capable counterparts happily resided in.

And the object of their infatuation lapped up every second of secret adoration from males and females alike.

However, despite the dubious sense of minimal respect that Ivan held for the youth, he could never turn away from the possibility of belittling him before his fawning classmates.

'Can't we talk about sport then, sir?'

Ivan slipped his hands behind his back and commenced to float slowly around the floor.

'Ah! By sport…do you *actually* mean…talk about…*you*, by any chance?'

The teenager grinned broadly.

'Well, only if you want to, sir. Perhaps it might also bring back a few memories of when you were fit and healthy. Relive some of your ancient achievements, eh sir?'

Mild titters emanated from varying points of the room although the sources were careful to remain undetected.

The syllabus dictated that Ivan began the year talking about sine, cosine, and tangents. However, his curiosity had now been pricked by the chance to engage in a battle of wits with the ever-willing participant sitting at the rear of the room.

'Are you playing soccer for the school this year, Mister Peterson?'

The boy laughed before spitting his response.

'Soccer? *Soccer*? Don't you mean *football*, sir?'

Ivan continued to sail toward the arrogant youth as he addressed the confusion.

'Please forgive my ignorance in the matter. Is there a difference, Mister Peterson?'

Peterson was now leaning forward in his chair and brimming with enthusiasm for the pending conflict and the surrounding interest it was generating. He loved the spotlight and never failed to embrace its glow.

'Yes…soccer is American. You mean football, sir. For all us *Englishmen*!'

Ivan continued to act dumb.

'Well, I suppose so, yes. But of course, I'm a Scotsman and a rugby man, myself. I broke my shoulder playing the damned game as well. It took me months to feel right. Even now it still hurts on colder days.'

More than a hint of slyness evolved on the face of the drooling teenage challenger.

'That's what I'm saying, sir. You played for too long! Got too old and couldn't admit it. The bones become brittle with old age, you know!'

Ivan pretended to chuckle as he finally locked in on Peterson's table and glared down at the preening young athlete.

'There is one thing that I can assure you of, Mister Peterson. That is to say, I am quite certain of the fact that, unlike me, you will not be playing competitive sport in *your* sixth decade. You might be a big shot on the cricket crease and soccer pitch…but not when it comes to real games.'

A silent class watched Peterson as he rose swiftly to snatch at the bait his teacher was preparing.

'Such as, sir? Name a *proper* sport, then! Go on! Do you mean knitting? That's what old people do when they've had it, isn't it? Knitting? You can knit yourself a balaclava for the winter, sir! And a shawl to keep your shoulder warm.'

The sound of thirty laughing fifteen-year-olds boomed out of the room and across the outer landing as they watched their teacher retreat slowly back toward the black board.

Behind his own chair once again he spun on his heels and uttered a single word to hush the din.

'Boxing.'

Peterson studied the teacher adorning the black mask.

'*Boxing*, sir?'

Now fortune would undoubtedly turn in Ivan Reynolds' favour.

'Yes, Mister Peterson…boxing. It requires dexterity and reflex; speed of thought and a stern physique…and above all…raw power.'

No further words were spoken by Ivan as he slowly removed his suit jacket, much to the bewilderment of the watching class.

Rolling up his right-hand shirt sleeve to the elbow, he then flexed his fingers and cracked each knuckle in turn. It was a sickly procession of sound that reverberated discomfortingly in the ears of all present.

Shaun Peterson could not resist obliging his raging sense of curiosity.

'So…what are you going to do now, sir?'

Ivan moved position to the side of the room nearer the door and beckoned Peterson to him with a crook of his forefinger.

'Come hither to me, boy. I wish to perform a quick exercise in comparison.'

With a combination of natural confidence and a slight pang of hesitancy, the pupil joined his teacher out front and listened attentively for further instruction as he wallowed in the scrutiny.

'Mister Peterson…I wish you to display your own brute power by slamming your fist into the wall.'

Now the youth was also as bemused as the rest of the pupils and more than a little wary of Ivan's ulterior intention.

A few seconds elapsed before the request was audibly repeated.

'It's very simple, boy. Punch the wall! There's no trickery involved in such a basic feat.'

Shaun Peterson was now feeling distinctly uncomfortable.

In his view the challenge was ridiculous.

It would prove nothing.

'I...I can't do that, sir.'

Ivan smiled without grace and moved his taunting features ever nearer to the boy's.

'Yes...you *can*. But...you *won't*. And why *won't* you?'

The confusing charade was becoming tiresome for young Peterson if intriguing for the audience, yet the pupil sensed increasing animosity from the elder man standing beside him.

'Because...because...it would hurt, sir.'

Feigning an expression of complete surprise, Ivan held both hands aloft.

'Ah! Are you saying you are not capable of doing this because it is painful? The great Shaun Peterson...unable to make the weight? Cowering from a challenge? Shirking the competition?'

The adolescent was now rendered completely dumbfounded by the proclamations of his maths teacher.

In the next instance, Ivan had drawn back his clenched fist and slammed it into the section of grey painted plaster.

There wasn't so much as a curling of the lips as the teacher returned his hand by his side and smirked.

Peterson, in tandem with the rest of the class, watched their tutor in concerned yet disbelieving astonishment at the spectacle they had just witnessed.

Then without further ado, Ivan raised his fist once more and repeated the act.

Then again.

And again.

Ten times his clenched right hand connected heavily and cleanly with the wall, leaving varying indentations in the small target area.

Matt Jenkins was teaching Third Years across the landing and was suddenly disturbed by the dim pounding that vibrated through the structure of the upper level. He did not attempt to fully respond to the understandable curiosity of his pupils aside from a half-hearted theory to allay their concerns.

Ironic that his absolute honesty was received as a jest.

'It's only Mister Reynolds punching the wall, again. Carry on reading. Ignore it.'

Finally, Ivan offered some calming assurance and explained the nature of the experiment.

'You may now resume your seat, Mister Peterson. That was a little lesson for you about supposed old age and its detrimental effects. When the body aches, the mind ably compensates. Now then, class. We must move onto the business of the day.'

Without further word of contention, Shaun Peterson placed himself back onto his chair with due embarrassment.

Aghast at the deed just witnessed, the entire class hastily engaged their full attention onto the fifty-nine-year-old maths teacher, who now proceeded to write on the blackboard.

As Ivan then turned and began to speak to them, each pupil in would afford themselves regularly brief and worried glances toward the testimonial marks in the wall behind him.

One potent thought prevailed over their eventual attempts at concentration.

As thirty pupils simultaneously reached the same conclusion.

Despite their youthful cynicism, Ironfist still reigned supreme.

8

Ivan lowered his briefcase and suit jacket next to his favourite armchair. The staff room was unusually quiet for dinner time. Carol Shaw was balanced on the edge of the seat opposite with a rather limp looking tuna sandwich in one hand and romantic novel in the other.

As his attention fell to his female colleague, she smiled back at him with her mouth full.

'It's no use indulging in fictional escapades, Carol. Harsh reality is always just beyond this door. There is no hiding place from the beasts that lurk in the forest.'

With a morsel still in her cheek, the Head of First Year nodded as she turned the page with her thumb.

'How was your first morning's timetable, Ivan?'

His reply was rapid and dismissive as he scanned the top of the coffee table for his newspaper.

'Bloody horrible bunch those fourth formers! Why do innocent little children have to evolve into such obnoxious brutes?'

Carol's mirthful expression had not altered.

'It's called growing up, I do believe. Plus of course they have possibly been influenced by you in the art of brutality, as you affectionately call it.'

'Do you think so? If so…I'm quite touched.'

Still hunting for his own read, Ivan mumbled in growing frustration as he continued the search. Phil Holmes entered the room whistling loudly, which caused the occupants to exchange amused glances.

Ivan dutifully opened the batting.

'They aren't all bad, I suppose. But that Peterson has turned out to be a real shit. If he were a lozenge, he'd suck himself! Now where's my blessed newspaper gone?'

Phil Holmes could not help but offer a typically brusque intrusion on the conversation.

'Loving the kids more than ever, I see? Doesn't bode well for the rest of your year if you're fed up after one morning, does it?'

Ivan halted his expedition to uncover the Daily Mail and looked up at the young physics teacher.

'I think age has made me less tolerant, certainly. Although, having said that, one or two First Year pupils have made a fair impression already…which is more than can be said for one or two of the teachers.'

Mister Holmes turned with mug in hand and again aired his views without invitation.

'All children should be treated equally. Classes of mixed ability should be taught as one. There should be no discrimination. Elitism is old hat.'

Having now stopped chewing her sandwich, Carol observed Ivan wide-eyed as he delivered a muffled verbal backlash whilst on all fours scrutinising under the table.

'Some pupils are worthy of special treatment because they stand out from the usual array of louts, ignoramuses and dirt mouths.'

The physics teacher sat down shaking his head.

'No! You're wrong! You can't be seen to favour individuals. It's against the ethics of our occupation.'

Finally conceding defeat in his quest, Ivan rose to his feet.

'Don't lecture me about bleeding ethics! So, what do you suggest doing with the bullies, graffiti artists, scrappers, and smokers, then Philip? Give them all a lollipop for their endeavours?'

Holmes had lost the contest again, whilst Carol bathed in the personal euphoria that always accompanied her in witnessing Ivan's little victories.

'Oh, blast it! I don't know where my newspaper is! I'm going out for a run around the park.'

*****

Ivan tied the laces of his training shoes and began to limber up outside the boys' locker room. He had always maintained a strict fitness regime since embracing belated National Service in his mid-twenties, and he had quickly discovered that a lunchtime jog was the perfect antidote to a morning of keeping simmering classrooms in check.

As he exited the red brick gymnasium and weaved his way around the playground and car park donned in white t-shirt and red shorts, various shouts of mockery and derogatory whistles accompanied his accelerating departure along the school driveway.

He paid the voices of predictable derision no attention.

Shaun Peterson was chief vocalist among the critics, but Ivan would not lower himself in attempting to take them to task.

He was far more interested in filling his lungs with fresh air and flexing his muscles.

The classroom was his much-preferred arena for tackling would-be hecklers, anyway.

There would always be another opportunity to exact a response.

Hardened experience had proven such a fact.

For now, it was high time for a little privacy in the midday sunshine as he veered out of the school gates and onward to the inviting greenery of the village parkland.

*****

The rousing symphony provided by 1RY was soon eradicated as Ivan appeared on the landing outside room ten to allow them access for afternoon registration.

Peace quickly prevailed as he waited patiently for his form group to divert their entire attention to the matter at hand.

With an open-palmed gesture to enter the room, the obligatory double-file inspection was carried out as the children scuttled past him and stood behind their chairs.

Closing the door gently, Ivan regally took his seat and nodded for the class to be similarly positioned.

He opened the register and began to announce the list of names and adhered to the respective replies.

Then a lone voice began to echo in his ear.

A grating female tone, the provider of which was evidently more interested in discussing the events of her lunch hour than obliging the form teacher with due civility as he checked attendance.

Ivan ceased reading immediately and looked up to ascertain the source of the disturbance.

Hilary Johnson's smirking features were focused across the room to where Wendy Bennett was sitting. Mugging gleefully at one another, they had developed the mutual distraction into an enjoyable game that had now eclipsed any minor interest in the business of the moment.

Stifling their giggles, both failed to acknowledge their form tutor as he stood up and began a slow meander toward them.

Hilary's emerging affinity for defiance had obviously bloomed in the past twenty-four hours and she was now fully prepared to run the gauntlet with the angered warrior that advanced stealthily toward her.

She continued to whisper across the room leaving her friend in mild hysterics.

Both were completely oblivious to the incoming storm.

Only when the shadow cast itself across her desk did Hilary detect his disapproving presence.

But it was far too late.

Ivan hooked his thumbs into the pockets of his waistcoat as he began the assault in low-key.

'You fancy a shot at the title do you, Miss Johnson?'

The girl observed him with her facade combining puzzlement and distaste.

'Eh? What you on about?'

Slowly shaking his head, Ivan's mouth formed a hard firm narrow pout below his black spectacles.

'Oh dear, oh dear...forgotten the rules already, have we?'

Still the expression of thinly disguised hatred remained on Hilary's face as she rolled her eyes and averted her disinterested gaze through the window.

Yet her careless whisper of abject disregard would immediately fall on the keenest of ears.

'…idiot…' she mumbled.

On hearing the insult that was obviously directed his way, Ivan maintained his air of untroubled calm as he leant forward to fully engage with the girl, who now found herself stranded at his mercy with no hiding place.

His words wormed around the cavities of her mind and her heart began to thump wildly with anticipation.

'Miss Johnson…please…be…upstanding.'

The girl opted to ignore Ivan's considered instruction as he slowly began to fume inside.

Indeed, as the seconds continued to pass, the insolent grin returned to her face in full view of everybody.

Yet this smile was now secretly borne out of quaking concern.

Not of carefree amusement.

Ivan waited patiently until deciding that a little more encouragement was needed. The rest of the class were now completely absorbed by the unfurling episode.

Yet even they could not have predicted the next scene in the chapter.

Accompanied by a yelp of rebellion, Hilary's chair spun from beneath her as his fingers clamped onto the back of it.

As a lion would return fleeing quarry to the den, the girl's sulking form was ordered to the front of the room for all observers to speculate upon.

Now they were finally witness to the legend.

Now the adrenalin of old flooded his veins once more.

Now the girl began to scowl with embarrassment as the teacher's temper refused to lighten.

He exuded authority from his very pores at that moment.

Classrooms on all floors of the building began to shake as Ivan Reynolds berated the pupil for her conduct.

His shattering vocals rattled the windows and door of room ten.

Yet his colleagues were quite adjusted to the shrill and deafening bark that Ivan was occasionally capable of producing.

But eleven-year-old girls had no idea how to respond other than to quiver helplessly under its powerful, unrelenting might.

It was all Hilary Johnson could do to cower in vain as her tutor's tirade rained down all around her suddenly insignificant, crumpled form.

Still his volume held firm in tandem with the constricting dry throats of the transfixed children.

1RY sat motionless, their emotions frozen due to the unfolding drama.

The lashing sermon ensnared the attentions of the entire upper floor landing for a full minute.

And then, finally, a tranquil silence rapidly resumed as Hilary was ordered to return to her seat.

Mentally beaten and battered to a crushing defeat.

A psychologically wounded animal; crawling back to safety.

The conclusion of registration was achieved to the backdrop of absolute peace.

The harsh lesson for Hilary Johnson was sharp, clean, and clinical.

And the effect had been established for all to see.

Ivan Reynolds was once again the master of his realm.

He remained the unchallenged king of the classroom.

And as 1RY had discovered for themselves in the previous two minutes, it was a wholly unwise decision to try and test the resistance of this most experienced of adversaries.

Closing the register, he spat across the room without emitting a shred of concern for the girl's display of apparent sufferance.

'Do not fish for sympathy, Miss Johnson. The waterworks may convince some, but certainly not I. You must accept consequence more graciously if you are so intent on encouraging it. I will not tolerate dissent - from *any* of you! Any more of the same and I will crush it without warning. Heed my words.'

The other pupils in the room dared not utter a syllable.

Ivan leaned back in his chair and checked his silver pocket-watch.

'All this distraction has made you late for your next lesson and my next group is now convened outside. Your English teacher will no doubt waiting impatiently for your arrival. Please apologise to Mrs. Hancock on my behalf when you finally attend with her. All stand. Class dismissed.'

The scraping of chairs drowned out the sorrowful moaning of the girl that dejectedly followed her peers from the room.

Ivan did not look at her as she passed his desk.

Yet he dearly hoped that she had learned from her mistake.

He waited until the final pupil had vacated before emerging triumphantly on the landing to address the two trembling lines of the Third Year mathematics group.

As he checked the parade of uniforms and startled ashen faces, Ivan Reynolds was comforted by one particular fact as he observed the incoming adolescents.

Despite his prior concerns that he may have become a little too relaxed in his final year, it came as an immense personal relief to have discovered that his unquestionable ability to enforce obedience, still stood as the unofficial benchmark to one and all.

9

The week's playground rota had been pinned to the teacher's notice board, dictating that Ivan undertake morning break-time supervision with Phil Holmes.

Ivan had never found the role to be overly enticing.

If nothing else, being seconded outside meant he was missing out on valuable newspaper and crossword time in his favourite staff room armchair.

Unfortunately, he was not alone in this viewpoint and so diplomacy decreed there was little alternative but to take his turn and bite his tongue.

However, with the young science teacher beside him, maintaining even a semblance of decorum would prove to be difficult.

Holmes had proudly emerged as Ivan's chief opponent among all his colleagues.

The friction between them was not obvious to all, but it was mutually tangible. The two men stood uneasily under the rain veranda and studiously observed the untypical peace that was currently residing among the pupils.

There was little of interest to divert the attention of either teacher, so it seemed inevitable that an exchange of words would eventually enforce itself upon the pair.

And despite dearly hoping against the probability, Ivan was quickly questioned by his younger colleague about the previous afternoon's disturbance at registration.

'It's reckoned they heard you shouting three villages away, yesterday. Quite unprofessional conduct for a man of your experience. Is it *really* necessary to lose your sense of composure?'

Ivan stared straight ahead, keeping a keen eye on the ever-changing flurry of activity before him.

The late summer sunshine had commandeered Ivan's spectacle lenses to turn jet black.

Not dissimilar to his mood at that moment as he covertly clenched his fists in his trouser pockets.

Reluctantly acknowledging the younger man's latest point of issue, Ivan turned to Mister Holmes whilst maintaining partial attention on the playground.

'Sorry, Philip…you have me at a disadvantage. To which incident do you refer?'

Phil Holmes shook his head slowly in utter disbelief.

'Yesterday afternoon! We heard you brought some poor wretch to tears. Johnson, is her name? It's not acceptable. We all get tarred with the same brush because of things like this, you know.'

Ivan shifted his weight from foot to foot as he mentally assembled an appropriate defence to the claims of the science teacher.

'Let's get this clear, Philip. I'm not under obligation to justify my actions to anybody. They are *my* form group and mine alone. If pupils show rudeness and disrespect, then I will deal with it as I see fit. It's a very simple policy. Although probably far too stringent and effective for you contemporary types.'

The younger teacher moved his position to stare through Ivan's disconcertingly dark visor. As expected, it hadn't taken much effort from Ivan to encourage the debate.

'If you mean that it's considered bad practice to lay a hand on the children, then yes…I'm all for the modern method. You can't just bully the kids into compliance anymore, Ivan. The Board of Governors doesn't like that sort of thing these days. The corporal approach is deemed outdated. And will hopefully soon be totally illegal!'

Ivan turned his head and sighed as he observed the beginnings of an unruly looking incident on the near side of the playing field.

'Well…in my old-fashioned little world…the firm-handed approach works. Anyway, the girl shouldn't take it too personally, Philip. My policy applies to all. I don't have favourites.'

A fistfight broke out in the short distance as Ivan uttered his last word on the subject.

Phil Holmes immediately began to panic.

Ivan placed a calming hand of restraint on his colleague's shoulder.

'Leave it for a moment, Philip. Let the pair of them swing a few. Let them tire a little. Then *I'll* take them. You'll only end up getting punched yourself if you wade in too soon.'

The science teacher twitched with anxiety as the two protagonists revealed themselves in full glory. Surrounded by a growing, heaving throng of cheering and jeering onlookers, the physical exchanges between the two boys became more intensive as the seconds passed.

As did Phil Holmes' urgent desire to intervene on the affray.

'We can't just ignore this, Ivan! We must step in and stop it! I don't care what you say. I'm going in…now!'

The elder statesman grabbed the younger teacher by the lapel of his jacket, turned his head and smiled in sympathy for his naivety.

'I will step in, Philip…all in good time. The timing is everything, you know.'

Still the fracas rumbled around the edge of the tarmac square like a thunderstorm that gathered more energy with each cloud swell.

Then suddenly, the eager spectators realised that the entertainment was moving slowly towards the two supervising teachers, who had remained stationary under the shadow of the veranda.

With blood now emerging on the faces of both fighters, Ivan decided that the moment was right to interrupt the entertainment. He waded through the tightened crowd and fought to gain access to the centre of the ensuing bout.

Phil Holmes watched Ivan in action as he shifted pupils out of his way to reach the designated targets.

Then with practiced ease, Ivan reappeared from the melee with a scrapper in each hand. With their school ties being held high and taut, the boys could do little else but follow the teacher as they were promptly guided forth.

Still leading his catch away from the audience, Ivan passed Phil Holmes without word and finally stopped his march at the brick wall base of the school building. He then heaved on the two ties, causing the bloodied young offenders to be positioned against the wall whilst rubbing their necks.

With the supporting crowd now dispersed completely, Ivan was left alone with the culprits, who rested their hands on their knees as they fought for breath.

'STAND UP STRAIGHT!' Ivan barked, giving each of the boys a sharp jab in the shoulder with his finger which served to knock them back against the wall once more.

Now both nursing the impact of their exchange, the pair seemed instantly sorrowful for the disruption to the usual civility of morning break-time.

Phil Holmes moved to position himself at Ivan's side as instructions were issued in a lowered, more reasoned tone.

'Third Year pupils should be setting an example to the younger ones. Both of you! Headmaster's office! Now! Wait outside until he's ready to see you. Tell him who sent you and why! Go!'

The dejected pair trudged regretfully toward the main doors of the school and disappeared into the corridor to face their mutual if uncertain fate.

Ivan turned back to scan the rest of the playground's occupants, who had now resumed their normal demeanour without any unwelcome distraction.

For once, Phil Holmes opted to say nothing.

Instead, he stood silently next to Ivan.

As deeply concealed pangs of admiration began to flourish.

10

The first week of the term had passed quickly. Seven days ago, the unknowing pupils of 1RY had been dealt their most dreaded hand.

And yet, as they settled down for the first form period of the year, there was a definitive sense of amiable familiarity between tutor and class members.

Although it could not be described as actual warmth, the initial sense of unbridled wariness in the children had diluted significantly.

Those that held Ivan Reynolds in high esteem felt no less about him.

Yet those bold individuals that might still wish to choose him as an enemy secretly felt more encouragement than ever as he stood with hands clasped behind his back and with eyes fixed on the sunlit scene through the windows.

'School diaries on your desks please! Cast your minds back. What did I say about school diaries, Mister Sims?'

The boy gazed vacantly at his form tutor, reminiscent of a young deer staring down the barrel of a hunting rifle.

Having finally remembered to discard his white socks after four days, he had now been chosen to highlight a pre-ordained task. A task that a substantial proportion of the class - himself included - had failed miserably to achieve, judging by the number of pink booklets that began to appear on the tabletops.

'Erm…we had to…get them…signed by you, sir…'

With arms now folded, Ivan's attention focused on the pale grey back wall of room ten as he continued to press for the answer he really wanted.

'And what else, Mister Sims? What *else* did I ask you to do?'

Trevor glanced down at his own diary, knowing full well that it had not seen daylight since the day he had received it.

'Don't draw on the cover and…get our mams to sign it as well, sir…'

Still Ivan stared straight ahead as he continued with the inquiry.

'I seem to recall something about covering them in brown paper. Did I or did I not give that instruction last week, Mister Sims?'

The youngster looked around the room at his wary classmates whose expressions were fully in tandem with his own.

Ivan began to walk slowly around the group until finding an example that pleased him.

Much to Jenny Douglas' embarrassment, Ivan chose to hold her diary aloft as if it were the Holy Grail.

He commenced to thumb through the first few pages as the class became increasingly uncomfortable with the expectation of an explosion.

'This...is what I anticipated from each and every one of you. Covered in brown paper and signed. And clean of any additional etchings. Congratulations, Miss Douglas.'

The girl blushed and wanted at that moment to disappear forever into a deep hole.

Across the aisle, Hilary Johnson held up two fingers and puffed out her cheeks to express her disapproval of Jenny's compliance.

Ivan resumed to hover around the desks, observing each diary and saying nothing whilst sniffing out the other failures among 1RY.

Then the roll call began as his knuckles rapped the desktop of every pupil who had not complied with his requests.

'Mister Scott. You have failed. Detention! Mister Pearson. Detention! Here! Tonight! One hour! Mister Sims. The same! Miss Bennett. The same! Miss Perkins! The same! Miss Johnson...the same...'

In all, exactly a dozen members of the form had been ordered to stay behind after three-thirty.

Of course, the reliable if lone voice of opposition among the group challenged Ivan's angry dictum as soon as it was given.

'Well, that's not fair...I didn't know that it had to be done for today! Stick your detention! I'm not coming tonight! No way!'

With conscience pricked and tongue armed, Ivan turned to face the source of rebellion as a psychological crack of thunder echoed around the corners of the room.

'Miss Johnson…if I set tasks for the group, I expect those tasks to be carried out without question. Do not try and absolve yourself with feeble excuses when others in the room heard me perfectly adequately.'

Colin Scott raised his hand in hope.

'But sir, I didn't have brown paper at home. I didn't know what to do.'

Ivan recoiled on the boy, whose whitened features displayed evident dread of his tutor's reply.

'Suffering in silence invariably leads to punishment, Mister Scott. You should have asked me what to do if you were not sure. As should the others who ignored my wishes.'

Hilary Johnson found herself compelled to interject on her classmates' behalf once again.

'*Ask* you? Ask *you* …what to do? Why? So that you can act the big man again and shout at us for being thick? About covering a pissing book!'

Ivan altered his expression to one of brimming fury as he closed in on the foul-mouthed young girl, whose game smirk betrayed her open intentions to cause conflict.

'Miss Johnson…yet again…may I suggest that closing the overactive hole under your nose more often is a policy I would advise you adopt to the letter. Your preference for profanity has just landed you detention *tomorrow* night as well!'

Hilary shook her head as Ivan made his way to the blackboard and rubbed it clean.

Colin Scott murmured further objection but was silenced by a relentless wall of sound that shook the upper floor of the building.

'1RY! THOSE OF YOU I HAVE READILY IDENTIFIED WILL BE PRESENT HERE AT THREE-THIRTY THIS AFTERNOON FOR DETENTION! THE SUBJECT WARRANTS NO FURTHER DEBATE! NOW…CAN WE MOVE ON WITH THE BUSINESS OF THE HOUR…please?'

Children in classrooms all around lowered their heads in the feint hope that the distant vocal hurricane beyond the door had reached its peak.

*****

Home time arrived far too soon for some.

Trevor Sims waited nervously at the front of the line that had amassed outside the locked door of room ten.

The minutes passed slowly, with no visible sign of the form tutor, although his presence lingered everywhere.

Colin Scott checked the display on his digital watch.

'This is stupid! It's a quarter to four! Looks like Hilary's gone home as well! She'll be on double detention tomorrow night for that!'

A whispered discussion ensued on the landing which was eventually interrupted by Sarah Green emerging from her own classroom opposite.

With an expression of understandable surprise, she quizzed the group of pupils as they looked straight ahead.

'Excuse me, boys and girls? I thought I heard voices. What is going on here? The final bell rang twenty minutes since. I presume you do all have homes to go to?'

Wendy Bennett's fragile voice pronounced the reason for the unusual congregation, which served to leave Sarah a little bemused.

'Are you *sure* you have detention? Tonight? Up here? In that room?'

With the arrangement confirmed with a nod of the head by all pupils, the teacher checked her own watch.

'No. Not now! You'd all better go home. I'll speak to Mister Reynolds when I see him and find out what he's doing. He must have been delayed downstairs. All of you…off you go.'

Watching the pupils wearily descend the stairs amid a veil of confused whispers, Sarah locked the door of her own room, as the latch clicked in the door opposite.

Grinning from ear to ear, Ivan emerged onto the landing.

'My dear, Sarah! You didn't happen to see some of my form group out here just now, did you?'

The younger maths teacher turned on her heel.

Pure bewilderment enshrouded the moment.

She walked over to her elder colleague whilst dropping the room key into her handbag.

'What are you playing at, Ivan?'

He continued to smirk unreservedly.

'What do you mean by 'playing', dear Sarah?'

'What I mean is…telling half your class to meet here for detention and then locking them out! What's the game?'

Slipping his hands in his trouser pockets, Ivan suddenly became disgruntled at the intrusive scrutiny of his arrangements.

'Do I take it you are responsible for dismissing my detention class?'

Her eyes widened as she sensed imminent confrontation.

'Yes…yes, I am! It's gone ten to four! How long were you planning to leave them standing out here? And furthermore, out of interest, when did you issue the detention and why?'

Ivan glanced cautiously at the mirror-shine toes of his shoes, knowing full well that despite her comparatively tender age, Sarah Green would be a worthy partner for an argument if she felt so inclined.

Feisty and enthusiastic, she unknowingly held the upper hand in this particular issue, as Ivan strived to think quickly on his feet.

'It was given this morning to those pupils in my form group who had not covered their diaries or had failed to get their diaries signed by parents.'

Sarah shook her head slowly as she watched Ivan's taunting smirk become a little broader.

He was fully prepared for her incoming response.

'You can't just make kids stay behind on a whim, Ivan! Parents should have at least twenty-four hours' notice. You must know the rules by now!'

'Rules? Bloody rules! I live by my *own* rules!'

Ivan stomped back into room ten for his briefcase and returned to the landing to lock up. Sarah watched in amazement as he brushed past her and began to descend the stairs.

'Ivan! You must let the parents know *why* their kids are being detained! It's called courtesy! Above anything else, it's a safety and welfare issue. And it's now an obligation for that matter!'

Her ruffled colleague did not look back as his reply capably echoed up the stairwell.

'Well, *you* can term it however you bloody well like. But *I* call it damned inconvenient!'

He halted his stride and glanced through the mid-flight window as Sarah followed and continued to advise him.

'Well put yourself in the parents' shoes! How would you feel if your son didn't make it home from school until gone five o' clock?'

He glanced up in her direction, now becoming tired of the discussion.

'Sarah…are you coming…or are you not?'

Trotting after him down the stairwell she felt evermore frustrated and wanted to understand the motive for his mysterious strategy.

'Ivan! You must write to the parents to let them know what's happening! Reception must send them a letter nowadays!'

Stopping again on the second-floor landing, his spectacles lightened their shade slightly as they became accustomed to the murk of the stair well.

'It's the bloody parents I blame, dear Sarah! The little buggers are thrown at us, and we haven't a clue what's coming. So, we deal with it as best we can. And that's all I ever intend to do. Deal with problems my way…as I personally see fit.'

Now off the lower flight of steps and into the main corridor, Sarah strove to keep up with Ivan's lengthening stride.

'It seems to me that you enjoy courting such controversy! You know you're playing with a hornet's nest. The Head is bound to find out!'

Again, he turned to face her as he walked.

His features became underlined by the constant smile of intended mischief.

'Yes, dear Sarah! Of course, he is!'

They reached the main double doors of the school reception.

The white walls and floor of the corridor dazzled in the late summer sunlight.

'Ivan. You haven't got long left to try and behave yourself. You need those kids this year. Try and get along with them for once!'

Now his smile instantly vanished.

A pursed line of adamant inner pride now replacing the fleeting dalliance with mirth.

'No…my dearest, Sarah. I don't need those kids. Those kids…need *me*.'

He pushed open the door to allow some warmth to bathe his face and blacken his mask once again.

Sarah Green shouted after him as he marched on toward his car.

'Not stopping for a quick coffee?'

Pulling open the driver's door, Ivan waved and thanked her for the offer.'

'No, thank you! I've had enough of the place for one day!'

Sarah shook her head and giggled.

Watching the metallic copper Princess reverse and then depart at speed down the school driveway, she closed the reception door before making her way to the staff room.

11

There was no sign of Hilary Johnson the next morning.

Ivan suspiciously closed the register and dismissed 1RY to their lessons. As silence eventually reigned supreme in room ten, he found himself to be rather curious as to the reason for her absence.

With a free period beckoning some hard-earned attention to the crossword and a much less appealing stack of exercise books to mark, he locked the door and made his way downstairs to the staff room.

The arena was occupied with the customary aroma of nicotine.

Not surprising really, as the sole occupant was Bob Davidson stirring a mug of tea. He turned to Ivan with a large drooping pipe hanging from his mouth and raised his hand as a good morning gesture.

Ivan nodded and set down his briefcase before reclining in his favourite chair and perusing the front page of The Daily Mail.

'I'm surprised you aren't hogging the bold print this morning, Ivan!'

Bob sat himself opposite and continued to suck on his pipe, the stench of which Ivan could not readily stomach.

'Me, Bob? In the headlines? Who on Earth is interested in little old me?'

Mister Davidson shook his head and grinned.

'Well...apparently that Johnson girl is in Taylor's office with her mother. What have you been up to this time? Old Geoff isn't too keen on bad publicity, you know!'

Ivan peered over the top of his read, now alerted to the possibility that the day's timetable might just be punctuated with unwelcome trouble.

'So...what does that have to do with me?'

Bob peered down his nose through the screen of smouldering tobacco before inhaling some more.

'Well, I'm no mathematician like you, but as she's in your form group and I'd say the odds are that you're the cause of the sudden parental interest, wouldn't you?'

Ivan pretended to chuckle at his colleague's astuteness but would not yet admit to being the centre of the problem.

'And…I suppose…two and two makes four in your non-mathematical eyes, does it?'

A wreath of tobacco smoke drifted across the void and temporarily separated the two men.

'It does in your case, Ivan! It *always* does in your case!'

Ivan smirked again, now aware that he must have been the main topic of conversation in the staff room that morning although he felt some comfort for the fact that his fellow teachers had been surprisingly careful not to talk about him within earshot.

And then, just at the wrong moment, Phil Holmes burst into the room. An untimely and unwelcome intrusion.

'Pardon me gents…forgot this pile of folders. Won't be a second! By the way, Ivan…rumour has it that you're about to get your arse kicked by the Head this morning! Or is it just the school grapevine jumping to conclusions again?'

Ivan glanced across to Bob, who cringed at the enticing faux pas that the young physics teacher had just committed.

The predictably derisory response was immediately shot from the barrel leaving Bob Davidson in hysterics and Phil Holmes lost for words.

'My dearest, Philip.'

'Yes, Ivan?'

'Be a good lad for me…and *bugger off*…and shut the door behind you when you've buggered off, will you?'

The perplexed science master sheepishly held the stack of folders under one arm whilst departing the staff room amid the resounding laughter of the man with the pipe.

Bob Davidson composed himself before offering a conclusive viewpoint.

'You can't stand him, can you?'

From behind the sports pages, Ivan's reply was implicitly well armed.

'Whatever gave you that idea, Bob?'

The French teacher recommenced his giggle fit as he began to mark some homework.

'Oh…just a hunch, Ivan. That's all. Just a hunch.'

*****

Less than twenty yards from where the staff room was situated, Geoff Taylor was stationed behind his desk with hands clasped as he listened carefully to the complaint being made by Mrs. Elaine Johnson.

Ever a loyal servant to the reputation of the school, the Headmaster listened with partially feigned enthusiasm as the mother promoted the innocence of her daughter, who sat beside her staring at the floor.

'It seems to me that he's blatantly victimising her, Mister Taylor. Hilary's a good girl. She can sometimes be a little quick to answer back, but she'd never show disrespect. But he likes to show her up in class, apparently. Shouting and slamming his fists. What example is this from a grown man? And as for making her cry…well I'd call that unacceptable. Wouldn't you? It's just not the right behaviour for a teacher, is it?'

Geoff Taylor removed his spectacles and rubbed his eyes. He had heard the allegations but was struggling to side with the emotive plea of the parent.

'The problem I have, Mrs. Johnson, is that Mister Reynolds has been a teacher at this school for many years. He has certain methods of child supervision which, whilst not seeming palatable to the pupils, are nonetheless, very effective. His teaching record is second to none and I have never had cause to question either his integrity or his professionalism.'

Elaine Johnson was not prepared to accept the Head's reply.

'So, you're telling me that no other parents have ever made a complaint about him?'

The Head cautiously considered his words before responding.

'So far as I am aware, there have never been any disciplinary problems among his classes, and furthermore, it is exceedingly rare for pupils to raise objection in this manner.'

Hilary's mother jumped the gun again.

'Don't you think he overdoes it a bit, though? Throwing his weight around? He needs a talking to! And if you're not capable then I certainly am!'

The Headmaster nodded eagerly before replacing the spectacles on the end of his nose.

'I will admit that he runs a very tight ship and runs it very well. But students have long accepted his methods of doing this. Indeed, they finish up with nothing but admiration for the man so far as I can tell. And as there have been no other issues of this nature, I may be so bold as to suggest that we simply have a clash of personalities between your daughter and Mister Reynolds which can be easily resolved.'

The angered features of the mother glared at the sulking expression of the daughter sitting beside her.

A few seconds passed whilst another angle of attack was considered.

'Do you honestly think she wants to get along with him after this? If they don't like each other, then surely Hilary has the right to be moved elsewhere?'

The Head leaned forward in his chair, closely examining the reactions of the two complainants sitting opposite.

'Mrs. Johnson. This is not a holiday camp. Hilary is here to learn and show compliance with school rules. Mister Reynolds is here to teach and has the authority to enforce those rules. She has only been attending Littleholt for a week. Seven days is comparatively nothing. Many pupils struggle to settle in for a good while. Sometimes for an entire term!'

Again, the maternal interruption halted the intended tide of diplomacy.

'My Hilary has never struggled to get on with people! She settles very quickly wherever she goes. She makes friends very easily!'

The Head sat back in his chair, now secretly becoming bored with the meeting.

There was no direct evidence of abuse on show and Hilary's silence spoke volumes.

So far as he was concerned there seemed nothing further to discuss regarding the matter.

'I cannot be seen to criticise my colleagues based on a single child's apparent displeasure. It would be inappropriate and unethical for me to question any of my staff's conduct without being presented with a much larger body of evidence.'

The mother was now becoming infuriated and gestured across the desk with a long, bony forefinger.

'But you just said there was a clash of personalities!'

'Yes, I did. But that should not imply that Mister Reynolds is in the wrong. There is teacher-pupil friction throughout the school. Indeed, throughout every school in the country. There always has been and always shall be. Unfortunately, that is all part and parcel of school life and children must learn to adjust.'

Again, the forefinger was jabbed sharply in the Head's direction to reinforce Hilary's vindication.

'Well, what about this business of detentions? Is there no control measure over keeping kids back after school?'

The Head nodded in agreement and appeased the increasingly irate visitor.

'There is, yes, certainly. I shall endeavour to speak with all teachers on the matter to clarify the school procedure regarding issue of detentions.'

Barely satisfied with Geoff Taylor and his ready stream of fair-natured answers, Elaine Johnson sat back in her chair. Her eleven-year-old daughter simply stared into space without uttering a word.

'So, I've wasted my time, this morning? Is that what you're saying? My girl should put up and shut up. Is that it?'

Now mildly perturbed by her attitude, the Headmaster moved quickly to defend his staff members once again.

'Might I suggest that your daughter adopts a different approach to her teachers? So that she sees them as a positive influence as opposed to figures that should be scorned and mocked. My staff members are only ever here to *help* children...not to upset them. And I assure you, if I ever suspected that any tutor was wilfully intimidating pupils for their own ends, then they would be answerable to me without delay. But, for the moment...'

Once more, Elaine Johnson could not wait for the Head to conclude his explanation.

'For the moment I'm to keep quiet and go away?'

'...Mrs. Johnson...I...don't think...'

'Don't bother saying anymore! I can see whose side you're on! Come on Hilary. You've got to get to your lesson.'

Geoff Taylor rose from his seat and eagerly ushered the Johnson ladies to the door.

'I hope it stops here, Mister Taylor! You tell him! You tell that jumped up little Hitler! He'd better leave her alone! Because if my Hilary comes home in tears again her dad will be paying you a visit next time! I can tell you now...you really don't want that to happen! My Steve will swing for him he will!'

The Head smiled graciously, whilst underneath, his temper fumed.

'Thank you, Mrs. Johnson. I will bear your comments in mind.'

Shutting the office door, he returned to his seat and rubbed his eyes once again, pondering the disgruntled exchanges of the last thirty minutes.

Whilst knowing full well that Ivan Reynolds was a very capable antagonist, it didn't seem correct at that moment to converse with him on the matter.

He hoped that a simple passage of time would erase any teething problems.

Yet as that very thought crossed his mind, Ivan was next door in the adjacent staff room, grinning like a Cheshire cat as he peered through the blinds.

Whilst watching Elaine Johnson make a very disgruntled exit along the school driveway.

*****

The morning could not have passed quickly enough for Ivan. The rumour mill was now in full swing and most First Years had listened to the exaggerated tales of how Hilary Johnson and her erupting mother had threatened to put the Headmaster through a window and burn down the school.

For Ivan's part, he was both amused by the wonder of childish imagination and generally apathetic about the actual truth.

Having passed Geoff Taylor in the car park at lunchtime, neither teacher had broached the issue. A courteous 'good afternoon' was exchanged as the Head made for his car and left the premises for a meeting with the local council about building improvements.

Evidently, Ivan was not to be reproached, despite the partially successful intentions of the scheming Hilary Johnson.

Opting not to go for his usual jog around the park, Ivan found himself to be unusually peckish and joined the throbbing queue leading into the dining hall.

Despite his attempts to make civil and casual conversation with other children in line, they were instantly wary of the domineering figure that had polluted their personal space, and subsequently kept mouths closed and eyes front.

They suddenly felt as though they were being studied and waited for that booming voice of discontentment to rage along the corridor.

Ivan Reynolds had such an unwitting effect on schoolchildren.

He also towered physically over the majority of Littleholt's pupils, which did not help diffuse the long-standing tension that arose when he was around.

So, in acceptance of the youngsters' right to remain silent, Ivan resigned himself to shuffling along in the queue without attempting to socialise with anyone.

Suddenly the aroma of the busy kitchen made its unpleasant impact with Ivan's nasal passages. It was a potent combination of burned cooking fat, braised beef, pungent custard and other sundry delights that served to alert his senses as to the vicinity.

Passing the stack of trays, he selected the top one and glanced along the array of savoury dishes that were on display atop the stainless-steel counter.

The lady serving main meals offered him a pleasant smile as she heaped his request onto a lukewarm plate. Handing across the pile of sausage, mashed potato, and peas, she thanked him for his custom and moved her attention to the next person in line.

With gravy liberally drizzled over his meal, Ivan selected some cutlery and turned to face the swelling, noisy inhabitants of the dining hall.

Searching vainly for a seat, he noticed pupils actively concealing vacant chairs to dissuade him from joining them.

'Oh, to be popular.' he mumbled, whilst scanning the room.

With tray held at chest height, he smelled his food and surprisingly became ever more eager to sit and sample it. Floating between tables, he sensed the scores of pairs of eyes warily following his every move.

Then finally, he spotted the table in the far corner of the hall. From a distance it looked to be unattended. Closing in on his destination, he found it occupied by a single, solitary diner.

Ever ready with his inherent manners, Ivan excused his intrusion.

'Miss Douglas? Would it be a problem if I sat here next to you to eat, today? Please say it's okay because my mash is going colder by the second.'

Jenny Douglas exhibited her genuine smile which was instantly book-ended by two red cheeks, the colour of which had been undoubtedly deepened by the unexpected appearance of her form tutor.

As was normally the case, she said nothing, instead desperately searching her empty plate for some distraction from the proximity of the teacher, who simply sat and began to eat.

But Ivan Reynolds was never one to allow silence to prevail for too long.

'So…how are you finding Littleholt so far, Miss Douglas? Do you like it here?'

The shy girl nodded, still blushing avidly.

'Its…okay…I suppose.'

Ivan swallowed his morsel before continuing the exchange with gradual enthusiasm.

'Do you like the subjects?'

Jenny nodded once again, now ever-so-slightly accepting to the amenable presence of her older companion.

'Are you making some new friends, okay?'

The eleven-year-old stared into space. A sudden and distinctive air of sadness tinged her expression for a moment as her attention slowly focused back on the teacher sitting beside her.

'I like *some* of my classes.'

'Good! And what about the teachers? Are you getting along with them?'

The delay in her response allowed Ivan to shovel in another mouthful of sausage. She was pondering the question with undue consideration, as though she had a reply ready, yet felt cautious of revealing her thoughts.

'Some of the teachers are nice.'

Ivan smiled as he swallowed again and reached across the table for salt and pepper.

'Are they really? Excellent. Tell me though…which teachers *aren't* so nice, then, Miss Douglas?'

She quickly diverted her gaze to the tabletop, yet her eyes flickered back to focus on Ivan's, despite the dispiriting ebony lenses of his spectacles.

'Mister Holmes. He's not that nice. I don't like him very much.'

Ivan wanted to laugh at the irony, but instead opted to veer away from the temptation of divulging his personal opinion.

'Okay…and who out of the teachers do you like best of all?'

Jenny Douglas suddenly stood up; her crimson visage almost ready to explode with youthful discomfort.

Yet for all her shyness, there was no hesitancy in the departing proclamation.

Or the honesty with which it was conveyed.

'You are…sir. You're my favourite teacher of all.'

With that, the girl with pig tails left the table under a shroud of earnest embarrassment and rapidly vanished among the crowd.

As Ivan sat somewhat aghast at the words she had just uttered, his concentration was interrupted by the instantly recognisable tone of Matt Jenkins who perched himself in the next seat.

He had obviously watched Jenny Douglas make her sudden exit from the scene and felt the need to venture a little sarcasm.

'Don't tell me you've upset another one, Ivan! Not your week, is it?'

The head of the Maths department could not help but smile gleefully at his younger colleague's woefully misplaced observations.

'For your information my dear Matthew, Miss Douglas has just informed me that I am currently her favourite teacher. And she is a pupil I find myself to be growing rather fond of even at this early stage of term.'

Matt sat back in his chair with knife and fork in hand and stared vacantly at the contents of his plate.

Feigning a reaction of stunned shock, whilst genuinely sensing a pang of disbelief at what his veteran colleague had just said, he murmured to himself.

'You know something, Ivan…I'm becoming seriously worried about you these days…'

12

The silver pocket watch lay in its owner's palm as Ivan impatiently awaited the arrival of the last straggler for afternoon registration.

He did not speak to Hilary Johnson as she nonchalantly stomped up the stairway and scuffed the soles of her shoes across the landing to join the rear of the two lines.

But he did notice the look of scorn she offered his way.

A stern glare of nothing less than absolute hatred.

Hilary carried the demeanour of a girl who was seemingly far from finished with her campaign to disrupt a generally very well-behaved form group.

Having mentally confirmed that all were now present and correct, Ivan held out his hand as an invitation for the group to enter the room. His mouth gradually turned up at the edges as each pupil in turn passed his position by the open door.

He purposely waited, still with watch in hand, as Hilary Johnson moved toward the towering teacher.

Yet, she was far from intimidated.

Unlike most of her peers, Ivan Reynolds did not instil into her that pure form of discipline that had become his trademark.

Instead, she made a point of stopping her stride to be out of earshot from the rest of the class. With just herself and her tutor on the top floor landing, she spat a poisonous declaration.

Ivan did not flinch as he received the whispered promise.

'You'd better be careful. My dad's coming for you if you don't leave me alone.'

Snapping shut the case of his watch he slipped the timepiece into his waistcoat. He had rarely seen such a rebellious streak in someone so young and without any obvious motive.

It only served to re-fuel the slowly decreasing fire in his belly.

He was more than ready for the challenge in the swansong of such an illustrious career. But he would not be drawn by the temptation just yet.

'My dear, Miss Johnson…if you would claim your seat…we are already late in taking the register…and you will certainly be delayed further for your next lesson.'

Jenny Douglas covertly watched Hilary move to stand behind her chair as Ivan closed the door. With the nod of the head given, the pupils seated themselves in silence.

Even before the tutor had re-positioned to his desk and opened the register, Hilary had begun whispering about her devious exploits that morning.

Jenny kept one careful eye on the young rebel a short distance away and the other eye on Hilary's perceived opponent sitting underneath the blackboard.

The expectancy of renewed hostility within the room was tangible.

Unusually yet wisely for the time being, Ivan chose to ignore the purposed distraction and proceeded to read out the list of names. Within seconds, the class was dismissed to their afternoon timetable.

It was noticeable to a few that Hilary was again dragging her feet as her classmates pushed their chairs back under tables and quickly exited the room as Ivan returned to the open door.

It was obvious that more fireworks were imminent, but the apparently pleasant smile that Ivan maintained as she sauntered towards him gave her the false impression that he was far from concerned about confrontation.

Calming the two gathering lines of incoming pupils, he raised a hand and asked for quiet. Hilary was rendered dumbfounded as he then re-entered room ten and closed the door, blocking her exit.

Looming above her, Ivan folded his arms and adopted a truly menacing air. Similarly, the girl mirrored the sentiment with a distasteful scowl.

It was a sign of juvenile defiance he had seen so many times in his career.

And every single opportunist had been vanquished without trace. Of course, this girl - in keeping with her predecessors - believed she was being original, smart and successful in her aim.

But she did not reckon on the resolve or experience of the particular teacher she had willingly adopted as her combatant.

His softly spoken question was unexpected.

'Miss Johnson…is there any problem you would like to discuss?'

Her answer was immediate and forthright.

'Talk…talk with *you*? I don't think so!'

His determinedly dark gaze remained fixed upon hers.

So young; so feisty; so foolish.

'Why did you not attend this morning's registration? Am I not entitled to an explanation of your whereabouts?'

The girl gripped the handles of her schoolbag somewhat nervously as Ivan began to move towards and then around her. She did not follow his movements as he silently encircled her position.

Suddenly, his rasping voice again broke her façade of supposed invincibility.

'You don't like being in my form group…do you, Miss Johnson?'

Growing consternation now smothered her response.

Yet she could not resist the inner desire to try and antagonize him.

'No. I don't like you at all. I think you're horrible.'

Taking deep breaths, she waited with increasing anxiety for the inflamed repost of her form tutor.

'Well…Miss Johnson. I do not care for your personal judgement. Sadly, we are deemed to be together by the powers on high. If you should find yourself needing to bring any issue to light…please feel free to enlighten *me* of your concerns first of all…before running to the Headmaster…or your parents.'

The girl sneered as she sensed Ivan's displeasure at the events of the morning.

But she would not be seen to weaken before him.

On the contrary, her resolve only hardened.

'Scared you, did it? Someone taking you on for once…instead of the other way round? Don't like it do you?'

Ivan continued to hover around the room as the class outside started to become boisterous in attempting to assess the cause of the delay to their lesson.

And still Hilary did not submit to engage the damning, ebony glare of the teacher.

Instead, she waited patiently for his acceptance of defeat.

Yet when Ivan finally spoke, she found his conclusion to be something of an anti-climax.

'Thank you for your time. You are free to go, Miss Johnson.'

Bemused by the outcome, the youngster carelessly swung her bag over her shoulder and left the room without further word.

Ivan followed her out onto the landing and watched her disappear down the staircase before turning his attention to the curious and highly vocal assembly of Fifth Years.

'Okay, you may enter…QUIETLY!'

*****

The bell that signified the end of another school day was music to Ivan's ears. He felt unusually fatigued and ready to escape from the asylum that Littleholt Secondary sometimes resembled.

Slipping on his suit jacket, he gave a quick visual routine check to confirm that the room was not too untidy for the cleaners. Moving to close one of the large windows that overlooked the playing fields, he saw that the afternoon's weather looked rather grey and unappealing compared to that of late.

With a humid summer throwing its last tantrum through the thick slate cloud, it seemed that autumn was perhaps closing in.

Ivan did not care either way for seasonal change, but nature's cycle dictated that his opportunities for positive progress at the allotment were now diminishing by the week, although one more full harvest was due to be reaped and collected by George Breeden.

With briefcase in hand, he locked the door and embarked on a decidedly weary descent. Having decided that perhaps a coffee in the staff room would provide an appropriate pick-up, he sauntered in silence through the recently vacated school corridors, relishing the quite that ensued now the children had dispersed.

In the staff room, a dozen or so of his colleagues had already found a seat and were either engaged in casual conversation about their day or marking exercise books.

Bob Davidson offered Ivan a nod from the other side of the room and gestured with an empty mug.

'Yes, coffee please, Bob. You know how I like it.'

The customary end-of-day buzz was brought to an abrupt halt when Geoff Taylor opened the door and poked his ever-furrowed features through the gap.

All mouths immediately closed in unison and all eyes fell to the Headmaster in intrigued expectancy of his business.

'Carry on, people. Don't let me disturb your recovery time! Ivan…have you a minute in my office, please.'

Carol Shaw glanced up from her marking with sudden concern but opted to conceal her interest from the others.

Placing the briefcase in his customary seat of choice by the window, Ivan held up a single forefinger to Bob as an indicator to put the drink on hold.

'Back in a tick, my friend.'

Now sensing the joint attention of the room to be fully focused on him, Ivan could not resist the chance to jibe back at his understandably curious colleagues.

'Well? What's up with you lot? It's not as if I'm in trouble again! Continue with your gossiping!'

Smirking triumphantly, Ivan left the room and made for the Head's office just along the corridor.

The door was ajar.

'Do come in, Ivan. This won't take long. Please…have yourself a pew.'

Ivan duly obliged and sat at the large, polished oak desk. The Headmaster observed the demeanour of his most experienced member of staff and smiled.

It was a warm, genuine expression that Ivan had received many times over the years, and it was always appreciated, although the circumstances in which he found himself immersed at that moment were relatively unusual.

Aiming to present himself to be as relaxed as possible, Ivan clasped his hands behind his head, crossed his legs and then with practised calm, decided to steal the honour and open the conversation.

'This is an unexpected pleasure, Geoffrey. What can I do for you?'

The Head fiddled nervously with the frames of his spectacles and pretended to straighten his tie. He was evidently ill at ease with the imminent subject matter.

'Ivan…exactly how would you describe the relationship you have with your First Year form group at the moment?'

Ivan smiled, now fully aware of the motive for the unplanned conference. He was also well versed in giving the answers that were required to be heard.

'Very amicable…so far. They're a relatively obedient collection of individuals. They seem to be toeing the line sensibly. No major problems that I'm aware of. Why do you ask?'

The Head sat forward in his chair and gazed at the top page of the writing pad on his desk. He appeared troubled by something though Ivan was certainly not about to try and allay his sense of discomfort.

In truth, he was eager for the Head to say his piece and be done with it.

'Ivan…there's been…an allegation of sorts.'

As there was no obvious emotional response from across the desk, Geoff Taylor continued.

'Not a formal complaint, mind you. More…an issue has been brought to my attention and I wish to attain your view of things before I make a judgement.'

Now Ivan uncrossed his legs and put his hands on his lap.

He had never been one for beating about the bush.

'By this…*issue*…you mean…Hilary Johnson, I take it?'

The Headmaster nodded cautiously, now almost embarrassed by the futile necessity of their dialogue.

His eyes widened with apprehension as he addressed his most senior member of staff.

'I don't care what's gone off, Ivan. And I don't particularly care for what might still occur. But I'm here to warn you. She looks like a trouble chaser to me. She had her mother giving me lectures this morning. The term is barely a fortnight old! Don't get caught up in the girl's game. I don't want you to be drawn in. Is that clear?'

Ivan Reynolds' blackened shades were now two deep dark windows that concealed an inner fury.

Geoff stared into those uncertain pools as he awaited a carefully considered reply.

'She is trouble, Geoffrey…I agree. But I haven't stepped over the mark if that's what you mean. I'm in full control of the form group…I can assure you.'

The Head placed his palms together as if ready to pray; sincerity sheathing his statement.

'I would never ever presume otherwise, Ivan. Like I say…this is to warn you that her general attitude is not favourable. We've seen her type before. She'll fabricate and connive, probably because that's all she knows. Junior school evidently let her rule the roost. But it's not healthy for you…especially with you having so little time to go.'

Ivan leaned forward in his chair now carrying a look of mild annoyance.

'Don't you mean…it will look bad for the school, Geoffrey? Isn't *that* what you're *truly* concerned about? If I upset people, it's the image of Littleholt that's under threat as opposed to *my* reputation…isn't it?'

Geoff Taylor began to shake his head, yet he would not be allowed to speak until Ivan had made his point.

'But dear Geoffrey, my reputation will matter not a jot after next April. I understand that the school's image needs to be preserved for the future. I sympathise. But I repeat…there has been no altercation or difference of opinion as far as I can recall…'

Ivan sat on the edge of his chair and raised his hand to affirm his standpoint.

'…nor…will there be one…'

The Headmaster smiled and stood up.

'You've nothing to prove to me, Ivan. I'm just tipping you off. That's all.'

Ivan rose to his feet and offered his thanks his for the advice.

'Geoffrey…please…have a little more faith in me. I haven't gone this far in the game without learning to keep my cards close to my chest.'

'No, Ivan…of course not. That will be all, thank you.'

Shutting the door behind him, Ivan made his way back to the staff room, which was now practically deserted aside Carol and Bob.

'Where is everybody? Scared the rest of the buggers off, did I? Where's my bloody drink?'

Bob Davidson hurriedly concocted Ivan's coffee and passed it over. He could not help but chuckle at his colleague's evidently disgruntled manner. Naturally, the open conveyance of his mirth did not serve to ease the situation.

'I don't know, Ivan …and here's us thinking you'd be in for a nice peaceful year.'

Ivan slumped into his chair, sipped the coffee, and instantly pulled a face of disgust.

'And that's got PISSING SUGAR IN IT!'

Bob laughed out loud as Ivan's features contorted.

'I reckon you need it to sweeten you up. Might do you some good, mate…'

Ivan offered no reply, instead opting to conclude the crossword.

13

George Breeden stood at the back step as Ivan pulled open the kitchen door to greet him.

'Hello mate! Come on in. Cup of tea?'

'No thanks, Ivan. On my way to set up the stall. Just thought I'd pop round and give you the nod about the veg. Could do with all you've got by the weekend.'

'No problem, George. I hope to make the most of time after school this week. Shame you can't hang on until next week when it's half-term. I'll have plenty of time then! You should have the lot by Friday night. It will probably be the last until next spring now. I've never been keen on winter harvesting!'

'Is it really half-term next week? Crikey…that's gone quick! The takings have been pretty good lately. I'll sort you out with a share.'

'Now George…you're my friend. Forget about trying to offer me money.'

'But come on…your supply has helped me out no end this summer!'

'No, George! I mean it! I do it for the therapy more than anything else. The way I see it you may as well let the locals enjoy the produce and you reap the rewards. Money makes little difference to me these days.'

Ivan crunched on a piece of toast whilst George pondered his friend's generosity and then conceded defeat on the issue. Ivan maintained a studious eye through the kitchen window in wait for the anticipated entrance of the tortoiseshell cat, which was now blooming rapidly into young adulthood.

'So, there's a market for you this morning, is there?'

'Yes, Ivan…got a pitch out at Shellbrook for a change.'

'Of course, yes…I know…I should remember after all this time shouldn't I! Well…shouldn't take long to shift that little lot once I've tended to it!'

Swilling down the toast with a gulp of tea, Ivan thought he perceived a glimpse of feline movement through the hedge bottom but couldn't be absolutely certain.

'You sure you don't want paying, Ivan?'

The teacher eyed his friend with insistence.

'No...*nothing...nothing at all*. Tell you what...take me for a pint to celebrate my retirement next Easter!'

'I'll be doing that anyway!'

Ivan smiled as he maintained close vigil on the scene through the rear window.

'Okay. Then we have a deal!'

'Right...well...have a good day at school...I'll perhaps see you Friday night, shall I?'

'No problem, George. See you then.'

Ivan watched his neighbour depart before shutting the door. After making the bed and adorning his usual armoury in preparation for another day of battle at Littleholt, he ventured back downstairs and checked the mail which had just clattered through onto the doormat.

One solitary electric bill was the only item delivered.

In the lounge he slotted the brown envelope onto the mantelpiece behind the carriage clock and combed his hair in front of the fireplace mirror as the seven-thirty breakfast time news crackled from the kitchen radio.

As he paid vague attention to the morning's headlines, confirmation of the date suddenly alerted his attention.

It was Tuesday the eighteenth of October.

A date of particular significance for Ivan Reynolds.

Exactly thirty-one years ago, his son had entered the world.

Nicholas was a quiet and contented baby, who all too quickly developed into such a handsome boy. And now, should he have inherited his father's mind, an undoubtedly intelligent grown man.

Ivan was temporarily inflated with paternal pride as he wallowed in the moment of unexpected nostalgia. If only he knew where to send the card and present.

He continued to study his age defying reflection. Not yet wearing his spectacles, he examined the whiteness of his eyes and the lines that surrounded them. The contemplation of time having passed by was a bittersweet experience, leaving him wishing that, just for a little while, he might be at liberty to re-visit those early days of family bliss.

But such a likelihood was now a mere pipedream; nothing more than a whimsical source of hopeful fantasy.

Harsh reality had moved life onward in its own direction as it often tended to do with annoying reliability.

And with the conclusion of the news bulletin, Ivan's brief immersion into his own history was brought to an abrupt end.

Cleaning the lenses of his spectacles and sliding the mask of duty into place, he reluctantly shuffled into the kitchen, flicked off the kitchen radio and readied himself for the journey to school.

*****

The first five weeks of the academic year had passed comparatively smoothly, and the statutory week-long half term break was imminent.

Ivan had purposely opted not to reveal his impending retirement to the form group, knowing full well that their recently learned sense of discipline may quickly erode should they discover their tutor was about to desert them.

Yet the underlying friction with Hilary Johnson had continued unabated. Though he had been sternly vigilant in identifying her regular bouts of wilful dissension, Ivan had also heeded the warning from the headmaster not to rise to the bait.

Of the entire First Year intake, it was plainly obvious that she was the willing ringleader in most unruly incidents occurring in and around the place.

Indeed, many of the First Year girls were now as fearful of *her* reputation almost as much as they were of Ivan's. He had become gradually thankful that Hilary Johnson's company was something to endure for only a few minutes a day, aside from the mandatory hour's form period each week.

Indeed, the timetable had become an accidental blessing that he was becoming increasingly appreciative of.

Yet this particular morning would bring with it another unforeseeable test of mettle as he ambled along the echoing corridors.

Sloping up the stairway to the top landing, he listened and then watched as the two lines of 1RY quickly acknowledged his light-footed approach on the steps with a deathly hush.

Yet he opted to cut through the veil of caution that always prevailed between pupils and their tutor at this juncture, with an untypically jovial greeting.

'Good morning, ladies and gentlemen.'

Most of the class responded accordingly with a united reply and even one or two smiles emerged among the throng.

Yet Hilary Johnson did not even look at him, let alone offer such a courtesy in tandem with her classmates.

And despite the fact she no longer wilfully spoke to her form tutor on any issue, she was always busy in her efforts to cause the mildest distraction to proceedings.

Persistently on the lookout for the opportunity to strike.

Ever ready to challenge Ivan's tenure.

Through his mystical shades, he stared without word at the somewhat subdued opponent for a few seconds before finally retrieving the classroom keys from his trouser pocket.

On unlocking the door, he performed the ritual inspection of uniforms, cosmetics, and jewellery as the lines of boys and girls passed nervously by.

Having assembled the class onto their chairs, he gently set down his briefcase as a knock at the door interrupted the morning routine before it had even commenced.

Carol Shaw's features appeared in the narrow gap and smiled gleefully at her colleague sitting a few yards away.

'Mister Reynolds…can I have a quick word, please.'

Ivan raised a discerning finger to give the order to 1RY to remain seated and silent.

He joined the Head of First Year outside on the landing and closed the door behind him.

'Yes, my dear Carol. What can I do for you?'

'It's old Eric. He's twisted his ankle at home and can't drive to school today. I said I'd cover most of his P.E. lessons this morning, but I've got a double history class after dinner. The girls can be taken care of by Miss Martin. You're free to do the lads on Tuesdays, aren't you? Be a love and help me out? I'm not much good at rugby!'

Ivan considered the opportune proposal for a moment to assess the possible implications.

'Which class is it?'

Carol smirked uncontrollably as she disclosed the answer.

'It's the Fourth Years. Your favourite group…Shaun Peterson and company.'

A broad smile underlined the eyes of ebony as the tempting prospect rapidly bloomed with infinite appeal.

'*Excellent*! Leave them with me. I shall be in the changing rooms at one-thirty after registration. Should be a nice surprise for them…shouldn't it!'

Carol gave Ivan an appreciative pat on the shoulder.

'Oh…I'm sure of that much! Thank you, Ivan. Don't go hurting yourself though! Look after that dodgy shoulder!'

Returning to the apparent obedience of room ten, Ivan resumed his seat at his desk and grasped the handle of the middle drawer where the register resided.

'My apologies to you all as we're now running a little late. I'll be as swift as is humanly possible.'

The drawer in question seemed a little stiff and flatly refused to slide open under his increasingly forceful grasp.

Becoming frustrated by the growing procession of hold-ups, he glanced down at the problem, already sensing the murmurs from outside the room as his incoming period one Maths class begun to gather on the landing.

Then the cause of the hindrance became obvious.

The drawer had been sealed shut with sello-tape.

With temper now simmering, Ivan looked up and engaged with the gallery of young faces.

And the culprit quickly revealed herself without a shred of fear or reservation.

Hilary Johnson's beaming smile easily identified her as the chief suspect as the other thirty juvenile expressions sported nothing less than undiluted trepidation.

Clenching his fists under the table, Ivan sat back in his chair and looked squarely at the villain of the peace.

It was evident that in the few seconds he had been absent from the room conversing with Carol, the girl had seized the moment.

He observed her through his dark facade before calmly standing to his feet once more.

'Miss Johnson…'

She did not speak or oblige the teacher with her gaze.

Yet she grinned broadly without a hint of contrition.

'Miss Johnson…my desk drawer has been tampered with. Could you possibly shed any light on the matter?'

The girl shrugged with amused indifference.

'So *what*? It's nothing to do with me! You can't blame me! You never saw me do it! You can't accuse *me*!'

Hilary muttered an insult as a lonesome figure at the rear of the end row of desks hesitantly held up her hand.

In her fingers was hooked a small pair of scissors.

Ivan duly marched to the generous provider and conveyed his sincere appreciation.

'Miss Douglas…I thank you for your valuable assistance in this unexpected crisis.'

Hilary instinctively swivelled in her chair to glare at Jenny Douglas and mouthed two words to convey her disapproval, causing the recipient of the insult to blush.

Unleashing the register from the drawer, Ivan then returned the scissors to their owner and slowly took his seat once again.

He glared without expression at Hilary Johnson as he delved into his jacket's inner pocket and removed a fountain pen, much to the confusion of the guilty party and her observing classmates.

Less than a minute later the attendance had been checked and the room quickly vacated.

Ivan sat for a moment, overwhelmed with anger that he should feel compelled to employ such a low-key reaction.

Yet Hilary Johnson knew the game she wished to play was fraught with danger.

And time was still very much on his side.

It even surprised Ivan that his patience had held thus far.

But even legends had their breaking point.

14

Bearing in mind his upcoming secondment to an afternoon P.E. lesson as urgent replacement for Eric Rogers, Ivan had opted to change into his gym kit at lunchtime and warm up with a gentle jog around the local parkland.

The thought had prevailed for most of the morning that if he were about to flex his muscles with an effervescent group of fifteen-year-olds, then he would not wish to run the risk of pulling a muscle at their expense or indeed for their entertainment. Besides, for Ivan, active participation was a major part of the attraction.

Trotting back towards the playground from his run, he noticed Trevor Sims and Jenny Douglas sitting together on a bench under the veranda. They watched from a short distance as their form tutor passed them without word and both observed his route into the gymnasium and changing rooms. Trevor contemplated the spectacle for a moment before offering an opinion on the athletic display just witnessed.

'I bet I can't run like that when I'm old like him.'

Jenny continued to stare straight ahead as she waited in vain for her favourite teacher to reappear.

She too carefully considered her reaction before conjuring the confidence to venture some modesty.

'I know I won't be able to! I can't run like it *now*, never mind when I'm an old woman!'

Trevor smirked and glanced across to his companion, whose vaguely attractive features now adorned earnest pleasure as she giggled in his company.

'What do you reckon to Mister Reynolds then, Jen?'

Still her attention remained fixed on some unspecified point across the playground. Yet to her surprise she felt at liberty to disclose her true feelings to her one and only genuine school friend

'You know what, Simmo? I think he's *brilliant*!'

*****

Alone in the boys' changing room, Ivan drank cold water directly from the tap and drenched his hair to cool down. Sweat poured readily from his brow and down his neck, yet he felt particularly fit and agile at that moment.

He was now pumped up and prepared.

Prepared for the joyous sight awaiting him in only a few short minutes; possibly the most enticing experience that Ivan Reynolds had endured in the entire first few weeks of the new term.

Throwing on a tracksuit top to preserve body warmth, he zipped it up and delved into the teacher's locker room for his silver pocket watch.

Ten minutes until show-time.

Remaining donned in his running kit, Ivan caused not a little consternation and considerable confusion from teachers and pupils alike as he meandered across the car park, through the corridors and up the stairway to room ten to mark the afternoon registration.

Reaching the double filed congregation of 1RY, they sniggered and pointed at their tutor's untypical regalia as he unlocked the classroom door.

Yet their opportunity for mirth was short-lived.

'QUIET PLEASE! I HAVE TO BE DOWNSTAIRS URGENTLY! AS SUCH…I WISH TO TAKE THE REGISTER WITHOUT DELAY! IN YOU GO!'

The form did not have to be asked twice to refrain from garnering amusement from their tutor's appearance and within two minutes they had been dismissed to afternoon lessons allowing Ivan to swiftly relocate himself back to the gymnasium.

*****

Having appeared for their lesson only to find the boys' changing rooms locked, the boisterous Fourth Year class had little option but to form a noisy and disorderly congregation outside.

Their customary vocal turbulence echoed around the walls of the narrow wood-lined corridor.

The highly audible bravado was typical for the peerage.

For all teenage boys, P.E. was the most anticipated lesson of the week.

However, the simmering adrenalin provided by the imminent games period was rapidly diffused, when they discovered who their stand-in coach was to be for the afternoon.

Ivan appeared discreetly from behind the blissfully ignorant melee and snaked his way slowly among the young men to appear victoriously at the front of the group.

Standing with hands on hips, he eyed the buoyant throng with an inflated sense of satisfaction.

With mouths agape, the dumbfounded youths simply stared back at him in innocent wonder.

At over six feet in height, Ivan was indisputably the tallest in the group, but not by much. His nearest rival in inches, Shaun Peterson, did not hold back in vocalising the murmured suspicions.

'God, no! Don't tell me, sir. Please…not *you*…'

An uncontrolled expression of superiority broadened below Ivan's dark lenses as he nodded and proceeded to unlock the changing room door.

'Oh *yes*…Mister Peterson…*me*! Mister Rogers is indisposed. Aren't you fortunate that I volunteered to take his place? Now in you all go…and change into your reversible rugger tops.'

Again, Peterson was the sole voice of adversity.

'But sir…we're supposed to be playing football until half term…not rugby!'

Ivan's aura of indescribable pleasure increased the severity of the lines around his eyes and cheeks.

'Mister Peterson…who said anything about rugby?'

The wave of confusion swept audibly throughout the room as the teenagers began to undress and don their kit.

'Where's old Rogers then, sir?' came another enquiring voice from the far side of the room.

Ivan unlocked a store cupboard and glanced upward to respond.

'How unusually considerate of you to enquire, Mister Thompson! *Mister* Rogers has twisted his ankle at home. Hence, you have the pleasure of my company for the next hour…or two.'

Another voice of frustration sounded from the centre of the room.

'Sir…that's not where the footballs are kept!'

Sliding open the wooden door of the cupboard, Ivan stood aside and revealed the tools of the particular trade that he had in mind for the session.

'And who said anything about football? Oh yes…I forgot to mention…you will all need to be wearing your plimsolls.'

A heavy silence prevailed as everyone's attention focused on the contents of the stock cabinet that Ivan had unsheathed.

Shaun Peterson again was the first out of the blocks with his objections.

'But sir…those are…hockey sticks…sir.'

Ivan blew sharply on the whistle that hung around his neck and casually tossed a small wooden ball from palm to palm.

'Gentlemen…on your way out to the Redgra pitch, each of you please take one stick each from the cupboard and line up sensibly facing the school building.'

The groans of dissatisfaction were veritable music to the teacher's ears. Almost preferable to any Roy Orbison record.

Not quite, but almost.

Grabbing the stopwatch from the hook in his personal locker room, he watched each boy in turn arm themselves with their weapon of choice, before plucking one for himself and locking the door behind him.

Once on the hockey pitch, the tangible sense of anticipation was worth coming to school for on its own merit, as he addressed the sulking, scowling faces of the youths.

'Gentlemen, you will undoubtedly be delighted to learn that as there are only fifteen of you, I shall join in and even up the sides to allow a game consisting of eight versus eight.'

The looks of sheer despondency carried domino-effect along the line as Ivan gestured to the middle of the group.

'This half…will reverse their shirts and play in yellow with me. The other half will remain in green.'

More grumbles ensued, further fuelling Ivan's brimming enthusiasm for the task.

He assembled his team into position, opting initially to play in defence.

Daniel Keeting, a tall and athletic-looking boy of Afro-Caribbean origin, unexpectedly offered Ivan a chance to taste some real glory.

'Hey…Mister Reynolds…play up in attack with me! We'll slay 'em!'

Ivan smirked at the proposition and saw that Shaun Peterson was already snarling as he gripped his stick with both fists and organised his troops. All things considered, the possibility of rubbing Peterson's nose into the dust of defeat held unlimited appeal.

Even to a fifty-nine-year-old teacher who should know infinitely better.

Perhaps this was the opportunity to teach him a valuable lesson.

'Very well, Mister Keeting. But I must reassure you, my speed will not be up to yours.'

Daniel grinned widely.

'No problem! I do the running. You do the scoring!'

Ivan had never taught Daniel, yet he had always admired the polite and affable boy from afar and felt he should have had far more encouragement in exploring his sporting potential.

A mutual thumbs-up declared Ivan's contentment with the plan as the bully-off for the game encroached and Ivan started his watch.

From the first whistle, the action was played at a fast pace and the challenges were hard and frenetic. So frantic was the tempo that Ivan found it increasingly difficult to both partake in the match and act as referee.

A few minutes passed before he opted to dispense with officialdom. Ivan pocketed the whistle and decided to fully indulge himself in the contest.

The clatter of gravel and sticks resonated across the pitch.

Legs and feet connected in hard fought yet fair and competitive opening exchanges.

But voices were rapidly becoming raised, and tempers were soon flaring.

Especially that of Shaun Peterson, whose side seemed somewhat disinterested in assisting him to the victory he so craved.

As Daniel Keeting proudly slammed home the first goal for his team, Peterson took a late swipe on back of the scorer's calves with his stick, which resulted in a fiery face-to-face confrontation.

With both boys armed and dangerous, Ivan stepped in quickly and separated the protagonists, but the aggressive tone of the contest was now firmly set for all players.

Every few seconds, yelps and winces arose around the pitch as the battle for supremacy reigned unabated. Ivan himself wisely took little of the brunt as the main nucleus of the conflict centred between the opposing captains, Peterson and Keeting.

They clashed heads and tangled bodies.

Elbows and shins collided, and the hostility raged further.

Ivan was intrigued by the evolving exhibition of combat to say the least.

He viewed male adrenalin as a wonderful ingredient for the mix as it was such a rare commodity inside the classroom.

Yet out in the field, ultimate triumph was the sole motive for the efforts of all. And soon, all sixteen players were fully enticed into the bear pit.

Ivan sweated and panted, dodged late tackles, and let the game flow with occasional bouts of praise for the young competitors.

That is, until Peterson's wild and reckless swing rendered the teacher inactive with a sharp crack around the ankle leaving Ivan hobbling off the pitch to soothe his bruises.

'THAT WAS A DELIBERATE FOUL, PETERSON!'

The smirking skipper offered little sympathy as he gasped for air.

'ALL PART OF THE GAME, SIR!'

Standing limply on one leg, Ivan pulled the whistle from his pocket and blew for half time. The score-line was duly confirmed as being three-two in favour of Ivan's team.

Before commencing the second period of the match, Ivan beckoned Daniel over, who listened intently to his teacher's words.

Ivan's whispered yet purposed instruction carried due weight as he sat lamely on the touchline.

'Whatever you do Mister Keeting…*don't* let Peterson score. Stop him playing! Do whatever you need to do. However, you wish to do it. The referee will show leniency. There will be no whistle from me…I assure you.'

Daniel nodded eagerly.

'No sweat, Mister Reynolds! Watch me *fly*!'

The second half endured with Ivan now hobbling in his team's defensive line due to a bruised and painful ankle bone. Time and again the game of increasing contact resulted in cries of discomfort and flying gravel dust clouded the moment.

Ivan checked his stopwatch once more.

'ONE MINUTE REMAINING, GENTLEMEN! ONE MINUTE!'

With the final whistle imminent, the teams were tied at five goals apiece.

And then it happened.

The moment Ivan Reynolds had prayed for and would savour for all eternity.

Peterson escaped his marker and was clean through on goal with only the goalkeeper to beat.

Twenty yards from knocking home the winner, he easily raced past Ivan who tried desperately to up-end him with the toe of his stick but fell woefully short.

Then, out of nowhere, came the hero of the match.

Like a streak of lightening, Daniel Keeting darted from the stranded pack of players and caught Peterson up just as he was about to take back his stick and shoot for goal.

In the next instance, Peterson was floored unceremoniously into the red stone shingle, writhing in agony due to Fenton's positively illegal yet supremely successful challenge from behind.

Ivan secretly observed the aftermath with quiet glee.

Back on his feet within a second, Shaun Peterson threw down his stick and made angrily for the challenger's throat. Now provoked beyond control, both boys opted to dispense with their sticks and an all-out fistfight commenced much to the joy of the rest of the class, who surrounded the violent grapple with unbridled excitement.

The spectacle was not pleasant to behold, yet somehow, Ivan gained a simple joy from actively encouraging Shaun Peterson's demise before his peers.

Ultimately, despite the entertainment it provided, the fight was short-lived.

Ivan reluctantly blew his whistle into the ears of the opponents, and they separated. Both breathing heavily, they eyed one another as blood ran from their noses and mouths.

'We'll finish this another time, Keeting!'

'Any time you want! You just tell me when!'

Further pushing and shoving occurred before Ivan offered another shrill blow on his whistle to signify the end of the game.

'IT IS NOW A QUARTER PAST THREE! SHOWERS FOR ALL PLEASE! STICKS BACK IN THE CUPBOARD AS YOU FOUND THEM! THANK YOU!'

*****

The post-match atmosphere became subdued.

With most of the boys having left the changing room, a supremely contented Ivan showered and got back into his suit. Unusually, yet perhaps predictably, Shaun Peterson did not offer any parting shot as he left for home.

As Ivan crouched down to tie his shoelaces, a shadow appeared in the doorway of his locker room.

The shadow was cast by Daniel Keeting.

Ivan smiled warmly at the loitering pupil.

'Yes, Mister Keeting? By the way…very well played!'

The teenager did not concur with the praise, instead pointing dejectedly to his left eye socket.

'Look, sir.'

The teacher moved closer to gain a better view of the golf-ball sized bruise.

'Peterson must have had a lucky punch!'

Young Keeting appeared concerned.

'Is it…very badly swollen, sir?'

Ivan shifted his glasses to the end of his nose and further inspected the injury being presented for his scrutiny.

'A little…but don't worry. All in a good cause! It will probably puff up overnight but be gone in a day or two. Like my blasted ankle!'

The teenager looked solemnly at his feet.

He was evidently worried.

'Something on your mind, Mister Keeting?'

'I don't want my father to see it, sir. He'll know I've been fighting. He doesn't like me fighting. I'll be in real trouble.'

Ivan stood up and placed a comforting hand on the young man's shoulder. He spoke with sincerity and assurance.

'Mister Keeting. Let me offer a piece of sound advice.'

The young man's eyes widened with hope.

'What's that, sir?'

'When asked about your eye…simply tell your father the truth.'

'The truth, sir?'

'Yes! The *truth*, my boy! The truth being that you got a smack in the eye during a hockey match.'

Daniel contemplated the teacher's logical and perfectly sound solution yet doubt still cursed his mind.

'But…my father won't believe that it was an accident.'

Ivan fully engaged with the discomforted gaze of the fifteen-year-old as the pair moved into the corridor.

Locking the changing room door, the Maths teacher repeated the insuring gesture of the hand on the shoulder.

'If your father doesn't believe you, Mister Keeting, then tell him to come and see me. I will gladly confirm your story. Okay? And as a bonus I'll also tell him what a fine hockey player his son is.'

Daniel smiled and nodded before turning for the outer door and heading for home.

'Thanks, sir! I'd sure appreciate that!'

The young man suddenly stopped his stride and turned to face the teacher once again.

'And...thanks for the lesson this afternoon, Mister Reynolds. I really enjoyed it.'

With suit jacket draped over his arm and briefcase in hand, Ivan smiled and followed Daniel into the car park.

'Don't thank *me*, Mister Keeting. I can assure you...the pleasure was all *mine*.'

For Ivan, life both at school and at home retained a relative peace for the next few weeks. During the half-term holiday, he had spent most daylight hours preparing the allotment for winter.

It was always sad to see such fertile earth being turned and practically left to seed, but it was also a necessary process if harvests could begin again as early as possible the following March.

Whilst it was common knowledge among most of his colleagues that Ivan's retirement was on the horizon, word had still not yet been given to the pupils regarding his imminent farewell.

Coincidentally, he had gleaned the distinct impression that the disruptive elements of earlier in the term had become slowly disillusioned with the purpose of making daily mischief.

Indeed, to the casual observer it appeared Ivan Reynolds' influence over 1RY had finally taken a resilient hold.

*****

The cold arm of early winter gradually strengthened its grip with both pupils and teachers alike more than eager for Christmas to make its entrance and herald the end of term.

However, for the staff at Littleholt, duty still presided over any personal wont. And it was on a particularly bitter December morning that Ivan had again been appointed the dreaded slot for playground duty.

Sympathetically, Carol decided to keep him company as both teachers observed the gradual influx of shivering pupils ambling down the driveway onto the school premises.

Of course, obliging the roster did not prevent Ivan from expressing his long-held negative opinion on the subject as the Head of First Year stood beside him with teeth chattering.

'I can't be bothered to check my watch, but I know its bloody twenty-five to nine and I'm freezing my bloody backside off! And for *what,* I ask myself? Why am I standing here? Are these kids deaf? Is our bell not loud enough all of a sudden?'

Carol giggled as she watched Ivan's grimly enthusiastic tirade progressively freeze as it hit into the sharp seasonal air. He often needed softening up first thing in a morning and she seemed to have acquired the knack of successfully altering his prickly moods with a simple line of humour.

'It's not all bad, dear! You look quite cute in your red hat and gloves.'

Ivan said nothing as cold air buffeted from his nostrils. He simply glared at her through the shining jet black of his spectacles which had been gradually turned so by the low profile of a watery sunrise.

Again, she guffawed at the sight of his exaggerated and almost pompous discomfort, which in turn prompted him to offer further exchange on the subject.

'*Cute*, Carol? Did you say I looked…*cute*? Hardly a word normally associated with yours truly, is it? Never…in my six decades…have I ever been deemed…cute! Even as a baby I was never cute! I'm an old man, you know! I shouldn't be out here! My blood's too thin. I bet it's turning my blasted nose blue!'

Carol supplied a short-term solution to the problem.

'Come on. Let's take a walk. Keep those ageing bones of yours moving!'

The pair slowly stalked the perimeter of the playground around the swelling throng of pupils amassing on the tarmac. The voices of the children seemed louder than usual, probably in an effort to keep out the chill.

They offered regular brief glances at the pair of teachers costumed in their woollen wear, but a casual interest was all they mustered this morning. And Ivan, to his own surprise, couldn't blame them one little bit.

'Jesus, Carol! This is ridiculous! I'm blowing the bloody whistle in a minute! I don't care *what* time it is!'

Holding a hand up to shield her eyes from the early glare of the sun, she looked across at Ivan for a prolonged moment.

Carol Shaw realised once again how much she enjoyed being in his company.

Even though as a person he had remained such an enigma to her and his other colleagues, she respected him dearly and held his teaching experience in the highest esteem.

Yet Ivan's homelife was still something of a mystery.

She knew he had a wife and son, yet he never spoke about them.

Indeed, for Ivan Reynolds to volunteer any information about his private affairs was unheard of. She had often wanted to delve into his psyche; to peel away the outer layers of his character, yet the moment never seemed appropriate.

And even as they walked, though having worked together for the better part of two decades, she could not compel herself to advance the conversation beyond basic civility.

'What are you doing for Christmas this year, Ivan?' she enquired out of genuine interest. 'Any exciting plans?'

He digested the perfectly reasonable question whilst continuing to stride beside her with leather-gloved hands firmly clasped behind his back.

'Oh…hadn't thought, really. Not my cup of tea anymore…this Christmas malarkey. Not these days, anyway. I'm a bit past all that frolicking and fun now…if you know what I mean.'

Carol did not probe any deeper as they turned the corner of the building and headed down toward the cycle racks.

This was a practiced haven for the young smokers in the school, although it looked as if they had been warned of the approaching inspection and vacated the area completely.

Although the evidence of their earlier presence lay strewn across the paving slabs.

'Looks like we just missed the fag brigade! Not much going on this morning, Carol. They must all be eager to get indoors. Shame, really. I could do with warming myself up with a little light confrontation!'

She noticed one of the bicycles sporting a holdall hanging from the handlebars.

'Better take that in! Someone will be looking for it in a few minutes. Talk about absent-minded!'

Having fully scrutinised the bike shed and surrounding area without detecting any sign of undesirable activity, the pair advanced toward the main entrance of the driveway.

To the pleasant surprise of both teachers, the minor diversion in the route proved rather fruitful.

Just beyond the school gates and along the pavement beyond, they simultaneously spotted the origins of an incident involving a small group of pupils with a very familiar figure at the hub of the dubious looking circle.

To the trained ear of Ivan Reynolds, the voice of Hilary Johnson was unmistakable.

Carol registered with his pang of familiarity as to the ringleader of the entourage.

'Ayup! Trouble at mill?' she quipped.

Ivan did not reply.

His attention was fully employed by the scene a few yards away. In an instant he had detected the aroma of a problem and quickly moved position to ascertain the identities of the others involved.

His senses had become finely attuned to Hilary Johnson's potential activity over the previous three months.

Wherever the girl was discovered, then something unpleasant was due to transpire or had just occurred. This particular case proved to be no exception and he did not hold back as he watched her launch a fist at the victim who cowered amid the cheering throng.

The voice of authority ricocheted along the street and brought the inglorious display to a shuddering halt.

'YOU THERE! ALL OF YOU! HERE! TO ME! NOW! THIS INSTANT!'

Carol stood back in concealed admiration as the half a dozen First Year pupils bolted to fearful attention.

Ivan vaguely recognised the faces of the other children as they warily approached.

He counted five girls and one boy.

The stick-thin curly-haired young man that had been the suffering subject of avid female interest looked up mournfully. His scarlet cheeks were cursed with wet and dried tears as he fidgeted and positioned himself uneasily before the teachers.

Ivan's tone of voice did not lower as he assessed the quivering youth with the intention of shaking the secret little union to the ground.

'YOU BOY! WHAT IS YOUR NAME?'

The callow youth began to mumble with trepidation as Ivan towered menacingly above him.

'Morris, sir. Steven…Morris.'

'AND WHAT EXACTLY IS GOING ON HERE, MISTER MORRIS? ANSWER ME, BOY!'

The fearful schoolboy looked across to the group of girls with some reticence before answering to the barked demands of the teacher.

'They were…they wanted…they were after…my dinner money…sir.'

Ivan looked up disapprovingly at the smirking collection of young females. They evidently felt no shame in perpetrating the act of wilful robbery. He then glanced across to Carol, whose authority was brought quickly to the fore.

'Miss Shaw. Would you like to deal with the culprits?'

The Head of First Year did not need further invitation as she gleefully bellowed her orders in similar fashion to her colleague.

'YOU GIRLS! HEADMASTER'S OFFICE! WITH ME! NOW!'

Escorting the would-be muggers to their fate, she left Ivan to speak calmly with the pale-skinned victim who was evidently rendered very shaken by the episode.

The teacher bent down and placed a protective arm around the boy's shoulder and afforded his voice to just above a whisper.

'Mister Morris…has this happened to you before?'

The youngster again wiped his eyes as he shamefully studied the floor at his feet and shook his head.

'Not to me, sir. But…it has happened to other kids I know.'

Ivan nodded with cunning insight.

'Of course, it has! And each time with Hilary Johnson at the helm, no doubt?'

Now Steven Morris suddenly felt the confidence to try and meet with Ivan's stern, dark gaze and willingly convict his attacker.

'Yes, sir! She's been doing it for ages.'

Standing back up to his full height, Ivan inhaled sharply.

'Okay, Mister Morris. Off you go to registration. Don't be late.'

The quaking boy looked up at the teacher with innocent concern in his eyes.

'But sir…what if…what if it happens again?'

Ivan smirked graciously and slowly shook his head.

'It *won't* happen again. Be assured of that much, Mister Morris. It *won't* happen again. Off you go. Registration!'

With a swish of his long winter coat tails, Ivan Reynolds turned on his heel and strode in the other direction back toward the bicycle sheds as the first bell of the day resonated around the school grounds.

*****

It was nearly a week later during the dinner hour when Ivan found himself having forgotten his packed lunch on the kitchen table at home. Strutting around the staff room emitting his frustration to a relatively disinterested and minimal audience, he finally opted to dine in the main hall as a last resort.

Braised beef didn't appeal, and pizza fell way below his expectations. So, with a packet of sandwiches and plastic drinks cup perched on his tray, he wearily scanned the bustling arena for the vague likelihood of a spare seat.

Yet again, as of a few weeks earlier, he eventually spotted Jenny Douglas at the far corner table and weaving in and around the busy throng of noisy young eaters, he attempted to reach her location.

It was obvious as he approached that, yet again, she was alone with her own company.

As she always seemed to be.

'Miss Douglas…would you mind awfully if I bothered you with my presence again? I trust this is not too much of an intrusion?'

Unlike the previous occasion, Jenny immediately looked up to her form tutor and smiled. Her bright young eyes shone like sapphires and yet for the briefest moment, Ivan supposed she may have been crying.

'No…it's fine…please, sir…yes…sit down.'

Ivan smiled and positioned himself in the chair next to hers.

Reluctantly peeling the cellophane wrapper from his sandwich, he eyed it with due suspicion and mournfully announced his conclusions.

'This filling…is apparently…cheese and cucumber…yet I fail to detect the presence of any cucumber. Looks like I shall be giving some of the kitchen staff a detention this evening!'

Jenny chuckled at the teacher's quirky sense of humour and watched him as he chewed slowly on a morsel. Even without observing the girl beside him, Ivan could sense that she was troubled about something.

Her unavoidable query was soon forthcoming.

'Sir…when are the mock exams starting?'

Ivan swallowed his food and had to think hard about the answer.

'I do believe…they commence next week, Miss Douglas. No doubt you have been revising avidly?'

The young girl nodded.

'Yes, sir. Will the exams be in here?'

'Oh no…they are not formal exams as such. Just basic written tests that you will sit during your normal timetable. They're just to ascertain your progress. Check that you've been listening for the past few weeks…that's all. Not a big deal. Not for someone with your intelligence.'

He pouted in mild disgust and ate some more sandwich as Jenny blushed and quickly glanced down to the tabletop.

She wasn't accustomed to receiving personal praise and hastily changed the subject.

'Just think, sir! Only three weeks until Christmas! Are you excited, sir?'

Sampling some of his coffee, Ivan grimaced again as his taste buds responded negatively to the lukewarm liquid.

'Yes…definitely a detention for whoever made this ditch water, as well! I'm sorry, Miss Douglas…you were saying?'

Stifling her giggles, she repeated the question.

Ivan could only obey his natural honesty as usual.

'I *used* to get excited about Christmas. Many years ago, well before you were born, in fact…but not anymore. Santa Claus doesn't leave presents under the tree for old miseries like me.'

Jenny seemed puzzled by his curious self-assessment and challenged his view.

'Won't your family buy you presents though, sir?'

Ivan shook his head whilst finishing the first half of his sandwich and swilling down more drink. Despite Ivan's evident persuasion regarding the subject, Jenny felt confident enough in her relationship with her form tutor to convey to him an opinion.

'You're not an old misery, sir. I think you're quite funny really!'

Ivan leaned closer to her and whispered softly.

'Yes…so do I, Miss Douglas! But sadly, most others in the school seem to think otherwise!'

Again, the First Year girl sniggered, causing her reddened cheeks to flush evermore.

Thankful for finishing his snack, Ivan pushed the empty plate to one side and emptied his cup of coffee in one gulp. He noticed at this point that his companion did not have any used crockery in front of her.

'Well, I must say that was a distinctly average lunch! What did you have for your dinner, Miss Douglas?'

She continued to stare at the surface of the table as though the question from her tutor had not registered. Ivan waited patiently for a reply, yet slowly got the impression that his inquiry had been deemed strangely inappropriate.

Further seconds of silence prevailed before the girl was tempted to respond.

'I er…I didn't…I didn't eat dinner today, sir.'

Ivan furrowed his brow at the admission.

His casual interest quickly evolved into a pang of concern.

'Why on Earth not? You must *eat*, Miss Douglas! We must *all* replenish ourselves! Even if it is this awful canteen food! The running engine must be regularly re-fuelled!'

Her mirth at his comments was short-lived as her rounded face developed an unexpected expression of misgiving.

The girl suddenly seemed sombre and clouded by unhappiness.

It was a signal in children that Ivan was not prone to ignoring.

'Miss Douglas? Are you okay?'

She did not look at Ivan when she spoke, as though feeling guilty at uttering the words that were on the tip of her tongue.

But she could not resist the comfort projected by Ivan's genuine interest.

She held him in high esteem as her form teacher and felt secure in confiding to him as a person.

'I don't eat some days…because…because…I'm fat…and need to get thinner!'

Evidently a moment for extreme delicacy, Ivan quickly picked up on her rabid self-consciousness.

However, he also felt it correct to impart some sound advice regarding the issue.

'Miss Douglas. Let me tell you something. You are far from being fat. As you grow older…the next couple of years…your shape and weight will change accordingly. Don't let your classmates bully you into thinking you're lacking in any way! I've seen this in children countless times. For most kids of your age, weight and size is barely even noticeable and infinitely changeable.'

Still she glared at the table-top; her mask of disdain not altering, despite the supremely welcome support of the teacher.

He didn't want to press the subject beyond the uncertain threshold of sensitivity and opted to let her think quietly for a minute.

Surprisingly, the girl eventually responded with a positive thought of her own.

'I'll be thinner by the time I leave school, won't I? I'll be thinner by then!'

Ivan smiled warmly and nodded.

'Oh yes! Well before then! Don't let the likes of Hilary Johnson get you down. Do you hear me, Miss Douglas? I want to know if any pupil in this school is bullying you about this! Am I clear?'

Jenny became muted again; lost in her train of thought.

But she felt at ease with the teacher perched beside her.

And her conviction in the reliability of his company led to the startling disclosure that followed.

'The other kids have never said I'm fat, sir. Not once.'

Now puzzlement descended on Ivan as he looked at the forlorn demeanour of the eleven-year-old sitting beside him.

'So, what is it that has made you think so negatively about yourself, Miss. Douglas?'

Eventually, she met his concern with moistened eyes and a blatantly half-hearted smile.

'It's…it's my physics teacher, sir. Mister Holmes. He said I need to go on a diet. He's always saying it. Every lesson he says I'm too big for the stool and could do with two.'

The young girl's innocent admission immediately struck an emotive chord with Ivan Reynolds. Fury began to bubble within him as utter disbelief enshrouded his typical clarity of mind.

Even so, he was careful to maintain a composed tone of voice.

'*Mister Holmes*? *He* honestly said these things to *you*? *Mister Holmes* did?'

Now shivering with a fearful uncertainty, Jenny Douglas already regretted unveiling the truth behind her prolonged despondency, yet she reluctantly nodded in a cautious affirmation of her allegation.

'I won't get into trouble for telling you, will I?'

Ivan's mind had already pondered the necessity for regular confrontation with his younger colleague. Now he had a cast iron motive. Lightly touching her upper arm, the teacher offered a few parting words of assurance to the furtive eleven-year-old.

'Miss Douglas. Rest assured in this. In you I have seen a warm heart and an honest soul. Two things that most of the blighters that attend this place can never hope to attain. And I include some of the teachers in that! You are a very nice person and a very competent student. I have high hopes for you. Never lose your self-belief. And never listen to bullies. One thing in life I cannot abide…is a *bully*!'

Suddenly embarrassed by Ivan's appraising monologue, Jenny Douglas awkwardly shoved her chair backwards and stood up.

'Thank you, sir. I'd better go, now. I'll see you at registration.'

Ivan tilted his head and watched her leave the table as she ambled toward the main doors and vacated the dining hall.

Now with anger burning at his core, Ivan reclined in his seat. He slowly began to scan the multitude of faces that bobbed and jerked in and around the near vicinity.

Having observed the noisy congregation for a good minute or two, he finally located his target of choice, sitting not three tables away, chatting with other colleagues.

He watched the subject eat his food; then drink his drink.

He watched the subject converse arrogantly with his peers; and laugh out loud at his own jokes.

Clenching a fist of now overwhelming vexation, Ivan Reynolds pondered his next move as he watched Phil Holmes from a secluded distance.

Figuring he had time aplenty to deal with the young physics teacher, Ivan rose to his feet and quietly departed the scene.

16

Ivan had carefully contemplated the stark and disturbing revelation from Jenny Douglas. In tandem with turning the unpalatable quandary over in his mind, Ivan's recent contact with Phil Holmes had been coincidentally minimal and, in a way, he was grateful for the fact.

At the end of another frantic school day, the overflowing staff room listened in respectful silence as Geoff Taylor stood before the full congregation of teachers with the weekly briefing.

It had also been another cold day outside and the winter sunshine had dispersed outside to make way for slate grey cloud, which hung heavily overhead, enshrouding the lifeless playground in an eerie semi-darkness.

Ivan gazed beyond the window, temporarily distracted from the headmaster's monologue. His mind was anywhere but in that room of loitering cigarette smoke, legislative referencing, and complaining counterparts.

The Head made the closing statement of his speech, causing Ivan to concentrate on the final few words as it signified that departure time was imminent.

'As you all know, the First Year parents' evening is in a couple of days' time. During the session, leaflets will be given to parents regarding the planned Christmas concert at the end of term. Carol will be announcing the event to pupils in tomorrow morning's assembly. Try and be a little promotional for the cause, ladies and gents. Who knows? Maybe one or two of you will even fancy trying your arm on stage with a little turn of your own? It should be a good way to help relations with the youngsters and a positive note on which to end the year. Anyhow, talk to Carol. She's in charge of the event. That is all. Goodnight!'

The Head finally vacated the room and paved the way for an erupting crescendo of chatter among the staff.

Now more than ready for the off, Ivan picked up his newspaper, coat and briefcase and made a supposedly inconspicuous route for the door.

However, his shrewd attempt at an escape was halted by Carol, who grabbed Ivan loosely by the arm and forcefully escorted him into the corridor beyond.

Instinct told him what was about to be proposed.

'Well, Ivan? You up for a bit of singing this year?'

A wry smile emerged as he shook his head.

'Me, Carol? Singing? On stage? You're pulling my bloody leg aren't you, woman? The kids would be throwing tomatoes as soon as I got up there!'

Her initially enthusiastic expression suddenly became acutely serious as her eyes narrowed through the thick lenses of her spectacles.

'No, I'm not pulling your leg! I'm pulling your bloody arm! I want you to be involved in this! Come on, Ivan! It's your last Christmas at Littleholt! Let's make it a memorable one, eh? If not for you...then do it for *me*?'

Mildly baffled by the affronting conclusion to his day, Ivan struggled vainly to think on his feet for once.

'But Carol! I can't sing a bloody note!'

The Head of First Year was far from appeased in her quest.

'Neither can the kids, Ivan! But they'll be more than up for a go if they can see that you're involved too!'

He grimaced as the mental list of feeble excuses rapidly evaporated.

Carol Shaw was a determined woman - especially when it came to dealing with Ivan Reynolds.

'Anyway - don't tell *me* you can't sing! We've all heard your Roy Orbison warbles! You've got a damned good voice in you! And you bloody well know it!'

Ivan gently prised his arm from her grasp, only to have it firmly re-clamped.

She cornered him. This was a dead end with only one exit route.

'I'm warning you, Ivan! I want a commitment here and now! I want you on that stage! It's the last chance you'll get! Just one little Christmas song. For me? Please?'

Ivan Reynolds was literally stuck for words.

Gazing vainly along the brightly lit corridor for absent inspiration, he finally relented to his only option and succumbed to her persistence.

'Okay, Carol! Okay! But I can't really sing *Only the Lonely* at Christmas, can I? Hardly a festive ditty, is it?'

Clapping loudly and jumping up and down on the spot, her joyful response caused him to shake his head in mock dread at the prospect.

'Ivan…you can sing what the hell you like! I don't care! Just enjoy it and make it memorable! That's all I ask! Positive participation is the key! Just think how much this will inspire the kids if they know you're going to be on the billing!'

Ivan again removed her hand from his elbow and began to sidle away toward the main doors of the foyer.

After a few strides he stopped in his tracks and pointed a forefinger in her direction.

'Alright, Carol! You've bagged your man. But there's one condition! You don't tell a soul! For the time being it's our little secret! Agreed?'

She swayed from side to side clutching her clipboard.

'Okay Mister Reynolds - anything you say, sir!'

Riding a wave of dubious relief, Ivan pushed open the main doors of the building, allowing cold air to rush past him into the corridor.

'Right…I'll think of something! See you in the morning.'

Carol's howls of euphoric laughter resonated along the walkway and up the empty stairwells as Ivan disappeared into the car park which was now shadowing quickly against the onset of another shrill winter dusk.

*****

Another chore of duty instantly awaited him the following morning; First Year assembly.

He listened in his customary location with arms folded. From the rear of the main hall, he stifled a yawn as the Head of Year addressed the pupils regarding all manner of school issues, ranging from internal exams, fund raising, parents' evening and the eternal debate on school uniform.

Then she began to reveal the plans for the end of term concert to the eager throng, whose interest was captivated from the first few words of the announcement.

'Anyone can take part and any acts are allowed. But they must be seriously rehearsed, and it goes without saying…not at all rude in content!'

The attentive gathering sniggered and whispered excitedly as the buzz rapidly began to spread throughout the hall.

'You may sing, dance, act, do magic tricks, tell stories…I don't really care. Prizes will be given for every act that goes on stage. Your parents are also invited along and will be given further information when they come to parents' evening tomorrow.'

Ivan watched Carol cautiously through his semi-shaded spectacles. Despite her pledge of confidentiality, he was fully expectant of being revealed as the supposed main attraction.

Yet to his pleasant surprise, she was unusually subtle in disclosing any confirmed details of the event.

'I can guarantee everybody that the First Year Christmas concert will be a lot of fun. That is…after all…the main objective. And there will be one or two surprises in store during the night, as well! So, it is well worth coming along to. Please get your thinking caps on. Come and talk to me about your ideas. Depending on the response over the next week, Miss Heaton may be supervising some after-school drama sessions to allow you some preparation time should you require it.'

As she finally brought the assembly to a conclusion, Ivan engaged distant stares with the Head of First Year, which quickly evolved into mutual nods of appreciation.

He slowly made his way from the arena, lost for a while in his own train of thought.

Unusually, he did not acknowledge the children in the corridor or even berate the uncontrolled din that their youthful enthusiasm had created.

Instead, a singular issue occupied his mind about one particular colleague, in those wavering seconds of deliberation.

It occurred to him that there weren't many souls in the world that he would oblige without a second thought, but Carol was definitely one of the few people in his life that warranted such time-honoured consideration.

She was a reliable, trusted colleague and perhaps if he allowed, even a good friend.

Indeed, he owed it to her to offer a solid contribution to the concert.

And to make it more than memorable.

17

Ivan had never particularly relished the prospect of parents' evenings.

Many times in his distinguished career he had been confronted by frustrated parents who believed that their child had been poorly taught or had in some way been mistreated or even excluded from certain classes as unjustified punishment.

Quite often, irate mothers and fathers would draw him into debates about other teachers in which he had no business intervening.

And his frequent attempts at imparting sound advice to such parents invariably fell on deaf ears.

In tandem with such futility, rarely did a mother or father commend the efforts of teaching staff or offer praise for the school in any general capacity.

And after thirty years, it still amazed him that a substantial proportion of parents had very little to say at all on any aspect regarding their child's education.

This was even more frustrating for those members of staff who had been sitting in the main hall since four o'clock, looking vainly for any glimmer of inspiration which would coax them to remain in their seat and not perform a desperate act of desertion.

In the corner of the chamber, Matt Jenkins' table was positioned only a few yards from where Ivan slouched. Matt watched his elder colleague as he rankled with the final two clues of the Daily Mail crossword puzzle.

'If old Taylor catches you doing that, you'll get short shrift!'

Ivan did not take his eyes from the page whilst offering Matt a curt reply under his breath.

'I am hoping that he *does* trot past, Matthew! Maybe he can help me finish this damned thing off! I've been struggling with it all bloody day! Or even better, maybe he could give me permission to bugger off home and finish it there!'

The younger maths teacher chortled as he slurped on a tepid mug of tea and lit a cigarette.

'How many appointments have you had tonight then?'

Ivan sat back and dejectedly dropped his newspaper onto the table. He pulled the silver pocket-watch into view and flicked open the lid.

'My dear, Matthew…I have been sitting here for over two hours and I have spoken to five sets of parents. I have had appointments for twenty! Not one of the conversations proved to be anywhere near inspiring or vaguely satisfying. Indeed, I have begun to understand why some of the pupils are so lacking in initiative and awareness. Their failings are sadly inherent!'

Matt's laughter resonated throughout the hall, causing those in close proximity to gaze curiously in his direction.

'Well, I think I'm about done here. I'll just finish this fag and be off.'

With his despondency growing by the minute, Ivan retrieved his paper and continued to pursue the solutions to his word puzzle.

The time continued to crawl onward.

A sudden influx of visitors was apparent around the seven o'clock mark, although none wished to speak with Ivan. Glancing over the rim of his now only slightly muted spectacles, he felt the fertile spirit of attentive tutorage beginning to fade rapidly with the onset of boredom.

Indulging once again in the newspaper, he opted to dispense with the crossword and scan the sports pages for the third time that day.

The minutes passed as he confirmed one or two headlining football stories in his mind that encouraged one or two murmured responses.

'I didn't know Shilton was at Southampton this season! Did you know that, Matthew? Whatever was Cloughie thinking of?'

The apprentice did not glance up from his magazine as he acknowledged his master.

'If you're talking about football…don't bother! I'm clueless!'

Ivan found the readers' letters section was always an amusing yardstick as to the lack of intelligence throughout the populace.

He shook his head in frustration at some of the feeble viewpoints laid out in print, before muttering a despairing conclusion in hissed tones.

'Bloody idiots…the lot of them! What hope is there for the kids if the adults talk and behave like morons?'

On emitting his whispered declaration, Ivan suddenly became aware of a solitary figure standing quietly at his table. Peering over the top of his page, he feigned delight at the diminutive vision of a woman in her mid-thirties.

She was vaguely attractive in the face but appeared to be without any make-up. In truth, the lady looked unkempt and careworn, as though she had just finished a long shift at work. Her hair was scraped back into a roughly assembled ponytail and her deep brown eyes conveyed a desperate need for sleep.

Ivan folded his newspaper and stood to greet the lone visitor with an outstretched hand of courtesy.

'Good evening, madam! Do you wish to see *me*?'

She appeared a little uncertain at first, but once Ivan had confirmed his name and form group, she began to warm to the conversation.

'Hello, Mister Reynolds. I'm Liz Sims. Trevor's mam!'

An instant broad smile emerged under the teacher's nose, alleviating any apprehension that may have accompanied her into the hall.

Obliging the invitation to be seated, she listened to Ivan's opening statement.

'Ah yes! Young Trevor! An enthusiastic pupil! Sharp-witted! Pleasant to talk with! Always late for registration! Excuse after excuse. But likeable in the extreme! A little rogue, for sure! How is he coping so far with his first term at Littleholt?'

Trevor's mother shuffled uneasily in her chair. Clutching her handbag on her lap, it was obvious that she was not accustomed to such a formal environment and such figures of supposed authority.

'Well…at first, he was a bit daunted. Especially when you told him off about his socks! But that was my fault! Then he couldn't find his way around the school. It's a big place for a little lad! But I helped him memorise the plan you gave him. He reckoned he learned it in one night!'

Ivan interrupted her engaging ramble.

'Yes...well...fair enough. And what does he think of *me*, Mrs. Sims?'

An expression of doubt cursed her features as though she was unsure of the question's motive or more pertinently, which answer would be acceptable.

'How do you mean, Mister Reynolds?'

Ivan leaned forward and clasped his hands together.

'Is he *scared* of me? Does he *like* me? Is he content with life in 1RY?'

Trevor's mother inhaled deeply before responding.

'Well...all junior school kids know about you, Mister Reynolds! But Trevor is not easily bothered about such things. He has an inner confidence. He's got a big heart. I don't know where it comes from. Certainly not me!'

Again, Ivan was prompted to interject.

'His fearlessness and courage at such a tender age can only derive from his upbringing, Mrs. Sims.'

She gazed at Ivan, pleasantly perplexed at his insightful proclamation.

He continued with an explanation of his theory.

'Do you know...one of the first things I asked the pupils to do was present an individual assessment of themselves in front of the entire class. Most were understandably nervous and hesitant. But Trevor did not hold back for a second! He was very honest about his parental circumstances. The absence of his father has created an inner strength in the boy. He is a credit to you, Mrs. Sims.'

Trevor's mother seemed quite touched by the glowing tribute to her only child. Ivan observed her weary features begin to brighten.

She evidently had little idea that Trevor was thought of so highly.

'I...didn't know he's spoken about it to anyone. We hardly discuss it ourselves these days to be honest. It only really hits home when he doesn't get his birthday card every year. And Christmas, of course. That tends to bring things to an emotional head these days! He still gets annoyed about that!'

Ivan nodded in sympathy.

'I know exactly what you mean, Mrs. Sims. But he is a brave young man. And I suspect he is also very protective of you. It must be difficult…being a lone parent…'

Her gaze dropped to the tabletop as she considered the next words.

She seemed unsure of how to proceed, yet Ivan Reynolds was an assuring presence.

'He's been brilliant since his dad left, to be honest. I just wish he could start enjoying life a little bit more. Sometimes I think he's had to grow up a bit too fast…if you know what I mean. He's missed out on a lot as a child.'

Ivan squirmed in silent agreement as he considered the situation for a moment.

'Does it help him having a male mentor at school?'

'*You*, you mean? Oh yes! He mentions *you* every day! He's always telling me who you've told off or who you've put on detention. He's very fond of you, Mister Reynolds. Very fond, indeed!'

Ivan sat back in his chair and rested his hands behind his head.

'So…my…shall we say…so-called formidable reputation…did not worry him at all?'

Trevor's mother giggled and shook her head.

'Oh yes! Just a bit! During the end of the six-week holidays he was crapping himself! Oops…sorry for swearing! Yes! He was quite daunted by the rumours! But kids always exaggerate stuff, don't they? Yet…even though he didn't know who his form tutor would be, he said he'd had this idea that it would be you. Weird, isn't it?'

Ivan watched her with great interest as she spoke.

He could see so much of the son in the mother.

The innocence and the honesty; the compassion and integrity.

The sense of comedy also seemed to have been passed down from his maternal side.

'A coincidence Mrs. Sims…certainly…'

'Of course, I was at a bit of a loss to help him, though! I mean…I work full time, so my mother and father look after him a lot after school. But I eventually found out that it wasn't meeting *you* that worried him!'

Ivan stared at the woman, eager for her story to conclude.

'Really? What was it, then?'

'It was whether *you* would like *him*! That was his main concern! He was dreading having a teacher that he didn't get on with!'

Although hidden to any witness, at hearing the declaration Ivan's eyes lit up behind his mysterious lenses.

'And so…you'd say that being in my form group is a good move for all concerned?'

'Oh yes, Mister Reynolds! He didn't enjoy school much before. But now it doesn't seem to worry him at all! And I put it mainly down to you. You've been very good for him in so many ways. And I'm very thankful for it!'

For once in his long school career, Ivan was rendered speechless for all the right reasons.

After years of inciting nothing less than alarm and wariness among the pupils of Littleholt, it felt inflating to be finally acknowledged to his face as a positive influence.

It was an unusual sensation and it felt rather good.

An alien feeling; yet all the more pleasurable for the fact.

He opted to end the conversation with parting word of appreciation.

Ivan rose to his full height and offered an open hand of farewell.

'Mrs. Sims. It has been a genuine pleasure to listen to your views. And it shall be a continuing pleasure to tutor your son. Academically I have no concerns. I like young Trevor…a lot! One of the brighter sparks in the school. It's nice to know that my input into his life carries rather more significance than it does in most of the others. This has been a most rewarding conversation. Thank you.'

The smile on Ivan's face remained as he watched Trevor's mother express her own gratitude before confidently making her way out of the hall.

Matt Jenkins had unavoidably overheard much of the dialogue and felt the inevitable compulsion to offer some commentary.

Albeit laced with a little customary sarcasm.

'Is she starting up a fan club then, Ivan? I knew you'd be top of the pops one day! You took your time though, didn't you?'

With the expression of satisfaction still on display under his clouded mask, Ivan turned to his younger colleague and jokingly raised two fingers in crude response.

'For your information, Matthew…I am just as bewildered as your good self. I never set out in this game to become popular! I suppose it must be down to the law of averages that someone was bound to like me eventually!'

Laughing heartily at Ivan's self-deprecation, Matt zipped up his coat and bid his elder colleague a good night with a wave.

'See you in the morning, Matthew. I might as well stop here for the night the way things are going!'

*****

Ivan wearily scrutinised the hands of his silver pocket watch.

Ten minutes to eight.

Ten minutes until he could grab his briefcase and coat and make for home.

The last ten minutes of a long, yet surprisingly fruitful day.

He had hoped to become acquainted with the parents of Hilary Johnson, but their no-show was indicative of the general disinterest that was so prevalent in their daughter.

It seemed that anything the Johnson family had to say to the school would be done so in the privacy of the Headmaster's office.

He was secretly hoping for a minor verbal conflict to balance out the amiability that Liz Sims had conveyed.

At the very least, Matt Jenkins would have enjoyed a front row seat on any ensuing spectacle.

Five to eight.

Ivan stood, yawned, swung his long black winter coat around his shoulders and slotted his creased newspaper into the briefcase.

'Ready for the off, Ivan?'

Carol Shaw's barking enquiry carried across the nearly empty hall. Many of his colleagues had been fortunate enough to accomplish their interview schedules early and seconded themselves to the sanctity of the staff room or luckier still, vanish away into the night.

'Yes, I am, thank you, Carol! Don't you think a twelve-hour shift is long enough for an old man like me?'

The Head of First Year giggled and headed away from the hall. As she did so, she nearly collided with a flustered looking man and woman, both dressed identically in blue jeans and blue anoraks.

'Good evening. Can I help you?' beamed Carol.

The woman looked a little startled by the offer of assistance and twitched with nerves as she replied.

'Oh yes…er…yes…we're here to see…er…Mister Reynolds…'

Carol nodded and guided the pair back across the hall, just as the teacher in question strode purposefully toward the trio.

'Ivan…a couple of late arrivals for you.'

The man and woman could not see the depth of overwhelming frustration in the eyes of the man they wished to talk to, nor could they hear the expletives that echoed unspoken around his mind at that precise moment.

Instead, he politely offered them a seat whilst placing his coat and briefcase onto the wooden floor next to the nearest convenient desk.

'You are cutting it very fine! I was just on my way home!'

The parents glanced at one another before the father introduced himself with a clammy handshake.

'Our daughter is in your form. Jenny Douglas. We are so sorry we didn't arrive sooner. She…she…er…didn't want us to come here tonight…but in the end…we felt we had to.'

Suddenly, Ivan had completely forgotten about his desperate need to evacuate the building as his attention became fully switched to the frightened looking couple in his midst.

'Yes! Miss Douglas! A charming young lady! Very clever! Exceedingly polite. I already have the highest of aspirations for the girl! Definitely one with university potential!'

The portly man's fatigued and stubbly expression did not alter as he placed himself onto a chair.

It was Jenny's mother that further initiated proceedings.

'We didn't want to bother you unnecessarily, Mister Reynolds. We know Jenny's a good girl and likes school. But there is something the matter and we are at our wit's end in trying to help her.'

The anger that Ivan had suppressed so efficiently over the previous week quickly began to bubble back to the surface. He remained shrewdly silent to glean what information he could from Jenny's mother.

'Please do go on, Mrs. Douglas.'

The round lady looked at her husband, whose gaze had now descended to focus on the floor at his feet.

She continued with the explanation.

'The thing is…she's been very upset recently. Well…the past two months to be right. About her looks…and about her weight. Now…she's always been a big girl. Well…you can see where she gets that for yourself. But it's never been a problem before. But lately she's gone right off her food. She's become moody. I've found her crying a few times. But she won't tell me what is upsetting her. She used to be such a happy child. But since coming here…something has changed her attitude. It's like…well…I'm just guessing…but I can only think that someone is picking on her.'

With fire of fury now raging in his heart, Ivan observed the love and concern etched in the mother's face.

Being only partially aware of the extent of Jenny Douglas' upset and her evident plight, he decided to tread carefully with her parents.

Ivan's mind whirled rapidly as to how to deal with the current situation.

He needed a smart plan which would incur the minimum of emotive reaction in anybody. Instinct told him that tonight was not the appropriate night to reveal what Jenny had confessed to him in confidence.

'Has she said who it might be that is making her unhappy at school, Mrs. Douglas?'

Ivan observed the woman's jowl wobble as she determinedly shook her head from side to side.

He continued to manoeuvre carefully around the issue.

'But she has intimated to you that a third party is causing her a problem?'

'Well...not in so many words. I'm just guessing. Call it mother's intuition. She was in tears again tonight before we came out. That's why we were delayed in getting here.'

Ivan nodded as he gritted his teeth.

The issue was obviously far more critical than Jenny had led him to believe in the dining hall.

The only apparent conclusion occurred to him quickly and he leaned toward her parents.

'This issue aside...are you generally happy with your daughter's academic progress, Mrs. Douglas?'

'Oh yes! She's very keen to talk about *you* as well! You're about the only thing keeping her spirits up at school at the moment. She *always* mentions you. Every night in fact!'

Ivan briefly considered the very amusing yet slightly perverse possibility that he may be currently vying for the role of favourite teacher of the year, but as always, it didn't serve to distract him from the business at hand.

'Is she considering entering the Christmas concert? It is planned for the day before we break up. A Thursday, I believe, but the date escapes me. Oh yes...here you are...there is some information on this leaflet.'

Jenny's mother studied the yellow piece of paper decorated with stars and Christmas trees and read the invitation.

'Oh no! She hasn't got the confidence to do that sort of thing! Her image of herself isn't up to much now. Not in the right frame of mind as you can imagine. Although she used to be quite outgoing at junior school.'

Ivan decided to end the meeting rather abruptly.

His mind now made up on the next move to make.

'Okay. Leave this in my hands. I shall deal with the problem. I will talk to your daughter and uncover the source of her trouble. Rest assured, Mister and Mrs Douglas…your daughter's upset will end very soon. Come…I will escort you both out.'

Walking from the hall and along the corridor, Jenny's mother turned to Ivan as he strode beside them.

'We don't want to cause you any trouble, Mister Reynolds.'

Ivan pushed open the main glass double doors of the building and allowed the parents to exit first.

'Mrs. Douglas…helping your wonderful daughter is anything but troublesome. It will be an act of honour and it is my duty! Goodnight. And please reassure Jenny that all will be fine in swift due course.'

The black sky above was decorated by a million stars as Ivan bid farewell to the Douglas family and unlocked his car.

Yet intense agitation was now his constant companion.

And remedial action was now the priority.

And whilst the season of good will to all men may have been just around the corner, a harsh lesson in professional conduct was absolutely paramount for one particular member of the Littleholt staff room.

As Ivan started the Princess and coaxed the temperamental choke into function, he silently declared to himself that the day of reckoning for Jenny Douglas' willing tormentor, was not only imminent, but decidedly overdue.

18

The following few days brought with them a gradually increasing sense of seasonal festivity among both pupils and teachers alike.

Internal examination results had been favourable, and Geoff Taylor had praised his staff for the encouraging progress of the First Year students during their inaugural term.

In turn, Ivan had commended his form group for their test performances, although one or two notable exceptions to the trend of achievement were expectedly castigated for their lack of effort and prolonged sense of apathy.

The penultimate day of term had duly arrived and the anticipation in the staff room regarding the evening's First Year Christmas Gala was at something akin to fever pitch.

Indeed, many of the teachers were more excited about the concert than the children, with the mystery surrounding Ivan's rumoured participation prompting a series of muttered conversations as he entered the main doors of the school that morning.

The indifferent smile etched under his formidable visage did not serve to allay or confirm the speculation that had been circulating among his colleagues.

Bob Davidson certainly did not feel compelled to reserve his opinion as Ivan made his way into the staff room and straight toward the tea urn.

'My, my! Look at this! Even old Reynolds looks game for a laugh, today!'

Preparing his drink, the target of gentle mockery was in an unusually upbeat and typically reciprocal mood.

'My dear Bob! Today I am happy because tomorrow is a day that marks our freedom for an entire fortnight! A long-held ambition will reach fruition by three-thirty, tomorrow afternoon!'

Matt Jenkins eyed the exchange from the other side of the room and naturally felt the urge to intervene.

'Never mind about tomorrow, Ivan! What about this evening? We've heard little birds telling tall stories. You wouldn't believe the whispers!'

Nonchalantly stirring his black, unsweetened coffee, Ivan made his colleague wait for a reply and perched in his favourite chair whilst unravelling the newspaper.

Determined to deflect any questions with customary good grace, he stared blankly at the front page as he responded.

'*Rumours*, Matthew? Rumours about what?'

With cigarette in hand, Matt mischievously pointed in Ivan's direction and could not contain a snigger or two.

'About *you*! About *tonight*! You dark horse!'

Feigning abject disinterest in the growing throng that had suddenly enveloped his chair, Ivan did not look up to engage with the mirthful gaze of his fellow Mathematics teacher.

'Tonight, Matthew? What of…tonight?'

Sarah Green now began to indulge herself in the scrutiny.

'You know what we mean, Ivan! The concert! Got a little surprise in store for everyone, haven't you?'

Ivan became suddenly overcome with disappointment at the high probability that Carol had indeed let the cat out of the bag.

Annoyance soon eclipsed his thoughts, and he quickly scanned the room to see if she had arrived.

He concluded that the benefit of the doubt would remain with the Head of First Year until he could confront her regarding the rumblings in the staff room jungle.

Meanwhile his aim was to douse the ever eager and somewhat frustrating sense of suspicion that had established itself among the staff before his arrival that morning.

'I don't know what you're babbling on about, I'm sure! Now do you mind? I'd like to begin the crossword in peace. I've only got ten minutes until registration!'

Dissatisfied with Ivan's vague denial of the allegations, the occupants of the staff room fell rather quiet for the next few minutes until the unwelcome intrusion of the morning's first bell compelled the teachers into action.

Without further word, Ivan gathered his things and quickly left the room, thankful for a few moments of solitude.

As he stalked the corridor to the bottom of the stairwell, pupils darted out of his flightpath, mistakenly believing he was about to pounce.

But that was not his policy today.

He had briefly glanced at the large Christmas tree that decorated the front of reception. The festive spirit was a reluctant visitor to him these days, but it was a pleasant change to see the pupils so buoyant and upbeat.

Smiles were aplenty and it struck Ivan that maybe he ought to try and lighten up for at least the final two days of term despite the cloud of extreme vexation that currently hung overhead.

Marching his ascent up the two flights of steps to room ten seemed to take on a more positive vitality this morning.

Indeed, he found himself mildly pleased to see his form group as they stood assembled on the top landing. Two practised military lines firmly waiting to attention. He greeted them with a broad and welcoming smile and unlocked the door. To his surprise, not one child in the group asked Ivan if he was participating in the imminent concert.

It struck him that the frustrating leak within the staff room must still be contained there. But as he took the attendance and dismissed 1RY to their last fully timetabled day of the year, the thought that Carol had let him down and breached their agreement plagued him intensely.

She pledged to maintain their arrangement as top secret.

Why should she feel the need to go back on her word so late in the day?

Her supposed actions had successfully tarnished the careful plan that he had devised for his role in the evening's bill of entertainment. But with professional duty still calling, it would be morning break time before he would be able to seek her out.

*****

Carol looked up into Ivan's dark spectacles and accentuated her vibrant defence with a jabbing pen.

'But I'm telling you that I haven't said a word, Ivan! I don't break promises to friends, and I'm insulted that you would believe otherwise. Somebody must have overheard our discussion and opened their big mouth! It's the only answer.'

He had located Carol in the main hall as she read through the list of acts that would be appearing that night. He looked up to the stage area which had been especially dressed and a full spot-lighting rig had been erected during the previous day.

The setting was effective to say the least, although it didn't serve to deter Ivan from his mission.

'Well then…you tell me who is spreading the good word…because quite frankly I'm at a loss.'

Carol shook her head, now becoming a little impatient with her elder colleague as he hovered insistently behind her.

'Listen, Ivan…nobody actually *knows* anything, do they? I don't understand what you're being so prickly about, anyway! You're only singing a bloody song for the kids! It's not exactly Live from Her bloody Majesty's, is it!'

Now his tone altered as internal frustration simmered over.

'Well, the way you begged me to take part in the bloody thing anyone would have thought the buggering Queen *was* attending tonight! Make it memorable, you said! Keep it a secret, *we* said. Not difficult, is it? You just can't keep your bloody mouth shut, can you? Not for five bloody minutes!'

Carol ignored him and walked toward the stage as she continued to scrutinise the sheet on the clipboard held tightly in her grasp.

He observed her for a few moments as she chewed her pen in concentration.

Eventually, the conversation resumed.

'Listen, Ivan. I haven't got time for this. I've got seven hours to organise a concert for two hundred people. You're either involved…or you're not. I can't concern myself with stupid tittle-tattle at this late stage.'

Ivan's voice raised an octave, causing some of the kitchen staff to offer a curious glance through the serving hatches toward the argument that ensued beyond.

'Tittle-tattle? *Tittle-tattle*? We're talking about a matter of trust here, Carol!'

Now she turned on him as her own temper began to fray.

'Trust? You sound like an agent from the KGB! It's a bloody kids' concert! Not a national security operation! It's supposed to be a bit of fun! To wish everyone a Happy Christmas! No lives are at stake, man! I don't know if anyone has told you, but we break up tomorrow! Please cheer up…or please just disappear completely! It's up to you, Ivan! I really am too busy for this!'

She turned on her heel once again to examine the lighting at the foot of the stage area and centred attention on assessing any potential tripping hazards. Looking down the proposed billing, she was relieved to discover that the greatest number of pupils on stage at any one time would be five. The microphone stands were in place and the school orchestra had set their instruments at the backdrop.

She contented herself that there seemed to be plenty of room to perform. Confirming her findings once more with the list of acts, she amused herself by looking at some of the names they had adopted.

The enthusiasm and invention of the First Year pupils were most gratifying. They had taken to the task of organising and rehearsing with gusto and the concept of live performance had really captured the attention of many of the youngsters.

Between the pupils, teachers and parents, the support for the event had been unprecedented. Having only mooted the idea of a concert three weeks earlier, Carol had now convinced herself that the night promised to be a riotous affair. As her own expectancy heightened, her attention shifted once again.

She turned back to where Ivan had been standing a moment ago.

He had vanished from the hall.

A stone-cold void left in his wake.

*****

The home-time influx in the staff room was rather more jovial than normal. Sausage rolls, mince pies and snips of wine and brandy were set aside as the staff sensed they were within touching distance of the finish line.

It had been agreed that the teachers should indulge in a little private party that evening, as home would be calling urgently for all come three-thirty p.m. the following day.

Laughter was in the air to mix with the soundtrack of some Christmas pop tunes as the noisy throng celebrated the fact that in just twenty-four hours, the school gates would be closed for a full fortnight.

Whilst in their own heads the pupils had now officially broken up for the festive holiday, they had been lured to attend on the official final day. The invitation to dispense with school uniform had been dubbed Dress Down Friday.

For all children, the prospect of attending school in clothes other than the regal greens and greys of Littleholt was very appealing, to say the least.

And even though their growing euphoria spilled over at the sound of the three-thirty bell, many familiar young faces would be back on site within a couple of hours having little comprehension of the wonders that awaited them behind the red curtain of the main hall stage.

Ivan sat alone, endeavouring to concentrate on seeing the daily crossword puzzle to completion. The hustle and bustle being created behind him was off-putting, but in the name of civility, he opted to keep his mouth closed and played along with the party atmosphere.

That is, until the distinctive and distracting voice of Phil Holmes carried piercingly across the room.

Ivan's ears twitched as his attention immediately diverted from the newspaper. Among the many voices resonating around him, Ivan could now hear only one. Maintaining a tactical position in the armchair, he listened as a vibrant and excited Phil Holmes shouted to be heard above all others.

Unbeknown to the physics teacher, the exaggerated announcement of his entry to the fuddle would prove to be a severe mistake. As would his reaction when he eventually spotted the elder statesman of the group sitting keeping his own counsel in the corner of the staff room.

His mouth was ever eager to volunteer a prediction as to the evening's likely outcome.

Yet as the younger teacher was about to discover, attempting to belittle Ivan Reynolds in front of his colleagues would also prove to be a grave error.

'So then, you old fart! Tell us what you're going to sing for us tonight! And don't deny it! I heard you talking to Carol a while or so back! You can't keep a secret from Phil Holmes, you know! I make it my business to find out *everything* around here! Especially where *you're* concerned!'

Double-pronged anger began to dilute Ivan's veins as he struggled to tolerate the physics tutor with the runaway tongue.

So, Carol *had* been true to her word, after all.

And Ivan had been completely wrong to accuse her.

It appeared that the source of betrayal was standing not five yards from Ivan's armchair, still intent on goading the head of the Mathematics department into a reaction as his mocking tirade continued.

'Don't tell us, Ivan! You're going to play the spoons!'

Raucous laughter emitted around the room as Phil Holmes continued to pitch his comical jousts at the unmoved and unmoving target.

'You're surely not dressing up as Santa Claus, are you? No way! You'd give the elves and kids nightmares if they lifted your beard and saw *you* underneath!'

The copious supply of supposed mirth was now beginning to penetrate Ivan's patience threshold.

Yet still the veteran remained calm and un-swayed by the science teacher's attempts to ridicule him.

Bob Davidson and Matt Jenkins watched expectantly as the fascinating episode unfurled before their disbelieving eyes.

Christmas may have been close.

But World War Three now seemed infinitely closer.

Ivan Reynolds was not in the habit of being patronised before an audience.

Especially when that audience contained people for whom he held the utmost regard, and who he presumed felt the same about him.

Turning the page of his newspaper, he swallowed a last morsel of his mince pie and waited longingly for the next nugget of comic genius to be hurled in his direction.

The timing was perfect.

'I know! I've got it! Its Scrooge isn't it! You're going to re-enact some Dickens for us, aren't you! Right up your street, you old misery guts!'

As the interest in Phil Holme's routine gradually dispersed, Ivan stood up and replenished his coffee mug. He checked to see that the physics teacher was out of earshot before whispering into the ready ear of Matt Jenkins, who was now fully aware of the inevitable aim of retribution that Ivan had in mind.

Nobody succeeded in making Ivan Reynolds look foolish.

But they might die trying.

'Matthew, do an old man a little favour and detain Holmes in here for as long as you possibly can. At least until the others have gone.'

With instructions successfully imparted, Matt moved to put the plan into motion whilst Ivan fixed his coffee and re-joined with his favourite seat and favourite newspaper.

*****

The minutes ticked by as Ivan inserted the penultimate clue of the crossword.

Ten minutes to five.

He flicked the lid closed on his silver pocket watch and cautiously glanced across the room, which was now vacant aside Matt Jenkins, Phil Holmes, and himself.

With the former two indulged in casual conversation, Ivan offered Matt a subtle thumbs-up as the signal to make himself scarce.

The hint was taken immediately.

Matt effectively dived for cover as he pulled on his coat.

'Well, gentlemen...I bid you a good concert - if you are going tonight, that is! I shan't be attending, though. Other plans.'

Matt looked at Ivan a little puzzled at the fact that he had remained in the staff room for well over an hour after the school day had concluded.

'Haven't you a home to go to, Ivan? You're *never* here after four! Hanging around for someone special, are we?'

Ivan stood, smirked, and addressed the would-be heir to the Reynolds' throne.

'Oh...no...not really. Thought I'd waste a little time here before I get into costume. Maybe do a little dress rehearsal as well! Have a good night, Matthew. Oh...and thank you.'

Phil Holmes was intrigued by the implication that Ivan had just laid down. He replicated the handshake of goodwill to Matt and conveyed similar sentiment.

Unfortunately, the physics' teacher's comment as Matt left the room was to be the most damning of all.

'I suppose I'd better come with you. Being stuck in the rush hour is far more enjoyable than being stuck in here with Scrooge!'

Less than ten seconds later, just the two opponents remained in the room. Ivan hooked his thumbs into the pockets of his waistcoat and faced his conceited yet hopeful nemesis.

The smile under the dark visor had now faded.

The mouth had become a severe, unwavering line of contempt.

He offered little clue as to the next line of conversation.

And Phil Holmes picked up on the uncertainty as he stuttered with woefully misguided judgement.

'I knew it! I bloody *knew* I hadn't been hearing things! You *are* in the concert, aren't you? You wily old fossil! I can't wait for tonight, now! I'm off home to get changed. Wouldn't miss this for the world!'

Ivan walked slowly across the room toward his oblivious target, checking that the blinds in the windows had been closed shut - as he closed in.

Still his granite-carved features carried no expression.

And still Phil Holmes continued blindly with his desperate quips.

'So, what's your turn, then? Back end of Rudolph? Front end of the fatted goose? The miserly old innkeeper? The world's your oyster really, isn't it? You could play anything and everything!'

Ivan continued to advance toward his inane antagonist until he was just within arm's reach.

And then, taking a slow deep breath, having located his final position of choice, Ivan stood still and began his response.

'A high opinion of yourself...haven't you, Philip?'

Holmes shook his head as characteristic smugness emerged across his face.

'Don't take yourself so seriously, Ivan. Look...it's all a joke! I didn't mean any harm by it!'

The unflinching mask of the avenger remained firm.

'No...no, of course not. No offence taken. Not by *me*, anyway. But of course...your true comic intent is not always adequately conveyed to the more sensitive souls under your address.'

Now the physics teacher looked more than a little confused.

'I don't understand what you mean. Explain yourself. Do you mean I *did* upset you? I don't believe it for a minute!'

The elder man shook his head from side to side as his tone became fortified by fury.

'Not *me*, Philip. You could never, *ever* begin to upset me. You intolerable...despicable...imbecile. I'm talking about the children. The youngsters that you take great pride in insulting and embarrassing in the name of acquiring a cheap...dirty... empty...laugh.'

Phil Holmes' mind now whirled with bemusement.

Ivan observed with a pitiful fascination as he waited for his younger counterpart to recognise the subject of their discussion.

'Look...I should advise you to stay off the brandy if it makes you like this! I don't know what you've heard, Ivan...but...if pupils are telling tales...'

Ivan raised a forefinger as a prelude to interruption.

His face moved inches from that of the enemy.

'Oh…but it's *you* who I hear, dearest Philip…because *yours* is the only voice to be heard. *Yours* is the mouth that must eclipse the sound all others strive to make. Especially the oh so young…and oh so defenceless…if…you get…my drift?'

Holmes furrowed his brow and waved a dismissive hand towards the elder teacher.

'If you're making any accusations, Reynolds, then please get on with it! Back up what you're saying with some proof! If, of course, there actually is any authenticity to your stupid riddles! You can't blind me with your words, Reynolds. You're not *that* smart!'

Now Ivan smiled.

Now the perpetrator was wriggling with desperation like a doomed rabbit ensnared in a net.

Now was the time to unveil the name at the centre of the issue that had so rankled with Ivan for so many days.

Now the time was nigh to defend the previously defenceless.

'Jenny…Douglas. Ring any bells…Philip?'

Phil Holmes' eyes whitened with guilty acknowledgement as the whispered name carried across the void to him. And it registered so heavily, dropping like a leaden ball into a tranquil pond.

Now at last, Phil Holmes struggled to speak.

Now the aggravator strived for an escape route that was no longer there.

Now he would be answerable for his gross abuse of responsibility.

And now, Ivan Reynolds unfurled his wrath.

'I need say no more…need I…dearest…Philip? Aside from offering a warning that I suggest you heed to the letter.'

The snarling expression of the physics teacher was jerked ever closer, as Ivan wrapped the fingers of his right hand around Phil Holmes' tie and wrenched him ever closer, lifting the younger man onto his tiptoes.

Ivan afforded his voice to fall in volume, so as only to be received by the ears of the intended subject.

'I trust implicitly the word of a frightened pupil, who tells me they are being bullied. Similarly, I would not trust an arrogant snake like you as far as I could throw you…and believe me, dearest Philip…I am very tempted to launch you through that window this very instant.'

Holmes began to squirm and tried to groan a feeble retort.

Ivan's grip became ever firmer and infinitely more restrictive as the overdue lesson continued.

'I may be hard-line to you, Philip…out of fashion…a relic of the past…but I am still the rooster in this particular hen house. One more peep out of you before I leave next Easter…and *you* will be retiring before I do! I will not hesitate to have you ousted you from your post. My four decades in teaching are unblemished. Your four months will be all you serve if you do not toe my line. Now get your things and get out of my sight.'

Without further word, the quivering quarry was released.

His expression rendered pale and fearful.

Phil Holmes snatched his briefcase and hurriedly made for the door, just as two cleaners entered to give the staff room a face lift and polish.

Now it was Ivan's turn to offer a parting shot to the retreating foe.

'Oh…and about tonight's concert, Philip…I shouldn't plan on turning up, if I were you. There's a good lad. I might not be in such a good mood later.'

The cleaners were efficient and gone again within a couple of minutes, giving Ivan the chance to make for his car before being discovered.

The unpleasant business with Phil Holmes was now placed to the back of his mind as the next priority mission honed into focus.

Poking his head beyond the staff room door, he checked the corridor was vacant before making a dash for the main exit with coat and briefcase in hand.

The time on the silver pocket watch declared five-thirty exactly. Carol would hopefully still be in the main hall overseeing the final touches to the stage with the other volunteers she had commandeered for the task.

With an hour to go until the audience would begin to arrive, this was Ivan's opportunity to change and maybe convince himself that he had learned his lines.

Then of course, he had to confront Carol once again and convince her into letting him onstage at all.

But she was an understanding woman.

He hoped.

Opening the car door, he noted the icy cold air of early evening and placed his coat and case into the back seat. On lifting the boot, he pulled out a large black dust jacket on a coat hanger, which housed all the chief accessories to his costume.

A pair of shining, black leather military boots were also removed from the rear footwell of the Princess, which he then duly locked whilst checking his surroundings for any passers-by that might have detected his suspicious presence.

With full regalia under his arm and renewed enthusiasm beginning to ascend once more, Ivan made for the gymnasium. The boys' changing room would provide the adequate solitude required for his undercover preparation.

Entering his adopted temporary hovel, he vainly ignored the ever-present aroma of stale sweat and turned on the showers.

Alone at last with his secret plan in place and ready to be executed, Ivan Reynolds' inner festive spirit began to burn brighter than it had done for many a year.

19

Thursday. Five minutes until seven o'clock p.m.

December the twenty-second.

Carol stood nervously on the chalk-marked centre point of the stage and rapidly ran through her notes dictating the order of billing. During the previous minutes, the initial murmur of the audience beyond the closed curtains had rapidly developed into a verbal myriad of vibrant conversation.

Failing to resist temptation, she succumbed to take a little look at the gathering throng. Covertly peering through the gap in the red velvet, the sight of the waiting masses thrilled her.

There was not a spare seat. Every single chair that she had helped place in position just over two hours earlier was now filled with pupils, teachers, and parents. Her heart began to race with anticipation. Everything was seemingly in order for a successful night.

In turn, the Head of First Year had made it a priority behind the scenes to welcome each and every participant in the concert and ensured that they were adequately prepared with costumes, make-up and any necessary extra helpings of confidence.

Backstage, the first act on the bill was almost in readiness and the excited young girl adorned in red and white exchanged a smile and thumbs-up with Carol as she hovered excitedly in the wings.

It was finally time to commence proceedings and as acting mistress of ceremonies, Carol gave the signal to switch off the grid of main hall lighting and illuminate the stage spotlight rig.

Generous applause greeted the concert host as the curtains swished open to the accompaniment of a short festive tune courtesy of the school band.

With an inflating combination of pleasure and pride, Carol allowed the wonderful applause to disperse of its own accord and she welcomed those present.

'I would like to thank everyone for attending this evening in what I am sure will be a night of intriguing surprises for one and all. I will state now that the First Year pupils involved in this concert are to be praised for their endeavours. I have only glimpsed the acts in rehearsal over the past week or so, and as you will see from your programmes, there are some strange sounding items in store! Anyway, this is their night and so with no further ado, I have the great honour of introducing the first performer. Ladies and gentlemen, boys and girls, please welcome…*Santa's Shadow*!'

Retreating hastily to the semi-lit wings, Carol watched eagerly as the inaugural turn of the night took position on the centre mark to the sound of generous appreciation coming from the now darkened stalls.

She was careful not to overbear the pupils as her daily authority would normally achieve. Instead, she made sure that her role was strictly reserved to keeping things moving behind the scenes and check that incoming acts would be ready for their curtain call.

Confirming the next turn on the billing and arranging the players backstage, she felt a pang of satisfaction as the sound of laughter echoed from the arena beyond. Although wishing to have more of an opportunity to observe the actual concert as it played out, Carol found herself constrained by various calls for help involving lost lipstick, torn fairy wings and an urgent need for a large safety pin.

No sooner had the second act been deemed ready, the Head of First Year was back on stage to introduce them. It was a frantic period of responsibility and vital for the structure of the show, but she revelled in the chance to make the youngsters feel good about their efforts and have the confidence to perform in public.

The audience were responding very enthusiastically, and the feedback was positive as the acts progressed through their assorted scripts and routines.

A comical sketch involving two girls about the joys of Christmas morning was followed by a choir of four boys in hats and scarves singing seasonal songs completely and purposely off-key.

A take on Santa's retirement increased the rate of sentimental amusement, whilst a fully costumed Hilary Johnson exceeded all expectations as she delivered a moving monologue which dramatically described the imagined hardships of life as one of Santa's elves.

The never-ending stream of impressively fertile invention rendered Carol and the other members of staff aghast with admiration for the tenacity and commitment of the eleven-year-olds.

The concert had been in progress for nearly ninety minutes as the Head of First Year introduced the penultimate entrant into the limelight.

Trevor Sims and Colin Scott sang an amusing parody of Rudolph the Red-Nosed Reindeer, which veritably brought the house down.

With just the final act left to introduce, Carol perched proudly at the side of the stage as a young quartet of wise men waited for her signal to stake their claim for a Littleholt Oscar.

As they stood tentatively in line, she could not help but giggle as well as offer some cosmetic advice.

'Is that tea-towel secured Simon?'

'Pull it back a bit we can't see your face!'

'Stop giggling, Neil! You're not supposed to laugh at yourself! That's the audience's job!'

'Right! Wait here while I go on and announce you. Then when I go off the other side, you follow me on and stand over the chalk mark. Okay?'

The four wise men nodded simultaneously under their cloth-covered heads as Carol turned and made for the microphone.

With the last of the bill finally making their entrance, she finally began to relax a little. The head drama teacher, Miss Heaton, congratulated her on organising the show, before revealing a surprise of her own.

'Er…Carol. I think you're going to have to make a last-minute amendment to the billing. It seems we've one more act after this one.'

Exhibiting an expression of sincere confusion, Carol quickly scanned the running order on her clipboard.

'No…that's it! The last act. Four wise men! The very last on the bill! According to this list, anyway! Goodness me…who have I missed out?'

Miss Heaton gestured with a thumb towards the rear of the stage and furrowed her brow.

'We have another wise man in the corridor who wants the chance to take to the stage, apparently.'

Now justifiably bewildered, Carol promptly weaved her way around the vibrant bustle of performers that were occupying the concealed dressing area.

On reaching the side door with more than a sense of concern that she might well have forgotten someone on her list, she hastily pulled down on the handle.

The sight that greeted her took her breath away.

Ivan stood with hands on hips, fully attired in his national dress. The half-smirk across his face conveyed a thousand humble apologies as he bowed his head.

'How do you like the kilt, Carol?'

Feeling both dumbfounded and yet inwardly delighted, she had a compulsion to laugh and placed a hand to her mouth.

But it wasn't mockery towards Ivan's eventual presentation.

Instead, she giggled in sheer relief that he had decided to appear after all. The release of inner gratitude overwhelmed her. But of course, a little teasing was inevitable between chums of old.

'I think you've come to the wrong place, sir. This isn't the knobbly knees contest!'

He merely saluted with a straight face and explained his regalia.

'Six generations of the Reynolds clan have donned this for formal occasion. The family tartan doesn't come out too often these days. But tonight…well…tonight is rather special, don't you think?'

She shook his hand and subtly moved her mouth to his ear.

'It is now, Ivan. It is very special now. Come on. Let's get you to the wings.'

Threading him through the busy throng of backstage activity, the young pupils looked on open-mouthed as the two teachers smiled at the admiring yet bemused observers.

Ivan duly spread some festive good will to allay the wariness that the youngsters were obviously sensing as he walked among them.

'Good evening, boys and girls! Enjoy your time in the spotlight? You all did very well!'

Some of them nodded in awkward silence.

Others were too taken aback to respond at all.

Only Trevor Sims had the natural confidence to enquire as to the reason for his form tutor's sudden appearance.

'Are you going out there, sir? On stage, sir?'

Ivan placed a hand on young Trevor's shoulder and looked into the boy's eyes, which glistened with anticipation.

'I certainly am, Mister Sims. I certainly am.'

'Brilliant! Come on, you lot!' Trevor cried; his enthusiasm quickly infecting the others.

The children followed the two teachers from the rear of the stage area and jostled for position in the murk of the wings. Ivan stood with hands behind his back, black boots gleaming and the silver buttons of his grey and red-chequered jacket glistening like diamonds.

The smile on Carol Shaw's face did not diminish as she waited for the four wise men to conclude their act to thunderous applause.

As she was just about to make for the centre of the boards, a familiarly soft voice sounded close to her.

'I'm so sorry, Carol. For earlier…accusing you…it was Phil Holmes with the loose mouth. Please accept my deepest apologies. And…thank you.'

Confused all over again, she looked at him and tried in vain to pierce those deep, dark spectacles.

'Thank me? For what?'

Ivan inhaled sharply and rubbed his hands.

'For inviting me to take part in this…of course!'

She did not have her usual instant retort ready in the barrel.

Instead, Carol Shaw was deeply touched by Ivan's evident remorse over the earlier argument. Besides which, she had never heard him apologise to anyone before and felt somewhat honoured by the rarity of the gesture.

Appreciating his very presence at that moment she simply stared at him for a moment or two of personal serenity before he ushered her into action.

'Go on then, woman! Get me on! Or we'll be standing here all bloody night!'

Taking her position at the microphone, she realised her trusty clipboard had been left behind in the dressing rooms. Yet it mattered not. For the next act was a last-minute Christmas bonus for all and would be announced as such.

'Ladies and gentlemen…boys and girls…I am quite sure you will all agree it has been a brilliant evening and wish to thank you once again for your attendance. Those involved have relished every second and I hope you've enjoyed yourselves as much as we have.'

Heartfelt applause interrupted her stride giving her no choice but to be quiet.

Finally, the audience calmed once more.

'Now…I know I said that the four wise men was the last act of the evening…but a little surprise has just materialised. And you will *all* want to stay and see this…I am quite sure! Now…I have no idea what is about to take to the stage, other than to say…please put your hands together…for…Mister Reynolds.'

A spilt second of disbelieving hush rocked the unlit banks of spectators.

Ivan began to walk slowly across the stage, hopeful that the shock of his appearance would kick-start an encouraging reaction.

The somewhat muted audience response to his reveal was matched by mumblings of wonder and giggles of understandable mirth from the unidentifiable voices in the stalls.

The reaction to seeing the most revered teacher at Littleholt donned in such attire, prompted more than its fair share of uninvited amusement.

Yet Ivan stood patiently and waited until the murmurs and finger pointing had dissipated.

Finally, he addressed the throng with microphone in hand as the audience swiftly became completely smitten with curiosity.

'At the request of Miss Shaw, I have to say it is truly an honour to stand here this evening and sing for you all. Please…should you wish to sing along with me…feel free to do so…in fact…I'm counting on it.'

Another momentary silence was the prelude to a gentle keyboard accompaniment.

Ivan quietly cleared his throat and began to enchant his now captive assemblage with a rendition of the classic Christmas hymn, O Come All Ye Faithful.

A solid lump of professional affection now lodged firmly in her throat, Carol Shaw lost herself in the moment.

With her arms folded as Ivan's captivating, pitch-perfect voice carried itself out to an astounded auditorium, she listened to the background organ and watched him through a gradually moistening gaze as he prepared to begin the second verse.

Holding the microphone casually in front of his chin, his reliable tones resonated capably across the dazzled spectators.

Among the transfixed throng, the younger sisters and brothers of the First Year pupils watched intently as the previously unheralded singer held their attention with the most anthemic of all the Christmas carols.

And of course, as the procession of verses was completed, the song travelled around again to the closing lines of the chorus, the leading man encouraging others to participate by raising his open hand as invitation to the enthralled crowd.

And join in, they most certainly did.

At first, only a smattering of reticent voices extended from the darkness. Then such a little confidence quickly spread, eventually compelling everybody to partake.

And by the end of the hymn, the accompaniment was full, controlled, and strong, inspiring the senior Mathematics teacher behind the microphone to conclude with a heart pumping finale.

As the keyboard played out to a conclusion, another split second of silence prevailed as Ivan watched and waited.

Then, it happened.

The eruption of applause raised the roof of the main hall.

Parents and children stood and cheered, with cries for an encore bouncing from every corner of the chamber.

Ivan glanced quickly to his left, where Carol covertly wiped her eyes under the lenses of her spectacles with a handkerchief, as she watched in undiluted, sensational astonishment.

Shrugging his shoulders as if to ask permission to continue, he waited for her instruction.

Finally, she answered his call with a distinctly proud slant in her reply as it drifted from the seclusion of the wings.

'Well? If they *want* more and you've *got* more…then *give* 'em more!'

The singer smirked before turning to the smiling Fifth Year girl sitting behind the large electric piano.

Exchanging brief nods of acknowledgement, the second song commenced its introduction and began to drift over the now tranquil and now fully transfixed congregation.

They sat patiently as Ivan commenced the ever-popular opening vocals of Silent Night.

Now completely engaged by the solo performance, the spectators began to hum along to the melody, so they might still here the sweet execution of the verse.

Now rendering his audience fully engaged, Ivan revelled in the spotlight for the duration and victoriously completed the song as he had begun it.

Two hundred spellbound concertgoers could do no more than be swept away by the beauty and power of Ivan Reynolds' voice and the undeniable potency of the songs he had selected.

Now there was no uncertain pause at the end as the entire audience out front and backstage stood to their feet once again and showed their brimming enthusiasm for the long-hidden talent that had unexpectedly paraded itself before them.

Joining in the tumultuous response, Carol observed the innocent faces of those youngsters who had already taken their turns on the evening's bill. In particular, she noted the entranced expression of Hilary Johnson, who had watched her form tutor in overwhelmed disbelief - and perhaps with a pang of admiration.

The calls for a further encore were united and earnest from all.

Every voice in the arena pleaded with Ivan to continue indulging them.

Gesturing for a little hush, the singer spoke to his adoring congregation.

'Your acknowledgements are fully appreciated ladies and gentlemen, boys and girls. I am humbled. And I must say I am very impressed with one or two voices in the audience! If you must insist on one more ditty…then I have an idea in mind that will *definitely* require *everybody's* assistance.'

Again, the cheers, screams and shouts echoed from the main seating area to the roof rafters of the hall. For a good few seconds, Ivan refrained from battling to be heard.

Eventually, a simmering peace descended again as he walked to the edge of the stage.

'Now…this next offering will be very familiar to you all. So…your instructions are as follows. This half of the audience will join with me on the even numbers…and the other half of the hall will support the odd numbers. I shall say no more. I guarantee you will soon pick it up…yes, I'm sure. Okay, Kerry…when you're ready.'

The keyboard player complied with the order and played the intro for a full ten seconds, leaving most of those present without any doubt as to their imminent role in the classic festive standard, The Twelve Days of Christmas.

The impromptu participation of the audience worked to absolute perfection. With Ivan conducting the choir of parents and children as to their cues, the hall brimmed with joyous laughter as the familiar hooks of the song cascaded and rose again by turn.

The conclusive countdown of all dozen lines was deliberately increased in tempo and volume to keep the supporting singers on their toes, and throughout the resounding finale the audience instinctively maintained the pace and never missed a single beat.

And for the very last line, the tempo was reduced dramatically, in order for one and all to rejoice in the final, joyful conclusion.

With the song finished and the act having reached its end all too soon for everybody, Ivan courteously expressed his appreciation and returned quickly to the wings, where he bellowed his instructions around the backstage area.

'HURRY UP! EVERYBODY MUST TAKE A FINAL BOW! COME ON! YOU TOO, CAROL!'

The audible volume of affection in the room increased greatly at the sight of the entire evening's billing returning to stage front and receiving the generous plaudits.

Ivan grabbed Carol's hand as he implored her to take her umpteenth bow before whispering in her ear.

'Come on! We need a closing speech! They're waiting for you!'

Nodding in avid agreement, she waited patiently by the microphone as the din of the effervescent audience began to slowly dissipate once more.

Carol reluctantly brought events to a close.

'I have to say, I am completely astounded both by the efforts of the players on stage and by your incredible responses. I wish to thank all the children involved for their relentless enthusiasm and of course…to the gentleman standing beside me in his family tartan, whose belated appearance I am sure will stay firmly in your memory for quite a while yet. I know it will in mine!'

Ivan politely removed the mike from Carol's grasp with an important word to say on his own behalf.

'Just before you make your way home, there is one person tonight who deserves more credit than anybody here, and yet has been barely afforded a mention. She had the original idea for the concert. She has done all of the organising and laid on the entertainment without a single hitch. Ladies and gentlemen…boys and girls…please show your undoubted appreciation for…the Head of First Year…Miss Shaw!'

Almost embarrassed by Ivan's gallant gesture of gratitude, Carol swayed uneasily as she wallowed in the tumultuous plaudits, now clutching her retrieved clipboard to her chest as a comforter.

The assembly hall lights were duly switched back on.

The spectators began to slowly trickle away, and the plethora of discussions and distractions backstage gave Ivan the chance he needed to try and make his exit unnoticed.

Through stealth and determination, he was soon alone again in the solace of the boys' changing room. Carefully removing the jacket and kilt and replacing them back in the dust cover, his ears were still ringing from the sound of success.

Attired once again in his teaching suit, he swiftly vacated the gymnasium and made his way around the outer building.

Dozens of other adults and children were congregated in the amber-hued pools of the car park, chatting avidly about the evening just witnessed and their unanimous vote for the undoubted star of the show.

To his relief, Ivan's prudent advance towards his car remained undetected.

He carefully laid his costume in the boot of the Princess and slid behind the steering wheel, thankful to finally be concealed by the shadows of night.

He sat in quiet contemplation for a full minute, mildly inflated by the adrenaline rush he had just encouraged in the main hall. It was gratifying to think of the positive reaction he had evoked in everybody.

Staring intently into his rear-view mirror, he vaguely recognised the silhouettes of various members of 1RY who had taken part in the event and one or two others with their parents who had watched from the stalls.

Ivan realised at that moment in the half-light of the car, that he had thoroughly enjoyed being appreciated and perhaps even *liked* by so many, even if only for just a few minutes of inspired generosity.

And now, alone again, he faced the prospect of home.

Nobody in the winter chill of the car park gave the Princess a second glance, as the driver somewhat reluctantly started the engine and glided silently away from the school grounds.

20

The last day of the autumn term was heralded by a clear blue December sky and un-seasonally pleasant sunshine.

With mug of tea in hand and still attired in slippers, robe and pyjamas, Ivan patrolled the frost-laden patchwork of his rear garden and scrutinised the fallow sections of the vegetable plot for any signs of the neighbouring feline.

Not that it mattered so much now.

Gardening was a hobby now fully in hibernation for at least the next three months.

He breathed the dawn air and lined his lungs with the fresh intake. It was sheer heaven to be out among the elements at first light. Mother Nature was truly his best friend and most reliable ally in that moment of splendour.

A semblance of peace that was duly interrupted by a familiar voice from over the boundary fence.

Jill Breeden's face appeared atop the wooden panel and bid Ivan a good morning.

'It most certainly is, dear Jillian. Most unlike the grey miserable weather of previous days.'

His friend and neighbour commenced to peg damp clothes on her line as she continued the exchange.

'Break up today, don't you, Ivan?'

Moving toward the fence, Ivan leaned over in order to lower the volume of his voice.

'Indeed, Jillian. Two weeks of freedom will soon be mine to embrace. Hope you don't mind the intrusion…but…a bit cold for hanging washing, isn't it?'

She did not look at him as she concentrated on draping several large bath towels.

'Don't know if this lot will dry today or not. Bit of sun should help, though. I could do with one of those new tumble drier things. By the way…what are you doing on Sunday?'

Ivan drained his mug and furrowed his brow above the dark shades.

'This coming Sunday? Why…I don't know, yet…should I have plans?'

Now Jill turned to her neighbour with a wry smirk.

'Yes, you *should*! You know full well that it's Christmas Day! What are you doing for your dinner?'

Ivan opted for humour to deflect from the melancholy truth of the matter.

'Well, once I've opened all the presents that I've sent to myself, I thought I'd indulge in some egg and chips in front of the box. A feast fit for a king. Don't you think?'

Jill's expression evolved from sympathy to fortitude.

'No, I *don't* think! George and I are having our Kevin and his family around. Please…why don't you join us? Don't sit all alone next door. It's not right, Ivan. Not at Christmas.'

Ivan Reynolds contemplated the generous and well-meaning offer.

'I know, Jillian. You are right, of course. But if I accept your kind invitation, do I have permission to bring some beer and get ever so slightly drunk?'

Jill laughed in relief at her friend's acceptance, slowly getting the feeling that he had hoped to be invited all along.

'Get as drunk as you bloody like! You'll be in good company with George and Kev! Ohh…I'm ever so glad you're coming! Made my week that has! By the way…how did your concert go last night?'

The reluctant star of the show simply smiled and lowered his head.

'It was…a success…shall we say?'

'Did you get up and sing as planned?' enquired Jill.

'Oh…yes…I went down fairly well…I think. I remembered all my lines, too!'

Ivan retreated from the fence to check the time through the kitchen window. The clock above the stove declared it to be five minutes to eight.

'I'd better be getting ready, Jillian. And thank you for the dinner invitation. I shall look forward to it.'

'My pleasure, Ivan. Honestly. And pop round tomorrow night if you want a tipple. And before you ask, tomorrow is Christmas Eve. We'll have plenty in!'

With sincerity in her gaze, Jill simply nodded as she watched Ivan wave and retreat indoors.

*****

Despite the last day of the school year being deemed non-uniform day, Ivan chose a charcoal grey suit. He examined the cloth of his jacket in the mirror. Not one of his newer suits, but it was bearing up rather well. Maybe an alternative would have to be selected for the start of the New Year.

Washed and brushed up, Ivan checked his briefcase in the hallway to check that he was not leaving anything behind that might be required. Geoff Taylor had insisted that the usual timetable be adhered to, but what teachers chose to do in their lessons today was down to their own discerning judgement.

Ivan examined his reflection in the hallway mirror before remembering there was one more task to undertake before leaving the house.

Back upstairs in the bedroom, he kissed Meg and Nicholas in turn and bid them both a Happy Christmas.

Holding them both simultaneously in his arms, his mind helplessly wandered back to far off days, when things were so different.

When life was different.

When perhaps, Ivan Reynolds was different.

Yet despite his apparently insurmountable failings, Meg and Nicholas continued to smile at him each and every day whenever he entered the bedroom.

Their earnest expressions of joy were never altered by mood or circumstance.

According to memory, Meg would now be nearly sixty-two-years-old, and Nicholas would have evolved triumphantly into his fourth decade.

Yet Ivan still coveted the images of them both as he remembered them best.

And as he pressed them close to his heart, he so dearly wished that he could be with them again.

Maybe, one day.

Looking deep into their eyes, he mourned the time that had passed and the errors he had made.

But such futile regret lasted only momentarily.

Kissing each of them once again and bidding farewell for the day, he replaced both photographs back in position on his chest of drawers.

The matching pair of ornate silver frames took pride of place among various other mementoes of Ivan's previous life.

Yet as ever, his wife and son remained unmoved as he dolefully departed the bedroom, descended the stairs and locked the front door behind him.

*****

Pulling on the handbrake, Ivan sensed that he was very much the talk of the playground that morning.

From behind the wheel, he observed the teenagers in his rear-view mirror pointing and gesturing toward his car.

Yet typically, not one dared come too close.

Climbing out and locking the Princess, he scanned the car park whilst adorning a combined squint and smile as his spectacles adjusted in the slowly rising winter sun. Indeed, he was the topic of debate, but alas he was not to be involved in the many discussions that abounded as he made his way across to the main doors and toward the staff room.

Matt Jenkins emerged to greet Ivan at the door and offered cautionary congratulations.

'Next stop the Albert Hall, eh, Ivan? Brought the house down so I here!'

Ivan smiled at the plaudit from his colleague.

He wasn't accustomed to receiving praise at all, let alone at such an early hour.

'Well…one does one's best in time of need, Matthew. Has the kettle boiled?'

Ivan brushed past his unofficial apprentice and entered the staff room to a round of unprecedented yet evidently earnest applause.

Many of those present had witnessed Ivan's triumph the previous evening and passed comment on his bravery and previously undisclosed sense of fun.

'Who'd have thought!' proclaimed Bob Davidson. 'Old Reynolds actually *entertaining* the pupils instead of hanging them from meat hooks!'

Ivan responded accordingly with a mildly forced and uncomfortable chuckle, yet he was secretly thankful of the acclaim from his peers. Before sitting down with a black coffee, he sensed the justifiably wary figure of Phil Holmes eyeing him intently from the far side of the room.

The physics teacher made not a sound and Ivan noted the younger man's exit soon afterwards.

'Phil's a bit subdued this morning.' Matt quipped, eagerly.

Ivan looked up from his newspaper and displayed a broad grin that adequately conveyed a thousand words. Every single one of which, Matt Jenkins understood to the letter.

With the registration bell signalling time for all to depart their comfort zone, the lethargic throng of teachers hauled themselves from their seats and clattered their empty mugs onto the worktop of the staff room kitchenette.

Ivan left his newspaper on the table and marched into the main corridor towards the echoing stair wells. Amid the din of a thousand young voices, Ivan did not identify a single word or any one pupil.

Instead, he continued the ascent among the swelling masses without exchanging so much as a syllable with anyone before reaching the top landing.

1RY obliged the normal procedure, with casual glances being offered in the tutor's direction as he waited patiently with hands in pockets before total silence prevailed among the two lines.

Discipline was still encouraged as a priority - even at Christmas.

Registration was taken quickly for the sake of everyone concerned and unearthed a major surprise in the process.

'A full house, 1RY! This must be a first! The last day of term and everybody is here! Miracles do happen at Christmas after all. Couldn't be anything to do with the absence of uniforms, could it?'

Aside from some half-hearted smiles, the class did not reply.

'Okay. You are all dismissed. See you after lunch.'

Ivan folded the register amid the customary backdrop of banging furniture and excited chatter. As the form group gradually streamed from room ten, Ivan sat back in his chair, removed his glasses, and rubbed his eyes, making the most of the minute or two of solitude before the incoming pupils would be howling at the door.

Staring vacantly into space, he did not detect the loitering presence of one particular member of the form, who abidingly stood next to his desk awaiting permission to speak.

Ivan looked up and scanned the well-mannered youngster through his quickly replaced black mask.

'Miss Douglas? You caught me unawares for a moment. Is everything okay? What can I do for you?'

The girl hovered next to Ivan, seemingly uncertain of how to proceed. She seemed strangely nervous and uncertain of her quest.

In her grasp, she carried a small box covered in red gift wrapping. Ivan also noticed a small white envelope.

He remained silent as she contemplated commencement of her speech and finally plucked up the wherewithal to deliver it.

'Sir…I…I…just wanted to say… I thought you were…absolutely brilliant…last night…in the concert.'

Ivan nodded in agreement.

'Thank you so much, Miss Douglas. I have to say I thoroughly enjoyed myself. I'm glad you were there to witness the show.'

The youngster's crimson gaze alternated between the small bounty in her possession and the intensive stare of the teacher.

Finally, she conjured up the courage to continue as the noise on the outside landing slowly became boisterous and distracting. Ivan raised a hand to her before standing up and sidled to the open doorway.

He addressed the melee beyond the threshold of room ten as a sergeant major would bark at his regiment.

'EXCUSE ME! I KNOW YOU'RE ALL DESPERATE TO ENTER THE LAIR AND REVEL IN MY COMPANY, BUT CAN YOU PLEASE CALM DOWN AND CLOSE MOUTHS? I CANNOT HEAR MYSELF THINK IN HERE! I WON'T BE LONG!'

Re-entering the classroom and shutting the door, Ivan sat back in his chair as Jenny Douglas cautiously whispered her message.

'I…I got you this present, sir. There's a card, too. My mum and dad said they really liked you when they met you at parents' evening. And they said you were very kind about me. You're the best, sir. I'll always remember this Christmas because of you.'

Ivan smiled.

But not his usual smirk of gamesmanship.

This was a genuine response of earnest delight.

Tentatively placing the card and gift on his desk, the eleven-year-old succumbed to inevitable embarrassment and quickly departed.

Gone without further word.

Leaving Ivan Reynolds completely stupefied by the unexpected and touching consideration he had just been shown.

He stared at the offering on his desk.

And he felt slightly relieved at the fact that the bearer had withdrawn from the scene when she did.

His throat suddenly became noticeably tight.

The very last thing he wanted at Christmas, was for any pupil to see him battling gamely with himself.

In his effort to avoid weeping.

*****

Thankfully for staff and pupils alike, the last day of term passed in the blink of an eye. Little was achieved during lesson time, but as was the long-accepted ritual, neither teachers nor children were willing or able to concentrate on their studies.

It was to everyone's immense relief when the final, liberating bell of the year droned throughout the building, prompting a rapid mass exodus that flooded the car park and playground within seconds.

The shouts and screams emitting from Littleholt's departing attendance were a joyous sound to embrace.

From his vantage point at the top of the stairs, Ivan observed the buoyant melee through the landing window whilst clutching the gift that Jenny Douglas had presented to him several hours earlier.

With the prospect of a fortnight being left to his own devices, covert desertion from the premises was very tempting, but he knew that informal goodbyes in the staff room would be nothing less than a civil requirement.

Forcing himself back downstairs to the smoke-lined congregation of his colleagues, he despatched farewell wishes relatively quickly, shaking hands with everyone present in the room and secretly hoping for a quick getaway.

Ivan was only mildly disappointed that Phil Holmes was not present to receive the festive message of good will.

Striding out with not a little relief into the car park, Ivan stopped and turned on his heel as a familiar voice carried after him from the main doors.

'Ivan! Wait up! I haven't seen you all day!'

He turned to see Carol trotting toward him.

'What's the rush? We're all off to the pub up the road for a drink. Why don't you join us for an hour?'

Looking more than a little uncomfortable with the idea, Ivan shuffled his weight from foot to foot as he vainly dragged excuses from the back of his mind.

'Yes...Matthew has mentioned it. I think I'll give it a miss this time if you don't mind, Carol. But thank you, anyway.'

The obviously disappointed Head of First Year observed her colleague.

He was evidently not in the mood for social contact at that moment. Christmas or not.

She also had cause to notice the red foil box he clutched in his right hand.

'My, my…you've done well! I didn't even get a card this year!'

Ivan looked puzzled until he registered the motive for her comment.

He moved a few paces toward her and eyed his prize triumphantly.

'Oh yes…from young Miss Douglas…to show her appreciation for last night. Amongst other things. She's a delightful student. Makes it all worthwhile if you only get one like her each year.'

Carol nodded enthusiastically.

'Bless her. I think you've got the makings of a fan club there! You certainly opened my eyes, Ivan. We didn't know you had it in you!'

His face moved closer to hers as affirmation lightened his ever-frowning features.

His voice softened slightly yet his words were direct and clear.

'Yes…*you* did, Carol! You yourself…told me specifically I had it in me! You were my sole inspiration for going on stage in the first place. So, I suppose I ought to be thanking you as well!'

Both teachers fell prey to a momentary awkward silence until the Head of First Year opted to run with instinct.

Much to Ivan's surprise, and possibly her own, she leaned toward her colleague and planted a gentle kiss on his left cheek.

He did not reciprocate, feeling distinctly uneasy on receipt of the unexpected yet wonderfully humane gesture.

'Happy Christmas, Carol…see you in January.'

She watched helplessly as this most mysterious of men faced the opposite direction and began to walk toward his copper-coloured car.

She loudly whispered her own festive best wishes but felt certain he did not hear her. With an unwelcome twinge of sadness in her heart, she pondered what might await him at home and the kind of Christmas he would encounter.

Back in the supposed bosom of his family that she had never met.

The family that she presumed loved him.

The family that he never spoke about.

A caring wife and son.

Maybe by now, grandchildren were on the scene.

But her natural preconceptions were based on an innocent ignorance of the truth behind the man.

Truth that he had strived to avoid divulging.

Ivan had never compromised his right to total privacy.

Yet contrary to what she might have believed in her heart, Carol couldn't quite envisage him as a family man.

There was a tangibly cold, almost callous streak that ran through him.

A shaft of inexplicable elusiveness in his personality that tended to drive people away with regular ease as opposed to drawing them closer.

She had always sensed it yet never truly understood the source of such a disposition.

Regarding the authentic nature of his character, she would never know just how poignantly adept her instincts were, as she watched the red rear lights of his car float silently down the school driveway and eventually beyond view.

21

The air felt sharp and crisp as the Christmas Day sunrise peered tentatively over the horizon, gently tinting the grey landscape with an orange sheen.

The only sound Ivan heard was that of his running shoes as they padded the deserted pavements of the local neighbourhood on route to the silent splendour of the parkland.

Dressed in shorts and a tracksuit jacket, Ivan looked to the skyline ahead and detected the familiar silhouette of Littleholt Secondary School, slowly displaying its uninspiring form as the daylight grew steadily brighter.

Yet, for all his physical ambition that morning, he had hardly slept a wink.

Having spent an hour or so with the Breedens the previous evening, he had been careful not to overindulge in alcohol.

Christmas Eve or not.

Ivan had planned to retain a clear head for this festive jog, which had become something of a welcome ritual over the past few years.

With nobody to greet him on this most potent of mornings, the concept of taking some exercise and breathing seasonal fresh air was infinitely more appealing than solitude at home.

Traditionally the most family-oriented day of the year was a prospect to savour for most.

However, for Ivan Reynolds, it only brought to bear the unavoidable fact that loneliness was his only truly reliable companion.

And with nature's palette beckoning him with another beauteous dawn, he had little hesitation in temporarily vacating the four echoing walls of an empty house, whilst also trying to leave behind an empty heart in the process.

For this hour, he would simply try and forget.

Just for this one hour.

But erasure of the past was a seemingly impossible feat.

Yet Ivan would not desist in trying to do just that.

As the sweat began to seep from his pores and his muscles began to warm, expand and flex more easily, adrenaline would ably revitalise the tardiness within his soul.

Yet any dormant thoughts that were linked to history were suddenly deemed indispensable and raw, deeming it necessary for him to make attempts to eclipse the constant millstone of regret that he carried.

Some seventeen years had passed since his wife deserted their marital union and fled with his only son.

Nearly two decades of wondering.

Of hoping.

Of wishing.

Yet as his stride slowly became more relaxed and fluid, the steadying rhythm afforded him time to ponder and replay the emotions of yesteryear in his mind.

Ivan always preferred to analyse his foibles whilst on the move, as if to mentally discard each item on the list of faults as he ran.

Certainly, his dalliance with paternity had been fraught with insurmountable hurdles.

Primarily, an unflinching, authoritarian attitude and an undying sense of omnipotence in all walks of life. Particularly at home.

The need to control and restrict and inflict order persistently bound his views and actions and indeed the views and actions of others.

But such inherent bloody-mindedness and an un-swaying arrogance had cost him so dearly.

It was ironic that such negative factors of his personality had proved distinctly attributive when in the guise of teacher.

Indeed, they had been the prime tools of his trade.

But belligerence and bigotry were not attractive qualities to flaunt within the realm of a family unit.

And if nothing else had been ascertained in the years he lived with Meg and Nicholas, his family left him quite assured of the fact that his demeanour and character had become wildly overbearing and unacceptable, to a once loving spouse and young son.

As Ivan flashed through the iron gates of the park, he noticed the white sheen that lay strewn across the varying patchwork of grassland.

Menacing, black-limbed trees reached out for him with spiny tentacles, but they failed in their efforts to touch him for the distance was too great.

He was beyond reproach as he plundered onward.

Ivan always believed that Meg and Nicholas had fled to the continent and settled down with her parents in Spain.

It was always a pipe dream of Meg's to return to her parental homeland where she was raised.

The thought occurred to him as he gently trotted across the wooden footbridge over the trickling stream, that Meg's mother and father would now be of a ripe old age themselves.

Not that it mattered a great deal, anymore. They had disliked Ivan from the moment they met him and would no doubt concur with such feelings even now.

Yes, even now. All these years later.

That is, presuming they were still around to tell their tale.

Ivan's steady pace caused him to dart out of the path of a disgruntled Yorkshire Terrier whose owner stood some thirty yards away belching smoke fumes from a pipe.

'Haven't you got a bloody lead for that thing?' Ivan whispered under his breath, as the dog scampered in retreat to its master.

Dogs and cats were still a literal pet hate for Ivan even at Christmas.

But the canine was only a temporary distraction from his pain.

Not a single word for seventeen years.

From neither an estranged wife nor a stolen son.

And remorse was now Ivan's gloating shadow as he forever rankled with his private losses.

The Breedens were aware of his parental downfall, having witnessed every ounce of despair that had seeped from that neighbouring house.

Yet they had always let their friend be at one with his sorrow.

It was a respectful if unusual interpretation of comradeship which Ivan had always appreciated. That is why, aside from being his geographical neighbours, Jill and George were also considered by Ivan to be the most loyal of confidantes.

Simply by refraining from wilful intrusion and natural suspicion regarding Ivan's years of torment, the Breedens had earned his implicit trust in a very short time, even though he rarely raised the issue of family in their presence, anyway.

Knowing they were there should he ever need to call on them was comfort enough. Analysis of events was wholly unnecessary.

Similarly, Ivan had been extremely cautious to guard the truth of his wife's desertion from work colleagues.

He had joined the Littleholt staff in Nineteen-sixty-one as a proudly married man.

So far as anyone at the school was concerned, he had remained so.

And would soon retire as such.

It was a closely maintained secret that Ivan considered vital to uphold. He had never once removed the band of gold that Meg had slipped onto his finger all those years ago.

It had become a symbol of his eternal belief that a sound family unit was intrinsically linked to success in education for both teachers and pupils alike.

It would not be conducive to positive reaction should Ivan ever admit that his wife and child had simply vanished one day, leaving no clue as to their destination or possibility of return.

But in his heart, Ivan knew that he had driven his family away.

And the only consolation he had nurtured from such a harrowing admission, was to maintain a silent and purposed dignity.

Thoughts of any alternative were the stuff of nightmares.

Subsequently, he had never attempted to trace their whereabouts aside sending infrequent and unanswered correspondence to Meg's parents on the continent.

He had gradually succumbed to accepting circumstance with the only the mildest semblance of understanding.

With his mind now having unravelled its usual daily conundrum as he galloped up the canal bridge, the route now began to head back toward home.

Out of the south gates of the parkland; back through the deserted town centre and beyond to the residential labyrinth of silent streets and houses.

He checked his progress for comparison.

The digital stopwatch on his wrist declared he had been running for thirty-eight minutes and by all estimation he aimed to be in a hot steaming bathtub by half-past eight with the radio playing softly in the background.

Perhaps then, a little breakfast.

Cereal or toast; depending on the mood and appetite.

Then maybe, if he felt like it, an hour of television.

The programme listings always improved dramatically this time of year. There was always something worth viewing on the Twenty-fifth of December.

And then, the pristine Christmas suit would be adorned.

A striking, navy blue three piece with matching tie, white shirt, and a large sprig of holly in the lapel to add a dash of festive colour.

All this careful planning should ensure that by midday, Ivan would be ready to attend for dinner with his friends, holding a bottle of Scotch in one hand and greeting card in the other.

Not a conventional celebration of the event by any means, but over time he had slowly become adjusted to going it alone.

He figured that he couldn't upset anyone if there was no one to share his company.

Everyone would be a winner.

*****

Having returned home and achieved his intended missions of the morning, Ivan sat down in full festive attire and checked his silver pocket watch. It was only eleven-thirty. No need to get there too early. Lunch was not planned until two.

Besides which, Ivan did not wish to arrive at the Breedens before their other, more important guests.

It seemed a little in the way of bad manners, somehow.

He sunk into the settee, vacantly staring at the flashing television screen, and occasionally chuckling as Laurel and Hardy struggled to ascend a flight of stairs whilst carrying a piano.

Casually gazing beyond the lounge window, his attention settled to the scene outside.

He noted that the sunshine was now at its highest point in the winter sky and had ably removed any evidence of the earlier frost.

Children had gradually emerged from the surrounding houses during the last hour and had proceeded to parade the bounty of gifts that they had discovered on waking from their blissful slumber.

Brand new shining bicycles of varying sizes glided up and down the road.

Boys on skateboards rattled along paving slabs interwoven by girls on roller skates.

Super-hero fancy dressers enacted battles with villainous arch enemies.

He stood at the windowsill to attain a better view of the bustling throng of young players and their attentive parents who watched from gateways and doorways still adorned in their pyjamas.

As the children rushed hither and thither on their new modes of transport and saved the world in their comic-book attire, not one of those souls beyond the glass offered a glance in the direction of their singular audience.

Not one person noted the appreciative smile that had spread broadly across his face.

Not one of them would understand the despair that accompanied his piercing sense of isolation at that moment in emotive, fathomless time.

He turned away from the frantic activity outside and suddenly a thought struck him.

The gift from Jenny Douglas was still in the car.

Hurriedly retrieving his keys from the hook in the kitchen, he ventured outside to the Princess and picked up the present and card from the passenger seat.

It was only when back indoors, he realised something particularly unusual had just occurred.

He had actually generated a mild sensation of excitement within himself. And for a fleeting, virtually unrecognisable second, Ivan found himself sated by the fact as he proudly re-entered the kitchen with his one and only Christmas present.

Slowly removing the rose-coloured foil wrapping, he was overwhelmed to unveil a chocolate orange. Slicing open the seal of the envelope, the card was illustrated by a painting of a lone reindeer in the sky heading toward the stars.

The handwriting was neat, consistent, and rounded.

Typical for a girl of her age.

The expression was concise and affecting.

To Mr. Reynolds - my favourite teacher and favourite singer.
Have a very happy Christmas.
Love Jenny D. XXX

Ivan proudly positioned the card and chocolate on the mantelpiece just as the sound of a car engine approached outside.

It was George and Jill's son, Kevin, with his wife and two little girls. Not wanting to interrupt the jovial procedure of their arrival, Ivan waited patiently until they had vacated the car and entered the adjoining house.

The silver pocket watch declared it was now ten minutes after midday. The loneliness was suffocating and grew more oppressive as the minutes passed.

The ghosts of his past were calling for him to go; pleading for him to leave that hollow chamber of echoes.

He had been patient for long enough.

One final act upstairs before departure.

Entering the bedroom, he held his wife and child in his arms hoping they might hear his unspoken sorrow.

And then, it was time to join the Breedens for Christmas dinner.

To join his friends; their son and daughter-in-law; their grandchildren.

To be able to feel, for only a few hours, that he was a small part of a family unit once again.

*****

'Ivan! Welcome! Come on in! Kevin and the crew have just turned up! What are you drinking, mate?'

Ivan shook hands with George in the hallway.

He handed over the bottle of whisky and card.

'Well…you could break the seal on this little beauty if you wanted!'

'Good idea! Come through. They're all in here!'

Ivan entered the kitchen, hugged Jill and pecked her on the cheek.

'Merry Christmas, Jillian!'

'My, my Ivan…you look very smart! Going somewhere nice?'

Ivan bathed himself in her compliment.

'Yes. Somewhere very, very nice indeed! Two wonderful friends have invited me for dinner!'

He was quickly re-acquainted with Kevin, his wife Sally and their two daughters, Sarah and Judith.

George observed the happy scene from the hallway before opening Ivan's card.

The familiar handwriting was classical, elegant, and poised.

The message, heartfelt and poignant:

To George and Jillian at Christmas.
Always yours; ever thankful for the fact.
Ivan.

An unavoidable pang of emotion pinched at George's heart as he rested the card on the lounge windowsill and re-joined his family in the kitchen. He watched as Ivan played the charmer with customary ease, acting the clown with the ever-receptive youngsters.

Ivan had watched the girls grow from their cots and had regularly admitted a fondness for them.

George was placated by the sight of his valued chum looking so contented for once.

Seemingly at peace with the surroundings.

And perversely, so apparently orientated to a family Christmas.

A treasured day in most peoples' lives.

And this day would prove to pass in the most pleasant manner.

Temporarily without care and with whisky in hand, the men and women, girls and boys laughed together; then they dined together.

Then they would doze and afterwards laugh and drink some more.

This was Christmas Day for Ivan Reynolds.

The unhappiest day of the year.

*****

New Year's Eve brought with it a novel twist.

The recently established new tenants of The King's Arms pub had decided to throw a celebration party for the locals as a token of appreciation for their continued patronage.

As regular customers of the inn, the Breedens had decided that they were going to attend the function and asked Ivan if he should like to encourage the arrival of the New Year surrounded by a throbbing room full of drunkards.

Fully understanding the fact that he was not a party animal in the least, to the immense surprise of his neighbours, he responded in the positive and even conveyed lukewarm anticipation of the event.

It was six o'clock p.m. on the thirty-first of December when George stepped over the low hedge that ran between the front of the properties and knocked excitedly on Ivan's door.

When it opened, George fully expected his grizzled neighbour to extricate himself from the evening's arrangement.

But he was in for a pleasant surprise.

Ivan was more than enthusiastic.

'Oh no! I'm definitely coming! I'm marginally looking forward to it. No, seriously - it will make a change. It's been a quiet holiday. I'm overdue a bit of fun and mischief, I think!'

George clapped his hands with glee.

'Brilliant, Ivan! By the way…what are you planning to wear?'

Ivan looked at his friend in bemusement.

'Well, it's a relatively important occasion so I thought…'

A hand of objection was raised and tersely interrupted Ivan's flow.

'Oh no! Not the bloody suit again! Shirt and trousers - yes! But…strictly…*no* waistcoat, *no* tie, and *no* jacket! Okay?'

Ivan pretended to shiver in the porch light.

'But it is quite cold, George! I'll need something over the top.'

'Whatever - so long as it's casual and modern. This is New Year's Eve! Not Crown Court! Okay? We'll take a gentle walk to the pub about eight. Give us a knock just before then. And remember, if you put a suit on, we're not bloody taking you! You can go on your own! Agreed?'

With a wry smirk of semi-reluctance, Ivan nodded, closed the door, and trudged upstairs to the bedroom.

Filing through most of his formal wardrobe, he eventually retrieved a pair of dark brown leather slip-on boots. To cover his legs, he pulled on light blue denim jeans and to complete the ensemble, a black, plain shirt.

Concerned about his lack of familiarity with the concept of casual clothing, he tentatively checked his appearance in the dress mirror.

Well, nearly sixty-years-old or not, he was mildly impressed with the look that had been assembled in the space of five minutes.

Pulling a comb through his hair and dabbing some aftershave here and there, Ivan began to feel a ripple of excitement regarding the imminent engagement.

Boldly pouring himself a double whiskey to grease the wheels, he lounged in front of the TV and let the alcohol slowly work its magic.

*****

On entering the lounge room of The King's Arms, the party atmosphere was electric. Scores of the pub's regulars were already in the swing of the New Year festivities and unusually, Ivan was finding himself to be slightly drawn into the desire for a good time.

Weaving his way in and around the heaving throng of revellers, he quickly became separated from George and Jill.

Scanning the room for a vacant seat, Ivan opted to prop up the bar cradling a pint of bitter as he watched the surrounding frivolity unfold.

It had been a long while since he had attended such an evening.

Never having been a lover of parties, he was unsure of how to proceed. However, he had decided to make the most of the invitation.

In the past few weeks, something elusive had altered Ivan's disposition about the way he lived his life.

He had sensed subtle changes in his outlook and desires.

He figured that maybe pending retirement was softening his rigid persona.

Perhaps it was a response to the knowledge that a pivotal age was upon him. Yet he didn't feel old, either in mind or in body.

Maybe it was the recent school concert that had persuaded him to alter his stubborn opinions about many things - including himself.

Whatever the mysterious mental process was entailing, he felt all the better for it at that moment.

And tonight, regaled in his blue jeans and black shirt, standing in the pub with drink in hand, he did not feel like Ivan Reynolds at all.

It was as if he had evolved into someone else entirely.

A new man with a new perspective.

With new discoveries yet to be encountered and enjoyed.

*****

'Ouch! That bloody hurt! Be *careful*!'

The final chorus of *RA-RA-RAs* was accompanied by the flinching exclamation of a female companion that Ivan had seductively procured for the duration of two dances.

However, with the liberal intake of drink now inducing serious misalignment of vision and control of limbs, dancing with a partner was proving to be a relatively hazardous practice.

Ivan and his accomplice had successfully waggled their way through The Birdie Song, but it was the Hokey-Cokey which brought their brief liaison to a shuddering halt.

'I do apologise, my dear. I'm all arms and legs this evening!'

Just about maintaining his focus on her anxious grimace of injustice, he had little other chance of retrieving the situation. In a flash of inaudible profanity, she was gone into the night to be quickly enswathed by a myriad of jigging bodies, flashing lights and tormenting shadows.

'Oh well…' Ivan chortled as he headed for the bar. '…you win some, you lose some.'

With replenished pint pot in hand, he turned and faced the room which seemed to swell and vibrate with the pounding beat. The clock on the wall offered a blurred representation of the time, but he gradually ascertained it to be around a quarter to midnight.

And then The Hokey-Cokey started playing again.

He smiled inwardly but having shamed himself with a perilous rendition last time, remaining leant against the bar counter seemed to be the safer option for one and all.

It also occurred to him that he was probably more inebriated than he had been for a good few years. Yet, unlike the majority of those present, Ivan's mood was inclined to become slowly more sombre when drunk, as opposed to most of mankind who became temptingly frivolous and increasingly flirtatious.

Despite hopeful expectation, the sense of isolation that he had successfully staved off all evening began to return tenfold and rapidly enshrouded him in despondency as he swiftly emptied his glass.

Choosing to move position against the wall among the flitting silhouettes, he found a seat and vacantly scanned the thumping dance floor for no apparent reason. So cocooned was his attention on matters beyond that heaving room, Ivan did not immediately notice the lady standing five yards away.

The attractive, slim, blonde-haired woman, whose rib cage he had unceremoniously clouted with his right elbow earlier that evening.

From the edge of the disco floor, she shouted to be heard above the melee, which seemed destined to destroy the possibility of a re-acquaintance with the silent subject of her whims, who continued to stare vacantly into the smoky void of flashing greens, yellows and reds.

A tap on the shoulder finally roused Ivan from his mental seclusion. He glanced upwards at the preening blond, fully expectant of another earbashing.

In view of such a prospect, he decided to get his retaliation in first and beckoned her closer.

'Look…I've said I'm sorry…okay? You'll have to find another partner who can actually dance without falling all over you and treading on your toes! And as I'm sure you are now aware…that partner certainly isn't me!'

Her disappointment was evident even to the casual observer and her reluctant retreat into the heaving crowd gave a relieved Ivan little cause for further contemplation.

Then a familiar voice resonated through the relentless throb of music and boisterous chatter.

George positioned his bulky frame next to his friend.

'What the heck are you playing at, Ivan? That little cracker has had her eye on you all bleeding night! And you've just given her the brush off! Are you *mad*? Do you know she's only forty-eight!'

Ivan was fully aware of his friend's possibly justified dismay but felt little in the way of remorse regarding the issue.

'Thanks, but no thanks, George! I haven't come here to find a girlfriend. Besides, I'm way too pissed to make good company now!'

'You must be bloody barking! You're the best-looking bloke here and you've passed up a chance with the best-looking woman in the room! I suppose you're going to tell me you're more interested in gardening!'

Ivan nodded in sarcastic affirmation as his tone increased both in volume and annoyance to rise above the din.

'Well…put it like this, George. I like talking to women…of course I do. And I like talking to vegetables. But I've concluded that I much prefer talking to vegetables!'

Now his friend had little option but to voice his bewilderment.

'But *why* for Christ's sake?'

Ivan's gaze temporarily rested on the attractive blonde currently under discussion, who had now taken to the dance floor once more and proceeded to swivel her hips and torso before him whilst knowingly under his vaguely disinterested scrutiny.

She was evidently not quite thrown off the scent just yet.

'Because, my dear George, vegetables don't bloody talk back!'

The music was only momentarily outstripped by the sound of George Breeden's raucous laughter as he stood up and headed for a refill.

The revelry was abruptly halted as the deejay called all to the centre of the room and to have a drink in hand. With only ten seconds until the stroke of midnight, the communal countdown to the end of Nineteen-eighty-three commenced in earnest.

Having played a subdued role in the charade, Ivan was glad to remain aloof as the scores of dancers began to trample the floorboards once again. Yet he felt inwardly frustrated at promoting his act of self-indulgence at such a genial time of year.

Flashes of differing emotion poked at his mind at intervals, as the alcohol finally rendered him totally vulnerable to the whim of his ever-present need for reflection.

Where most cheerfully welcomed the incoming year with hopes of prosperity, Ivan could see only a long, unyielding, dark tunnel.

The imminent cessation of a life's work and career was the one guarantee that awaited him in the coming months.

As he listened to glasses colliding, feet stomping and chants erupting around the cavities of his head, the omens predicted anything but a Happy New Year for Ivan Reynolds.

WINTER TERM 1984

22

The tenth. The second Tuesday in January.

A different year; a different story.

A familiar beginning; an uncertain ending.

Standing tall in his new work outfit, Ivan could not shrug off the nagging sense of time eroding away as he half-heartedly scrutinised his image in the bedroom mirror.

The first, tentative step toward retirement was to be taken today.

The final term of his tenure at Littleholt Secondary.

The last parade as Head of the Mathematics department.

The last stand of an undefeated warrior.

Inspecting the cut and cloth of his deep grey three-piece suit, he mentally assessed encroaching time and its accumulative fate.

Future passing minutes would quickly evolve into lost hours.

Precious days ahead would amass and collate into weeks.

Nearly four months would helplessly slip through his fingers and then, the name Ivan Reynolds would only be occasionally whispered in fleeting reference to the past.

A mere myth. Linked by rumour to a bygone era, in a school community that would no longer feel compelled to tread lightly in respect of his presence.

No more to be the dominant phantom of the corridors, but to be a dead ghost. Finally, to be taken by progress and immediately relegated to annals of vague memory.

A man who would no longer cast his daunting shadow upon those brightly lit classrooms.

An icon would be gone.

A legend would be no more.

The truly plaguing notion was that thirty-five years in teaching would soon be rendered into a virtual irrelevance.

He had long since attained the ambition to prove his worth as some academic commander after undertaking the hardships of military regimentation as a callow youth.

But that timid boy soon became a man.

A man who had confidently kicked out against the conformity that bound his upbringing, redefining it as his own sword of power to wield according to his own preference.

Forging a personal path, he had enforced a new authority upon susceptible people, and it had been accepted as the benchmark of his educational ruling for nearly four decades.

But such a quest for near godliness had encouraged inevitable casualties.

He had administered painful scars on the battlefield; both in the family home and among the generations of youngsters who dared question his burning yet baseless desire for cultural immortality.

Self-propelled in his mission to exert maximum superiority over those around him, he felt little for those that had strayed helplessly in his relentless wake.

And it was this strange addiction to such hollow victory that still motivated him so.

Or so he believed until very recently.

Yet now, with all willing foes seemingly vanquished, the fuel for his inner fire was running steadily dry.

And the angst of carrying such knowledge was never more apparent than at that moment of self-analysis in the dress mirror.

The drug that he had gorged himself on for so many years was in imminent depletion. The hunger was still in evidence, yet the source of sustenance would soon vanish.

The soul-driven habit of affecting, motivating, and influencing needy young souls would soon rebound unto him from an empty shell.

No more the chance to expose and confront; to punish and redeem.

To nurture and enlighten; to encourage and support.

In short, the essence of his very core was soon to become redundant.

And the prospect terrified Ivan Reynolds as he straightened his tie and traced a moist fingertip across both eyebrows.

Then the tempting thought dawned.

Maybe, just maybe, it would be appropriate to indulge in one last feast at the table.

A farewell sampling of the conflict he so enjoyed.

One final hunt in the forest.

The last duel before hanging up the holster.

To bloat his yearning appetite in the hope it would remain sated forever.

Perhaps now was the moment for true glory and the lasting establishment of his status.

As he clasped the silver-framed yet dormant images of his far distant loved ones and gazed upon their static radiance, the irony became stiflingly cruel.

That he had ably managed to mentor, guide, and advise so many for so long. Yet he had never accomplished the same feats with his own flesh and blood.

Indeed, far from it.

Embarking on his curtain call, the real fears of a secretly vulnerable man encroached, again clawing him back to the horrendous misgivings of his past.

A very real possibility lay before him awaiting discovery.

The galling truth, that his role as a supremely successful teacher had merely been an inadequate substitute for that of a dismally failed father.

The infinite harshness tore into him as he set the photographs gently down onto the dresser, being careful not to avert his gaze from that of his wife and child.

The renewed notion of guilt stayed with him and accompanied his descent to the hallway.

The agonising reality drilled into him, that when his duties as an accomplished educator are eventually relinquished, it would only stand to logic and reason that all that would remain, was a failed father.

*****

Ivan could not recall any previous Christmas leaving him with such a bitter aftertaste. The festive period had simply served to highlight the elements of his life that filled him with nothing less than heartache.

As he drove to school on the first day of the new term, his anxiety and resentment had never simmered so threateningly close to boiling point.

He had always believed he loved teaching.

Yet now thought he hated it.

History stalked him relentlessly.

He had shown bigotry to his family; and now dearly wished to accommodate them so.

No music accompanied his journey. The entertainer that had triumphed in the school concert had now receded; banished by demons that would not weaken in their cause.

In with the New Year; and soon to be out with the old, cold, bold figure of folklore.

The mere sight of the school building encouraged the bitterness to swell within him. That now so offensive silhouette hung against the lifeless backcloth of a winter sky, churning his stomach with fury.

The first damning indictment greeted his arrival.

His usual parking space was occupied. Cursing the driver responsible, Ivan swung into another spot and wrenched on the handbrake.

Blinkered by a frothing anger, he locked the car and made for the main school doors, acknowledging nothing and no-one as he waded past the busy throng of pupils in their woollen hats and scarves.

On entering the bustling staff room, he exchanged forced pleasantries with favoured colleagues and ignored the polite greetings of the younger influx of teachers.

All in the room could see the black cloud hovering menacingly over his head as he reclined with the crossword.

Most strived to vacate the room to avoid the imminent storm. But a few others braved the uncertain stare of dark ice and opted to try and shatter Ivan's evident despondency.

'Enjoy the break?' chipped Matt Jenkins.

'Someone's obviously glad to be back!' quipped Bob Davidson.

'Not long now, Ivan! Happy New Year!' added Sarah Green.

Grunts and nods were representative of Ivan's feigned act of sparse civility. Failing to summon the will to expend any further effort into the charade, he duly rose from his armchair and left the room as the registration bell droned.

Emptying his pigeonhole outside reception caused another reason for barely muttered profanity as he clutched the handful of memos.

'Damned waste of paper. It's all *bullshit*!'

Carol Shaw overheard his low-key outburst and readily offered her support as she protruded an inquiring head from the stationary office doorway.

'Thought I recognised those jovial tones! You alright, Ivan? You look and sound fed up!'

'That's because I *am* bloody fed up!' he snapped.

Both the receptionist and Head of First Year watched bemused as he strode determinedly away down the corridor, not sure if his comments were directed at them or some other unseen unfortunate specimen.

Stomping his ascent to room ten, the mood thickened and swirled. His turn of pace had beaten the incoming congregation of pupils. The landing was empty.

Locking himself in the silent classroom, he dropped his briefcase to the floor and threw the internal correspondence on the desk.

Removing his spectacles, Ivan wandered among the empty tables and rubbed his tired eyes as if attempting to encourage some foresight into what the day might bring.

He listened to the distant voices emanating from the playground below, which gradually became the louder voices outside the door after the first bell of the day continued to toll relentlessly.

Noises and voices that penetrated his thoughts.

So stark; so unruly; so untamed.

He would shut them up.

He had not been banished from their schedules just yet.

Checking his pocket watch, he waited for another full minute before inhaling deeply and moving to the door as the din created by dozens of pupils gnawed at his conscience.

With a turn of the key and the click of the latch, he appeared in the open doorway to stand imposingly before them.

The unkempt and excitable group of pupils instinctively swivelled to attention as their master appeared.

Now it was back to hostilities.

To the final offensive.

'TWO LINES! IN SILENCE! NOW! YOU CANNOT HAVE FORGOTTEN THE RULES IN TWO WEEKS! I SAID *SILENCE*!'

Partially obstructing the doorway, Ivan observed each red-cheeked face as it nudged tentatively passed him. He had amused himself by the conveyance of power he effortlessly exuded. The children, having slowly filed in, stood obligingly behind their desks, awaiting the order to be seated.

With the order duly given, the entire room remained soundless in anticipation of the attendance check. Just as Ivan opened the register, the door burst open, revealing the panting form of Trevor Sims.

His classmates watched with bated breath as the interrogation began, with Ivan immediately jumping back to his feet to accost the young latecomer.

As the teacher forcibly slammed the swinging door to secure his belated victim inside, the second eruption of the day commenced in earnest.

'MISTER SIMS! LATE AGAIN! THE FIRST DAY OF TERM AND YOU ARE LATE! TWENTY PRESS-UPS! NOW!'

The boy's expression altered from relief at having made it to school to one of instant disappointment as he dropped his rucksack and knelt at the teacher's feet.

'DOES THE CLASS GET AN EXPLANATION, MISTER SIMS? ARE WE NOT DESERVING OF SOME APOLOGY FOR THIS RUDENESS?'

Ivan stood over the boy with hands clasped behind his back.

A tiny, breathless voice emitted the latest excuse.

'My…my…new bike…chain…came off…sir…' puffed young Sims as he began his punishment. The room remained quiet as the discomforting spectacle played itself out.

'SO WHY DO YOU NOT GET A BICYCLE THAT IS SUITABLE, MISTER SIMS? FAULTY EQUIPMENT WILL ALWAYS LET YOU DOWN! COME ALONG. THAT'S ONLY ELEVEN!'

'I…had to push it…from the train station…sir…it snapped…sir.'

Ivan peered at the bobbing head of his quarry as he counted out loud for the benefit of all present.

'AND I SEE THAT, YET AGAIN, YOU HAVE OPTED TO ATTIRE IN WHITE SOCKS! HOW MANY TIMES, MISTER SIMS? HOW MANY TIMES WILL YOU PERSIST?'

Now there was no reply from the unwashed juvenile, who continued to address all his efforts into completing the penance.

'THAT'S YOUR TWENTY! GET YOURSELF TO YOUR FEET AND TAKE TO YOUR SEAT…WRETCHED ARTICLE!'

Trevor hauled himself upright, grabbed his bag and shuffled disconsolately to his desk. Wiping his perspiring forehead as he claimed his chair, he briefly noticed a look of intensive sympathy from Jenny Douglas.

The register call was duly commenced with all boys answering in the affirmative. The girls duly followed suit, but the process came to a shuddering halt when Ivan reached the letter J.

He waited patiently for exactly five seconds whilst Hilary Johnson made faces and threw pieces of pencil rubber at her classmates across the aisle.

Sitting calmly in his chair, he continued to observe the exhibition of insolence as his inclination to explode was encouraged ever further.

Not a word was said as he rose to his feet yet again and moved quickly towards the wilfully ignorant offender.

Finally, she turned to face front after an eleventh-hour warning came from her friend, but it was far too late.

Yelping in surprise, Hilary was startled as she felt her left arm become clamped in the grip of the form tutor.

Limply rising from her chair, she followed his lead from her desk and across to the door.

Ivan did not utter a word as he escorted her through the doorway and onto the landing.

Without warning, he released his hold on her arm. Unexpectedly liberated, she stumbled before losing her footing completely.

She then fell into the hanging line of coats, groping at the jutting wooden pegs in her struggle for balance before concluding the move by ending up on the floor.

Hilary Johnson's emotions began to stir. A combination of upset and shock overwhelmed her as she engaged glares with her irate form tutor.

Yet even in the face of towering authority, her resistance held firm.

'You'll pay for that, Reynolds. My dad will have you now!'

Ivan stood motionless as the gravity of what had just transpired swiftly pummelled his conscience.

He was suddenly in mental freefall.

He knew instantly he had administered a grave error of judgement.

Succumbing to regret, he turned away, leaving Hilary to pick herself up from the floor of the top landing. She barely heard the door of room ten slam shut behind her as she whimpered outside, leaving her form tutor to finish taking the register against a soundless backdrop of stifling apprehension.

Finally, the pupils of 1RY were freed from their keeper.

As they trailed from the room without a single whisper, Jenny Douglas hesitated by the door. She quietly observed the teacher as he slouched forlornly into his chair, very possibly regretting the episode just enacted.

She saw his evident torment yet failed to comprehend its cause. Clutching her schoolbag, she hovered hoping he might just acknowledge her wavering presence. Ivan sat with hands clasped on his lap, watching the back wall of the room through his intimidating black mask.

And still she waited, until the last possible instant, when eventually a soft, mellow tone carried towards her and halted her intended exit.

'Miss Douglas…'

She nervously twitched in response yet felt so thankful that he had recognised her desire to speak.

Yet he still did not look directly at the girl with the pigtails.

'Yes…sir?' she replied, tentatively.

Ivan unclasped his fingers and folded his arms.

He maintained an averted gaze, which had now been slightly re-directed beyond the window toward the distant low winter sun.

'Miss Douglas…please…forgive me for my bad manners. I am somewhat…unsettled…this morning. And I owe an apology.'

Jenny became puzzled; almost concerned as she offered some support.

Yet she felt confident enough to venture an opinion.

'Hilary is very rude, sir. She hasn't learned very much. She deserved it. But…Trevor didn't, sir. You've really upset him.'

Now Ivan finally turned to look at the young girl standing determinedly in the classroom doorway.

'I did not refer to the others. My apology pertained to *you*…Miss Douglas. There is something I have to say to *you*…and…as yet…I have not done so.'

Jenny became suddenly wary of her solitude and potential vulnerability, yet she felt no fear.

'*What* is it you forgot to say to me, sir?'

He titled his head forward, directed his attention to her, and peered over the rim of his spectacles so she might see the humility in his eyes.

'I wish to say…thank you. Thank you for the Christmas present you gave me. It was a wondrous gesture on your part.'

Jenny Douglas wanted to continue with the exchange, yet the appropriate words escaped her when she most needed them.

Instead, she simply nodded in overwhelming embarrassment and hastily left the room.

Now contemplating the undoubted consequences of his foolhardy and reckless behaviour, the disgruntled teacher slowly rose to his feet and moved to address the incoming class.

Dejection and remorse being his unshakable dual companions as he did so.

23

Ivan greeted the arrival of morning break with an unfamiliar sense of unease. According to reports, Hilary Johnson had not appeared at her lessons after the incident during registration.

Word had begun to break about the possible causes for her absence and Ivan was in full preparation for the inevitable inquisition that would follow.

Trooping a preoccupied descent to the ground floor, he felt the desperate need for a black coffee and some quality time in seclusion with the newspaper.

Entering the staff room, he felt the eyes all around immediately boring into him as he weaved a path to the drinks station and retrieved a mug from the shelf.

Bob Davidson wasted little time in conveying a low-key warning of the ensuing rumours that had surfaced.

'Not the best start to the new year, is it? For a man flying so high recently you've crashed and burned pretty sharp-ish! Don't tell me you laid a hand on the girl, for Christ's sake! Don't tell me *that*, Ivan!'

Ivan was already tiring of the expected curiosity but upheld the vital necessity to appear unfazed under scrutiny.

'It was nothing, Bob. The kid's a bloody nuisance and I dealt with her. I haven't the patience these days for pupils that try it on. She knows the rules and still fancied a shot. Well…she picked the wrong bloody day, today. Simple as that.'

Silence followed Ivan's mildly defensive stance, although both teachers knew that repercussions on the issue were unavoidable.

Matt Jenkins walked in the room and made straight for the Head of Mathematics.

Lighting a cigarette, Matt leaned close to Ivan and whispered.

'You're lucky I found her. Otherwise, small as she is, I think she'd have been keen to kick the door off its hinges to have a go back. A feisty one is that Johnson girl.'

Ivan stared through the developing smokescreen.

He brushed past his apprentice and made himself comfortable in the usual armchair.

'You seem to be forgetting something, Matthew. Whatever happens…it doesn't really matter anymore, does it?'

Matt drew heavily on his nicotine as he argued the point.

'That's total *rubbish* Ivan and we both know it! Don't try and tell me you're not bothered! No one believes that for a second!'

Appearing from the corner of the staff room, Phil Holmes joined in on the conversation, evidently relishing the prospect of again seeing Ivan in strife over his actions.

'Taylor will have you for this, Reynolds! You won't get away with it this time. It's going to be made illegal to touch the kids, you know! The corporal approach is going to be a thing of the past! Did you not know that? The bill is being submitted to Parliament.'

Ivan did not avert his eyes from the front page as he sipped his coffee and hissed a reply.

'Stay out of this, Holmes. And play another bloody record. I've heard this one much too often. Mind your own damned business for once in your bloody life.'

The younger opponent was unwilling to let things lie.

'Oh…but that's the whole point, isn't it! We *can't* stay out of it, can we? Because your prehistoric stupidity won't allow us to, will it? Every move you make represents the entire staff at this school! Every word you utter *is* our business. The Board of Governors will want your head on a stick, mate!'

Now severely vexed by the unwelcome attention, Ivan dropped his newspaper onto the table and stood up with fists clenched.

'I am anything…but…your…*mate*! This is *my* battle, Philip. I am quite capable of mopping up any mess without arrogant upstarts such as you unnecessarily stoking the fire further.'

The smug grin on the face of the physics teacher caused Ivan to grind his teeth and take a sensible step back from the confrontation as the goading persisted.

Phil Holmes detected the sudden vulnerability in his elder colleague.

'Well, at least you admit to messing up! I'll give you that much, you old fossil. Good luck! I think you're going to need it!'

Satisfied he had made his point, Phil Holmes turned on his heel and left the room, which had now become engorged with eager colleagues wanting to know the facts behind the morning's hot gossip.

Ivan eyed the speculative throng through his protective dark visor, fully aware that he was indeed likely to be facing calamitous consequences.

Considering his only current option to be that of a steadfast silence, he sat himself down once again and re-shuffled the Daily Mail to the crossword page.

*****

Whilst never willing to openly surrender admission to the extreme unlikelihood of a mistake, Ivan privately recognised he had committed an almighty blunder as the remaining day's lessons played out to an atmosphere of distinct tension.

The usual banter with the older pupils was noticeably absent.

Indeed, Ivan's intolerant mood had manifested itself for the duration and he reacted vehemently to the mildest provocation.

As he wrote instructions on the blackboard for his Third Year class after morning break, the grating tone of a digital watch alarm resonated from the rear of the room.

Spinning in anger, Ivan launched the stick of chalk at the supposed culprit, just missing the teenager's face by inches.

'TURN THAT OFF AND REMOVE IT FROM YOUR WRIST, BOY! IF I EVER HEAR IT DISRUPT MY CLASS AGAIN THERE WILL BE HELL TO PAY!'

The corridors had become threaded by varying accounts of the Hilary Johnson debacle and a rather erratic Ivan Reynolds was now in evidence for all to see.

The lunchtime bell afforded him some welcome respite from the microscope, and he purposely delayed dining until the last sitting had all but cleared from the main hall.

Alone and facing the bleak view of the playing fields, he forked at the tepid portion of fish pie and lumps of mashed potato. He juggled morsels around his mouth with aching regret tormenting his every chew.

It was true to say that the first few hours of the new term could not have elapsed more disastrously. In weary concession to the meal before him, Ivan placed his cutlery on the half-full plate and pushed it across the table.

In his own mind he perceived echoed whispers of distrust and fingers of contempt poked toward him as the accused. He believed that words of derision were now being associated with his impeccable name and whilst he maintained an air of indifference, the knowledge of such discussion among the staff and pupils cut him deeply.

Notoriety and respect had been his greatest allies in previous years, yet now, at the supposed peak of his repute, such negativity from all directions was a painful burden he did not wish to court.

His legacy lay wounded; no longer quite so revered.

And he had been solely responsible for the instant decline in his own once admirable standing.

This long-time paragon of discipline and order was now reduced to eating in solitary confinement. Now declared by many to be a bully, a monster, and a tyrant. Yet unbeknown to most at Littleholt Secondary, such sentiment was not entirely unfamiliar to him.

Ivan now perceived the notion that most pupils viewed him with undue caution and possible resentment.

Most pupils; but not all.

As he gazed vacantly into noiseless space, a familiar voice suddenly sounded beside him.

Turning attention to his right shoulder, he saw the diminutive figure of Trevor Sims awaiting the opportunity to speak.

Instantly pleased by the unexpected approach, Ivan smiled and softened his voice to reassure the boy.

'Mister Sims? Can I be of some assistance?'

Young Trevor shifted weight from foot to foot, unsure of the wisdom behind his ambition.

'I wanted to speak to you, sir. If that is okay?'

Ivan found himself wholly gratified by the unexpected company and invited him to be seated.

'The stage is yours, Mister Sims. How may I help?'

The eleven-year-old ruffian never averted his attention from his form tutor.

'You don't look…very happy, sir…are you alright? I didn't mean to be late today. But me mam likes me to do a paper round for pocket money and I was late for that and then me chain snapped on the way to school and…then me white socks…I didn't mean to make you angry.'

Ivan turned fully in his chair and engaged with the heart-wrenching sincerity of the young man perched beside him.

He took Trevor's comments on board and gently replied.

'Mister Sims…I was very wrong to berate you earlier. For that…I am eternally sorry. Please accept my sincerest apologies. My day started badly and has continued in steep decline as you've seen for yourself. Are we still friends? I dearly hope so as I fear that after today, I won't have too many friends left! Please say you are still on my side, Mister Sims.'

Shocked by his form tutor's semi-humorous yet emotive admission, Trevor remained in his chair desiring to continue with the exchange.

'You're still my favourite teacher at the school, sir. Don't worry about that. But I'm worried. Will you be banned, sir? They say you will be in trouble for what happened to Hilary. We hope not. She's horrible. She asked for it.'

Ivan sighed deeply as he considered his uncertain position.

'Mister Sims. *Trouble* is my middle name. But please do not concern yourself with my problems. I shall live to fight another day.'

The rough-looking boy smiled.

An impish yet relieved smirk conveyed a genuine sense of support for the teacher sitting before him.

'I don't want you to be in trouble, sir. And I'll wear different socks tomorrow. I promise. Me mam has had to work a bit over Christmas. She says we're a bit behind with the washing.'

Ivan smiled in response.

'Don't tell me…its wash day today, yes?'

Trevor nodded eagerly.

'Run along, Mister Sims. Don't waste what's left of the lunch break talking to an old misery like me. Go and play. It's soon time for the bell. And by the way…thank you so kindly for coming to speak to me.'

With that, the urchin was gone, having deposited a little softness into a stony, cold heart.

The possibility that he may well have misconceived reaction to his error began to inflate Ivan with hope.

It had not occurred to him for one moment that the children may well have been grateful for his actions. Yet young Trevor Sims had unwittingly set the seed for some overdue positive thinking.

*****

Ivan did not loiter around the premises at home time. No sooner had the bell signified the end of the doomed day, than Ivan had locked up room ten and ventured covertly to his car.

It was a painfully irksome for him to think that he may have lost the respect of his pupils.

Respect had been the pivotal factor to his years of success.

As he drove homeward, thoughts turned over in his mind about the past and the future.

Without respect, a teacher is rendered impotent.

But even more worrying was that a sense of self-doubt had slowly and progressively encroached during the day.

Maybe Hilary Johnson was not the devilish child he perceived her to be. Maybe, just maybe, his hardy principles were outdated and could rightly be deemed unacceptable by the modern bodies of authority.

Perhaps he was indeed a bully; a tyrant; a monster as the potential rumours may have established.

Could it be that this long-time paragon of law and order had got it so badly wrong?

The solitude at home did not allay his concerns.

His loneliness only heightened the inner tension he vainly fought against. The quandary ground away within the cogs of his brain, providing nothing in the way of illumination to the suffocating darkness.

Yet still the inner conflict raged as the night wore on, until his mindset finally cemented some direction.

Professional and personal pride could not allow him to show contrition.

An example needed to be made of the girl and he was the ordained person with the responsibility of setting that example.

He had never - and nor *would* he never - cower away from duty.

When called to arms, Ivan Reynolds was nothing if not immediate and precise.

Yet, even as he half-heartedly convinced himself of the purity of his principles, the inescapable photographic proof of his penchant for failure sat staring back at him as he slouched on the edge of the bed in his pyjamas.

With nightcap of whiskey in hand, he dared not look back at their knowing gaze.

Despite having taught many lessons over many years, the realisation that he himself had possibly learned very little, was the one gnawing thought that accompanied his eventual surrender to slumber.

24

'Taylor's had a word, Carol. I'm in at nine for the summit with the Johnsons.'

'I'll go up and take your register. You'd better prepare yourself.'

The Head of First Year's tone of cautious assurance was little crumb of comfort to Ivan as he dejectedly sat in the staff room draining his coffee mug with an angered slurp.

The first bell of the day had tolled and as his counterparts slowly vacated, Ivan felt very pensive with his thoughts.

Searching vainly for initial crossword answers, his mind remained blank, forcing his gaze to divert temporarily beyond the window to the empty playground.

The time on the pocket watch declared that he had five and a half minutes left until his presence was required in the Headmaster's office just along the corridor.

An accusation of assault had been levelled.

As defendant, Ivan Reynolds would need to provide a sound argument against such a damning allegation, fully aware that being found guilty of such gross misconduct would certainly bring a premature and bitter end to his teaching career.

Carol remained by her colleague's side as he aimlessly began to wander the room. With her own thoughts centred on his potential plight, she was startled by the sound of Ivan's mug being slammed on the work surface next to the sink.

He peered above his ebony mask to usher her away.

'Thank you, Carol. You'd better get up there and see to them…run along and…I'll…probably see you later.'

She hovered in the doorway, imparting one final offering of consolation.

'You'll be okay. Just don't…don't lose you temper. Say the right things. Play the diplomat.'

Ivan turned to face her with a forced smirk of incredulity underscoring his black spectacles.

'The right things, Carol? I did the *right* thing in the first place! It's what I've been doing for the last thirty bloody years! It's called teaching! And now suddenly, I'm not allowed to do my job without some little blighter wanting to change the world because they got a clip around the ear! In fact, it didn't even classify as that much! Bloody kids…'

She took a deep, sympathetic breath whilst placing one foot in the outer corridor.

'Well…like I said. Keep your anger under wraps! Times are changing, Ivan. I don't like it any more than you do. But you can rise above this little episode, I'm sure. Don't let it get the better of you. Not this late in the game.'

Ivan shook his head and purposely increased his volume.

'It won't *work*, Carol! Soft-soaping pupils is a path to *disaster*! You mark my words! If that is the future, it will soon be the end of discipline in all schools! The pupils will be in charge and good men like Geoff Taylor will be out of a job!'

Carol pointed at the irate head of the maths department with a jabbing finger of warning.

'Just play the game. Even if you don't mean it! Go through the motions wherever possible. Don't give Taylor any cause for doubt and he'll come down on your side. You'll see!'

Ivan displayed a mildly sarcastic thumbs-up and gestured beyond the door.

'Tell my form group I hope I'll see them this afternoon, will you?'

With a departing nod of tentative relief, Carol was gone, leaving Ivan to ready himself for the microscope.

*****

'Mister Reynolds…do come in! Take a seat. Meet Mister and Mrs. Johnson.'

Hilary's parents eyed the disenchanted entrant with due suspicion; their mutual expressions conveying little other than grave hostility.

Ivan closed the door behind him and stood tall with his shoulders pushed back.

Presenting the image of the smooth, experienced professional, he offered an outstretched hand of greeting to the visitors, adorned his expression with a false smile and bid them good morning.

Reluctantly, both parents reciprocated the gesture of civility, although their perhaps understandable coldness towards him was also very apparent.

Ivan calmly pulled a chair across the carpet and sat adjacent to the headmaster's large oak desk.

All four occupants of the room endured a temporary atmosphere of very uneasy silence until Geoff Taylor commenced proceedings as tactfully as possible.

'I've asked Mister Reynolds to join us as I feel it would give some balance to the issue at hand. Perhaps if he presented an alternative view of things, it might affect our current perception of the matter. Maybe help us come to some positive conclusions.'

Hilary's father was a spiteful-looking brute with short brown hair and a drooping moustache.

He eyed Ivan with contempt before snarling his first contribution.

'What you *actually* mean is…give him the chance to wriggle out of it? Is that what you're after? I can't say I'm pleased to finally meet you Mister Reynolds. But I'm looking forward to hearing your answers. And they'd better be bloody good ones and all!'

Trying desperately not to display his unflinching disinterest in the scenario, Ivan crossed his legs and began to fiddle with his wedding ring by way of distraction.

Geoff Taylor, meanwhile, was anxious to dampen down any aggressive slant that may be present by re-capping the truths of the matter.

'Now, as I understand it, Hilary became upset during registration yesterday morning and was accompanied to reception by another teacher, Mister Jenkins. From there, the school contacted you and you collected Hilary from the premises. Is this correct?'

Now it was the girl's mother who sprayed her anger across the void.

'Dead right, it is! And I'd only just got to work, too! I lost a full day's pay yesterday because of what he did to my daughter! And I wouldn't have thought I'll get paid for sitting here talking about it today, either!'

Ivan remained silent and motionless staring blankly at the wall opposite. He seemed barely aware of the Johnsons' very audible and double-pronged offensive, which only served to fuel the vexation of the girl's mother who quickly noticed Ivan's apparent indifference.

'Totally distraught she was, yesterday! Beside herself! Inconsolable! Are you listening to me? It's not right for teachers to go around attacking kids! He should be sacked! At the very least, investigated and suspended! He's a disgrace!'

The Head raised a hand to quell the sparking friction whilst casually glancing in Ivan's direction.

Still the disposition of his colleague remained unimpressed at the predicament he found himself immersed in.

'Well…as I said…this is why I have invited Mister Reynolds along this morning. So that he can hear your comments for himself and establish some facts in response.'

'ARE YOU CALLING OUR HILARY A LIAR?'

Geoff Taylor suddenly realised his unintended faux-pas and became aware he might just be verging on digging a large hole for himself and the accused.

'Mister Johnson…I am suggesting nothing of the sort. But in these emotive situations, events can easily become distorted.'

Ivan sensed that the time may be near for him to present his case. But still he remained sitting contentedly beside his superior, concentrating on the varying pieces of Littleholt memorabilia that decorated the shelves and walls of the office.

He had made a strict pledge to himself not to utter a single word until requested to do so.

However, the Headmaster's regular glares at his most senior member of staff suggested that it might just be appropriate to offer some form of a response on his own behalf.

Yet still Ivan retained his rightful distance from the debate, causing not a little frustration for the plaintiffs facing him.

'Seems an open and shut case to me!' snapped Hilary's father.

'A silent man is a guilty man!' claimed his wife. 'He's got no answers because he bloody hurt my little girl! He's done it alright! He's nothing but a bully! And he knows he's been found out! So…Headmaster…what you going to do about him?'

Geoff Taylor could no longer avoid the inevitable.

'Please…Mister and Mrs. Johnson…let us all now listen to what Mister Reynolds has to say. I'm sure he can allay your concerns.'

Hilary's father folded his arms and slouched back into his seat. With features resembling granite, he was evidently not in the mood to have his mind changed easily.

'I doubt it, sunshine! I doubt it very much!'

A blanket of unease was thrown upon the room once again. The Head was beginning to recognise certain familiar signals from Ivan that he had become vaguely accustomed to over the years.

Having believed that the Head of Mathematics might just crumble under the strain of such business, it quickly dawned on him that Ivan was indeed more than ready to respond and would never wilt under such pressure.

And the eventual acceptance of this fact also brought with it an overdue sense of relief.

The unprecedented lack of emotion that Ivan performed so ably was in fact the calm before one almighty storm.

And Geoff Taylor now had little option but to invite the clouds to break.

'Ivan…please…help us out here? Talk to the Johnsons. We all require some level of clarity on what actually happened yesterday.'

Ivan observed his accusers through the concealing lenses of his spectacles, now relishing the opportunity to strike back.

He eased himself up from the chair, stood beside the Headmaster and defiantly folded his arms to match the gestures of the opposition.

The Johnsons studied his every move with natural suspicion.

The first distant clap of thunder was accompanied by intermittent spots of acidic rain as Ivan's initial tirade began to grind into first gear.

'Mister…and Mrs…Johnson. I have sat here in graceful peace…with my professional integrity at your mercy…and only now…even with my unequivocal guilt etched firmly in your minds…you afford me the dubious honour of mounting a so-called…defence.'

The icy silence remained as Ivan continued.

'Well…I am afraid…I will not be lowering myself to enter this unfounded and frankly irritating argument. Please do not ask me to expand on my reasoning, because my own personal opinions will undoubtedly be in conflict with your own. This circle of unjustifiable intrigue must not be permitted to turn any further and I for one will not assist its futile cycle.'

Geoff Taylor felt a combined pang of allegiance and pride having considered his colleague's articulate response. Yet similarly, he detected rapidly increasing unrest from across the table.

As he rightly suspected, the Johnsons were far from finished in their quest to tarnish the name of Ivan Reynolds. Hilary's father jabbed an accusatory index finger as he interrupted the teacher.

'So, you're saying that nothing happened yesterday? That our little girl is making it all up? THAT YOU NEVER TOUCHED HER?'

Ivan fingered his chin as he observed the man's frothing features. Hilary's parents were slowly being ensnared into a dead end by the man they wished to see reprimanded. The Headmaster was now powerless to retrieve them from a certain defeat.

More vitriol was offloaded by the parents upon the unwavering target.

Yet their mission to discredit Ivan was losing ground by the second as they began to lose their tempers and subsequently lose sight of the argument.

Against the backdrop of vocalised anger, the so-called perpetrator remained stoically quiet until he opted to intercede and shower the parental jury with some hard truth.

'Mister…and Mrs Johnson. Let me reassure you of some facts in this matter. My experience, credibility, and exemplary record display ample evidence of my ability to teach. Your cries of derision cannot…and will not…blemish me. The secondary factor of this circus will no doubt give you cause for remonstration. However, this is beyond both my control…and concern.'

Clearly bemused by Ivan's monologue, Hilary's mother hissed her disapproval from the other side of the desk.

'Why don't you talk properly? Why speak in this fancy language? Talk straight and stop the riddles, man!'

Glancing briefly at the Headmaster, Ivan continued with his statement.

'As I was saying…the secondary factor. In the months since making my acquaintance, your daughter has proved herself to be thoroughly insolent and knowingly ignorant. She is an unwilling pupil and an uncooperative distraction for many. She possesses no manners and portrays herself to be a callous and rude individual.'

The mother and the father moved to the edge of their chairs with burning fury simmering to escape.

Yet still the accused stood defiant and continued to disarm them.

'Furthermore, I can quantify and perhaps enlighten the both of you to the fact that your daughter is an adept bully and proven thief. All these despicable characteristics have been honed and nurtured long before she came to this school. I therefore conclude that the blame for her disposition and personality…cannot ever…and will not ever…be laid at my door.'

Temporarily stunned by the belittling proclamations, Hilary's parents sat speechless for a few contemplative seconds. But the eventual registration of Ivan's standpoint only prompted further protests from the red-faced father.

'What do you mean…a bully…and a thief? How *dare* you? Who the bloody hell do you think you are? *You're* the bloody bully, sunshine! *You're* the one going around smacking children! *You're* the bleeding lunatic around here!'

Still Ivan remained un-swayed.

Still with arms folded and still maintaining the position adjacent to Geoff Taylor's chair, the defendant returned serve.

'Mister Johnson…I suggest you be very careful with the slanderous remarks. The influences over your daughter poisoned her soul long before I came into her life. Perhaps I could propose that you both look closer to home in attempting to discover why she is such a disobedient and affronting young girl.'

Hilary's father roared back his reply.

'HANG ON A BLOODY MINUTE! ARE YOU BLAMING *US*? ARE YOU SAYING IT'S *OUR* FAULT THAT YOU CAN'T CONTROL YOUR PUPILS? YOU ARE UNBELIEVEABLE, MATE! YOU ARE AN ABSOLUTE CLOWN!'

Ivan smirked without remorse and raised a forefinger to exaggerate a sense of establishment.

'Ahh…Mister Johnson…that word you use so freely…a word so important in school life. Control! *All* children need controlling! It is a vital part of their education. But be very wary. Please do not surrender the power of control to teachers and then question their interpretation of that power. If you are not careful, you will erode the very authority that education exudes. This is a very dangerous path to follow.'

'So, control to you means manhandling the children then, does it?' sneered Hilary's mother.

Ivan raised his head high and engaged his gaze with the cabinet on the far wall that contained the school's sporting silverware.

With a deep, assured breath, he continued.

'I have never…ever…willingly upset any child in my care.'

'Except for our Hilary, you mean!' rasped the father.

'As I have already conveyed…and you yourselves have noticeably failed to dispute…the girl is an accomplished liar! Her word is not to be trusted! But apparently, my word is to be trusted even less so. I proclaim this debate to be beyond any amicable resolution. How much more time must I waste talking to these people, Geoffrey?'

The Headmaster was jolted at the mention of his first name.

And was jolted from a temporary personal fascination with the exchange.

Reverting to the realm of ceremonial master, he readily attempted to bring matters to a close.

The Johnsons were expectant of some form of apology from either teacher but were about to be disappointed.

In his heart of hearts, Geoff Taylor found himself bound by unquestioned loyalty to his colleague.

'Okay…it is evident that continuing this meeting will get no one anywhere fast.'

Ivan concurred with practiced assuredness.

'There is no argument from my corner, Geoffrey. If anybody wishes to cross examine my aptitude and application, by any means deemed appropriate, then they should feel at liberty to do so…'

The Head of Mathematics then turned to the extremely disgruntled and dejected parents slouched before him.

'…but do not sit there on your self-appointed backsides…flinging mud…in the vein hope that some of it might just stick! It is a road to inconsequence and a plan that is doomed to fail.'

Hilary's father now jumped up from his chair and waved a fist angrily at the chosen subject of scorn.

'So, you're not even going to say *sorry*? For my daughter's state of mind and the inconvenience you have caused everyone? The first day back after Christmas and you carry on like this? And you show absolutely no concern whatsoever?'

Ivan remained completely unfazed by the gestures and posturing of the shorter, infuriated father and replied with simple logic.

'Mister Johnson…the incidence of time is barely relevant. The cause of your daughter's problems is…not me…I'm afraid….'

'YOU'RE TALKING IN BLOODY RIDDLES AGAIN!' the father barked.

Ivan stared down at the irate figure.

'Maybe it is *me* who warrants an apology…for your scurrilous attempt to denounce my good name? After all, I gave no permission for her to leave the premises. We can't have children wandering out of the place willy-nilly, can we? It's against the rules!'

'But you threw her out of the class!' the father chomped.

'I simply removed a disturbance. I did not tell her to go home!'

As a stark indication that the accusers were now aware of their imminent defeat, Elaine Johnson left her chair and moved toward the door.

'Steve…come on! We've wasted our time! I knew they wouldn't want to listen.'

The teachers watched without further word as Hilary's parents hovered angrily in the doorway.

'You're not wrong, there. I thought this school had a good reputation. The idiots seem to be running the asylum these days!'

'Steve…COME ON!'

The Johnsons exited into the corridor and slammed the Head's office door behind them. Ivan placed his hands into his trouser pockets and watched studiously through the partially closed blinds.

Confirming the departure of the aggrieved visitors, he smiled and pulled out his pocket-watch, oblivious to the swelling frustrations of the man sat beside him.

Unexpectedly, it was now Geoff Taylor's turn to launch an offensive.

'For Christ's bleeding sake, Ivan! You've got *one* term left to go! Twelve bloody weeks! What is your problem? What's with the sudden desire to instigate a one-man bad publicity campaign?'

Mildly perturbed by the Head's reaction, Ivan smiled and slipped the watch back into his waistcoat.

'My problem, Geoffrey? Why would you assume I have a problem?'

The Headmaster rolled his eyes and removed his spectacles. His reddened cheeks appeared ready to combust with teeming bewilderment.

'Well…alright, Ivan…why do you insist on giving ME a problem? Parents banging my door down! The *same* bloody parents…I might just add…who were in here last term for the same bloody *reason*!'

Ivan's dispiriting explanation was laced with flippancy.

'What can I say? They have a consistent daughter…' he grinned.

Geoff Taylor was less than impressed, however.

'I know what's bugging you! You've been here too bloody long! That's what it is! You've become an immovable object. A damned millstone hanging around the necks of everyone but yourself!'

'Why…thank you, Geoffrey…I'm touched by the compliment.'

The Head was now exasperated by Ivan's insistence on pouring humour on the issue.

'GET OUT, IVAN! JUST GET THE HELL OUT! AND TRY NOT TO BRING TROUBLE TO MY DOOR AGAIN BEFORE EASTER! CAN YOU MANAGE THAT MUCH?'

Ivan nodded with profound inner satisfaction and headed for the door.

Despite being appeased by the outcome, his sense of victory was short-lived as the Headmaster ushered close behind him.

'You know, Ivan? Things in education are quickly evolving. And I'm certain you'd never change with them. But that's not your fault. That's just life. But you've had your day, now. You do understand…I've got to concern myself with the *future* picture…not the people that are still living in the past.'

Ivan's previous sense of injustice now began to brim back to the fore.

He could not resist the chance to vent his spleen in response to such patronising commentary.

'Well don't overly concern yourself on my behalf, Geoffrey! You'll soon be shot of this old bird! Then you'll see the bloody changes alright! This school will be rendered vulnerable to the unruly. And then you'll all soon wish I was still bloody *here*! You heed my words. If you want the new order…you're welcome to it! But it won't work…it'll never, ever work…And do you know what else? I might not tell any of the kids I'm going! Let them keep thinking I'm around. Just to keep them on their toes. So that I'm haunting you buggers until you take your last breath in the wretched place!'

The Headmaster observed the sudden pained anger in the features of his most senior member of staff as he digested the words Ivan had conveyed.

'Are you kidding? Have you not informed any pupils, yet?'

'No…not yet. I haven't found the right moment.'

The Head sat back down behind his desk and again rubbed his eyes.

'Well…don't take much longer, will you? And…let's just try and have a bit of peace, eh? Just for the next few weeks?'

Frustrated, Ivan simply turned into the corridor and gently pulled the door into the frame behind him.

Geoff Taylor replaced his glasses, pondering the explicit warning he had just been given as he stared at the space Ivan had just vacated.

It was fair to say that the legacy of Ivan Reynolds was unsurpassed and would certainly be impossible to imitate. And the theory he had just delivered on the pending changes in the field of education carried more than a hint of foreboding.

It was an undeniable probability that without him around, the future for Littleholt Secondary would prove to be, at the very least, shrouded in uncertainty.

25

Ivan's air of intolerance failed to lighten for several weeks afterwards.

Consumed by a cloud of untypical yet unrelenting despondency, he had become distinctly colder towards colleagues and pupils alike. Compounding his sullen disposition, the belief gradually encroached that Geoff Taylor might just have been correct.

Ivan had slowly convinced himself towards the potential truth, that the traditional way he performed his role was now something akin to antiquated.

In himself, he now felt nothing other than borderline obsolete.

The message had been tactfully conveyed by the Headmaster yet carried discernible viability.

It appeared to be the popular view that when Ivan Reynolds was finally gone from Littleholt, it would be to the eternal benefit of all concerned.

Yet, through this phase of self-pity and doleful reflection, there was at least one singular voice of support that continually penetrated his hardened shell with a positive barb.

Carol Shaw had opted to join Ivan as he performed his scheduled playground duty on morning break. Despite being the middle of February, the air was strangely mild for the time of year.

Spring was firmly on the horizon, which served to offer some consolation for Ivan as he stared vacantly into the bustling activity of the school grounds.

'I hear you haven't announced to your form group about retiring.'

Ivan stared at Carol through his tinted frames before averting his gaze back across the bustling pupils.

'Is nothing decreed valid enough to be kept secret anymore? No, I haven't…not yet. I told Taylor that I might not bother, *either*!'

'Oh, Ivan! Don't talk so silly! Most of the kids really look up to you. I know you won't believe me, but they were so pleased when the trouble blew over. It's not fair to keep them in ignorance.'

He sighed in dubious agreement.

'I know, Carol…I know. To be honest, I've become rather attached to a few of them myself over time. Especially the younger ones this year…the poor blighters!'

Puzzled by Ivan's description of the First Years, she asked for further explanation.

'Why are they poor blighters? What do you mean by that?'

Ivan swallowed as a sentimental chord chimed upward from deep in his heart. Yet as always, the good-humoured sense of detachment served to camouflage his true feelings.

'Well…they're going to be losing me, aren't they? You're all…going to lose me. It…won't be long now.'

Carol studied the indeterminable masked posture of her colleague, searching for just a hint of emotion.

'Gone yes…but never forgotten, Ivan!'

She suspected he was not looking her way as he offered a conclusive murmur.

'Maybe…maybe not.'

Carol forced herself to avert her own gaze as latent sensations began to churn. The time for sorrow was not there and then, however. Instigating a throw-away quip, although conveyed in jest, still pained her beyond all expectation.

'Well…*I'll* miss you, anyway…God knows why…you unapproachable old sod…'

Whilst thankful of his colleague's offer of light-hearted solidarity, Ivan's attention was centred to the far side of the playground where a familiar figure honed into view from the crowd beyond. A figure that was evidently in some distress and required assistance.

'MISTER MORRIS!'

Ivan's bellowing address carried across to the subject who, teary-eyed and sniffling, obeyed the beckoning forefinger of the Maths teacher.

Shuffling toward the caller in the long black coat and dark glasses, the boy wiped his eyes and awaited the inquest.

'Mister Morris…why the tears? Not girl trouble again, is it?'

Carol smirked at Ivan's mild sarcasm and moved a few paces away, which afforded the uneasy youngster some confidence to reveal the source of his upset. Ivan leaned closer and whispered.

'Well, boy? Who has caused you grief this time?'

The callow youth shook his head and glanced around the near vicinity. His moist green eyes scanned the playground as he considered disclosing the culprit.

'It's…Martin Howe, sir. He's in the second year. He kicked me…down there, sir…where it hurts most…sir.'

Partially concerned by the unfortunate episode, Ivan lowered his frame to allow them both some temporary privacy.

'And why would he do such a terrible thing, Mister Morris? Did you deserve such treatment?'

Again, the boy checked the surroundings before expanding on the cause of his pain.

'Because…sir…I wouldn't play in goal. So, he kicked me.'

The teacher rested his hand on the young man's shoulder and conveyed a meaningful nugget of advice.

'Now…Mister Morris…do you know why you are such a pleasurable target for such vile creatures?'

The boy winced innocently.

'No, sir. Why?'

'Because they see that it upsets you. And because you do not respond in kind. Would you like to know how to fend off bullies in future, Mister Morris?'

Now intrigued by the forthcoming pearl of wisdom, the boy's enthusiasm eclipsed the searing discomfort between his legs.

'Don't be a pussycat, Mister Morris. Be a *lion*! Hit the buggers back. And hit 'em back so hard so they learn not to bother you ever again! Now…go and play soccer!'

Ivan watched with inner satisfaction as the grinning young man scampered back to the football match that he had been unceremoniously ejected from.

More than a little entertained by the incident, Ivan re-joined Carol near the veranda as the bell signified the end of morning break.

*****

Lunchtime was embraced by unseasonably warm sunshine which encouraged Ivan to take a run into the local park. Pulling open the gymnasium door he almost collided head-on with the figure of Daniel Keeting who emerged with a ready smile.

'Sorry, sir. My fault.'

'Not at all, Mister Keeting. Not at all. Haven't seen you around school for a while. How are you?'

'Good, sir. Good. I'm starving hungry, though!'

A hiatus in the exchange prevailed which was quickly erased by a query from the young man.

'What are you doing here, sir?'

'Oh…just changing to take a little run in the park. Helps me to unwind.'

Ivan stepped into the corridor and allowed Daniel to pass, but the teenager seemed a little hesitant and hovered in the doorway.

'Something the matter, Mister Keeting?'

The youth looked at Ivan through deep brown eyes before revealing his thoughts.

'Sir…do you mind…*would* you mind…if I join you? For the run, I mean?'

Ivan smiled and waved the boy back into the changing rooms.

'Mister Keeting…it would be…an unexpected pleasure and a privilege.'

Within a minute both emerged in their training kit and proceeded to jog gently through the car park in full view of those in the playground. Murmurs of suspicion and fingers of mockery followed the pair as they entered the top of the driveway leading to the school gates.

The voice of Shaun Peterson predictably carried above all others as they passed the bicycle sheds.

Surrounded by his usual array of courtiers, Peterson could not help but jibe at the spectacle.

'Jesus, Keeting! Struggling for company or what? Is he your new bodyguard then?'

Neither runner responded to the inane commentary, instead focusing their energies on the task at hand. Leaving the laughter in their wake, they headed from the school premises and toward the parkland.

As they jogged, Daniel felt himself becoming steadily impressed with the elder man's levels of fitness and easiness of stride. The Head of Mathematics was barely drawing breath as they navigated the route through the housing estates and reached the wrought-iron entrance to the public park.

As he began to steadily perspire, Daniel felt compelled to compliment the teacher.

'You…keep yourself…in good shape…don't you, sir…'

Ivan did not immediately answer, choosing instead to venture an enquiry of his own as they cantered along the tree-lined pathway.

'I never got the chance to ask until now. Your father…did he ever mention that eye injury you sustained in the hockey match a while back?'

Daniel felt himself to be falling slightly behind the pace and marginally increased his output to keep up with Ivan.

'You told me to tell the truth, sir. So, I did. And I was amazed! My father is a very strict man…and very suspicious…but I mentioned you…and he didn't seem to doubt my word…in fact…he never spoke about it again…'

The pair passed across the footbridge that spanned the trickling stream and then flanked the children's play area. The younger runner was astounded by Ivan's stealth and stamina as they moved across to the adjacent path.

'Do you…do this…everyday, sir?'

Ivan did not interrupt his breathing whilst providing a response.

'Only when I feel like it, Mister Keeting. That's always the best time to exercise…when you feel like it. Work the body and switch off the brain. It works a treat in the middle of the school day!'

Now passing out from the park grounds, Ivan led the gallop as they entered the town and picked up the route leading back to school.

On reaching the entrance to the school driveway, he motioned for them to stop running and walk the distance back to the changing rooms.

'It acts as a warm-down. It stops the muscles cramping later. By the way…very good pace…Mister Keeting.'

Predictably, Shaun Peterson lay in wait with a contribution to greet their return, but both joggers continued onward without acknowledging the tedious banter.

Having showered and re-dressed, the pair sat in the stench-riddled changing rooms drinking tap water from plastic cups. Ivan looked at the younger man as a question emerged.

'Mister Keeting…what do you plan to do after leaving Littleholt? Any ideas for what job you might enter next year?'

The teenager was a little bemused by the query, mainly because it was not even an issue that he himself had considered before that moment.

'I don't know, sir. My exams aren't until next summer. My dad says there might be a position at the company where he works. But it's early to say.'

Now prompted by curiosity, Ivan slipped on his suit jacket and continued to convey his genuine interest.

'Really? What does your father do for a living?'

'He drives trains, sir.'

It was not customary for Ivan Reynolds to offer career advice to fifteen-year-olds, but he had developed an inspired affinity for the young man in his presence.

'Mister Keeting…might I be so bold as to make a suggestion?'

The youth smiled whilst nodding enthusiastically.

'Have you ever considered sport as a career? Your physique is commendable…as is your temperament. I feel you'd make a good role model.'

Daniel's brow furrowed in light of the unexpected praise. Ushering him to his feet, Ivan led the pair from the gymnasium and into the car park.

'Well...I like athletics, sir. I've always been a good sprinter. But I've never really taken to team games. Not like footy, sir. Shaun Peterson's your man for that, really.'

Ivan continued to stride in front as he checked his pocket-watch.

'Mister Peterson is far too sure of himself to earn a living from his ability. He hasn't got the correct attitude to those around him. But you have, Mister Keeting. You definitely possess what it takes.'

'Attitude, sir?'

'Yes...attitude...confident...not cocky. Arrogance is a most unattractive trait in young men...especially sportsmen. It drives people away instead of drawing them closer.'

'I'd not really thought of myself in that way before, sir.'

'No...that's exactly what I mean, Mister Keeting. That is what I like about you. Your quiet modesty. Even though I have never taught you in class, I see a young man who is full of humility and consideration. You are a credit to your father. You make sure you tell him I said so! I'll bet you he believes *that* as well!'

Chuckling with an inflating inner pride, Daniel followed the Head of Mathematics to the main doors of the reception area as Ivan turned to him once again.

'You want to know something, Mister Keeting? Come sports day this year, I should have liked to have put myself forward as your team captain. We would have cleaned up on the track! I can see it now!'

Confused by Ivan's declaration, Daniel screwed up his nose and shook his head.

'So why *not* put your name forward, sir? My last three sports day captains haven't really been interested. It would be great to have you lead us.'

Ivan's gaze monitored the buzzing crowds of pupils as they darted hither and thither in the midday sunshine.

He then inhaled deeply on finally deciding to reveal his secret.

'Well...sadly for us both, Mister Keeting, sports day typically takes place in early July.'

The youth became ever more bemused by the remark from the teacher as he vainly tried to see through the elder man's dark lenses.

'Yeah…so? Put your name forward for skipper, now! It's ages yet! I'm in the Nightingale team.'

Ivan tried to smile as he spoke but found such a task impossible as emotion threatened to douse his words.

'Yes…I know you are in Nightingale, Mister Keeting. I've already confirmed that for my own curiosity. But I cannot be captain…because I will not be here in July.'

Open-mouthed astonishment was the young man's reaction to the statement that echoed unsteadily in his mind.

'I don't understand, sir. What do you mean…you won't be here?'

Ivan lowered his head and whispered.

'Come Easter…I will have retired from teaching. I won't be at *any* school. But do me a consideration, Mister Keeting…don't tell anybody else, will you? There's a good lad. You're the first pupil I've confided in.'

Quickly stunned by the announcement, Daniel also sensed a pang of honour at being Ivan's first choice for disclosure. He looked away and across the playground as the puzzling harsh truth gradually dawned on him.

He turned back to continue the dialogue with the teacher, requiring some further explanation regarding the impending departure.

But Ivan Reynolds had vanished into the building before any response could be given.

Ruing the lost opportunity, Daniel Keeting shuffled from the steps and perched himself underneath the rain veranda, pondering the very real implication that he might never have chance to talk with Ivan Reynolds again.

*****

Pushing open the staff room door, Ivan stopped his stride and gazed further along the corridor.

A familiar looking figure sat hunched on a chair outside the Headmaster's office. With elbows resting on knees and sulking white features framed by his palms, the boy looked to be the very image of dejection.

Ivan walked slowly toward the feeble form; a sense of wonder pressing him to announce his concerns.

'Mister Morris? Why are you sitting outside Mister Taylor's door?'

Two large guilty green eyes diverted attention sheepishly from the floor and fixed firmly on the tall inquisitor towering above him.

No explanation was forthcoming.

Ivan, although mildly aggrieved by the lack of a response from the boy, maintained an air of calm as he crouched down to his eye-level and again broached his curiosity.

'Mister Morris…what are you doing sitting here?'

With great reluctance, the boy finally opted to speak.

'Well…sir…I did what you said, sir.'

'What do you mean?'

'Well…I was sat having dinner and…Martin Howe…came from behind me…and knocked the back of my head with his elbow…on purpose, sir.'

Bubbling amusement began to gather momentum in Ivan's mind as he eagerly continued to listen.

'Yes? And then what happened, Mister Morris?'

'Well…then I thought about what you said to me at break time this morning, sir.'

'Yes? And then…what exactly *did* you do, Mister Morris?'

'I stood up…turned around…and punched him hard…in the mouth…and he dropped his tray…sir.'

Stifling his brimming mirth, Ivan stood up straight and glanced up and down the corridor.

'And so…why are you here? Who told you to report to the Headmaster?'

'Mister Holmes did, sir. He saw the whole thing. Will I be expelled, sir?'

Seeing the boy verging on upset yet again, Ivan checked the corridor once more to confirm the absence of any witnesses.

'Does the Headmaster know you are out here?'

'No, sir. I've been out here for twenty minutes! I don't really know what I'm supposed to do!'

Watching as the young boy wiped his eyes, Ivan hastily conjured up a plan.

'I'll tell you what, Mister Morris. Make a run for it! Go on! I'll speak to Mister Taylor and explain everything if he asks. Well…off you go, lad…before he appears!'

Astonished by the undue leniency of the teacher, the boy named Morris said nothing more and grabbed his school bag before disappearing from sight.

Now exhibiting a very satisfied smile, Ivan made his way triumphantly into the staff room.

'Coffee?' offered Matt Jenkins.

'Yes please, Matthew.'

'You've had a good morning by the looks of you.'

Ivan did not return the gaze of his unofficial apprentice but replied with vigour as he sank into his favoured armchair.

'Yes…*excellent*…actually.'

Soon immersed in the puzzle section of his newspaper, Ivan barely heard the staff room door crash open, which allowed Phil Holmes to enter looking red-faced and very agitated.

'Ivan! I've just spoken to young Morris! He's playing football in the playground! Is it true what he's just told me? That you sent him back out?'

Inserting the clue to seven across, Ivan duly responded to the complaint of the despairing physics teacher.

'Probably, Phillip. I reckon you can trust Morris's word. Don't you?'

Phil Holmes did not even attempt to return volley.

The argument was already lost.

The resulting slam of the door signified another small victory for Ivan, who dropped his newspaper onto the table and shut his weary eyes until the afternoon bell called all back to duty.

The imminent half-term break was very timely.

26

With winter reluctantly handing over the baton to spring, Ivan and George became fully immersed in the scheduled re-vamp of their allotments.

Ivan had already prepared his back garden during the half term break in February and set the ground in readiness for the hope of sunshine making increasingly regular and prolonged appearances.

The brighter evenings had slowly begun to promise much, assisting Ivan's climb out from his inexplicable pit of morbid self-analysis.

Now the bigger task was also almost nearing completion. It was the simplest of pleasures for him to revisit the partially fallow rows of earth and invigorate them back to life. The odour of creosote was also a welcome accompaniment to the surroundings as many fellow allotment owners opted to re-coat their sheds for the summer months.

Meanwhile at Littleholt Secondary, the final days of Ivan's reign were looming on the horizon. Acceptance of the end of his career had been a gradual and uneasy personal process, but he had become accustomed to the premise of having much extra spare time to follow his horticultural dreams.

Plus, the West Indies cricket team was due to tour England in the summer, and both George and Ivan had pledged to treat themselves to a test match ticket apiece.

As for the rest of the Littleholt staff, the pending departure of the Head of Mathematics had barely been mentioned in the staff room due to preoccupation with post-Easter exam preparation.

This in itself was something of a consolation for Ivan.

The fact that he would not be subjected to the unavoidable stress of the upcoming exam period eased the imminence of retirement. It was a time of year in the curriculum that always added to the daily strains of a teacher's already busy day.

*****

Wednesday. The Fourth of April.

And still, Ivan's imminent farewell remained undisclosed to the pupils.

With just nine days left until he officially departed the school permanently, Geoff Taylor had again voiced the opinion first thing that morning that it could only be considered appropriate courtesy for Ivan to announce his retirement to the pupils of 1RY.

Indeed, the Headmaster held the view that Ivan had not handled delaying the revelation as well as could be hoped but accepted the teacher's reasoning for withholding his secret.

The one and only pupil privy to developments, Daniel Keeting, had evidently kept his word and upheld Ivan's trust, as not one single voice had breathed one single syllable about Ivan's situation during the course of the previous days and weeks.

But now Ivan himself had to concede that informing his public was a task now woefully overdue.

The inevitable had evolved into the unavoidable.

Ivan had specifically chosen his penultimate weekly form period as the moment to announce his news. Yet during the two days that preceded the announcement, he felt himself becoming ever more reticent about the prospect.

Since Christmas, his attitude to saying goodbye to his career had wavered from cynical relief to heartfelt regret almost on a daily basis.

Yet now, as he sat before his final ever form group waiting for their undivided attention, he felt a strange numbness of the emotions.

Carol Shaw had urged him to reveal the news far earlier in the year, but Ivan's penchant for stubbornness had proved to be an efficient obstacle to her proposal.

Perched patiently in his chair behind his desk in room ten, he watched the children as their interest in one another gradually settled into a joint focus on the teacher waiting to speak.

The main tasks of the lesson had been accomplished.

Ivan had deliberately delayed until the last ten minutes of the period were upon the class.

He let them simmer down in their own time, checking his pocket-watch and for once having little inclination to berate them for their natural juvenility and effervescence.

He was aware that the eventual moment of revelation would encourage an unpredictable reaction among them.

From behind his darkened lenses, he visually acknowledged the varying faces and personalities that were now so familiar to him.

In turn they returned his dubious stare, themselves sensing some uncertainty as to the nature of what was to come.

A large proportion of 1RY had remained as they had first appeared the previous September.

Obedient and well mannered; keen to learn and always obliging.

There was also the minority who had affected their own individual influence on matters and had probably learned some valuable lessons in the process.

Dealing with both ends of the pupil spectrum had perhaps subconsciously played its due part in Ivan's delayed decision to unveil his news.

But now evasion of the issue was not an option. With everybody present in the room and time at a premium, there was simply no evading to the speech he was about to deliver.

With the group eventually enshrouded in a very unsettling silence, Ivan wearily pushed himself out of his chair and stood dominantly in front of the blackboard as he had done thousands of times before.

Yet his uncharacteristic body language now consisted of nervous glances beyond the window and hands sliding in and out of his suit jacket pockets.

And the reality of the moment suddenly struck him, as the pupils anticipated his voice to carry across the void.

Saying goodbye to his last ever form group was going to be a far more testing and emotive experience than he could ever have imagined.

He continued to scan their innocent, inquisitive faces through his mildly blackened visor, so wishing that the episode would pass and perhaps allow him complete avoidance of the responsibility.

Then in the very next thought, he searched for the correct way to begin informing them of his long-planned farewell.

And as the seconds passed and the pupils maintained their bemused attention directly to him, commencing the mission became ever more difficult to achieve as his head began to whirl.

This declaration was going to be acutely disconcerting.

For them.

And for him.

Finally, with a courage-inducing deep breath, Ivan clasped his hands behind his back and leaned gently back against the blackboard to steady himself against the rapid-fire and contradictory messages ricocheting around his mind.

He studiously focused his eyes on the back wall of the room to avoid seeing the faces of the children.

As they sat in their pairs, behind their tables, awaiting their form tutor's next ordainment.

And as he felt their inquisitive natures beckoning him to speak, the ultimate realisation rapidly dawned on him.

That he did not actually want to say goodbye to the children at all.

Then as this resolution registered, he fought it off and began to make his confession through a controlled, stoic tone.

'Boys…girls…ladies…gentlemen…this is going to be a rather different form period this week…because…as your form tutor…'

Ivan interrupted himself as the roaring upset began to simmer within his gut and in his heart.

The next words of his statement instantly deserted him.

The children engaged with him now in curious wonder.

They could detect his buckling disposition.

Desperate not to engage with the blank curiosity he had encouraged from all in the room, Ivan switched his focus to the emerging lush greenery of the treeline beyond the window as it swayed freely in the early spring breeze.

Yet the potency of the form group's emerging confusion seared into him, tearing at his soul.

They did not respond.

They continued to wait for their teacher to resume his monologue.

All eyes and ears centred on one man.

The premise of his veritable abandonment of them as a class, now began to cut deeply as Ivan strived to deliver the news.

Yet his act of indifference was visibly faltering.

And just as he prepared to continue, a rock-solid lump of emotion swiftly formed in his throat, threatening to convulse and explode should he relinquish his self-control even by a fraction.

But for a man who apparently adored the sound of his own voice, thought seemed infinitely preferable to speech at that moment.

But finally, his albeit frail courage prevailed.

'I have taught here at Littleholt for many years…and have seen many wonderful things…and taught many…wonderful pupils. But alas…age ultimately works against everybody. So, the time has come for me to take my final bow as a teacher at this school.'

Again, inhaling deeply as his diaphragm twitched, Ivan could feel the initial stirring reactions of the children as they remained absolutely transfixed by the mentor standing before them.

For all the natural authority he may have exuded as a standard bearer, Ivan Reynolds would not identify the irony that his direct influence over any class in his entire career, had never been as inspiringly powerful as it was at that moment in time.

The children watched him.

Awe struck and totally attentive. Justifiably concerned and intrigued by their suddenly stumbling, bumbling leader.

Where was his customary assuredness?

Who were his eyes trained on, behind those bleak, black lenses.

What was it he was trying to tell everybody?

And still Ivan fought so gamely not to crumble in their midst.

'A week on Friday…the thirteenth of the month I believe…is when the school breaks for the Easter fortnight. And that is also the day I shall be saying goodbye to you all…for the very last time. I am sixty-years of age early next month…and as such…I will be retiring from teaching.'

Now exhaling with a combination of nausea and relief, he finally dared to slowly let his gaze wander across the captive throng.

Unsurprisingly, there was not a single word of protest.

Nor was there one single utterance of pleasure.

Indeed, there was no vocal strand of response expressed among any of the fifteen boys and sixteen girls within the walls of room ten.

The arena lulled itself into an eerie stillness that Ivan could not ever have expected from such a reliably boisterous group.

Then his mind and vision cleared temporarily, and the reasons for the uncharacteristic absence of sound became painfully clear.

Every innocent young face in the room had become instantly etched with the effects of an emerging, genuine, personal sorrow.

Each child, sitting obediently behind their desk as he had inducted them to do so competently, had succumbed quietly to their own individual process of registration.

The teacher remained positioned with the back of his suit jacket pressed against the blackboard and he digested the altering expressions of his pupils.

And the process of reaction began to strengthen its grip.

The boys and girls of 1RY wiped their eyes with their fingertips.

But to no avail, as the tears did fall again.

And as they freely shed their uncontrolled remorse, their teacher observed the pained communal release without further comment.

Ivan's attention was drawn in particular to those children who had made his final terms at Littleholt so memorable.

Jenny Douglas; Hilary Johnson; Trevor Sims; Colin Scott; Wendy Beattie. They cleaned their noses on their sleeves and sniffled helplessly at the realisation of their imminent loss.

And this teacher of supposedly daunting repute, for the very first time in his career, felt completely without inspiration to say anything more to them.

This man, who had bellowed his orders in classrooms and corridors for nearly four decades, was now reduced to a humbled figure of reticence as he watched his pupils weep openly without shame or resistance.

Glancing down to check his pocket-watch once again, the atmosphere was suddenly pierced by the bleat of the lunchtime bell.

And Ivan was never more gratified to acknowledge its irritating, jolting tone.

Totally stunned by the news they had just received, 1RY slowly trudged one by one from the classroom, as their teacher stood alone by the window in contemplation of the future.

The deed was done.

And unsurprisingly, Ivan felt little consolation for the fact.

Within the hour, the entire school would no doubt be aware that Ivan Reynolds' tenure was soon to end.

And as he observed the playground become occupied by the lengthening queue for the dining hall, he wondered whether in fact he himself was ready to embrace that very fact.

For all his satirical exhibitionism and staff room pontification, the teacher that regularly proclaimed to be more than content to be shipping out, was in fact now accompanied by one sensation and one sensation only.

Sheer, enveloping desolation.

*****

As anticipated, the news did indeed travel incredibly fast.

The afternoon was spent fielding predictable questions about what life would bring for Ivan Reynolds after Littleholt.

The lessons with the Third and then the Fifth formers were good humoured and upbeat, but he could not shake off the prior vision of his own First Year form group and their earnest displays of upset.

Never did he ever suspect that their affection for him lay so near to the surface.

Naively, he had expected cynical shouts of celebration and maybe sarcastic cheers of thankful relief.

Never did he anticipate the outpouring of genuine despondency that followed his disclosure.

It had been a long, tiring day.

Unusual for one reason, yet typical for many others.

And akin to its beginning, the day was not to end as planned either.

Glad to be finally making toward his Princess with briefcase in hand, he admired the orange-copper sheen that glimmered in the relatively mild sunshine.

Placing his belongings in the car, he closed the passenger door.

It was at that moment Ivan thought he heard a distant cry for help.

A female shriek; vaguely familiar, yet indeterminable as to its whereabouts.

He listened carefully once again.

And the desperate call was repeated.

Leaving his car, Ivan began to walk to the rear of the school building and toward the bicycle sheds. Hoping to uncover the source of the shouting, he found the bike racks to be deserted.

Encroaching confusion was soon eclipsed by another high-pitched scream emanating from the seemingly short yet obscured distance.

Walking at increased speed, Ivan strode the length of the bike racks and past the science block.

Just as another, slightly louder bark of evident urgency descended on his ears.

Then, on reaching the entrance to the science block and turning the corner towards the playground, he discovered the scene of the action.

At the edge of the biology pond, four Second Year pupils had in their claim a younger victim and having taken a firm hold of each of the younger girl's limbs, were evidently about to douse their quarry into the green-tinged waters.

Ivan stopped his stride and observed the episode from his secluded vantage point.

And then it hit him.

The identity of the squirming victim about to be submerged slowly revealed itself.

Hilary Johnson.

The seconds passed as she continued to wriggle within the vice-like trap.

And as those same seconds passed, Ivan considered his potential role in the ensuing melee.

He might turn his back on the scene and walk away.

This was certainly a tempting option and most definitely, a personal preference.

But Ivan Reynolds was still a teacher at Littleholt Secondary.

And professional decorum still rose above any private whim as he bellowed for a cessation to the fracas.

'YOU THERE, GIRLS! STOP THAT AT ONCE AND COME HERE! ALL OF YOU! HERE! TO ME! NOW! QUICKLY!'

All five pupils looked up, evidently startled by the intruder on their mission.

All five trudged toward the teacher as he stood with hands clasped behind his back and the blackest mask of doom parading itself.

'WHAT ON EARTH IS GOING ON, HERE?'

The tallest of the Second Year pupils mumbled in reply.

'Well, sir…this First Year girl has been taking my younger sister's dinner money and picking on her after school. So, we thought…'

'WHAT *DID* YOU THINK, MISS DIXON? YOU THOUGHT YOU'D TAKE THE LAW INTO YOUR OWN HANDS? YOU THOUGHT YOU'D TEACH HER A LESSON?'

All five girls let their gaze drop to the floor as Ivan declared his conclusion.

'GET YOURSELVES OFF HOME! I'LL DEAL WITH THE FOUR OF YOU IN THE MORNING! LEAVE MISS JOHNSON TO ME!'

Without further word, the older pupils relished the invitation to make their escape and avidly scampered from the scene.

Ivan then focused his attention to Hilary, whose wet hair and damp green pullover displayed evidence that he had missed out on the early stages of the revenge plan.

She did not look up into his ebony-glazed stare, preferring instead to maintain her attention at the ground around her feet.

'Miss Johnson…'

She reluctantly returned the teacher's gaze in anticipation of a further remonstrative tirade.

Ivan smiled before completing his assessment of her predicament.

'Miss Johnson…in truth…I hope that those girls *have* taught you a lesson. Now please…if you can do so without any further chance of a fracas, will you get yourself safely home…'

With a broad grin quickly underlining her brightening eyes, Hilary Johnson realised that she had not only been rescued, but also duly pardoned.

Seconds later, she was gone from the school premises amid a cloud of contented disbelief, leaving her form tutor alone to make his way back to the car park.

*****

On departing the school grounds, Ivan decided to stop by the allotments and spend an hour or two in the early evening sunshine.

Come the beginning of April, the weather was now habitually unpredictable, by the hour verging between being very mild and windy, on to snow flurries and occasional hail showers.

But it was the fresh air and intoxicating aroma of newly turned earth gave Ivan great comfort.

He was fully aware that George was at market and wouldn't be keeping Ivan's company that evening. As such, the visit to the allotment was cut somewhat shorter with the absence of his friend and so Ivan quickly checked the progress of his vegetable rows and replenished the bird feeders that hung from the roof of his shed.

Reflection on the day's events was the main occupation of his mind as he drove home.

He could not erase the image from his mind.

The little ones and their timid sadness.

The wrenching dismay that had contorted their faces.

Pulling onto the driveway he wistfully emerged from the Princess and gave Jill a wave as she appeared at her lounge window, evidently awaiting George's return.

It did not take long for her to relocate to the back fence as he walked down the side of the house to access and assess the welcoming scene of the back garden.

With the distinct feeling that the mischievous cat from the houses beyond had paid its customary visit, Ivan crouched down to observe his lawn for growth and cast attention to the newly laid seedlings.

Still with briefcase and suit jacket in hand he stood tall once more.

More than ready to bemoan the vexing sight of any feline deposits, he was suddenly alerted to the familiar tone of his neighbour.

'Well…how did the kids react? I take it you told them as planned?'

Ivan slowly turned to face his friend, who's inquiring features bobbed up and down along the top of the fence.

'Well, Jillian…they were…I do believe…rather upset. All things considered it was pleasantly surprising to think that they might just hold me in their hearts, after all! In fact, I got the definite impression that I might well just be *missed* around the damned place! Can you believe *that*?'

Jill chuckled at Ivan's self-deprecating tone.

'Oh…I'm sure you'll be missed alright! No doubt about that! By the way, the postman didn't come until after dinner. I didn't see if he called to your house or not.'

'Okay, Jillian. Thank you. Speak to you later.'

Ivan nodded his appreciation as he scanned the vegetable patch one final time before departing the scene and marching back down the side of the house to the front door.

Ivan let himself in and discovered that there was indeed an item of mail underfoot.

Retrieving the single white envelope from the mat, he placed his briefcase and jacket in the hallway and moved onward to the kitchen.

Filling and flicking on the kettle, his casual interest in the envelope was suddenly alerted by the handwritten address and an unusually distinctive franking mark.

Then a daunting realisation dispelled his initial confusion.

It had been posted from Spain.

It had to be from his wife.

Or maybe, his son.

Time stood still for a moment as he continued to scrutinise the blue, inky stroke of the writing.

Poignant images from the past raced through his mind in a kaleidoscopic montage of his own chequered and flailing history.

Communication with Meg had ceased to exist long ago.

Any letters Ivan had tried to send had not been responded to and ultimately, the quest to retain contact with his estranged family had fallen completely flat despite all efforts to ensure the contrary.

To receive correspondence after such time was something of a major shock.

Ivan prepared a large black coffee and sat himself down in the lounge. Conveying another inspection of the envelope in his trembling grasp, its weight suggested it didn't contain anything other than a letter of no more than two or three pages.

Tentatively peeling open the seal, all thoughts regarding the events of the school day were completely eclipsed by the realisation that his wife had possibly made much belated contact.

His heart began to beat faster, and his palms became clammy with cautionary expectation.

But for all his reserved excitement at the prospect, he could not fathom a single reason why she would need to write to him after their separation had endured for so long.

Then, as the seal became completely broken, an immensely perturbing possibility encroached.

Perhaps Nicholas was in trouble.

Perhaps his son needed help in some way.

Perhaps the letter contained bad news.

The potentials were almost frightening.

Before he dared pull the notepaper from its case, Ivan sipped a taste of coffee, noticing that his hand was shaking uncontrollably as he held the mug to his mouth.

The delay of execution was both overwhelming and enticing.

Yet he upheld the nagging sensation that positive news was not the motive behind the correspondence.

Almost slamming the coffee mug back onto the table, he freed the letter and unfolded the single leaf.

Focusing his mind on the words written in the distinctive hand that seemed to have become more elegant with time, the disappointing truth of the matter quickly became clear.

Yes, his wife's motive was one of personal urgency.

But it was not reconnection that Ivan's wife required.

Far from it.

The tone of the script was cold and impartial, as though written in haste in the manner of a message for the milkman.

He read it rapidly the first time, then endeavoured to study the content more deeply as a sense of fogged inevitability descended.

By the second analysis of the letter, it was soon obvious that the closure of his school career would occur in tandem with the abrupt conclusion of his marriage.

He visualized Meg's once adoring face as he scanned the words for a third, thoroughly disheartening time.

Ivan,
As a matter of courtesy, I write personally to inform you that I have instructed my solicitor here in Marbella to commence proceedings with regard to petitioning for divorce.
The relevant paperwork will arrive for your approval sometime in the next few weeks and it would be appreciated if you could respond accordingly with your own legal representation to enable both sides to perform the necessary protocol and allow things to progress without unnecessary delay.
Procedure in such matters is rather more efficient here than in England and in order to take advantage of this fact your full cooperation would be most welcome.
I trust you will not begrudge me this final honour as I behold the presumption that you would positively encourage our contract of matrimony to be annulled.

As an aside, Nicholas is very well and living happily with his wife Alexia in Gibraltar.
You may or may not be interested to know that you have become a grandfather in your prolonged absence.
Sara is three years old. I have enclosed the most recent photograph I possess.
It is to be hoped that a policy of compliance on your part will provide for this matter to be resolved with relative immediacy.
Yours faithfully
Margaret.

Still clasping the letter between thumb and forefinger, Ivan let his arm leadenly drop onto his lap. With his spare hand, he enticed the colour photo from the envelope and studied the portraits of his handsome son and blond-haired, beautiful granddaughter.

Both shared the same smile, which beamed from the sunlit snapshot, in turn temporarily illuminating the long-shadowed recesses of Ivan's mind.

Yet the instant sense of detachment that rapidly overwhelmed him at that moment on the settee was nothing less than agonising.

The complete lack of compassion and harsh formality of address in Meg's note needed no explanation.

Her long-standing animosity was coolly evident.

She had merely sent him a polite warning that a legal business was about to ensue.

A business that, in his heart of hearts, Ivan never wished to confront.

A business that would remove any chance for the reconciliation that he still craved in the warmest part of his heart.

A business that signified the end of a once-happy union.

The final division of a family and effectively, the crushing of unspoken hope.

Alone with his sorrow, Ivan clutched the note and photograph to his chest and surrendered.

He wept alone.

He wept until he could weep no more.

The grief roared openly from his very depths; echoing around the walls of that house that he very begrudgingly called home.

A grief that he had been waiting to discharge for an entire generation; yet had resisted with all his might until this day.

The demons of intensive remorse that had haunted him would now finally triumph.

Long into the night; and beyond to the following dawn.

The only chance of respite was to sleep.

And with that sleep, claim a temporary peace.

27

The piercing sound of birdsong accompanied Ivan's reluctant arousal from slumber the next morning. Still fully clothed on the settee, he was enswathed in the cool air of the lounge and the relentless beat of a searing headache.

Harsh reality quickly enswathed the moment as he pulled himself upright and re-positioned his spectacles. His vision immediately located the letter and photograph on the floor at his feet.

He did not wish to move.

He did not wish to see.

He did not wish to breathe.

Blinding sunlight streamed into the lounge, coating the furniture in a golden sheen. He squinted through the windowpane, but the stinging sensation was too much to bear.

He simply sat for minutes on end, his dry throat clamouring for coffee. His now empty heart, pleading for the pain to end.

Eventually, Ivan dragged himself from the sofa and shuffled into the kitchen. Gazing across the scene through the rear window his concentration centred on a different issue. The hunched form of the tortoiseshell cat sheepishly covered its mess with two front paws and scampered back into the safety of the undergrowth.

But the feline visitor would be in no danger this morning.

For the old man was trapped inside; trapped by regret and a wish for his lot to be so different.

And yet, despite his quandary, another test soon awaited him.

It may already have proved to be a most extraordinary day, but Thursday was still a school day.

And the clock on the kitchen wall declared that the odds were against him should he plan to arrive at Littleholt on time.

Eclipsing his torment with the need for positive action, Ivan trudged upstairs and prepared himself for duty.

*****

His complete disinterest in the surroundings was all too obvious as he laboured his way through the school timetable. In no mood to engage in depth or socialise on any level, the underlying air of aloof hostility he conveyed was readily identified by colleagues who wisely gave him a wide berth.

A few enquiries from varying faces of 1RY were answered truthfully and politely, but Ivan did not particularly wish to indulge in conversation even with his own class.

He forced icy smiles and acknowledged the expressions of well-wishing from his pupils, but the demoralization he felt was prompted by events far away from Littleholt.

When the three-thirty bell tolled to signify the liberation of all it had never sounded so good to his ears.

Dismissing the Fifth Year maths class and snapping his briefcase shut, Ivan sat back in his chair and relished the opportunity for a few minutes of sanctity in room ten.

And as his pricking consciousness willingly returned once more to the graveyard of the past, the ghosts reappeared to taunt him and thwart any attempts to immerse himself in solace.

Ivan removed his spectacles as the tears fell again.

Dripping from his cheeks and onto his white shirt and black tie.

He rocked silently in his chair, allowing the tide of release to take him as he cradled his face from view and succumbed to the finality of his unexpected, regretful loss.

At one with the swell of emotion, he floated from the past back to the present and back to the past again.

And as he wept, desperately fighting to restrain his vocal releases, he did not see the face at the classroom door, staring through the window to ascertain why he might still be encased in the room.

Observing the man in his plight and recognising the unerring sound of his distress, Carol Shaw did not interrupt the moment.

Tiptoeing away from the scene, she opted instead to wait for him downstairs.

*****

Over thirty minutes passed in concerned anticipation until Carol heard the gently echoing footsteps, before eventually observing the silhouette of Ivan's slow descent down the lowest flight.

His tall, lean frame appeared to float from the bottom step, into the shadowed corridor and on toward the staff room.

He did not detect her covert position in the girls' cloakroom, and he was completely unaware that his outpouring of earlier had been observed.

But Carol could not ignore what she had witnessed.

She was his colleague; his friend; and a confidante in waiting.

'Ivan…' she muttered, allowing her greatly softened tone to carry gently in his wake.

After one more stride, he stopped and turned his head.

'Carol? Is that you?'

In consideration for his likely state of upset, she walked cautiously along the corridor to join him.

She tried to smile but was wary of it being received as wholly inappropriate.

'So…your news is common knowledge.'

They continued to tread tentatively along the route to the staff room, from dark shadow into brightly lit corridor.

'Yes…that is correct. Everybody knows now. No more the big secret. The party can start. Reynolds is going at last!'

Struggling to keep up with his increasing pace, she nudged him in the arm to regain his attention.

'Ivan…it isn't like that at all…believe me. You've known this day has been coming for months. Now it's arrived…well…it's difficult for *me* to comprehend to be quite honest.'

He did not look at her as he walked.

'Yes, well…it matters very little now does it, Carol?'

Identifying his misplaced disgruntlement, she threw a suggestion into the wind.

'Listen, do you fancy a drink? A *proper* drink, I mean. Just the two of us? None of the others. Unless you want to ask them?'

Ivan did not reply immediately.

Yet his eventual response was loud and concise.

'NO! I mean…*yes*…I *do* want a drink…but yes…just…you and me. That would be…very nice.'

She felt more than a semblance of comfort on realising that Ivan was in the mood to talk to at least one of his colleagues that day.

'When do you fancy? The weekend, perhaps? We could make a foursome up if you wanted. I'd like to meet your wife. We could…go for a meal…maybe? It will probably be our last chance to socialise before…well, you know…before you go.'

Ivan stopped walking and engaged the Head of First Year's mildly confused stare.

'No…we'll go for that drink *now*, Carol. Now is the perfect time. Come on. I'll drive.'

*****

It was the first occasion Ivan had ever carried female company in the copper Princess. Pulling to a stop in the car park of The Arlington Arms, he gently applied the handbrake and looked across to his passenger.

'I'd just like to say thank you for this, Carol. It's very much appreciated.'

She was a little bemused by the statement.

'You're supposed to thank me afterwards, silly! Who knows, we might have an argument in the pub and then the thanks will be a little premature won't they!'

Ivan pushed open his door and stepped out.

'Believe you me…I'm in no mood for arguments. Shall we sit outside? The weather's lovely this afternoon.'

Nodding in avid agreement, she found a suitable bench under an ivy drenched pergola whilst Ivan ventured inside the pub's main entrance. As he emerged a couple of minutes later with two drinks, she could not help but offer a semi-humorous complaint in attempting to lighten his mood even further.

'You never asked what I wanted! That's quite rude, you know!'

Almost taken aback by her comment, he stood and wavered before her, his visor now fully blackened by the late afternoon sunlight.

'Well…I *am* quite rude…haven't you heard? In fact, I've made a bloody career out of being quite rude, you know! Besides…your favourite tipple has always been a half of lager, hasn't it?'

'But I might not have *wanted* half of lager.'

Ivan perched opposite and pushed the smaller glass across the bench-top toward her.

'So…what *did* you want to drink, then?'

Carol glanced down and giggled.

'A half of lager.'

Ivan shook his head and raised his glass.

'Oh, shut up, woman! Come on! Let's have a toast. To history…and all who sail in her! Cheers!'

Both sat sipping their beer as the spring sun began its gradual descent below the rooftops. The air turned slightly chillier, and Carol could not ignore the heavy clouds that Ivan was evidently trying in vain to fend off.

It was a friend's prerogative to offer support.

'Ivan…I'm…I'm not sure how to say this, so I suppose I'll not beat about the bush. It's just that…I saw you crying earlier…at your desk. I didn't want to intrude. I know leaving Littleholt's a major wrench. But no one could ever have guessed it would affect you so deeply.'

Downing a large gulp of lager, Ivan stared straight ahead through his ebony spectacles and scrunched up his nose. In turn, Carol suspected he may have been embarrassed by her confession and was careful not to press the matter further.

It was only after a full minute of total silence had elapsed that he reluctantly attempted to quantify his feelings.

'I wasn't crying over bloody retirement, Carol. In a way, I'll be glad to get gone. It all feels a little bit pointless now…as though I'm hanging on for dear life knowing full well that the trapdoor will soon open anyway. I reckon the next week is going to drag beyond recall. God help the kids…'

Carol chortled and sampled some more of her own drink as she endeavoured further to study the man sitting across the table from her.

'So…what made you have your little moment of emotion, then? Was it the sudden thought of not seeing me again?'

Ivan smirked briefly at his colleague's jovial accompaniment.

Then, with a straight face, he stared directly at her which allowed her the opportunity to fully observe the lean and handsome features that lay persistently disguised by his ebony visor.

'Likewise, Carol. I won't beat about the bush, either. Put quite simply…I found out last night that my wife is intending to file for divorce.'

Carol's complete astonishment at the disclosure evoked instant bewilderment and the immediate emptying of her glass.

'Jesus Christ…Ivan! I'll get us another drink in…won't be a tick.'

Now fully prepared to divulge the unpleasant business surrounding his personal life, Ivan suddenly felt a weight gradually lifting from his shoulders. Sensing that the burden would be off-loaded a little, he felt at ease in revealing some detail of his private affairs that had caused so much wonder among colleagues over the years.

He watched Carol return with the replenished glasses.

He was now smiling; she was now in a full state of shock as she reclaimed her seat and tried to select the appropriate response.

'But *why*, Ivan? After all these years? Not much of a retirement present is it!'

He shook his head, prompting further curiosity from his companion. He was struggling to engage in the exchange without emotion intervening.

'Ivan, I know I shouldn't pry, but is there…you know…another man involved?'

His answer was frank to say the least.

'I've absolutely no idea! And I care even less! I haven't seen her myself for twenty years!'

Now Carol was completely at a loss for words as the rapid intake of alcohol very slowly began to make its mark.

He knew she wanted to know more.

For him to unravel the finer details of his life and the reasons for its gradual dissipation.

However, she did not need to plead for expansion.

The explanations came without prompt.

'We loved one another, Carol. Of course, we did. At first, anyway. But I'm afraid…that as a younger man I was pretty unbearable when I came out of the military.'

'How? In what way were you so unbearable?'

'I think a modern term would be control freak…bully…general chauvinist pig. Generally, a walking nightmare. And a sometime alcoholic. So, you see…she'd secretly had enough of me long before Nicholas arrived on the scene.'

Carol listened sorrowfully to her friend's confessions.

Her heart wrenching in sympathy with every new revelation.

'I hadn't been at Littleholt all that long. I can't remember…it's all a bit vague now. I came home from work one day to find a note on the kitchen table. Classic Dear John stuff, really! Meg said she'd gone with Nicholas to her parents' house in Spain and wouldn't be coming back. I tried phoning and writing. But to no avail.'

'Couldn't you have gone after her, Ivan? Don't tell me you just gave up on your family?'

He looked at his colleague with a twinge of indignation.

'Hold your horses, Carol! *She* gave up on *me* if truth be known! Might sound terribly defeatist…but it's true. We'd had many rows over the years. But I suppose it was no environment for a child.'

The conversation progressed ever deeper as Carol's long held fascination was slowly sated.

'Did things ever get…well…you know…*violent*?'

Ivan focused his attention onto a car that pulled into the space beside the Princess.

His unease was evidently rising back to the fore once again.

Though he maintained a semblance of control as he continued to speak.

'Yes…yes…I hit her…but she hit me back much harder! It was ridiculous! Comical almost! Like I say…it's so long ago now. I couldn't even tell you what the fights were about. I hoped one day that we might be a family all over again, but that was just a very silly pipe dream. And now…with me finishing the teaching…that very silly pipe dream has taken on far more relevance…and then, of course…yesterday…the letter arrived.'

'And what are you going to do?'

Ivan finished his second pint in record time and set the glass gently down on the table.

'Give her the divorce she craves, of course! Bloody shame really. I don't suppose I'll ever get to meet my granddaughter, now.'

Against all whim, Carol Shaw began to cry.

In turn, Ivan breathed deeply in solemn gratitude for her barely concealed affection.

'Come on, Carol…don't shed tears on my account. I'm hardly worth it.'

Ivan's most trusted colleague removed tissues from her handbag, wiped her eyes and re-engaged her stare with his.

'You are to *me*, Ivan! You're worth it to *me*. And you always have been.'

She shifted from her seat, re-positioned herself next to her friend and colleague and hung her arms around his shoulders. The impulsive embrace endured for several minutes, which allowed the closeness of the moment to gradually dispel the mutual flow of emotion.

She finally drew away and once more focused with Ivan's features through moistened eyes.

'So…what does life after teaching hold for you, now? Without a family…without a career? What will you do with yourself?'

He smiled and stared directly into the dropping sun.

'Play around on my allotment, I suppose! Watch some cricket. There's not much else for me to do, is there? I can't cause too much trouble with a spade, can I?'

Carol placed her hand on Ivan's, noticing his wedding ring as she did so.

Her sympathy for him was something she refused to hide.

'I can't believe you've spent most of your time at Littleholt living life alone as a single man! How could you have accommodated such anguish? Such...uncertainty? Every single day...carrying that secret inside you...and still managing to be the best bloody teacher that the school has ever known!'

Ivan did not respond to her open praise.

Because he hadn't the first clue how to react.

Flattery was something he was certainly unaccustomed to.

Instead, he opted for another slice of self-mockery.

'I don't know about being the best teacher, Carol. But I do know this. To think that perhaps all these years I've spent making enemies...what I'd give now to have a friend around.'

Grasping his hands tightly, she looked through his shades and attempted to see into his soul, sensing herself melt with admiration as she did so.

'You've got *one* friend, Ivan. You've got at *least* one.'

28

Ivan's final week of active duty for the school saw him enter the main doors on Monday morning in the least hospitable of moods.

Proceeding to bite the heads off any unwitting souls crossing his path, Ivan had inadvertently turned room ten into a veritable hell for the pupils.

And yet in his heart, he so wished his natural impulse could extend some amity toward those around him.

Inexplicably on edge, his senses were actively aware of the mildest sign of dissent. At a time when all at Littleholt could have justifiably expected his approach to incline towards that of lenient, the exact opposite was applicable.

Especially regarding the members of his form group.

During Tuesday morning registration, many in 1RY were naturally vibrant about the fact that their leader was in the final throes of his reign.

It was a combined sensation of tentative relief and sombre regret. Whilst conforming to the accepted rituals of good manners and discipline that had been drilled into them over previous months, the group's banter had reached a level of juvenile excitement that, unbeknown to them, had rapidly breached the radically shortened threshold of their teacher's patience.

Ivan was half-way through checking the register when he detected a whisper from the back of the room.

Having mentally identified the culprit, he rose to his feet and moved slowly toward the blackboard behind him.

All attention in the room focused out front as he took the board rubber in his grasp and slowly swiped it in a circular motion across the dark grey canvas, creating copious clouds of chalk dust.

Then in a flash, Ivan had turned on the spot and hurled the rubber towards the wall. The clatter of the impact against plasterboard instantly silenced the class, as it ricocheted onto the floor.

In the same movement, the teacher then reverted to the blackboard.

He hastily scrawled a self-explanatory order in five pre-dominant capital letters.

QUIET.

The underlying message was clear for all to see.

He might have been within touching distance of his last horizon.

But Ivan Reynolds had not retired just yet.

*****

Wednesday brought an underwhelming and unpleasant surprise for Ivan to discover, even before sampling his first coffee of the day, that he had again been listed to supervise the playground during his last lap of honour.

Fully intending to oblige routine with the crossword puzzle, his hopeful entrance into the staff room was dashed by the enthused gesturing of Matt Jenkins pointing avidly toward the rota list on the staff room wall.

'And guess who's been posted with you!'

Ivan placed his briefcase on the floor next to his favourite chair before replying to his younger colleague's sarcastic poser.

'Matthew…please tell me it's not the bloody physics teacher. Not this week. Anybody but bloody Holmes this week.'

There was no need for vocal confirmation.

The answer was perfectly evident from Matt's inane grin.

The sigh of resignation acknowledged another layer to Ivan's overriding dismay.

'No point in me hanging around here then, is there? When he shows up…tell him I've already gone out. And Matthew…stop bloody laughing!'

Taking his coffee with him, Ivan trudged outside into the spring breeze and positioned himself next to the biology pond where he hoped at least the goldfish would divert his mind from the eternal drudgery of playground duty.

Phil Holmes was not far behind, and much to Ivan's inner chagrin.

He stood right beside him to speculate on the throng of incoming pupils.

Ivan did not hesitate to lay down one or two guidelines regarding how the next few minutes should transpire.

'If you want polite conversation, Philip, please don't bother. I'm not in any kind of sociable persuasion.'

The younger teacher shook his head in disbelief.

'No change there, then! You know…most people in your position would be having an absolute ball this week! Not moping about feeling sorry for themselves.'

'Yes, Philip…well see how you feel when you retire. Personally speaking…I don't find it to be a charming prospect.'

The conversation stunted, Ivan now feeling fully justified in standing perfectly still and saying absolutely nothing.

Watching him from the other side of the playground, Trevor Sims and Jenny Douglas sat together underneath the veranda, discussing the board rubber throwing incident of the previous day.

'He's miserable, isn't he…I thought he'd be more cheerful this week. We'd better be careful, Jen. He might chuck a chair at the next kid who annoys him'

Jenny listened to her friend's musings without response.

Her inner sorrow had only grown since learning of her favourite teacher's rapidly approaching farewell.

So far as she was personally concerned, Ivan's departure was a severe loss to one and all, and the belated nature of the revelation only made her feel even more aggrieved about the matter.

So much so that she could not even bring herself to begin discussing how she felt inside.

Despite his sometime thorny nature and naturally imposing presence, Ivan Reynolds had been a figure of nothing less than total reverence in her eyes.

The prospect of her future schooling without him was too much for a young girl to bear. Even just to look at him that short distance away was quietly causing her heart to break.

She was certainly not looking forward to Friday.

For Jenny Douglas, it was already a day to dread.

And she anticipated that the final goodbye would hurt beyond all expectation.

Ivan's attention was fixed firmly into the depths of the past when Phil Holmes tapped him on the arm. He did not hear the words spoken by his younger colleague.

Or the tone, which had adopted a distinct air of concern.

'Come on! Time for action! A fight's kicked off on the main field.'

Ivan remained unmoved by the information and finished his drink.

'Did you hear me, Ivan? There's a fight over there! Let's sort it out before the whole school converges!'

The Head of Mathematics remained stationary without reply and simply watched as pupils left the playground and gathered around the pair of protagonists exchanging blows by the canal.

The distant shouts of encouragement carried back across the playing field to the two teachers.

The children glanced in Ivan's direction as they passed him, but his expected shout of prohibition did not come forth.

Yet again, Phil Holmes pleaded with his elder colleague for some assistance.

'What are you doing, Ivan? You're supposed to stop this kind of thing you know!'

Ivan did not avert his gaze from the oblivious goldfish in the pond as he finally responded with casual disinterest.

'*You* deal with it please, Philip. I've shown you how more than once. I'm going back inside.'

Phil Holmes watched in helpless amazement as Ivan tossed the dregs of his coffee mug onto the ground, turned on his heel and sauntered in the opposite direction back towards the main doors of the school building.

*****

'Aren't you supposed to be outside?'

Ivan did not even summon the will to look at Matt Jenkins as they passed one another in the corridor beyond the reception office.

With a sigh of utter dejection, he simply leaned against the wall and let his tinted gaze drop to the floor.

'Yes…Matthew…yes…I am officially on playground rota. But alas…today…I simply cannot be bothered.'

Deciding to leave Ivan alone with his own counsel, Matt bemusedly ventured onward into the staff room.

Silent seconds passed. Ivan was eventually nudged from a world elsewhere as the piercing bell announced the end of morning break, and the relative solitude was once again decimated by a gradually increasing crescendo of echoing voices.

Teachers dashed in and out of the adjacent door to gather books and get to their classrooms for the next period. They did not hesitate to ponder Ivan's dubious presence in the corridor.

It was a good few minutes after the bell had ceased before a young physics teacher appeared, accompanied by two very familiar faces.

Phil Holmes glared angrily at the Head of the Mathematics department as he brushed past.

Shaun Peterson and Daniel Keeting also offered Ivan a tentative glance as they were escorted to the vacant chairs outside Geoff Taylor's office.

Both were smeared in blood and bruises and were evidently the source of the conflict that had attracted most of the school's attention during break time.

They reservedly took a seat apiece before both teenagers briefly scrutinised along the corridor, as Phil Holmes walked up to deliver confrontation of his own to the Head of the Mathematics Department.

'Thanks for your help! I could have done with you out there! These fourth formers are big lads to try and separate these days, you know! Look at me! I'm covered in the stuff! This shirt's ruined!'

Ivan's smile broadened under his bleak visor as he observed the blood stains on the Physics teacher's tie.

'You'll survive, Philip. It's called cutting your teeth, lad! You don't need me to hold your hand, anymore! It's good training. In a few years' time the whole school will be punching one another at break time if you modern types get your way.'

Mister Holmes gestured to both boys who looked on nervously as his tirade continued in a lowered tone of voice.

'I wouldn't mind so much…but it was *you* they were fighting about, for Christ's sake!'

Ivan swiftly found himself to be mildly intrigued by the episode.

'*Me*, Philip? They were fighting about *me*?'

'Yes! Peterson was overheard saying he would be glad to see the back of you…or something along those lines. The next minute, apparently Keeting's heard him, lost his temper, and tried to defend your honour with his fists! Can you believe that?'

Ivan looked affectionately towards the two boys whilst ignoring his younger colleague's evident frustration.

As he digested the moment it offered a pang of satisfaction that at least *one* pupil was prepared to stand up for Ivan's honour.

The Head of Mathematics removed his back from the corridor wall and floated over to the pair of scrappers.

They observed his approach with inherent wariness.

But this time, Ivan was not angry.

His smirk was motivated by genuine gratitude, as he stood before the battered youths with his hands in his trouser pockets.

'Brawling over me, eh lads? Wonders will never cease…will they?'

Shaun Peterson stared straight ahead without comment.

Daniel Keeting gazed sheepishly at Ivan and began to stutter.

'I'm sorry, sir. I don't know what came over me.'

Ivan's smile broadened further, and he nodded in appreciation.

'Please don't be sorry, Mister Keeting. I'm extremely humbled by your loyalty…'

Daniel's eyes widened with shock as Ivan continued.

'…but I must apologise in advance, because I have absolutely no idea what excuse you're going to give your father for that black eye this time.'

29

The day of reckoning had arrived.

April; Friday the Thirteenth.

Due to the pending Easter fortnight break, the day's timetable was scheduled to end at lunchtime but there was one unusual proviso to the arrangement.

Every pupil and teacher in the school had been invited to attend the main hall once the dining equipment had been cleared.

There was to be no afternoon registration.

Amendments had been made to accommodate a special event.

It was a particularly subdued 1RY that waited attentively outside the closed door of room ten, awaiting the teacher's appearance to take attendance that morning.

Being fully aware that today was the day they would bid a final farewell to their form tutor, the group's usually vibrant interaction and frothing camaraderie was strangely absent.

Still stunned by the revelation of just over a week ago, the majority of his First Year form group carried a downbeat demeanour.

Uncertainty was now their overriding feeling.

Uncertainty regarding how the day would elapse, and indeed uncertainty regarding what the future had in store for the form group.

Ivan had fully endeared himself to them without even realising it and in turn, the class respected him for the succinct authority that he effortlessly exuded.

Through the duration of just two terms, Ivan's influence on those young minds had been immense.

Although his tenure was now almost at an end, the legacy left by him would live in the minds of those thirty-one pupils for a long time to come.

But today, there were no voices to be heard on the landing.

Two uniformed files stood silently in wait for their master to emerge.

Fifteen boys and sixteen girls faced straight ahead.

They found no cause for distraction in each other this morning.

Only one person mattered now.

And the children sensed deep sorrow for the fact, that after leaving the premises today, they would likely never set eyes on their beloved form tutor ever again.

And just as the wary despondency began to enshroud the hushed group, as if by magic, he appeared majestically before them.

In pristine grey suit, red tie, and white shirt, with shoulders pushed back and head held high.

His spectacles ever-so slightly darkened by the spring sunshine that appropriately flooded the classroom. Ivan Reynolds invited his form group to enter room ten and be seated.

For the final time in his life.

For the final time in theirs.

He attempted to crush his emotional inner battle as he claimed his own chair and opened the register with trembling hands.

The names were announced.

Loudly and clearly.

Tentatively.

Fittingly, a full attendance was confirmed.

Without word, Ivan closed the register and slipped it back into the desk drawer.

For the final time.

Teacher and pupils eyed one another as the subsequent awkward seconds became a thoughtful, peaceful minute. He leaned forward in his chair, rested his elbows on the desk and clasped his fingers together.

He eyed those thirty-one wonderful children studiously.

Yes. He would indeed miss them.

And again, without prompt, the tears of those wonderful children began to fall.

Now sufficiently persuaded by their earnest upset, he stood up, moved to the door, and beckoned the incoming Fifth Year pupils to wait quietly outside as he had something to attend to.

Replacing the door back into the frame, he then began to walk among his class.

Ivan hovered in the aisles between desks, desperately trying not to engage with the release of innocent and genuine anguish that had descended on the room.

But his power over the group had now completely dissipated for all the right reasons.

And it was he who now felt the compulsion to follow their lead and attempt to soothe their discomfort.

One by one he moved to each desk and shook the hand of the pupil sitting before him.

Each time, the same message was repeated after the pronouncement of their names.

'Behave. Good luck. Goodbye.'

And in turn, those children did attempt to reply as they fought back against their unbridled, impassioned release.

With remorse now replacing her customary, disparaging glare, Hilary Johnson placed her hand into Ivan's and though her throat danced with the imminent strife, she issued a startling confession.

'I'm so sorry, sir. I'm so sorry for all that I did. I didn't mean it.'

Ivan looked at the girl with kindness.

'Don't be sorry for *anything*, Miss Johnson. Without the likes of you…my job would be so boring. Thank you…Hilary…'

Ivan nodded to her and continued his parade of well-wishing.

Trevor Sims eyes streamed as he gripped the fingers of the teacher with all his might. Trying in vain to see beyond the elder man's darkened visor, the boy's grief was tangible, and it cut the elder man deeply.

Ivan gazed at the unkempt urchin, whose undiluted distress brought to bear his own sadness.

Ever the consummate professional, Ivan managed to summon humour through his own verging tears.

'I see…that you *still*…have those white socks on…Mister Sims?'

For some strange reason, Ivan's thoughts instinctively turned to his own son, as he watched Trevor Sims attempt to retain some composure, albeit through bubbling nostrils.

Ivan reached into his inside pocket and produced a handkerchief.

'Dry those tears please, Mister Sims. And wipe that nose. And by the way, you can keep the hanky.'

Responding to the timely moment of jest, the thirty-one children laughed in unison.

But the mirth was only a temporary respite from the hurt.

Never had this teacher witnessed such a united show of unabashed affection.

Never could Ivan Reynolds ever have anticipated the bond he had established with those fifteen boys and sixteen girls.

And as he moved along his pupils imparting his good wishes, the sixteenth girl of 1RY waited patiently to express her youthful despair.

As he stood before the very last desk in the very end row, the occupant leapt to her feet and embraced the teacher tightly around his midriff with all her might.

Her unguarded grief only served to heighten Ivan's own acute sense of sorrow.

'Miss Douglas…please…don't upset yourself unnecessarily.'

She clung unto him as though she would instantly wilt without the comfort of his presence.

Ivan respected her right to display her feelings and remained motionless as she wept, before placing his arms around her.

And as he looked up and gazed around the room, he saw that the entire class had now left their chairs and had surrounded him.

Thirty-one pupils. His pupils.

One teacher. Their teacher.

It was a spontaneous and completely disarming exhibition of honour that Ivan had never experienced in all his years of teaching.

And for that tender moment, he willingly trapped himself in time, wishing that things could have been so different before.

Wishing. Always wishing.

Never looking forward.

Always looking back.

*****

One-thirty p.m. The main assembly hall.

No more double filing outside room ten.

No more fearful commandments on the landing.

No more 1RY.

No more Ivan Reynolds.

The last time he had stood behind the red curtains of the stage he was about to enter the Christmas spirit and lead an inspired chorus of festive joy.

Now, as he waited patiently on that same deserted, lonely spot, surrounded by the flitting shadows of history, it would be to say goodbye to Littleholt Secondary School.

Forever.

When once the children applauded him for his singing voice, they would now applaud him for his body of achievement as the longest serving teacher at the school.

He listened to the muffled myriad of hidden discussions beyond the wings and then inhaled deeply as Geoff Taylor endured with his opening speech.

Without warning, the curtains parted.

And Ivan Reynolds could not believe the scene that greeted him beyond the stage.

The arena was packed to capacity and then some.

All pupils of all age groups were assembled across the entire breadth and depth of the room.

All were standing.

All were clapping.

All were acknowledging the imminent departure of a legend.

And along the back wall of the hall stood every single one of his colleagues, united in expressing their acclaim.

Ivan observed the forty-two faces of his peers and counterparts.

Each one smiling in solemn reflection.

Each one indulging in their personal celebration.

Acknowledgement of a most distinguished and influential career.

The like of which may never be repeated.

The Headmaster had given his most senior member of staff a glorious introduction and now stood aside for the subject of the occasion to say a few words on his own behalf.

With posture rigid and proud, Ivan nervously linked his hands in front and continued to gaze appreciatively around the hall.

A thousand faces stared back; each carrying an individual exterior expression, yet inside, the possessors sensed the similar tidal swell of emotion as they conveyed the ovation.

And finally, the chamber descended to a level of complete quiet, presenting Ivan with the opportunity to speak into the microphone.

He purposely cleared his throat whilst simultaneously contesting with a gnawing melancholy.

One deep intake of breath.

And then he began.

'Knowing me as well as you all do by now, you will all probably understand that…it is…*not* very often in life…that I find myself to be flattered. Yet today is certainly one of those days. Because now…at this particular moment standing before you…I feel completely overwhelmed by the warmth that has been shown toward me on my day of retirement.'

All present in the hall were transfixed by the solitary figure on the stage as his tribute continued.

'I fully realise that I may have been a subject of dubious repute and undoubted endless debate throughout my career. And that's just in the staff room. And that some of you will remember me for…shall we say…the *less* savoury encounters.

However, aside from the apparently harsh day to day responsibility of guiding young people into adulthood and beyond, you may be surprised to discover that I do carry a deep-rooted affection for my pupils. Those that have left this school…and those that remain here…will always leave a little of themselves behind in my supposedly cold, old heart.

And yet it is only now…now that my own personal journey within these walls is at an end, that I see the bigger picture. I see the effect of my endeavours. I see the progress in you all…you wonderful young people. And…it makes me eternally humble to think that I have perhaps, even if in only some *small* way, helped to engineer your development. But of course, I must also pass on my appreciation to my fellow staff members…without whom…I would surely have remained untamed and virtually uncontrollable!'

Laughter abounded around the dining hall yet subsided quickly as the entire throng hung on his next word.

Ivan spotted the knowing smiles of Matt and Carol. He also acknowledged with a gentle wave, the tear-strewn features of Trevor Sims and Jenny Douglas standing in the front row.

With obvious increasing difficulty to remain composed, he ventured to continue.

'But the greatest compliment I can pay to all you fine people… as I take my final bow…is that I have suddenly realised something. A sensation that I have never really experienced until this exact moment…'

Ivan swallowed back a hardened emergence of despair as he strived to complete the endearing monologue.

'…because you see…I don't really want to retire at all. And I wish for you all to know that I shall miss you all very much…and I am quite sure…for a fact…that you will all miss *me*. Thank you for having me. Behave yourselves. Good luck. And of course…goodbye.'

A split second of silence preceded the inevitable reaction.

Then the room instantly erupted with vibrant, thunderous applause.

Ivan smiled and raised a hand, thankful that his shaded lenses ably hid a steady trail of emotion that would remain unseen by most.

Retreating to the wings with mission satisfactorily accomplished, a newfound if exhausted hero sat alone on the steps of the stage door, awaiting the oncoming rush of congratulations.

But before the pats on the back, the hugs, and the kisses, he obliged a personal whim.

Ivan Reynolds removed his spectacles.

And he wept alone.

*****

As per the plan, the pupils were given permission to leave school early, giving opportunity for Ivan's fellow teachers to complete their process of farewell in the staff room.

It was a rare occurrence to find every single member of the Littleholt staff simultaneously convened in that smoky little recess of social interaction.

But today, everyone was there to shake the hand of the departing elder statesman.

One by one, Ivan filed among the group, accepting gifts, cards and vocalising his gratitude.

A proportion of those in his company barely knew the man.

Some of them still had the majority of their teaching careers ahead of them and would be enjoying their roles for the next thirty years or more.

But today, they saluted an inspiration.

The soldier returned from service, having now completed his full tour of duty.

Bob Davidson took Ivan's hand firmly in his.

'Don't forget. We've booked a table. We're taking you out for your birthday next month!'

'Of course, you are, Bob. Dear me…rub it in why don't you?'

Sarah Green kissed her Head of Department on the cheek.

'Oh, about that heavy syllabus you mentioned, Sarah…'

'Yes?' she gleamed, teary-eyed.

'I've every faith you will cope. By the way, with Matthew's full agreement, I've nominated you.'

Sarah appeared puzzled.

'Nominated me for what?'

Ivan drew back and placed his hands on Sarah's shoulders.

'To be my replacement as Head of Department, of course. No finer woman for the task.'

For once, Sarah Green was shocked into silence and could do no more than clutch her palm to her chest and mouth the words *Thank You*, as Ivan moved along to his next colleague in the line.

Matt Jenkins edged forward and presented Ivan with a large bottle of Scotch.

'Something to remind you of us…and *home*!'

Ivan whispered into Matt's ear.

'You know…somehow…this place has always reminded me of home in a way.'

'How's that?' enquired the unofficial apprentice to the one-time Head of Mathematics.

'It's filthy and full of strangers! Keep upping the ante, Matthew!'

Geoff Taylor hugged Ivan who now slowly veered ever nearer to the exit.

'Well, Geoffrey. You finally got shot of me!'

'Thank you, Ivan…for everything. See you soon for your party!'

And finally, Carol Shaw, whose professional respect and personal fondness for the man standing before her ran far deeper than he would ever realise.

A gentle kiss and quick embrace needed no further verbal addition.

Their thoughts were almost simultaneous and were mutually acknowledged with a lingering, moistened gaze.

And then, just as he believed that freedom was finally his to embrace, the one person yet to offer his best wishes emerged from the crowd and led a rousing chorus of his own.

'THREE CHEERS FOR IVAN, EVERYONE! HIP, HIP!'

The young conductor ended the raucous tribute, before turning to Ivan, who now carried his familiar indeterminable smirk.

The older man outstretched his hand and engaged the full attention of the physics teacher.

'Put it there, Philip…thank you. And I mean it!'

Phil Holmes suddenly seemed to be losing composure as he shook hands with his most favoured opponent.

'Goodbye and good luck…you old fossil.'

But Ivan had not quite finished with the sermon.

'And by the way, Philip…don't be afraid of being old school. Despite the opposing theorists such as yourself, it does still tend to work best, you know!'

The physics teacher chuckled avidly as Ivan's last lesson registered with telling resonance.

And then, the legend was gone.

Having loaded the boot of the Princess with the bounty of cards and gifts, he despatched one final wave through the driver's window, before cruising along the driveway and away from Littleholt Secondary.

But Ivan did not look back at the buoyant scene of his colleagues in his rear-view mirror.

Now, it was all about the future.

If he could ever manage to let go of the past.

The second. The first Wednesday in May.

The morning of his sixtieth birthday felt no different to any other morning of any other day in any other year in his life.

Six full decades on the mortal coil had forged a mindset that allowed for little distraction from preferred habits.

With no alarm clock to disturb him, it had been the gradual rise of the spring sun that had encouraged his arousal from deep slumber. Having donned his dressing gown, Ivan forced himself downstairs to make a welcome mug of tea and retrieved the newspaper from the doormat.

The postman had delivered one solitary item of mail.

An advertisement for life insurance, which duly sailed into the kitchen waste bin.

Back in bed, mental immersion in the front-page news caused him to completely miss the first knock at the door.

The secondary rap echoed loudly around the hallway and up the stairs, this time successfully breaking his concentration from the Daily Mail.

Considering his comfortable position under the bedclothes, Ivan opted not to answer to the visitor.

Then the sound of a clattering letterbox pricked his curiosity further.

With partial intrigue passing for a mild denial of excitement, he hauled himself off the mattress once again and descended the stairs. The large yellow envelope lay on the brown mat, promising content he could only pretend to guess at.

The birthday card portrayed a painting of a fisherman by a stream, sitting on the bank being bathed in sunshine. It was an image of contentment, but which puzzled Ivan as he had never professed to be a fisherman in any sense.

The inscription inside was written in delicate hand.

From George and Jill.
Happy retirement and Happy Birthday, Ivan!
PS. You're on the committee at last!! xxx

Taped to the inside of the card above the message was a silver key.

The key to a padlock.

The padlock that secured the allotment gates.

Yet whilst such a touching surprise achieved a long-held ambition, Ivan could not shrug off the sense of despondency that had already threatened to overshadow his supposed day of celebration.

Subsequently, preferring not to venture to his neighbours' house and express his thanks, he sat alone for the entirety of the day.

There was a knock at the door at least twice which he duly ignored.

The telephone rang several times which he did not pick up, knowing full well that it may be one of his ex-colleagues from Littleholt confirming arrangements for the evening's retirement-birthday meal that they had planned for him.

But in truth, Ivan did not feel like celebrating his birthday this year.

He did not even feel like walking in the rear garden for fear of being seen by his neighbours.

In truth, at sixty years of age, Ivan Reynolds had never felt so empty inside.

A spent force.

A man with no company, aside from the thoughts in his head.

Ironic that his legacy would indeed live on into the distant future.

Whilst he remained aloof, fighting the hourly temptation to dwell on the distant past.

But the searing truth of the matter was unavoidable.

And it troubled him to accept it.

The reign of The King of Littleholt Secondary was over.

The Last of the Old School was no more.

EPILOGUE

The twelfth. The second Thursday in August.

Nineteen-ninety-nine.

The man oversaw the final gardener depart from the allotment grounds and after peering among the lengthening shadows, he gave one final check on the premises before hobbling steadily toward the exit.

The creaking sound that had accompanied the swinging of the green-painted mesh metal was more piercing than ever. Despite oiling the hinges numerous times, it remained a persistently incurable annoyance.

Positioning the large double gates, he secured the silver padlock in place with his key.

The key given to him some fifteen years earlier by his late neighbour and dearest friend as a retirement present.

The man then shuffled to his car and climbed behind the steering wheel to head for home.

*****

Later that balmy, summer evening, he sat with his neighbour on the rear patio and together they attempted to complete the Daily Mail crossword.

'I'm struggling to *read* the blessed clues these days never mind solve them. George used to have it finished in one sitting.'

'Well…to be perfectly honest, Jillian, I've never been any good at the damned things anyway. In thirty-odd years of trying I don't think I've finished one yet! Often get close…but no cigar!'

'It's getting a bit nippy, Ivan. I think I'll be off.'

The man always escorted Jill next door after she had visited.

Making sure she got inside her house, he then turned back toward his own abode, only to find a stranger standing at the end of the driveway.

He studied the loitering figure, who appeared lost for direction.

Not one to hide his suspicions regarding any matter, he approached her and inquired as to whether he could be of any assistance.

The slim, attractive lady with blond hair eyed him with unwarranted caution.

Yet her initial wariness was gradually subdued by a brilliant smile which only served to add to the man's mild confusion.

He moved closer to her; his eyes squinting over the rim of his reading glasses to ascertain the possible identity and business of the unexpected visitor.

Despite a studious examination, he was certain he did not readily recognise her face.

Yet he could not help but feel that the lady felt familiar in some way.

Similarly, her jovial expression suggested that she definitely knew *him*.

'Can I help you, my dear?'

Still, she stared back; still smiling but without response.

'Are you looking for someone?' asked the man.

The young lady nodded.

'I think I've just found him.' she finally replied.

'What do you mean?'

'I hope you don't mind the intrusion…but…you are…Ivan Reynolds…aren't you? The ex-teacher from Littleholt School?'

A myriad of images flashed rapidly across his conscience as long redundant memory banks began to re-activate. Pushing his shoulders back, he stood to his full height and stared down at the visitor.

'I am indeed. And who might you be, may I ask?'

The woman came a step nearer and offered a hand of greeting.

The man eyed her with continuing bemusement as he willingly returned the gesture.

'Well…it's been a while…a good few years in fact. My name is Jennifer Young. I was in your final form group at Littleholt. Just before you retired.'

Now the man's eyes illuminated with the pleasant relief at solving the puzzle.

'*Miss Douglas*! Of course, you are! I couldn't place you! But now you've said your name…the girl who gave me the chocolate orange for Christmas! Room ten…last row…end table.'

The young lady laughed as the scene of reminiscence evolved between them.

'You've got it, sir! I've changed a bit. I was rather…shall we say…bigger…back in my school days…mind…you said I would change in time! And you were right!'

The man looked her up and down, still peering over his reading spectacles.

'Well…it's not appropriate to call me *sir* anymore, I assure you. I bet I've changed too, haven't I?'

'Well, you seem a bit smaller. A bit less intimidating. But that's probably because I'm a bit taller. You're a bit greyer here and there. And a little bit older looking. But apart from that…'

'I know, I know…flattery gets you *everywhere*…I don't look a day over seventy-five!'

Chuckles preceded a short hiatus in the conversation which prompted him into making an invitation.

'Would you…like to come in for a drink of something…Mrs. Young?'

She nodded with enthusiasm and followed him through the front door and into the kitchen. At the table she noticed the open newspaper and the unfinished crossword.

Next to it lay a silver pocket-watch on a chain.

'Oh wow…that brings back memories!' the lady exclaimed.

'Well, you can always rely on old timers, my dear. That's what I always say! I'll make a pot of tea…if that's agreeable with you?'

She took a seat at the dining table and casually glanced around the kitchen and then beyond the window.

'It's a lovely view through the back. You've a well-kept garden.'

'Yes…that's about all I *do* get up to these days. Biscuit?'

'No…thank you! No sweets for me!'

He positioned himself opposite the welcome guest and folded up the newspaper.

'So…the inevitable question arises, Mrs Young. What brings you here…and however did you track me down?'

The visitor was evidently overjoyed to have been reunited with her ex-form tutor. Her expression veritably beamed with enthusiasm as she spoke.

'Well, sir…it's a simple tale, really. About a month ago, there was a school reunion for the Littleholt leavers of Nineteen-eighty-eight. Everybody had a great evening…chatting…showing off old photographs and what-not…and then the subject of our old teachers caused some debate.'

The man stirred the steaming teapot as he interrupted.

'I've told you. It's not *sir*, anymore. Please, call me Ivan.'

'Okay. Ivan. Well, we talked about those teachers we liked and those we didn't like. But of course…the one person we all remembered…was *you*!'

He smiled gently whilst setting two mugs into place next to the pot.

'Was I remembered for good reasons…or for bad ones?'

Jennifer Young laughed heartily before continuing.

'To be honest, BOTH! But everyone could remember the day when you left. It was so upsetting. Can you recall me holding you round the waist? I cried all the way home! I remember it like it happened yesterday!'

Ivan Reynolds got up once again to retrieve milk from the fridge.

He returned to the table before pouring tea into the mugs as he interjected.

'You know…I can't remember the entire class…but one or two faces are coming back to me. Sugar bowl is there should you take it.'

Jennifer Young twitched in her seat with the thrill of nostalgia.

Now growing fully absorbed by the exchange, the man became amused as her evident glee at locating him grew by the second.

'Go on then…Mrs. Young! You describe some pupils and I'll try and name them. See if my memory still works after all this time!'

The visitor hunched forward in her chair and leaned both elbows on the table.

'Well, remember the skinny curly-haired lad who was always getting picked on?'

He fingered his chin whilst flicking through the mental files of history. Eventually, a name rolled off his tongue.

'Morris, wasn't it? He wasn't in my form group though, was he?'

'Not 1RY, no. But you know who I mean! He's now a computer programmer!'

The man sat back in his chair and winced as hot tea burned his tongue.

'Splendid! And what of the ginger haired boy...freckles. Scott something, wasn't it?'

'Colin Scott! He's now bald as a coot and runs a butcher's shop. Your old sparring partner came to the reunion, too!'

He seemed momentarily puzzled by the reference, but his first guess was correct as he put a hand across his lips.

'Hilary! Hilary Johnson! Is she still a living nightmare?'

Jennifer laughed out loud and rocked back in her seat.

'Yes! A nightmare with two kids! But she's married and doing well for herself.'

'Oh dear! May God help their little souls!'

'Believe it or not, she went to drama school. She's been on telly in a few things! But wanted to settle down and be a mum.'

'A commendable option, indeed. And what of the scruffy little urchin? The one who was always turning up to school in white socks! He must have done more press-ups than everyone else in the class put together!'

The female caller suddenly adopted an air of intense solemnity.

'You mean...Trevor?'

'Yes! That's it! Trevor Sims! What's he up to now?'

A distinctly uncomfortable silence encroached.

Jennifer Young glanced down to the tabletop and then diverted attention back to the elder man as she stammered her revelation.

'Trevor...Trevor died...when he was seventeen...got knocked off a motorbike. He never knew a thing.'

Amid a pang of sorrow, the former teacher shook his head in sympathy as the flashbacks continued.

'He was an only child, wasn't he? He lived alone with just his mother. His father wasn't around as I recall.'

Jennifer nodded, obviously very touched by the accurate recollection.

'That's right. Trevor was a lovely lad. He was my first boyfriend. I'll never forget him.'

The ex-mathematician studied the anguish that suddenly etched itself into the young lady's radiant features.

An uneasy hiatus ensued before a change of mood was called for.

'Did you ever hear anything of any other ex-pupils from the school? Daniel Keeting? He was a couple of years older than you. Do you know whatever happened to him?'

The lady's moistened gaze suddenly lit up with an injection of vigour once again.

'Was he the one who won the athletics scholarship at Southampton?'

Ivan Reynolds nodded as a broad grin stretched from ear to ear.

'I've no idea…but I sincerely hope so! I don't think I met many other First Year pupils that weren't in my last form group.'

His gaze diverted to the lengthening shadows beyond the kitchen window, before another piece of the puzzle required itself to be tackled.

'Tell me, Mrs. Young…how did you get this address?'

'When the reunion was organised, we offered Carol Shaw an invitation through the school secretary. She looks older now as well. She's been retired about six years. She left Littleholt to become Headmistress of an all-girl's school. She certainly has fond memories of you. She said you wouldn't mind if she gave your details.'

Continuing to sip his tea, the former Head of Department allowed his mind to wander.

'It all seems so long ago now. How are your parents doing?

'They're good. Very well, thanks. They still remember you as well!'

'That's good. I recall their visit to parents' evening before I finished. I'm glad they highlighted the fact that you were struggling with that nasty issue.'

Jennifer looked at the expression of the elder man and felt confident enough to broach a question that had burned in the back of her mind for the better part of fifteen years.

'You know when I revealed to you that I was being bullied by that physics teacher called Holmes…'

Her former form tutor smiled with anticipation.

'Oh, yes. I recall. Why?'

'…well…I always wondered…what did you do after we spoke about it? Because it never happened again.'

He nodded with pleasure.

'Let's just say he was made to see the error of his ways and he understood very quickly that he was in danger of being exposed. You see, it's not just the pupils that need to be ready to learn. Sometimes…on occasion…teachers need to be educated, too.'

Jennifer Young smiled, opting not to dig for more detail on the matter.

Ivan Reynolds, Last of the Old School, drained his mug and pondered another polite query.

'So, tell me…Mrs. Young…what are you doing with your life these days aside from being a loving wife to *Mister* Young?'

Her visage became ever further effusive on hearing the question.

'Well…I stayed on and did my A-levels at Littleholt. And then went to training college for my degree.'

'Really? That's *excellent*! What was it that you specified in?'

With a glowing conveyance of pride, Jennifer Young revealed her fully realised ambitions to her sole source of inspiration.

'Actually, I've just qualified! I'm a teacher, sir! Just like you!'

*****

Both parties said their goodbyes with a sense of buoyant finality.

Ivan felt most gratified by the unannounced visit of his former pupil. After bidding Jennifer Young farewell and good luck, he retreated into the encroaching dusk of the back garden.

One aspect of their conversation had lingered pleasantly.

As she walked down the drive to her car, she suddenly turned and echoed a sentiment that touched him deeply.

You were the best!

To receive such an appraisal lifted his spirits no end.

The summer evening was now alive with the sound of birdsong, and he decided to perch himself among the dancing groups of insects that flitted in the diminishing shafts of sunlight.

Positioned on the bench by the vegetable patch, Ivan looked down to his left hand and the now ring-less finger, where treasured memories were once signified by a gold band.

Then, as he momentarily dwelled on times previous, a dark shape emerged from the undergrowth and advanced steadily toward him across the rear section of lawn.

The tortoiseshell cat approached without caution and proceeded to snake its tousled form in and around the old man's legs before clawing at his trousers as a request for affection.

Compelled not to frighten the animal, Ivan began to stroke it.

The sensation was soothing, and for the first time in their relationship, the protagonists looked like agreeing a peaceful policy of mutual acceptance.

Surprised by his lack of traditional hostility toward the feline invader, Ivan watched the cat as it struggled to manoeuvre with its ageing physique.

He even felt compelled to speak to the animal as it purred contentedly at his ankles.

'Christ! That's a thought, puss. I've just realised something. *You're* older than *I* am these days!'

In response to the man's mumbled musings, the cat looked directly up at Ivan and offered a quiet meow of confirmation.

Then in the next movement, it wandered gamely onto the vegetable patch and proceeded to dig a shallow hole with its front paws, in which to deposit the business of the hour.

Never taking its eyes of Ivan for a second, the cat completed nature's task and duly covered over the remnants of its visit before disappearing back into the hedgerow.

Tail in the air; swagger firmly on display.

Initially bewildered by the feline display of affronting bravado, Ivan also found himself slightly amused by the indigenous defiance of the animal.

'You are about the only one who ever did have the better of me, you little sod…'

Then the initial amusement at the incident evolved into a giggle.

Which rapidly developed into a raucous, booming laugh.

A laugh that echoed around the back garden and beyond.

In the relentless grip of his unbridled mirth, Ivan rose to his feet and admired the distant red sun as it offered a last glimpse above the rooftops of the distant neighbourhood.

And simultaneously, a pleasant realisation occurred.

Ivan Reynolds found himself sincerely thankful that the same sun would return in a few hours and bring with it another glorious day.

For the first time he could recall in his life, the Last of the Old School found himself relishing the prospect of what lay ahead.

Instead of being shackled to history.

The future beckoned him.

Perhaps even enticed him.

And a pledge was made.

From that moment on, he would always be looking forward.

Never again, looking back.

ACKNOWLEDGEMENTS

I wish to thank the following people for their invaluable expertise and support in helping this book gain wings:
Ron Clements; Samantha Thornton; Hannah Bliss; Charlotte Wilson; Robbie Wilson; Carole Thornton, Chris Bliss; Charlotte Bliss; Jeanette Taylor Ford; Sue Hayward; Ford Wood; Beverley Latimer; Karl Gregg and last but certainly not least, David Slaney for his superb cover design.
I couldn't have done it without any of you.
I am forever indebted.
RJT

Also Available on Amazon
by Richard John Thornton

DELIVER US FROM EVIL

AT HELL'S GATE

THE SWANS AT CLEARLAKE

WITHIN THESE WALLS

A PRAYER FOR MARTIN

Printed by Amazon Italia Logistica S.r.l.
Torrazza Piemonte (TO), Italy